FIG

Steve Rasnic Tem has pu[blished ...] [...stories,] seven novels, and ten collections during a career spanning forty years. He is a past recipient of the World Fantasy Award and the British Fantasy Award, and his 2014 novel *Blood Kin* won the Bram Stoker Award. His latest novel, *Ubo* (Solaris, 2017), is a dark science fiction tale about violence and its origins, featuring such historical viewpoint characters as Jack the Ripper, Stalin, and Heinrich Himmler. *Yours to Tell: Dialogues on the Art & Practice of Writing*, written with his late wife Melanie, also appeared from Apex Books in 2017.

FIGURES UNSEEN

selected stories by

STEVE RASNIC TEM

Introduction by
SIMON STRANTZAS

VALANCOURT BOOKS

Figures Unseen: Selected Stories by Steve Rasnic Tem
First edition 2018

Published by Valancourt Books, Richmond, Virginia
http://www.valancourtbooks.com

ISBN 978-1-948405-01-0 (hardcover)
ISBN 978-1-948405-02-7 (trade paperback)
Also available as an electronic book and an audiobook.

All Valancourt Books publications are printed on acid free paper that meets all ANSI standards for archival quality paper.

Set in Dante MT
Cover by Henry Petrides

CONTENTS

INTRODUCTION

It's strange that you hold this book in your hands. Those of us who have counted ourselves Steve Rasnic Tem's devoted readers since his work first appeared in the late seventies remember a time not too long ago when, beyond a few chapbooks from nascent publishers and a lone novel, *Excavation*, there was no single place one could read all or even a good chunk of his work. It wasn't until the year 2000 that a book-length collection of Tem's short fiction appeared, and even then it contained only a small selection of the numerous stories he'd by then published. Were he any other horror writer he probably would have faded away as soon as the boom ended, dissuaded and discouraged by a lack of markets and sales. It happened to so many, after all. The reason it didn't happen to Steve Rasnic Tem is probably because he isn't like most horror writers.

For one thing, he's never stopped writing short stories. There's been a steady stream of work from him over the decades and he shows no sign of stopping now. For another, I have trouble summoning the name of another writer for whom the old adage "his early work was better" is so consistently proven false. Tem has always written at a level above his contemporaries, and continues to do so even as those contemporaries disappear and are replaced by newer voices. And, of course, it's impossible to forget just how prolific Tem is—if it's the writer's job to fully explore her or his craft, both in terms of how and why, then Tem has done so with fierce dedication, with both his analysis on the craft of writing, as well as investigating how his muse works in horror's satellite genres like fantasy, science fiction, and mystery. And, yet, no matter which of these genres he touches upon, or how many simultaneously, it never feels as though he's simply visiting, nor is it not recognizably his work. A Tem story is like no other. Perhaps Joe R. Lansdale put it best when he said: "Steve Rasnic Tem is a school of writing unto himself."

It could be because Tem's work is difficult to pigeon-hole. We classify it as horror because there aren't many other options available. But by horror we don't mean the genre's conservative face. Tem's work does not follow horror's tropes or trends—you'll rarely come across a monster in the pages of this book, and other than one seaport town you'd be hard pressed to connect anything here with what has come before. Instead, we mean horror's transgressive face, where it becomes a catch-all for work that comfortably fits nowhere else. Where horror becomes and/or overlaps with weird fiction. It's here in the interstices that Tem works best, with stories that operate simultaneously in all the different modes of fantastical fiction to tell intensely personal tales of loss and failure. Let me be clear, however: I don't mean to suggest the stories you'll read in this book are personally about Tem—no more so than all stories are about their authors to some degree. Rather, I'm suggesting that each of Tem's stories is written from deep within the space of the personal, where all humanity's hopes and fears are rooted. In many ways, these stories are masks he's constructed for you to wear. A new set of eyes through which to see and experience the world. Tem's fiction gives you insight into the lives of people who want something they can't have, and it allows you to suffer their failures as though they were your own.

Allow me to go back a few sentences and re-emphasize the word *experience*, because that's what Steve Rasnic Tem writes instead of stories. He writes experiences. You are meant to feel them. This is why plot is often not the point in Tem's work. Instead, it acts as the frame on which to hang those experiences he wants to convey. A lot of horror fiction tends to be investigative: where stories are plot-driven explorations into a mystery whose solution turns to horror. It could be a small town with a secret the protagonist discovers, or an ancient book whose contents set a group of people on a quest. It could even be the trials of a person as they slowly uncover the horrible thing that's been done to them. There's a plot, an A to B path that the characters travel down to meet their often untimely end.

Tem's style of experience horror is more uncommon in the field. With his work, we don't worry about where characters are traveling or what mystery they are solving. Instead we worry about who they are as people, and its through understanding them that we better understand ourselves. How does that skinned rabbit unnerve us? What are those dead child's opening eyes asking us? How does that cabinet's contents fill the void in ourselves? This fiction doesn't lead the reader along a path toward a discovery; it instead tries elicit a transformation in the reader by brute force. It wants to change some fundamental part of you. It wants you to come away affected. What's remarkable is how often it succeeds.

That success stems from Tem's ability to place the reader into the center of the tale. The stories here are highly subjective—the prose often becomes an extension of interior dialogue, with sentences that end halfway through, rewind and repeat. Words echo, and both situations and environments can alter drastically in the space between two periods. What Tem does with great effect is disconnect the reader from the passage of time, and this disconnection further amplifies their subjectiveness by inducing dreamlike rhythms. The combination unmoors the reader from the stories' realities and creates the potential for the superreal to impose itself and transform even prosaic events into the fantastic.

But this is only part of the answer to why the stories here are so affecting. The techniques above attempt to explain the "how", but the "why" is due to Tem's subject matter: namely, the complications of family, of trying to do right by those you love, of succeeding when everything has prepared you for failure. Tem's stories are, again, deeply personal, because they deal with personal issues, with personal stakes. The threat of physical death is not as important as the *fear of it* in these stories, and their characters and their readers are made even more fearful by other obstacles—the fear of loss, the fear of regret, the fear of powerlessness. They are powerful and universal concerns, and the act of facing them might be more terrifying for the reader than any vampire or cosmic monster could ever hope to be.

I don't think I know for certain which was the first Steve Rasnic Tem story I ever read. A case could be made for "Underground", originally published in Dennis Etchison's marvelous anthology, *Metahorror*, but perhaps I think that because the story has remained with me over decades since that reading. What I do know is that Tem's work continues to impress me as much now as it did then. His were the first small press chapbooks I ever bought, and I vividly remember fantasizing in the nineties about becoming a publisher so I might issue collected editions of all his work (a notion that seems terribly premature in retrospect). I simply couldn't comprehend why the world wasn't singing Tem's praises. To be frank, I still can't, but time has shown me that I wasn't the only one who noticed Tem's name and work in that string of anthologies, nor was I the only one who kept them close to the heart. A surprising number of these readers grew into authors in their own right, bringing with them the understanding of how important Steve Rasnic Tem's work is and continues to be. If anything, I think his work has become even more relevant now to the horror genre than ever before. The entire movement of weird horror that is currently so prevalent seems to be rooted in the same intersectional spaces that Tem has been exploring for decades. He's been here for a long time, showing us the way, and it pleases me greatly that people are finally starting to listen. This retrospective being only the latest concrete proof of that.

Between these covers you'll find almost three dozen waiting experiences to be had, each one transformative in its own way. Whoever you are now, reading this, is not who you'll be when the last page is turned. You'll be older, wiser, and in many ways too broken to be fixed. But you'll have lived almost three dozen lifetimes, experienced almost three dozen moments of pain and confusion and heartbreak. If you can survive that, maybe there's still hope for you yet.

Simon Strantzas
Toronto, Canada

Simon Strantzas is the author of five collections of short fiction, including *Nothing is Everything* (Undertow Publications, 2018), and is editor of the award-winning *Aickman's Heirs* and *Year's Best Weird Fiction, Vol. 3*. His fiction has appeared in numerous annual best-of anthologies, in venues such as *Nightmare*, *Postscripts*, and *Cemetery Dance*, and has been nominated for both the British Fantasy and Shirley Jackson awards. He lives with his wife in Toronto, Canada.

CITY FISHING

After weeks of talking about it, Jimmy's father finally decided to take him fishing. Jimmy's friend Bill, and Bill's father who was Jimmy's dad's best friend, also were to go. Their mothers didn't approve.

Jimmy wasn't sure he approved either, actually. He had somewhat looked forward to the event, thought that he should go, but as the actual day approached he knew fishing was the last thing he wanted to do. It seemed to be important to his father, however, so he would go just to please him.

"Now, look what we have here, Jimmy. Everything you need to get along in the wild." Jimmy's father was tall and dark-haired, and the deep resonance in his voice made his every word seem like a command. He gestured toward a display of tools, utensils, and weaponry. "Hunting knife, pistol, wire, gunpowder, hooks and sinkers, poles, small animal trap, steel trap, fish knife, stiletto, Bowie, .22, shotgun, derringer. You have to have all this if you're going to get along in the wild. Remember that, son."

Jimmy nodded with hesitation.

Bill had run up beside him. "See what I got!"

Jimmy had already seen out of the corner of his eye a dark shape in Bill's left hand. As he turned to greet his friend he saw that it was a large, dead crow, its neck spotted with red.

"Dad caught it, then I wrung its neck while we had the feet tied together. I thought I'd bring it along."

Jimmy nodded.

Loud noises were coming from the house. Jimmy could hear his mother weeping, his father cursing. He walked up to the front steps and watched through the screen door.

He could make out Bill's father, his father, his own mother, and a young red-haired woman back in the shadows who must have been Bill's mother.

"You can't take them!" He could hear his mother sobbing.

Then there was a struggle as his dad and Bill's dad started forcing the women into the bedroom. Bill's mother was especially squirmy, and Bill's father was slapping her hard across the face to make her stop. His own mother was a bit quieter, especially after Bill's mother got hurt, but she still cried.

His father locked the door. "We'll let you out, maybe after we get back." He chuckled and looked at Bill's father. "Women!"

It all seemed very peculiar.

As Jimmy's father pulled the battered old station wagon out of the driveway he began singing. He looked back over his shoulder at Jimmy and winked. Jimmy figured that singing was all part of fishing since first Bill's father, then Bill, joined in. Jimmy couldn't follow the words.

"Make a real man out of him, I think," his father said to Bill's father. Bill's father chuckled.

They didn't seem to be getting any farther out of the city. If anything, they seemed to be driving into the downtown section. Jimmy had never been downtown.

"Are you sure this is the right way to the stream, Dad?"

Jimmy's father turned and glared at him. Jimmy lowered his head. Bill was gazing out the window and humming.

They passed several old ladies driving cars with packages and shopping bags filling the back seats. His father snickered.

They passed young girls on bicycles, their dresses fluttering in the wind. They passed several strolling couples, and a man with a baby carriage.

Jimmy's father laughed out loud and punched Bill's father on the shoulder. Then they were both laughing; it sounded as if they were almost crying. Jimmy just stared at them.

The shopping malls were getting smaller, the houses darker and shabby.

Jimmy's father turned to him and said fiercely, almost angrily, "You're going to make me proud today, Jimmy."

Bill was beginning to get fidgety as he looked out the window. Every once in a while he would gaze at the back of his father's head, then at the buildings along the street, then back out the rear window. He began scratching his arms in agitation.

Jimmy gazed out his own window. The pavement was getting

worse—dirtier, and full of potholes. The buildings were getting taller, and older, the farther they drove. Jimmy had always thought that only new buildings were tall.

They passed a dark figure, wrapped in rags, crumpled on the sidewalk.

Jimmy's father chuckled.

They had left the house at noon. He knew it had been noon because he'd just eaten the lunch of soup and crackers his mother had fixed.

The sky was getting dark.

Jimmy put his cheek against the car window and tilted his head back so that he could see above the car. Tall smoke stacks rising out of the dark roofs of the buildings across the street blew night-black clouds into the sky. The smoke stacks were taller than anything he'd ever seen.

Jimmy felt a lurch as the car started down the steep hill. He had been in San Francisco once, and there were lots of hills that steep. He couldn't remember anything like that in their city, but then, he had never been downtown.

Bill was jerking his head back and forth nervously. His eyes looked very white.

The buildings seemed to get taller and taller, older and older. Some had columns out front, or wide wrap-around porches. Many had great iron or wooden doors. There didn't seem to be any people on the streets.

It suddenly occurred to Jimmy that the buildings shouldn't be getting taller as they went downhill. The bottoms of these buildings were lower than the ones farther up the hill, behind them, so their rooftops should be lower, too. That was the way it had been in San Francisco. But looking out the back window he could see that the roofs got farther away, taller still as they descended the hill. The buildings were reaching into the sky.

Dark figures scurried from the mouth of an alley. Jimmy couldn't tell what they looked like; it seemed to be almost night-time out.

Jimmy's father and Bill's father were perched on the edge of their seats, apparently searching every building corner. His father was humming.

Bill began to cry softly, his feet shuffling over the rumpled carcass of the crow.

The street seemed to get steeper and steeper. Occasionally they would hit a flat place in the road; the car would make a loud banging noise, bounce, and then seemingly leap several feet into the air. The car was going faster.

His father laughed out loud and honked the horn once.

It was black outside, so black Jimmy could hardly see. The two fathers were singing softly again. The car was picking up speed with every clank, bounce, and leap. Bill was crying and moaning. Jimmy couldn't even see the sky anymore, the buildings were so tall. And so old! Bricks were falling into the street even as they passed. Stone fronts were sagging, the foundations obscured by piles of powdered rock. Beams were obviously split and cracked, some hanging down like broken bones. Windowpanes were shattered, curtains torn, casements grimed. Jimmy couldn't understand how the buildings held themselves up, especially when they were so tall. Miles high, it seemed. If he hadn't been taught better, he would have thought they hung down from the sky on wires.

He was bouncing wildly up and down in the seat, periodically bumping into Bill, who was crying more loudly than ever. The car was like a train, a plane, a rocket.

A loud clank, then something rattled off to his left. He turned and saw that a hubcap had fallen off and was lying in the street behind them. Shadows moved in a side doorway.

The car was groaning. Bill's wails were even more high-pitched.

"Daddy . . . daddy. Bill's afraid!"

His father stared at the windshield. The car dropped another hubcap.

"Daddy, the hubcaps!"

His father remained motionless, his hands gripping the wheel. A brick fell and bounced off the car. A piece of timber cracked the windshield.

The car squealed, roared, and dropped further and further into the heart of the city. They seemed to have been going downhill for miles.

It suddenly occurred to Jimmy they hadn't passed a crossstreet in some time.

"Daddy ... please!"

The car hit a flat section of pavement. The car body clanked loudly, the engine died, and the car rolled a few feet before stopping. They faced an old building with wide doors.

Jimmy looked around. They were in a small court, faced on all sides by the ancient buildings which soared upwards, completely filling the sky. It was so dark he couldn't see their upper stories.

He looked behind them. The steep road rose like a gray ribbon, disappearing at the top. It was the only road into the court.

Everything was quiet. Bill stared silently at his father. The dead crow had been trampled almost flat by Bill's agitated feet. The floorboard was filled with feathers, pieces of skin, bone and blood.

There were shapes in the darkness between buildings.

Jimmy's father turned to his friend. "Bottom. We made it." He began rummaging in his knapsack.

He was handing Jimmy the rifle, smiling, laughing, saying "That's my boy!" and "Today's the day!" when the dark and tattered figures began closing in on the car.

ANGEL COMBS

The morning had sharp edges. Annie could see them.

Her mother had gotten her up an hour before dawn—the earliest she could remember ever getting up, except for that Christmas Uncle Willy had stayed with them, and she knew she was getting something nice that Christmas because she had seen a half-moon sliver of the doll's face with the long blonde hair in the big brown sack Uncle Willy had carried in. That night she hadn't slept at all. She had dreamed of the doll's hair, how it might be arranged, how long it might grow. Maybe the doll was a little magical and the hair might grow forever. She dreamed of it stretching around her little room, catching her other toys up in its waves, carrying them along like colorful boats in a river. She dreamed of drowning pleasantly in the flood it made. Most Christmases it didn't much matter. Most Christmases Momma couldn't afford much of anything.

Her bedroom window looked out on the back yard. Under the brownish streetlight she could see the rough darkness of her dead father's old car, wheel-less, drowning in weeds. The occasional razor-sharp gleam of a discarded tin can.

Annie kept thinking maybe they should clean up the back yard a little. Maybe turn it into a garden or something. They could have fresh vegetables, their own peas and lettuce and corn. But Annie was too scared to be in the back yard very long: the weeds were too tall, and sharp, and things were always moving there. And her mother kept saying she just didn't have the heart.

There was usually a little bit of a fog in the back yard. A mist. This morning was no different. This morning the fog looked torn, like some ferocious beast had ripped into the middle of it, pulled it to shreds. Great long pieces of it hung from tree branches, eaves, and junked machinery like fingers, or teeth. It fascinated Annie, but it also made her nervous to look at. Eventually she turned away and started getting dressed.

She could hear Momma getting dressed in the next room. Humming, happy. Only now and then snapping at one of the twins to get a move on. "Tommy! You don't want me to dress you! Nossir. You don't want me to squeeze your scrawny little butt into them tight jeans!" Then she'd go back to humming, singing, as if nothing had happened. It had been a long time since they'd made, as Momma put it, "a major purchase." She always said that with a soft, serious voice, like she was talking about somebody that'd died. Her mother was almost funny when she talked like that.

Momma had found this ad in the paper. "Bedroom Sets. REDUCED! $40!" And they had just a little over forty dollars saved. The little over would go for the tax, Momma said. And if the tax didn't take all of that, they could use the left over for an ice cream treat. The twins were excited by that, all right. They didn't care much for the idea of bedroom sets, but the prospect of a special ice cream, a separate one for each of them without having to share, that had kept them talking most of the past evening.

Her mother said it was like a miracle, the way they'd just gotten that very amount saved, and for sure a hard saving it had been, too, and here this furniture store comes out with this nice sale. And them needing the bedroom furniture so bad. Like a dream, Momma said. A fantasy come true. She'd shown Annie the picture in the paper. It was a drawing so you really couldn't tell that much. That's what Annie had told Momma, but her momma had said, "No. They couldn't do it up in the paper like that if it wasn't true." And of course that wasn't what Annie had meant at all, but she just nodded and let her mother point out each piece and tell her how fine it must all be.

There was a bed with four posts (the sketch in the paper showed wood grain so Momma said it must be oak and "oak is about the best there is"), a bedside table with two drawers (not just one like most bedside tables had), a set of drawers, and a little dresser with an oval mirror ("They call that fine detail.").

"Now maybe I can buy my children something that will last," Momma said.

Maybe it was because Annie hadn't shown enough enthusiasm about the "major purchase" to satisfy Momma, or maybe it was the way Annie had looked at that dresser. But last night, after she'd gotten the twins into bed, her Momma had said, "You know I've been thinking. I think maybe you should have the dresser. I've got that dresser Grandma Smythe willed me, and it's special enough. Why, it's an antique. And you need a private place to comb your hair. Every woman, or about-to-be-a-woman, needs a private place to comb her hair."

Without really thinking about it, Annie began stroking her long, brownish-blonde hair with her palm, then opening the fingers slightly—as if they were the teeth of a huge, heavenly comb—and catching her hair now and then with those finger-teeth, using them to melt away the day's filth, making the tangles and snarls vanish one by one into the cool night air.

Annie had looked up at her mother, seen her mother's satisfaction, and then realized what it was she'd been doing. And stopped it immediately. She'd seen herself in that dreamed-of oval mirror, seen herself combing the hair that was so much like her mother's, hair that was the only thing even remotely special about her. Hair even the rich girls in her class envied. She'd seen herself combing herself in that fine and private place that once was her bedroom, that special place because the dreamed-of dresser was there.

And at that moment Annie was almost angry with her mother because of the dream.

They arrived at the furniture store only a few minutes after it opened. There were a few other customers already inside: two well-dressed women, an older man in a ragged overcoat with dark spots on its sleeves, and a tall young man casually dressed, but Annie thought his clothes might be expensive since she'd seen some just like that on one of her favorite detective shows.

Her mother looked a little panicky when she saw those other customers. She'd wanted to be at the store before it opened, but the twins had gotten in a fight at the last minute—Momma tried to slap at least one of them but they got away from her—and then their old car had stalled three times on the way over. Annie had been wondering the whole time how they were supposed to get the new bedroom set back to the house. Surely they just couldn't tie it to the top of the car. She'd heard about having things delivered but she didn't know if the furniture store would do that, especially for something on sale like that, or even how that sort of thing was done. She doubted Momma knew how that sort of thing was done either. It would be just awful if they couldn't get the bedroom set after all because they didn't have a truck and somebody who had a truck got there first, or because they didn't have enough money to pay for the delivery.

Again, Annie found herself absently stroking her hair, seeing her reflection in each display case they passed, something glinting between hand and hair, and almost hating her mother. Suddenly she just wanted to get out of there. She just wanted to go home where no one could see her.

Her mother made her way quickly to the back of the store, clutching the newspaper ad, looking around to see if any of the other customers were looking at the bedroom set.

As they stood there waiting for someone to notice them, Annie looked around the store. Nobody seemed to be paying them any attention. A man in a blue suit and tie was talking to the casually dressed young man, who was looking at sofas. Two other men in suits were talking to the well-dressed older women, showing them something in a huge book on one of the counters. The man in the dirty overcoat was going from chair to chair, sitting in each one, occasionally saying something aloud to no one. Nobody seemed to be paying any attention to him, either.

All the bedroom furniture had been shoved into a far corner of the store. From that distance Annie didn't see anything that resembled the picture, but she reminded herself that you really couldn't tell anything from those sketches. One of the well-dressed women was making her way toward the bedroom furniture, and Annie's mother was watching the woman, licking her lips nervously, her back rigid, hands fisted tight. But still she didn't try to get the attention of one of the sales clerks. It was all crazy. Annie's face was growing warm with anxiety and unfocused embarrassment. The man in the filthy overcoat looked at her and grinned with broken, brown teeth. Annie closed her eyes and imagined herself combing her hair with a beautiful curved, silver comb. Gazing into a mirror that made her look far better than she thought possible. Combing away all her nervousness, all her fear. Combing peacefulness and beauty back into her body.

"May I help you?" a male voice asked.

Annie opened her eyes. A tall man in a suit leaned over them. Annie's mother bobbed her head spastically, as if she had just awakened from a trance. "This ad," she said, shoving it into the salesman's hands. "We'd like to buy . . . to purchase that bedroom set." Then, anxiously, "You still got it, don't you?"

"Oh, yes. Several, in fact. Right over here." The salesman started toward the bedroom furniture. Annie's mother breathed deeply, relieved, and hurried after him. For all her hurrying, Momma was trying to look queenly.

"Here we are. A fine set. And a very good price."

"Oh yes, a very good price," her mother said. "We're not against paying the money for quality, mind you," she said hurriedly. "But why pass up a bargain, I always say." Momma laughed off-key.

"Hmmm. Yes. Of course. Anything I can tell you about this particular set?"

Annie could see that her Momma could hardly look at the set, so nervous she was. She just kind of moved her eyes around the furniture, going "Hmmm, hmmmm, yes, oh yes," all the time. Not really seeing anything. Annie, on the other hand, looked at every piece. It wasn't much like the newspaper sketch. A slightly different style, and of lighter color than she had imagined. Certainly not oak. The color, in fact, was unlike any wood she had ever seen. She went around to the back of the headboard and the set of drawers and discovered some other kind of board with little chips pressed into it, and plastic. But still it was nice enough looking. Certainly better than anything else they had.

And the oval mirror was real nice. Not expensive and elegant like they'd imagined, but clear and shiny. Her hair looked good in it. It caught the highlights. At a certain angle her hair seemed to grow dozens of brilliant sparkling places, as if she had filled it with all these tiny silver combs.

Someone touched her hair, softly. But she didn't see anyone in the mirror, and when she turned there was no one there.

Her mother was crying. Louder and louder, until she was almost wailing. People were turning around. The two elegantly-dressed women were whispering to each other. Annie saw all this, looking all over the store before she could bring herself to look at her mother.

"But the ad says forty dollars!" her mother cried.

The salesman looked embarrassed and a little angry. He was looking around too, as if he were trying to find someone to come help him, to help him shut up this bawling, embarrassing lady. For a panicky moment Annie imagined him calling the police. "That's forty dollars reduced, ma'am. The price has been cut by forty dollars. Four sixty down from five hundred. It's . . ." He looked ready to plead with her. "It's still really a very good price." He looked around, maybe to see if his boss had shown up yet. "Maybe you could finance?"

Annie's mother looked thunderstruck. The casually dressed young man was looking their way, smiling. The raggedy old man was smiling, too. Annie wanted to kick them both in their smiling mouths. Annie wanted to kick them all. Something cool and metallic was in her hair, stroking it. She turned to the salesman. Her mother was like a doll, a dowdy mannequin. "We can't . . . finance," Annie told the salesman. "We don't have the money."

The salesman nodded, and for a moment it looked like he was going to reach out and touch her hair. But her mother had moved behind her, and now was breathing cold and sour into her hair. "How dare you," her mother whispered harshly. "We're going," her mother told the twins.

"What about our ice cream?" one of the twins cried. Annie didn't know which one.

Her mother turned around and grabbed both the twins by the arm and started dragging them toward the door. They both screamed, and her mother had to threaten them with slaps and worse before they faded into sniffles and whimpers.

Annie took one last look at the mirror. In her reflection, sharp-edged glints of silver seemed to be attacking her hair. She broke away and followed her family out to the car.

That night Annie had been sitting in the kitchen, just staring out the window, absently stroking her hair. Her mother came into the room, looking drawn and pale, but at least she had calmed down. She pulled an old purple brush out of her robe and began brushing Annie's hair. "I just wanted to get you something nice," her mother said.

Annie squirmed away from her mother and walked quickly to her bedroom. Her hair felt warm, uncomfortable.

The next morning Annie found the first comb under her pillow. She had had bad dreams all night, of sick smiles and dirty poor people and of teeth, mostly teeth. Biting and ripping, or sometimes just pressing up against her soft skin and resting there, as if in anticipation.

When she woke up she'd still felt the teeth, working their way into her skull like the worst kind of headache. Then she'd lifted her thin pillow and discovered the comb. Long, curved metal. Not silver, she didn't think, but something like it. The teeth long and tapered, spaced just the right amount apart, it seemed, so that they wouldn't snag the hair, but pass through softly, like a breeze through the woods.

Tentatively she pressed the beautiful comb into her hair. It was as if all her nerves untangled and flowed as softly as her hair. She could hear a soft buzzing in her ears. Her skull went soft as moss. She hated to take the comb out of her hair. Her hair clung to the comb, making it hard to take away. She could feel her skull pull toward the comb.

Annie took the comb, holding it like a baby to her chest, into the kitchen where her mother was drinking coffee. "Oh, Momma. Thank you," Annie said.

Her mother looked up at her out of ugly, red-rimmed eyes. "What's that supposed to mean?"

Annie was suddenly confused. "The comb. You put it there, didn't you?"

Her mother pursed her lips, put her coffee down. "Let me see that thing."

Anxiously, Annie handed her mother the comb, already thinking about what she would do if her mother refused to hand it back. Her mother dropped the comb onto the kitchen table. It made a musical sound, like a triangle or a very small cymbal. "You steal this at that store yesterday?"

"Momma! That was a furniture store! Besides, I don't steal. I found it under my pillow this morning; I thought you had given it to me for a present." Annie felt on the verge of tears.

Her mother grunted and stood up, took her coffee and started back to her own bedroom. Much to Annie's relief, the beautiful metal comb was still on the kitchen table. "Well, I don't care if you stole it or not," her mother said as she was going out the door.

When Annie walked back to her bedroom, moving her beautiful new comb through her hair rhythmically, in time with her steps, she thought she saw two silver wings resting on the edge of her bed. When she got a closer look, however, she could see that they were two small, metal combs, only a couple of inches long.

Something unseen whispered through her hair. Insects buzzed at her ears. The comb moved rapidly through her hair, dragging her hand.

Annie thought she could see bits and pieces of her reflection in the air around her. Slivers of face, crescents of shoulder. Long flowing strands of hair, floating through the air like rays of silver dust.

Row upon row of long silver teeth dropping through the morning air.

"You dream too much. You eating junk before bed?" her mother said, when Annie told her about the eight metal combs she had found around her bedroom.

"Just a glass of milk." Her mother looked at her skeptically. "But see," Annie said, reaching into a worn paper bag and dropping the musical assortment of combs onto the table. "This isn't a dream."

It gave Annie satisfaction to see the dumbstruck look on her mother's face. Her mother stared at the assortment of combs for a very long time before actually touching one of them. "This one's cool," she said, running her finger along the spine of the longest comb. "Like ice." She picked up the smallest comb, one so curved and delicate it resembled the skeleton of a tiny sunfish. "And I swear this one's warm as a kitten." She stared at them a while longer, then looked up at Annie. "But what good are they goin' to do us?"

Over the next few days Annie discovered combs everywhere.

In the silverware drawer, nestled cozily among the forks and knives. Arranged in a circle under the front door mat. Hanging from the ivy that grew up the back wall of the house. Flowering from otherwise dusty mason jars in the cellar. Planted in rows in her mother's flower boxes. Jammed into the house foundation's cracks along with leaves and twigs. Raked into the weeds that had swallowed the back yard. The combs' positions changed a bit each day, so that Annie imagined a steady drift of combs, grooming the weeds into ornate stylings.

Annie felt blessed, richer than she could ever have imagined. Who needed a fancy mirror when the combs seemed able to make each window, each shiny surface the clearest of mirrors? She tried out each comb she found, at least once, spending hours sitting, humming to herself, the combs harvesting all the tension from her head.

And still it was the original comb, the one she had first found under her pillow, nibbling at her head, that was her favorite. She let it mouth her long hair every chance she could.

But her mother was not as enamored with the things. "They scare me," she'd say, "all these shiny, sharp, toothy combs. Where'd they all come from? Can you tell me that?"

Annie just smiled a lazy smile, the only kind of smile she could manage these days. Broad smiles, grins, they all seemed just a little angry to her now. "I don't know. Does it matter? Maybe the angels left them," Annie said.

"That's crap," her mother said, trying to remove a particularly sharp-toothed comb that had gotten snagged on her sweater. She got it out finally, but in the process lost a small swatch of material.

Annie just smiled.

Like their mother, the twins grew to dislike and distrust the combs. They'd sit down in front of the TV to watch cartoons and a wayward comb would work its way out from under the living room rug, snag their socks and scrape their ankles. They'd reach into their toy boxes for a truck or gun and one or several combs would bite them. And early one morning Tommy found his pet kitten stiff and matted in the front yard, a long shiny rat-tailed comb protruding from one ear.

More and more the family found combs soiled with the occasional fleck of red.

At dinner a spoon might arise from the soup with a small comb nestled in its hollow. The hamburger grew crunchy with their discarded teeth. They collected in boxes, in bags, in suitcases and every unused pocket. They gathered in the cold dark beneath the steps. They held meetings in the mailbox.

"I'm gonna sell some," Annie's mother announced one day. "You can keep that first one you found; you seem to like it best anyway. But we need the money. I'm sellin' the rest." She waited for Annie to say something. The twins were cranky, complaining about going with their mother, afraid to help her pick up the combs. They didn't want to touch them. Annie said nothing, just continued stroking her hair with her favorite comb. Her mother looked almost disappointed that she didn't get an argument.

Not bothering to repackage them, her mother carried them away in the vessels in which they'd naturally gathered. She filled their old car with suitcases, jars, bags, and boxes, cans and glasses and pots and pans full of combs. The car jangled musically as she and the twins sped off for town.

While they were gone Annie dreamed of unseen presences, riches by the bagful, and a quiet place where the combs could make love to her hair. For hours she waited for her family's return.

"They wouldn't take 'em, none of 'em!" her mother shouted, slamming through the door. "The recycle man said they weren't any metal he'd ever seen, and all the other stores said they weren't good as combs anyway. Too sharp. Might hurt somebody, they all said."

"Where are the combs now?" Annie asked quietly, stroking her hair.

"At the dump, that's where! That's where they belong—bunch of junk! Lord knows I wasn't going to haul 'em all the way back here!"

If her mother expected an argument, she wasn't going to get one from Annie this time, either. Annie held her last remaining comb to her ear, and then looked up at the ceiling. Her mother looked up, too. "What the hell?" she began.

"You wanted things. That was your dream," Annie said, as the metallic rain began. "You gave me the dream, Momma. And now we're rich. Just listen to all we have."

The sound on the roof was unmistakable. Metal against metal. Metal against gutter, against shingle. Comb against comb, a steady downpour.

Her mother ran to the front window. Annie could see past her, through the window and into the front yard. Where thousands of combs fell in a shimmering, silver-toothed deluge.

Her mother turned from the window. "Annie!" she screamed. Her mother dashed across the room. The twins were bawling. "Annie!" Her mother reached for her, angry and scared. "Annie, give me that comb!"

The comb flew from Annie's hand like an escaping bird. It landed in her mother's hand, pulled her mother's fingers around it like the individual bits of a fancy-dress ensemble. Then it pulled her hand to her head and began to comb.

Annie smiled her lazy smile. The floor grew soft with the thick pile of her mother's harvested, blood-clotted hair, her mother's discarded pain.

THE POOR

The poor are grinning in his waiting room.
Waiting in his room are the poor grinning.
The purposes of his office are to help and serve the poor.
To serve and help the poor are his purposes.

They come every day, mobs of them. Some get in line at six in the morning, knowing he won't arrive until nine. He has driven by that early, after reading about their early arrival in the newspapers, just to confirm it for himself. There are hundreds of them, some days thousands. All waiting to see him.

He reads in the newspapers that he has money to give away, jobs, coupons exchangeable for food, gift certificates, and new toasters. But the central office never sends him these things. The poor frequently tell him all about new benefits being offered, but he never sees them. The poor know much better than he himself how his office is run.

In his evenings at home his wife asks him how things went during the day, what he did, if he accomplished anything, and how the poor people in line were, if he had been able to do anything for them yet.

He doesn't know how he will pay for his son's college tuition next semester, how they will be able to afford a Christmas like last year's, how they'll be able to maintain their standard of living in general. And she asks him about the poor.

He cannot imagine how the poor can live, how they can live at all. How do they meet expenses? How do they keep up with the rising cost of food?

He sometimes wonders if the poor are real at all, or actors hired by someone who hates him, hired to disturb the regular pace of his day, to corrupt his dreams with their thin faces.

Or perhaps they're an illusion, and he simply minds an empty office all day. For why else would the central office ignore him, all his letters requesting funds, his many phone calls?

You worry yourself sick, you don't enjoy life, his wife tells him. You're brooding about them all the time. Them? he asks. You mean the "poor." Can't you even say the word?

His marriage is falling apart. What if he told them that? Then would they stop lining up outside his office?

He decides to arrive early each day. Talk to them. Get to know them. Show them he wants to understand their many needs.

When he arrives early he discovers that the line is much longer than ever before. Is that any way for them to show their appreciation? They're backed up outside the building and around the parking lot. He has to shove and kick his way into the building; some of them think he's one of them, and try to force him back to the end of the line.

He walks up and down the line attempting to make conversation, but they won't reply to any of his questions, merely nod or shake their heads, wring their hands. A few weep quietly. Can't they see he's trying to help them?

At nine he gives up, unlocks his office door, and sits behind his desk. There is some shuffling outside as a committee of the poor checks their line-up sheet to see if anyone's missing or wants to trade places, and then they send the first one in. It is a tall, thin, quiet man with dark circles under his eyes. He looks as if he hasn't slept, or eaten, for a week. He sits down in the chair before the desk, and stares.

The poor man stares for several minutes, making him feel like an intruder in his own office. Then finally the poor man says, "I want a wife."

He stares at the poor man in fascination. How could he request such a thing?

I'm afraid I cannot provide that for you. I'm sorry, he tells the poor man.

"I'm lonely, I need someone," the poor man tells him.

He rummages through his desk trying to find a form for the poor man to fill out, some kind of application, anything to distract him. He slides a form in front of the man. "Do you need a pencil?"

The poor man starts to fill out the form. It's a request for an emergency gallon of gasoline. He hopes the man won't be able to tell the difference.

Perhaps I could give him my wife, he thinks, and is ashamed of the thought.

There seems to be a gradual change in the poor, the first change he can remember. The line seems to have broken down into little groups, little conclaves. What could the poor be planning?

Perhaps they're plotting for more bread, sex, and rest? Or maybe they're planning to kill police officers, politicians, social workers?

Each day he goes home, his wife asks him, What are they doing today?

They're plotting, he tells her. They're seeking to overthrow our present form of government.

She nods in feigned interest.

He and his wife seem to have little time for each other any more. It's too time-consuming just making a living, trying to maintain current standards, trying not to be poor.

The poor have moved into the trunk of his car.

He went into the garage this morning, opened the trunk to load his briefcase, and the old poor man who'd requested a wife was lying curled up in the trunk.

You can't be here, he told the poor man. This won't do at all.

The poor man just stared at him sadly. No doubt waiting for his wife.

You can't have my wife, he told him.

At work the poor were in his office. You can't be here, he told them.

But they said nothing. They sat on his desk. They lay under his desk.

Several had tried to sit in his chair, but the chair had broken.

The poor were in the bathroom, hundreds of them, living and sleeping there. The poor filled the parking lot with their cooking pots and sleeping rolls.

The poor are everywhere, he tells his wife in the kitchen at home. Several poor people are sitting at their kitchen table.

There are twelve poor people living in his garage, and six more on the patio.

I know what you're planning! he tells them hysterically.

One morning he finds a poor woman with her lips clamped around his car's exhaust pipe.

Another afternoon there is a poor couple trying unsuccessfully to make love in his back seat, their starved and tattered forms smacking together futilely. He finds one in his living room, lying in front of the TV, and he beats it with a broom.

He finds one hanging from the lamp in his bedroom and he violently jerks it down.

He discovers one curled under his easy chair and he stomps it until it's dead.

The poor are living in his trash.

They're living in his bed with his wife.

The poor are dying. He beats them and they're dying.

He finds the dead bodies stacked in his garage like cordwood. He finds them piled in the study.

Small, emaciated bodies, the flesh fragile as paper, the mouths pulled back in a rictus.

The poor want too much from him. They want all the little things he has. How can he take care of himself?

The bodies of the poor fill his bedroom. He can't even find his wife any more. The dead hands try to catch his clothes; the dead, widening mouths want to eat him.

They know they will always be poor. They know the wealth will never filter down through all the widening hands to their own thin hands.

No, no! he tells the dead bodies spilling over his bed. I have an office. I'm there to help.

But the mouths say nothing.

The poor are his.

A HOUSE BY THE OCEAN

She had to park the rental car out on the main road and walk the rest of the way, taking just a few clothes and a present for her niece in the backpack that had been her carry-on. If things went well enough with her sister—and there was just no predicting—maybe she could come back for the rest of her luggage. Maybe they had a pickup or something that would run on that debris- and sand-laden lane the sign promised was Ocean Way. Or maybe not. Her sister Karen had always been dismissive of things other people thought practical, or even essential.

Lauren's annoyance gathered as she stepped carefully through the tangle of branches and fallen leaves under the canopy of tree limbs, the sounds of her progress disappearing into the unstable soil that covered the invisible road. But she was twenty years out of practice being angry with her sister—she couldn't maintain it, even in the aftermath of all those years thinking Karen was dead. As the wind picked up and rattled the limbs above, the fragmented shadows swarming like the spirits of a thousand broken birds, she began to cry as both regret and anxiety fought to consume her.

She made her way out to where the trees stopped altogether and the ground dropped swiftly into the oceanfront. The demarcation was so defined she wondered if the shoreline might have changed because of some calamity, or the ocean had receded after having taken its last bite. She'd never spent much time near the ocean, and was sure this visit wouldn't change that. How did her sister live with that constant rumbling wall?

For a few minutes she simply stared at the heaving, changing waters. The view held neither the sameness nor the peacefulness she might have expected. There was such a lack of defining form, such terrible possibility—how had those early sailors crossed its landless expanses without their minds dissolving in the terror of its scale?

Even perched a couple of hundred yards from its edge, she felt at risk to body and soul. She was an educated person, but what she saw made no sense to her, inspired silliness and superstition: the ocean appeared so high, what held it back? Suddenly it had made her a child again.

Her eyes had been on the house for several moments before she realized what she was seeing. It stood among those huge rocks not too far from the beach, and had that same sort of blockiness and a similar coloring of dark gray going to black in spots. It leaned a bit, or seemed to, away from the ocean, and she couldn't tell if some of the odd angles above the windows and just under the roof were purposeful examples of eccentric craft or simply evidence of structural damage. It looked abandoned—no curtains she could see, or anything outside indicating a family lived there, and there were great bands of crystalline silt deposited near the bottom, as if those parts upon occasion had been submerged.

Lauren had called her once, after Hurricane Fran landed on the North Carolina coast in 1996. She used to have a torn piece of paper on the refrigerator with the phone number scribbled on it. "Why wouldn't I be okay?" Karen had snapped, as if it had been an offensive question. "I can take care of myself!" And then she'd hung up. It was the same old argument they'd been having ever since their mother died. But Lauren was the older one—of course she felt some added responsibility. If she came off too strong sometimes it was only because she cared.

She'd called that number again in 1999 after Floyd hit. It had been disconnected. She wrote a letter but it was returned. She'd contacted mutual friends. No one had heard from Karen since the hurricane. She thought about flying out there then, but she had her job, and Karen would have just dumped all kinds of abuse on her for her troubles. So finally she'd let it go. She'd done her share. Let Karen contact her if she wanted to stay in touch.

The lane began to fade halfway along the slope and eventually disappeared among the scattered clumps of salt grass. There were no signs of ruts, so she assumed Karen must not own a vehicle. Maybe she shouldn't have come, but Karen had called at last, needing her, sounding nothing like the resentful younger sister from their last conversation. The weight of the ocean air pushed against her face brought her to the verge of tears.

"Sis?" Her sister's voice had sounded thin and reedy, and even further away than North Carolina. There was a hiss on the line, and the occasional watery echo that might have been interference, or a sob, or the surrounding ocean, rising.

"Karen? Honey, it's been a long time."

There was just a moment's hesitation, and in that moment Lauren thought she heard a child crying. "Sis ... we need you to come out here," Karen sounded stressed out of her mind. Another pause, and in that a child's intemperate scream. A girl, maybe. Lauren had never had kids, but for a child to make a sound like that, it unsettled her.

"Karen, is there a child there?"

"Julieee ..." The name trailed out, in sadness, or because her sister was trying to calm the child, Lauren couldn't tell.

"I didn't know. Is she yours?"

"Seven years. Please come, soon as you can ..." Karen's voice had a hollow sound.

"Is it the same place? Did you move?"

"Same ... always been here ..." Her sister's voice was lost to the echo and static hiss.

She'd tried several times to call her back with no luck. The line sounded weak or distorted, or there was no sound at all, not even a ring. The next day she purchased her plane ticket. She bought Julie a doll on her way to the airport, a floppy thing with huge, aimless eyes.

Lauren found the entrance to the house, a single narrow door that faced the ocean, but it had been placed about a third of the way up the structure, on a porch apparently accessible only by means of several sets of stairs that were staggered across the rocks and appeared to have been constructed from old water-logged timbers, many with cracked and collapsed surfaces and splintered ends, and decorated with scattered white furry streaks she assumed to be some variety of mold.

The whole assemblage appeared unsafe for a child, or anyone else, for that matter. She was feeling a familiar, nagging outrage over her sister's irresponsibility, before it occurred to her that of course Karen couldn't possibly live here. She must have abandoned this ruin ages ago, and for some reason assumed Lauren had her newer address.

But then something up on the porch caught her eye, some shape near one corner, almost but not quite out of her line of sight. Rough-formed head and maybe a beak, some sort of huge dark sea bird peering down at her. Unmoving, patiently waiting. And that led her eyes to the window above and to the right of it, and the face of the little girl on the other side of the glass looking out.

Lauren went up a few steps carefully. The wood was mushy. Moisture was weeping out around her shoes. She took another few steps and could feel the timbers shifting, barely gripped by the wet and rusted nails. A large flat expanse of rock made a landing before the next flight of steps began at its far end. She walked across the rock feeling more secure; the next steps looked drier, but groaned when her feet came down on them. The rough-hewn stair stringer wiggled, but the rickety frame held. She came to the next landing, which was just a few planks attached to an old beam bolted to another rock. It was too narrow to be safe, she thought, especially for a little girl, and she stepped quickly on to it and off again, and after a few more nervous steps—she seemed so high now—she was standing on one end of the porch.

The ugly sea bird stared at her, its neck bent awkwardly. It was just a strange and heavy twist of driftwood, she now saw, which someone had apparently treasured enough to risk a dangerous haul up here for display.

She walked slowly over to the window. The girl's face looked up at her, then vanished into the grubby darkness of the room, but not before Lauren had been struck by the remarkable family resemblance to Karen, to their mother, and to Lauren herself.

She went to the heavily-weathered door and knocked, waited, and knocked again. She tried the greenish knob and after the momentary resistance of swollen wood the door popped open.

It took a while for her eyes to adjust, and when they did she was disappointed by the dust-furred interior, the ridges of grime on the floor, the dirty bottles and corroded pans, the water stains on the walls as large and complex as duotone landscapes, the stench of mold.

Her tears welled up—she hadn't realized just how much she'd hoped—when the ocean hissed behind her as the dying waves raced over the pebbled shore, and Karen drifted in and wrapped her arms around her, whispering "Sis", and folding her seemingly weightless body into Lauren's embrace.

They held each other and cried, and over Karen's shoulder Lauren watched as that lovely little girl came in and smiled, holding up a lantern, and in that warmer light she could see how mistaken she had been. The room was poor but clean, and invited her with its array of quilts and pillows and cushioned chairs, hand-crafts hanging on the walls, and everywhere she looked an array of colors and intriguing shapes. The decay and disorder had been a product of the shadows, she thought, and the angle of the light, aided by her distress and fatigue.

The two sisters talked long into the night, Julie asleep across a blanket at her mother's feet. She held the doll Lauren had given her lightly in her hand.

"I was afraid to tell you," Karen said again. "I've messed up so many times." She sat with her knees up, narrow arms binding herself to herself. Her face was worn, and wearied with stress lines across her forehead, slashing over her cheeks so deeply they looked like scars in the spongy, unhealthily pale skin. Lauren couldn't ever remember her sister being so frighteningly skinny. And yet it oddly made her look younger than she was, like an undernourished teenager. She was also rocking, so subtly that at first Lauren hadn't noticed it. Then she realized it closely matched the rhythm of the waves breaking outside. In fact the whole house appeared to have a sway to it, but that had to be the wind, not the waves.

"We all make mistakes, hon," she told her, reaching out her hand, but for some reason reluctant to touch that fragile body wound so tightly. "If you'd been around you'd have witnessed far too many of mine."

Karen nodded ever so slightly, but didn't look at her. In fact Lauren had noticed her sister's eyes had so far completely avoided any direct contact. The poor kid seemed so ashamed, so distracted, her mind hardly there in the room. Was she at least partly responsible? She'd been the one to raise Karen those last few years of high school.

"I had a husband, Paul. He drowned when Hurricane Fran came ashore. I know I was harsh with you on the phone that time—you'd just wanted to see how I was— but I'd never even told you I was married, so how was I going to tell you my husband was dead?"

"We were pretty distant then, as much my fault as yours. But, honey, that doesn't matter now. 'Water under the bridge', like Mom always said."

"You always told me I made bad choices. It was true. I had no business being with him. Neither one of us knew what we were doing here. Paul was full of ideas, but he didn't know how to do anything."

"Look at me, Karen. Please, look at me." After a few moments her sister glided her head around, pointing her face at her. But Lauren could still tell she wasn't actually looking at her. Karen's eyes appeared as pale and unfocused as smoke. Maybe that was the best her sister could do for now. She was obviously, seriously, damaged. "It's not your fault. You've done the best you could. I'm sure." Of course Lauren had no idea if Karen had done her best—in fact, that possibility seemed quite remote, but what did the truth of it matter now?

"I've been so lonely since then," Karen said to the window, and the ocean moving so invisibly, and largely, out there. "I've had nothing to do."

Julie stirred then, turning her head to the ceiling. Her face was so white and perfect—like a mask floating up from the depths of her head to the surface and then settling back down again. Lauren yawned. She was exhausted. She'd have to go to bed soon.

"Well, obviously you met someone later, right? And then you had this angel to take care of. That's not exactly nothing."

Karen had closed her eyes. "Nothing," she repeated.

"Before we both fall asleep, is there a spare bedroom? I mean, whatever it is it'll be fine. Or I could sleep right here."

Karen got up without speaking and helped Lauren up a steep

and narrow flight of stairs, leaning against her as they ascended, snuggling like a sleepwalker. There were pictures on the walls of people Lauren did not know. Finally they reached a snug little room at the top, a low sprawl of a bed, a skinny window with an eavesdropper's view of the dark waters, the occasional long lines of serrated white illuminated by a full moon. Lauren fell into the covers without undressing, aware of only a whispered goodnight, the cold breath across her face, then oblivion.

She dreamed she fell into the ocean, and even though she couldn't swim all that well the dream didn't bother her, and when she woke up there was no anxiety, only the feeling of a long and tiring trip completed, with Karen waiting at the end.

But somehow she must have fallen out of bed, because now she lay in a sprawl of dirty rags. She looked around—the sun blazed through the narrow curtainless window. And clearly there was no furniture in the room—just these piles of filthy rags, and a few crumbling boxes of warped, waterlogged books, and chewed bits of debris all over the floor, as if rats had been up here doing all the things rats do. She must have wandered away from the guest room upstairs into another, similar room—maybe on the other end—a room that was no longer being used, but then Karen really should have locked it, because Lauren didn't like the idea of Julie wandering in, playing in here.

She went over to the decaying boxes and spent a few minutes looking at the books. They smelled like earth, like the bare moist ground under a big rock you've just pulled up, the exposed worms crawling all around. There were several ancient hardcover novels by authors she had never heard of, an early Southern history, a slim volume concerned with cooking okra, a study of barns of the Carolinas, and a collection of letters between an early governor of North Carolina and his children. If the books had been in better shape, and if she were to stay here for a while, she might have tried to read them. Maybe she still would.

She pushed her face against the window and looked out at the ocean. It was a dark bluish gray today, the sky a stirred expanse of cream above it, heavy with clouds. Visibility was poor. She thought she saw the shape of a distant ship, but it could have been a bird, or driftwood, or anything. She knew, of course, that the rest of the world still carried on while her sister and her niece kept themselves locked away in this isolated house on the coastline. But none of that felt very real while she was here. Time seemed to have given up, because there was nothing to count off, nothing to look forward to. From this angle she felt quite high up in the air; she could feel everything swaying. And yet the ocean was still higher, seeking to invade the sky, and only a trick of physics kept it from invading the land. It all seemed impossible.

She felt vaguely ill, watching the mass of it churning. It was like gazing at a nearby mountain suddenly gone liquid. The roiling waves revealed dark pockets which appeared to have something in them, creatures or spirits or passage to somewhere else, but the pockets collapsed too quickly to tell. She supposed it was akin to seeing shapes in shadow or cloud, but she still could not stop herself from staring and wondering.

As she leaned against the glass she was surprised to feel it give. An arm and a hinge mechanism had been designed to open the window, but the handle was missing so there was no way to pull it shut tightly or latch it firmly. The window was partly open, so she pushed it open some more to lean out for a better look. Maybe she shouldn't have done it, but surely Karen would know how to fix it closed.

She had a good view of the coastline this way, a mile or so north and south. All along the shore the land was dissolving into the aggressive edge of that great body of tortured gray liquid. She had no idea if this meant a storm was coming or if this was the way it looked every day.

She dropped her gaze and saw a large pale bird making its way precariously along the slick rock surfaces between this house and the precipitous edge. Occasionally it would lose its balance and land on its side, then struggle up with hands and feet. Lauren gasped. It was Julie.

"Julieeee ..." The sounds of her niece's name floated, stretched out and thinned atop a rising gust of wind. Lauren searched frantically for her sister, and then saw Karen struggling up the rocks on the southern edge of the formation, her pale dress soaked and clinging like tissue to her skinny frame. Then Karen was racing across the black and gray stone, but Lauren couldn't see how she could possibly get there in time. So Lauren began shouting "Julie! Julie!" hoping the child would stop and turn around. The wind reached out and snatched the syllables out of her mouth and flung them at the sky.

The child neared the edge. It was like watching a movie so intently you felt you were actually participating, but then something happened to remind you that most decidedly you were not. Karen's back was blocking Lauren's view of the child. Then a wave hit, drenching them in obscuring spray.

Lauren raced down the stairs, her hands grazing the furry bits of wallpaper and plaster, the cracked walls beginning to come apart and showering the steps in dust and grit. An array of crooked empty picture frames, their surfaces stained green and mold black, shook and tumbled off around her. She had to push her way through a tangle of broken chairs and rotted cardboard at the bottom of the staircase, and maneuver around the collapsed table at the center of the room. Broken fragments of crockery and rusted pans edged a large hole in the warped, stinking floorboards, gaping onto the dark spaces below the abandoned house. Nothing could live in such a place. Nothing could long survive such destruction. Finally she dragged aside the ruins of the half-open front door, the bottom scraping in anguished protest, and stepped gingerly over the trembling porch, careful to avoid the missing and rotted planks.

She found Julie and Karen resting in a shallow place in the rocks. Karen's thin arm lay across the girl's body. Lauren imagined the worst. Then the child's face turned from somewhere within that jumble of wet cloth, pale flesh, and hair, and looked at her, and began to speak, but even getting down on her hands and knees and leaning over as close as possible Lauren could hear no words.

She moved her hands between them, but her fingers would not grab. Their skin was soft, and seemingly edgeless, and moved slowly, or not at all. But eventually they disentangled. Julie sat cross-legged a few feet away, staring out at the ocean. Karen had pulled herself into her sister's arms, and clung there, weeping. Lauren herself was shaking and kept touching Karen's body with her hands to reassure herself, and rubbing her cheek along

Karen's face, and kissing her, and softly apologizing, but she wasn't sure if Karen could hear, or feel her at all.

"I wish . . . you could take her . . . with you." Karen rasped out. "I never could take . . . the proper care. Is it really too late?"

"Oh, honey, she's yours. She loves you. I can tell."

"No. No," Karen insisted, crying. "It's no good. Please . . . please . . . you can't understand."

Her sister brushed vaguely against her, and she seemed so small, it was like they were kids again, and Lauren wanted so badly to protect her, but didn't know how. It felt as if Karen weighed almost nothing at all. Lauren didn't know if her sister could ever come back from this; there really was no time. She pressed her hands against her, swearing to herself she would never let her go, but it felt as if she already had.

They made their way slowly across the rocks toward the house, Julie in the lead, now moving almost playfully, skipping, with no indication of the danger she'd just been in. Lauren felt unsafe and tried to call the child back, but Karen was so weak, barely there in her torn and disintegrating garment. Lauren couldn't quite get her mouth to make the words. Karen suddenly sighed deeply, and Lauren could smell the stink on her sister's breath, the rotted weed and spoiled fish of it, and the sourness of her hair, like cotton left to soak in rancid water.

She didn't want Julie to reach the house before them, not with all that rotted wood, that grime and rust and breakage, those walls decorated in regret, that life collapsing into ruin. She didn't want to go back in herself, to see again what she'd seen when she came back down the stairs.

"Karen, who is Julie's father? You never said."

The answer came slowly, a whisper wet with emotion. "I don't like . . . I don't think about that."

"It wasn't, well, it couldn't have been Paul, could it? That would be impossible, of course. She's far too young for him to be her dad. Was Paul her father?"

"Yes," her sister sighed, and seemed to fall into nothing, to spread thinly over her, until all Lauren could feel was the damp.

It was then that Julie crossed the rock between Lauren and the sun. In that brief shadow Lauren looked down for her sister, and, not seeing her, turned, and turned again, but Karen was not there, even though Lauren would swear later that she could still smell her on her clothes. Lauren waited for Julie to reappear so that she might hold and reassure her, take the child back with her and make her her own.

She waited the rest of that day and most of the next, then found her way back up the ocean road to her car, and returned home alone.

WHEATFIELD WITH CROWS

Sometimes when he sketched out what he remembered of that place, new revelations appeared in the shading, or displayed between the layering of a series of lines, or implied in a shape suddenly suggested in some darker spot in the drawing. The back of her head, or some bit of her face, dead or merely sleeping, he could never quite tell. He was no Van Gogh, but Dan's art still told him things about how he felt and what he saw, and he'd always sensed that if he could just find her eyes among those lines or perhaps even in an accidental smear, he might better understand what happened to her.

In this eastern part of the state the air was still, clear and empty. An overabundance of sky spilled out in all directions with nothing to stop it, the wheat fields stirring impatiently below. Driving up from Denver, seeing these fields again from such distance, Dan thought the wheat appeared nothing special. He made himself think of bread, and the golden energy that fed thousands of years of human evolution, but the actual presence of the grain was drab, if overwhelming. When he'd been here as a child, he'd thought these merely fields full of weeds. But so tall, they had been pretty much all he could see, a sea of weeds, wild and uncontrolled. But when he was a child everything was like that—so limitless, so hard to understand.

In the decade and a half since his sister's disappearance, Dan had been back to this tiny no-place by the highway only once, when at fifteen he'd stolen a car to get here. He'd never done anything like that before, and he wasn't sure the trip had accomplished anything. He'd just felt the need to be here, to try and understand why he no longer had a sister. And although the wheat had moved, and shuddered, and acted as if it might lift off the ground to reveal its secrets, it did not, and Dan had returned home.

Certainly this trip—driving the hour from Denver (legally this time), with his mother in the passenger seat staring catatonically out the window—was unlikely to change anything in their lives. She'd barely said two words since he picked her up at her apartment. He had to give her some credit, though—she had a job now and no terrible boyfriends in her life as far as he knew. But it was hard to be generous.

Roggen, Colorado, near Interstate 76 and Colorado Road 73, lay at the heart of the state's grain crop. "Main Street" was a dirt road that ran alongside a railroad track. A few empty store fronts leaned attentively but appeared to have nothing to say. The same abandoned house he remembered puffed out its gray-streaked cheeks as it continued its slow-motion collapse. The derelict Prairie Lodge Motel sat near the middle of the town, its doors wide open, various pieces of worn, overstuffed furniture dragged out for absent observers to sit and watch.

Every few months when Dan did an internet search, it came up as a "ghost town". He wondered how the people who still lived here—and there were a few of them, tucked away on distant farms or hiding in houses behind closed blinds—felt about that.

"There, there's where it happened," his mother whispered, tapping the glass gently as if hesitant to disturb him. "There's where my baby disappeared."

Dan pulled the car over slowly at this ragged edge of town, easing carefully off the dirt road as he watched for ditches, holes, anything that might trap them here longer than necessary. They'd started much later than he'd planned. First his mother had been unsure what to wear, trying on various outfits, worrying over what might be too casual, what might be "too much". Dan wanted to say it wasn't as if they were going to Caroline's funeral, but did not. His mother had put on too much makeup, but when she'd asked how she looked he was reluctant to tell her. The encroaching grief of the day only made her face look worse.

Then she'd decided to make sandwiches in case they got hungry, in case there was no place to stop, and of course out here there wouldn't be. Dan had struggled for patience, knowing that if they started to argue it would never stop. It had been mid-afternoon by the time they left Denver, meaning this visit would have to be a short one, but it just couldn't be helped.

As soon as he stopped the car his mother was out and pacing in front of the rows of wheat that lapped the edge of the road. He got out quickly, not wanting her to get too far ahead of him. The clouds were lower, heavier, leaking darkness toward the ground in long narrow plumes. He could see the wind coming from a distance, the fields farther off beginning to move like water rolling on the ocean, all so restless, aimless, and, by the time the disturbance arrived at the field where they stood, the wind brought the sound with it, a constant and persistent crackle and fuzz, shifting randomly in volume and tone.

It occurred to him there was no one in charge here to watch this field, to witness its presence in the world, to wonder at its peace or fury. No doubt the owners and the field hands lived some distance away. This was the way of things with modern farming, vast acreages irrigated and cultivated by machinery, and nobody watched what might be going on in the fields. It had been much the same when Caroline vanished. It had seemed almost as if the fields had no owners, but were powers unto themselves, somehow managing on their own, like some ancient place.

Dan took continuous visual notes. He itched to rough these into his typical awkward sketches, but although he always kept sketching supplies in the glove compartment he couldn't bring himself to do so in front of his mother. He never showed his stuff to anyone, but his untrained expressions were all he had to quell his sometimes runaway anxiety.

So like Van Gogh's "Wheatfield with Crows", Dan saw long angular shadows carved into the wheat beginning to lift out of their places, turning over then flapping, and rising into the turbulent air where they became knife rips in the fabric of sky.

"She was right here, right here." His mother's voice was like old screen shredding to rust. She was standing near the edge of the field, her head down, eyes intent on the plants as if waiting for something to come out of the rows. "My baby was right here."

The wheat was less than three feet tall, even shorter when whipped back and forth like this, a tortured texture of shiny and dull golds. At six, his sister had been much taller. Had she crouched so that her head didn't show? Had she been brave enough to crawl into the field? Or had she been taken like his mother always thought, and dragged, her abductor's back hunched as he'd pulled her into the rows of vibrating wheat?

Out in the field the wheat opened and closed, swirling, now and then revealing pockets of shade, moments of dark opportunity. The long flexible stalks twisted themselves into sheaves and limbs, humanoid forms and moving rivers of grainy muscle, backs and heads made and unmade in the changing shadows teased open by the wind. Overhead the crows screeched their unpleasant proclamations. Dan could not see them but they sounded tormented, ripped apart.

His mother knelt, wept eerily like a child. He had to convince himself it wasn't Caroline. He stepped up behind his mother and laid his hand on her shoulder, confirming that she was shaking, crying. His mother reached up and laid her hand over his, mistaking his reality check for concern.

A red glow had crept beneath the dark clouds along the horizon, and that, along with the increasingly frayed black plumes clawing the ground, made him think of forest fires. But there were no forests in that direction to burn—just sky, and wheat, and wind blowing away anything too insubstantial to hold on.

Suddenly a brilliant blaze silvered the front surface of wheat and his mother sprang up, her hands raised in alarm. Dan looked around and, seeing that the pole lamp behind them had come on automatically at dusk, he turned her face gently in that direction and pointed. It seemed a strange place for a street lamp, but he supposed even the smallest towns had at least one for safety.

That light might have been on at the time of his sister's disappearance. He'd been only five, but in his memory there had been a light that had washed all their faces in silver, or had it been more of a bluish cast? There had been Caroline, himself, their mother, and Mom's boyfriend at the time. Ted had been his name, and he'd been the reason they were all out there. Ted said he used to work in the wheat fields, and Dan's mother said it had been a long time since she'd seen a wheat field. They'd both been drinking, and impulsively they took Caroline and Dan on that frightening ride out into the middle of nowhere.

Ted had interacted very little with Dan, so all Dan remem-

bered about him was that he had this big black moustache and
that he was quite muscular—he walked around without his shirt
on most of the time. Little Danny had thought Ted was a cartoon
character, and how it was kind of nice that they had a cartoon
character living with them, but like most cartoon characters Ted
was a little too loud and a little too scary.

"I never should have dated that Ted. We were all pretty happy
until Ted came along," his mother muttered beside him now. She
hadn't had a drink in several years as far as he knew, but like many
long time drinkers she still sounded slightly drunk much of the
time—drink appeared to have altered how she moved her mouth.

This was all old stuff, and Dan tuned it out. His mother had
always blamed ex-husbands and ex-boyfriends for her mistakes,
as if she'd been helpless to choose, to do what needed to be done.
Just once Dan wished she would do what needed to be done.

When Dan had come here at age fifteen it had been the middle
of the day, so this oh-so-brilliant light had not been on. He hadn't
wanted to be here in the dark. He didn't want to be here in the
dark now.

But the night his sister Caroline disappeared had also been
bathed in this selective brilliance. That high light had been on that
night as well. No doubt a different type of bulb back in those days.
Sodium perhaps, or an arc light. Dan just remembered being five
years old and sitting in the back of that smelly old car with his
sister. The adults stank of liquor, and they'd gotten out of the
car and gone off somewhere to do something, and they'd told
Danny and Caroline to stay there. "Don't get off that seat, kids,"
his mother had ordered. "Do you hear me? No matter what. It's
not *safe*. Who knows what might be out there in that field?"

Danny had cried a little—he couldn't even see over the back
of the seat and there were noises outside, buzzes and crackles
and the sound of the wind over everything, like an angry giant's
breath. Caroline kept saying she needed to go to the bathroom,
and she was going to open the car door just a little bit, run out
and use the bathroom and come right back. Dan kept telling her
no, don't do that, but Caroline was a little bit older and never did
anything he said.

The only good thing, really, had been the light. Danny told

himself the bright light was there because an angel was watching over them, and as long as an angel was watching nothing too terrible could happen. He decided that no matter how confusing everything was, what he believed about the angel was true.

Caroline had climbed out of the car and gone toward the wheat field to use the bathroom. She'd left the car door part way open and that was scary for Danny, looking out the door and seeing the wheat field moving around like that, so he had used every bit of strength he had to pull the car door shut behind her. But what if she couldn't open the door? What if she couldn't get back in? That was the last time he saw his sister.

"I left you two in the car, Dan. I told you two to stay. Why did she get out?"

Dan stared at his mother as she stood with one foot on the edge of the road, the other not quite touching, but almost, the first few stalks of wheat. Behind her the rows dissolved and reformed, shadows moving frenetically, the spaces inside the spaces in constant transformation. He'd answered her questions hundreds of times over the years, so although he wanted to say *because she had to go to the bathroom, you idiot*, he said nothing. He just watched her feet, waiting for something to happen. Overhead was the deafening sound of crows shredding.

There used to be a telephone mounted below the light pole, he remembered. He and his mother and Ted had waited there all those years ago until a highway patrolman came. Ted and his mother had searched the wheat field for over an hour before they made the call. At least that's what his mother had always told him. Danny had stayed in the car with the doors shut, afraid to move.

He guessed they had looked hard for his sister, he guessed that part was true. But they obviously did a bad job because they never found her. They also told the officer they had been standing just a few feet away at the time, gazing up at the stars. What else had they lied about? The brilliant high light carved a confusing array of shadows out of the wheat, Dan's car, and his mother. His own shadow, too, was part of the mix, but he had some difficulty identifying it. As his mother paced back and forth in front of the field, her shadow self appeared to multiply, times two, times three, more. As the wind increased the wheat parted in strips like hair, the stalks writhing as if in religious fervor, bowing almost horizontal at times, the wind threatening to tear out the plants completely and expose what lay beneath. Pockets of shadow were sent running, some isolated and left standing by themselves closer to the road. Dan could hear wings flapping over him, the sound descending as if the crows might be seeking shelter on the ground.

"She might still be out there, you know," his mother said. "I was so confused that night; I just don't think we covered enough of the field. We could have done a better job."

"The officers searched most of the night." Dan raised his voice to be heard above the wind. "They had spotlights, and dogs. And volunteers were out here the rest of the week looking, and for some time after. I've read all the newspaper articles, Mom, every single one. And even when they harvested the wheat that year, they did this section manually, remember? They didn't want to damage—they wanted to be careful not to—" He was trying to be careful, calm and logical, but he wasn't sure he even believed what he was saying himself.

"They didn't want to damage her remains. That's what you were trying to say, right? Well, I've always thought that was a terrible word. She was a sweet little girl."

"I'm just trying to say that after the wheat was gone there was nothing here. Caroline wasn't here."

"You don't know for sure."

"What? You think she got ploughed under? That she's down under the furrows somewhere? Mom, it's been years. Something would have turned up."

"Then she might be alive. We just have to go find her. I've read about this kind of thing. It happens all the time. They find the child years later. She's too scared to tell all these years, and then she does. There's a reunion. It's awkward and it's hard, but she becomes their daughter again. It happens like that sometimes, Danny."

He noticed how she called him by his childhood name. Danny this and Danny that. It was also the only name Caroline had ever had for him. But more than that, he was taken by her story. To argue with his mother about such a fairytale seemed too cruel, even for her.

He barely noticed the small shadow that had fallen into place not more than a foot or two away from her, a dark hollow shaking with the wind, perhaps thrown out of the body of wheat, vibrating as if barely whole or contained, its edges ragged, discontinuous. At first he thought it was one of the large crows that had finally landed to escape the fierce winds above, ready to take its chances with the winds blowing along the ground, but its feathers so damaged, so torn, Dan couldn't see how it could ever fly again.

Until it opened its indistinct eyes, and looked at him, and he knew himself incapable of understanding exactly what he was seeing. If he were Van Gogh he might take these urgent, multi-directional slashes and whorls and assemble them into the recognizable face of his sister Caroline, whose eyes had now gone cold, and no more sympathetic or understandable than the other mysteries that traveled through the natural and unnatural world.

His mother wept so softly now, but he was close enough to hear her above the wind, the hollowed-out change in her voice as this shadow gathered her in and took her deep into the field.

And because he had no right to object, he knew that this time there would be no phone call, there would be no search.

CRUTCHES

A tap, a thump. A tap, a thump. Michael listened to his mother pacing her room with the crutch, just overhead. He had awakened to the sound, three a.m., and that was two hours ago. Two hours of steady pacing, and how many before that?

He slipped on his robe, trying not to awaken Doris, and climbed the stairs slowly. He paused on the landing, where a great bay window displayed the western slope of the Rockies, the dark houses at its base, and the slow drift of snow like sleep falling from the peak. A narrow road ran between Michael's borrowed house and those darkened houses, a passageway that held few cars this time of year. A few local vehicles, certainly, but as the snow season reached its height even they would no longer be venturing out. People in Elkins Park took out their cars only when they needed something from another town, or if they were going on vacation. Otherwise, they walked. Or made their way cross-country on skis.

He reached the top of the stairs and looked at the bottom of her door. The light was still on, and now he could hear the tap-thump of her one crutch, although much fainter than it had been downstairs. Once again he blamed himself for dragging his mother up here, but they really had no other place to go. Joe Jensen had offered him the place rent free for a year, just to take care of it, and Michael and Doris had both been out of work for almost two years at that point. And afraid of failing again, Michael thought, then shook himself irritably. Elkins Park did have its advantages—it was cheap to live here, and a quiet place for Doris to do her painting.

There was no energy left in the marriage; there hadn't been for some time. Lack of money only made it worse. At least sometimes money could buy the energy: concerts, plays, ski trips. They seemed to have no more words for each other. And finally here, in this house, time had stopped completely. They didn't go forward, but with some relief Michael realized things weren't falling back, either.

He paused in front of the door, then knocked before gently swinging it open.

His mother stood by the window, gray hair hanging over her cheeks, her tattered housecoat bunched into odd, shapeless lumps; she appeared suspended from the one crutch like a broken scarecrow. A cigarette dangled from the front of her mouth, the long ash suspended impossibly from its tip.

"You'll burn yourself, Mother."

She reached up and jerked the cigarette out of her mouth. "I'm sorry," she said softly, and turned to the window.

Tap thump. A hollow sound, and for a moment Michael imagined that her entire leg was wood.

She had gone downhill fast since the accident. Their first day there she had fallen through a rotten board in the front steps. Michael had thought, momentarily, of suing his good friend Joe, who had no homeowner's insurance for this old derelict, but his family wasn't the kind to sue. What happens, happens, as his mother had put it at the time.

She looked awful. The broken leg seemed to have sapped the strength from the rest of her body. He remembered the way it had swollen, so quickly, and even at the time it had seemed the swelling was draining her face, her eyes, her long narrow fingers of their small store of vitality.

"You should try to get some rest," he said.

She looked at him as if he couldn't possibly know what he was talking about. Then she gazed out the window again. "I can't sleep."

"You look worried."

She gazed at him distractedly. "I'm going to be on this crutch for the rest of my life."

"That's nonsense. You're healing fine. You never let anything like this get you down before."

"I was never this old before. I can feel it, Michael. Something's different inside me. I won't be letting go of this crutch until the day I die."

Michael started to speak, but thought better of it. At least she was up out of bed; she'd stayed in bed for a long time after the accident. She wouldn't even try. Then the town doctor brought the crutches—he said there was a man in town who carved them himself—and she'd pulled herself up on them, so at least she could pace. There was something about the crutches that moved her, pulled her right up out of bed. Michael'd seen the look on her face when the doctor brought them. As if they were arcane objects, mysterious and magical.

"You're scaring me, Mother." It was embarrassing to say, but he suddenly realized it was true.

"I don't mean to, son."

As he started down the stairs he noted the change in sound. She had taken the other crutch out of the closet and now she was using two.

Tap thump tap. Tap thump. Tap thump thump.

The next morning Michael didn't get out of bed immediately. His wife was already up, and that made it easier for him to stay in bed. If she were still there in the room she would be able to see he wasn't really tired at all, and he'd feel too guilty to stay in bed. There was nothing to do. He should have been out looking for a job, he thought irritably, but he knew he wasn't going to even try for a while.

It was the same every day. The same thoughts, the same worries. The lack of energy. It was the sameness that was wearing him down. He thought it was the sameness that would finally kill him.

The same. Each day. Always. Tap. Tap. Thump.

Elkins Park was a poor place to find work in any case. The general store and gift shop, the trail guide center, were all run by people who had been in Elkins Park for some time. It seemed unlikely there would be any more openings. Most of them had no more on the ball than he did, but they'd got here first and settled. They wouldn't budge. Jacobs at the guide center was a failed lawyer. Matthews at the gift shop a failed crafts store owner. The gift shop was owned by a friend in Denver and he merely worked there.

Michael didn't know a single person in town who hadn't failed somewhere else. The realization troubled him. It was as if they had all gathered here. He couldn't figure what was so attractive about the place.

The next day he had to go into town for supplies. Willis had had the grocery store in the Park for over ten years. But before that he had had a chain, ten of them all along the Front Range. He'd lost them all in little over two years. Tap. When Michael walked through the door . . . tap . . . Willis looked up and smiled wanly. Thump. He had a crutch. Michael wasn't surprised.

"What can I get for you today, Michael?" Tap tap.

Not wanting to talk to the man, Michael just handed him Doris's list. Thump.

While Willis was filling the order Michael wandered out onto the wide wooden boardwalk fronting the store. The day already seemed to have turned cooler since the morning. He hunched his shoulders inside his jacket and turned to walk down the street. But he was stopped by the sight of dozens of crutches stacked haphazardly in the alley next to the store.

A bearded man in a checkered shirt lumbered into view, rearranging the crutches into a neat stack. Michael could see now that the crutches looked hand-carved—like the others he had seen around town, like the kind his mother had—each one slightly different.

The big man stopped and stared at Michael, seeming to appraise him, then returned to his workbench set up deeper in the alley.

"Hey, wait!" Michael cried, and ran after him.

The man picked up a rough-shaped crutch and began smoothing it with knife and sandpaper.

"What are you doing?"

The man edged a crutch forward to the front of the bench. "Crutches," he said.

Michael peered at the man. He could swear there were tears in his eyes. "Everybody needs a crutch now and then, eh?" He wasn't sure why he said it. "What does a pair cost?" he asked, and immediately regretted it.

"I only sell one at a time," the man said softly. "And you don't seem to need one, not just yet."

Michael glanced away. The man was grinning now. "You think

this a pretty good joke, don't you!" Michael suddenly shouted, and slammed his fist on the crutch on the bench. It snapped like a twig. Michael's eyes widened. "Why . . . why it wouldn't support a kitten!" he cried.

Tap. The man said nothing. Tap. After an awkward moment Michael turned and left.

He drove home quickly, trying not to glance at pedestrians. But every now and then he couldn't help looking to the side, and seeing that a quarter of the people were using crutches. Tap tap. Tap tap.

Workers were renovating an old house on the outskirts, just before the turnoff to Michael's own residence. Hammer shots echoed in the winter stillness. Tap tap tap tap. He tried to ignore the sound. Beams had been propped up against one side; the house leaned precariously, as if the beams were all that held it erect.

One of the workers pulled tools out of a metal box, then tossed them one at a time into the tall weeds behind the structure. Then he sat down on the box, and rubbed his legs.

Michael drove more slowly the rest of the way home, afraid he might miss something. Something was happening in Elkins Park.

When he got home he found all of Doris's painting supplies in the trash, along with most of her paintings. He picked them out one at a time, sadly, examining torn canvas and broken frames. Some of her best work: that old lady back in the city, her grandfather's house, Michael's own portrait.

She was sitting on the couch in the living-room, watching television. "Why'd you do it, Doris?" he asked, feeling uneasy about the trembling in his voice.

"I'm giving it up, Michael. There just isn't any point." She looked years older than she had that morning. Tap. Michael was numbed.

"You've felt discouraged before . . ." Tap.

"It's different this time. I have nothing to paint about, nothing to say." Tap. "Painting is about the last thing I want to be doing with my time." She turned her head and locked her eyes onto the television screen.

Michael watched her face glaze over. "So what do you want to do with your time?" He knew it must sound sarcastic. Tap. But she didn't react. Tap. It was as if she hadn't even heard him.

Suddenly she was looking up at the ceiling. Examining it. As if she were looking for the point of contact of his mother's crutch and the floor. Tap. As if she might see the sound. Her eyes out of focus, glazed.

His mother hung over the bed, her hips and belly gone to fat. She glided over the covers and suddenly it seemed to Michael that she was a great dark poisonous spider. He stared at the wall and moaned. It was true—the shadow had eight legs. He turned to see her creeping up over his face, and was almost relieved to see it wasn't his mother at all, but a small spider made larger in shadow by the porch light, crawling up his bedclothes. But then he looked more closely, and saw that the spider had no legs at all, but eight crutches supporting its fat, limp abdomen.

In the morning, when he opened the front door to receive the mail from the carrier, he saw that the bearded young man was leaning weakly on a crutch. "Won't be coming out here anymore; they'll have to replace me. See, my leg here . . ."

Michael shut the door in his face.

Normally he worked around the house on Saturdays, then read out on the enclosed front porch. But he couldn't bear to be there that weekend; he couldn't sit still: Doris with the TV going the whole time, staring at it silently, his mother pacing with her two crutches in hollow syncopation on the loose floorboards. He saw the way Doris watched his mother sometimes now—the glow of excitement in her eyes. Following the movement of crutch, arm, and leg as if it were some sort of ballet. Tap thump. Tap thump. The noise wasn't very loud, but he found it impossible to ignore. He found himself listening for it, focusing his hearing, holding his breath until he could make out the faint tap tap thump, becoming more and more irritated.

Michael threw down the paperback and got into his coat. He opened the door, hesitated at the first blast of sharp cold wind, then plunged ahead. And almost jumped at the sound of the screen door bouncing off the inner door. Tap tap tap tap. Following him.

He had no idea where he was going. The snow made the road

all but impassable; there would be virtually no traffic. About a half-mile before town he looked off towards the Carter place up on the hill. A tiny figure in a red coat, shoveling snow. It looked awkward, crippled. Michael shielded his eyes, squinted, and could just make out the crutch wedged under one arm.

He turned and picked up his pace towards town. And saw someone not more than ten yards ahead of him, standing by the side of the road.

A large bearded man. With an armful of crutches. Michael turned.

Tap tap tap tap behind him.

Michael was out of breath by the time he got back to the house, his lungs almost splitting from the cold and exhaustion. He couldn't quite see the details of the room once he stepped through the door; the snow had blinded him. But he heard it. Tap thump. Tap thump. With a slight variation in rhythm. Two slightly different rhythms.

He walked into the kitchen. "Hello, son." His mother's tired voice. Tap.

"Michael?" Tap tap tap.

As his vision cleared he could see them by the stove—wife and mother. Doris had borrowed his mother's second crutch. They stared at him. And he couldn't bring himself to speak.

She woke him up in the middle of the night, every night the next few nights. Tap. Hobbling into the bathroom. Tap tap. Going to the kitchen for some milk. Thump. Letting the cat in. Tap thump. Doris, or his mother—he soon lost track. His mother pacing. Doris moving. Back and forth in the darkened house. The syncopation of their crutches. The synchrony.

Tap thump. Tap thump. No peace. No peace.

After the snow melted that year he was able to walk in the woods again. Until the little boys and girls drove him out. The children were the worst. On their crutches. Breaking their dogs' legs so they could strap on miniature crutches. Tap and tap and tap in every alley, on every sidewalk. The bearded man made them, as he made all the crutches; Michael had seen him pass them out to the kids. The kids just playing with their pets. But when they ran out of dogs, they started putting even smaller crutches on the cats. Then they were out in the woods, looking for squirrels, birds, anything they could catch, bundles of tiny crutches bunched in their fists like flowers.

Michael stopped pretending to seek work and spent most of his time hiding from his neighbors. He hadn't been bothered yet, but he was the only one in town without a crutch. It made him uneasy, and now he was seeing the large bearded man and his evil-looking sticks of wood everywhere he went.

Doris certainly didn't notice; she didn't notice him at all these days. Unless he stood in front of the TV.

Each night he awakened from a fever dream. Suddenly he was frightened. He could not remember how long he had lived in the town, if he had lived in the town forever, if he would be returning to the city after the summer. If he had ever lived in the city at all. His wife slept untroubled beside him, her shoulders, her shadowed face seeming older than he remembered. Had they been there that long?

He stands up out of sleep and reaches for the bedpost. It is soft wood. Seductive. He pats it. Tap tap tap it replies. Thump. There is energy in the wood. The first energy, the first aliveness he has encountered in some time. And he is so tired, and his life is so much the same, again and again the same. He has no energy.

He runs his hands down the sides of the wood and is soothed by it. He turns to the bedroom window and sees the face of the bearded man behind the glass. Grinning. Tap tap tapping with two stubby fingers against the glass. And amazingly, Michael realizes he is not afraid. He strokes the wood, taps it. It is vaguely comforting and he thinks, tap tap, maybe, tap tap tap, tomorrow it might support him.

LEAKS

"A family's got to do things together, each and every day," Owen's father always said. "And do things best as you can, like you mean them. That's what makes right living. Those little things you do every day. Like working in the garden, or working on the house, even going to a ball game together. You do them regular and it's just like praying. Even if you got nothing else but that, everything'll turn out okay."

His father's rituals. Owen used to think they'd drive him crazy. Maybe they had. Maybe he should have asked his wife if they had—Marie would know. But he hadn't even talked to her on the phone since she'd left him two years ago. He had no idea where she was. She hadn't even tried to contact their older son Wes, and that surprised him. Her leaving in the first place had surprised him. As had her taking Jimmy, the younger, and leaving ten-year-old Wes alone in the house that day. Owen couldn't imagine what she'd been thinking.

He hadn't really known Marie at all. And now, he had to admit, he knew his sons even less. His family must have been slipping through his fingers for years and he hadn't noticed a thing.

"I hate it here." That was Owen's mother. But it might have been Wes. He'd said that when they weren't more than three feet inside the doorway of the old house. Owen had felt like hitting him. "I hate it here," she always said. The regular, ritualistic complaints, day after day. "Everything's so damp. I can't leave any of my clothes in the trunks for fear they'll mildew on me. And it's so plain. It's like living in a box!" Then she'd drag Owen to her closet door and make him look in. The mildew spread over the old floorboards like pale green paint. It nauseated him. He'd look back over his shoulder at his father, who watched them from just outside the door but never came in. It embarrassed Owen, the way she'd show him things wrong with the house as if his father wasn't standing right there.

"It's a great deal, hon." That was Owen's father. "County used to use it for storage, I think. Marine equipment, or something. That's why it's plain. But hell, doesn't have to be that way forever. We'll fix 'er up. Besides, it's the only way we're going to get a house right now."

"But it's so wet here. Makes my skin crawl. Like I'm always tasting bad water."

"It's close to the water, don't you know," he said, and laughed each time. Each time Owen's mother trembled, and after a few years in that house Owen understood why.

The voices were so clear, only slightly muted as he recalled them. As if they'd leaked from the walls that had stored them these many years.

His father's attempts to placate his mother were useless. Owen didn't think he'd really tried. Most of the time he ignored her complaints, as if he had other things on his mind and counted on the rituals to make things right in the family.

"Almost sunset. Let's get those chairs ready and head down to the creek bank." He never said it loudly, but the firmness of his expectation was clear. It was something the family did every night, even in the coldest weather. "Owen, you shut the door behind your mother." Always the same instruction.

The family trooped the hundred feet to the creek bank, a hundred muddy feet most of the time, the brownish-yellowish grass lying flat over the wet loam like a badly done toupee, Owen's father always in the lead. "In case of water snakes," he said, and winked at Owen's mother. A little cruelly, Owen always thought. One evening she'd been terrified to distraction by one of the enormous earthworms that were always lying around, forced out of their holes by all the water that saturated the ground near the creek. Owen had to admit it was the biggest earthworm he'd ever seen. Freakishly big.

They each carried a lawn chair. "Okay, now you sit there, Mother. And you there, Owen." His father stared at them as they struggled to unfold the stiff old chairs. It always made Owen terribly self-conscious. And then inevitably his father would grab the chairs out of their hands and show them how to grip the aluminum tubing, how to snap the chair out just so. "Why can't you people ever learn the proper way to unfold a lawn chair?" Then they'd all sit facing the creek. "Good to do things together," his father would say several times during the next hour. "Family needs its routine." And that would begin the lecture for the evening.

They'd sit there, watching the sunset redden the greasy water below them, dark water that seemed too thick somehow, too substantial, that lapped at their feet so hungrily.

"Beautiful evening," his father would say. "And look at how pretty the water is!" Owen could taste the creek—the air was full of it. It was like drowning.

That was a long time ago. Now he and Wes were back.

The first day back in the house Owen wandered aimlessly from room to room. Wes stayed in the back yard and complained. Sometimes Owen would catch a glimpse of him through a yellowed window pane. At thirteen he was tall and lanky, a dishwater blond much like Owen himself, much like Owen's father. Owen felt a sudden pride in his son at that moment, but he doubted he ever would tell him. Something made it too hard.

Several times Owen had to stop Wes from throwing rocks at the house. He was rapidly losing his patience; he was sure if Wes didn't stop he'd take a backhand to the boy. He couldn't understand why his son would do that; he couldn't understand why he was so angry all the time. He'd talked to him, when he could, about Marie's abandoning the two of them, and Wes really seemed okay about all that.

But Owen knew he was overstating things—Wes certainly wasn't angry all the time. He just had a talent for picking the wrong times to be unruly.

Once during that first afternoon in the house Wes brought Owen flowers. "For the lady of the house," he said with a grin.

Owen was touched. "Lady?"

"Sure. You've been hanging closer to home than an old maid, Dad."

Owen sighed. "I am being a little silly I guess." He laughed when Wes nodded in an exaggerated, comic fashion. Owen smelled the flowers. "Terrific. Where'd you find these?"

"Out by the back gate, near the woods. They're all over the place out there.

"Yeah. Seems like I remember my father having a bed of perennials out there." He looked up. "I'm sorry, Wes. How are you doing?"

Wes let loose a lopsided grin. "Hey, no sweat. I just feel a little strange out here is all. What can I do for you?"

"You're already doing it, Wes. You're already doing it."

He left his own and Wes's meager pile of belongings in the front hallway, right where they dropped them. He traveled light, never thinking of any particular place as home, determined not to let his own possessions tie him down.

Very little had changed in the house in fifteen years. In his mother's sewing-room a swatch of bright blue cloth was still wedged under the needle. The dust had only now begun to accumulate; his father had been dead a week, the house untended for two.

He knew the house would dirty quickly. There seemed no end to the work required to maintain a house. Owen found himself listening to the walls.

"It doesn't stop! I've cleaned the floor twice today already!" His mother was on her hands and knees, her back hunched, scrubbing at the kitchen tiles. No matter how much she scrubbed the seams still looked muddy. Her face was red. Her hands raw, nearly bleeding. She was sobbing.

In his father's den a newspaper from last month was neatly folded on his overstuffed chair, the same soft brown chair Owen remembered. The house had been a lifetime of work. His father's lifetime.

His father had seen Wes only once or twice; he'd never seen Jimmy at all. "Can't come out there now, Owen. The house needs too much work right now." The same excuse, again and again. "No time for visiting with all this work to be done."

"I can't do this anymore!" His mother said it almost daily, ritualistically, her hand clutching a filth-encrusted rag, her eyes red from the dust and crying. The mold came back no matter how thoroughly she scraped it away. The tiles peeled from the floor. The window sills warped. The paint flaked away. "This house! This house!" She complained all day when his father wasn't home, complained just to Owen, and to those always damp, clammy walls. His father made her sound crazy.

"It's that fancy house your mother's folks own." His father spoke to him as if his mother wasn't standing right there, slamming pans around as she fixed dinner. "It's got her spoiled, I think. Your mother doesn't seem to know about working to make something good. Like this house. It'll be a showplace someday. If we all aren't afraid of a little work."

A lifetime of work. Owen knew he should have sold the house, or denied the will, anything other than, in fact, to take possession of it. But his father had worked so hard. His father had told him again and again that children owed their parents, and Owen believed that. His father had manipulated him as skillfully and persistently as he had manipulated the rules by which houses fall into disrepair.

All the furniture and appliances looked new in that house. It was only by looking very closely that Owen could see the countless, minute indications of repair—the re-weavings, the welds, the glue repairs, the parts replaced by parts of ever-so-slightly different color. Such fine repair work. So much effort spent to gain such small results.

He could smell the dampness in the house.

It was only after dark that Owen realized he and Wes really didn't have to stay in the house. Wes had known, had insisted, they didn't have to stay, but Owen had other voices to listen to.

"We can leave all our stuff here, Dad. None of it really matters that much; isn't that what you're always saying?" Owen gazed at his son in surprise. Wes was almost in tears. Owen wondered how the boy could even know.

A battered suitcase and a few boxes of clothes and paperbacks. Owen could hire an agent to handle the sale of his father's house.

He gazed at the new woodwork around the doors and windows, the new paint that had replaced the old, the carefully wrought repairs in the furniture. It was insane, the amount of wasted labor, wasted life that had gone into keeping this house alive.

When next he looked out the window it was dark. Wes had fallen asleep on the couch. He could hear the creek lapping at the muddy bank only a short distance away. A damp sensation crept into his throat. Suddenly Owen was afraid to step out on to the soft, fog-shrouded ground that surrounded his father's showplace. Wes was asleep; it was best to spend the night. Owen covered him with a blanket—it had always been easy to catch colds in this house.

Owen left their things in the hallway and slept upstairs that night. First he tried his old bedroom, but after gazing at all its carefully repaired toys he discovered he could not sleep there. He used his father's old bedroom.

His mother left the house, and the creek, when Owen was thirteen. He never saw her again. He knew it was that nightly ritual that finally did it, for his mother had always hated that creek. She said she'd never seen water like that anywhere.

Owen woke up on his second day in the house with an enormous headache, his chest sore and his body riddled with aches and pains. Opening his eyes seemed unusually difficult, as if the wet headache were pushing his eyelids down.

The wooden floorboards creaked—too loudly—as he padded his way towards the bathroom. He stopped at the bathroom door and looked down. He felt dizzy. The floor looked warped, buckled towards its center. He grew nauseous and fled into the bathroom.

He hovered over the sink, barely able to control his sickness, his arm supporting him against the wall. The wall tiles felt slick, slimy beneath his palm. He wanted to remove it from the tile, but he hadn't regained his balance yet. He stared down at the faucet. Water was flowing in a silver line into the drain, noiselessly, with almost no splash, like an unbroken tube. He suddenly couldn't bear the thought of touching it, of breaking its symmetry.

He dressed quickly and went downstairs. Wes's bags were gone. He started to call him when he heard the footsteps overhead, in his old room. He couldn't suppress a smile as he walked past his stuff and opened the front door.

With his first steps outside he noted how quiet it was. You couldn't even hear the creek.

He walked around to the patio facing the garden. The cement slab was cracked—you could see the traces of patching material. It had cracked every spring when the water pushed the ground up under it, and his father had repaired it every spring with the same patching compound, which made the slab good until the next spring. Owen looked out on the garden; it was badly in need of weeding. Several potted plants left out on the gravel pathways had tilted where the gravel had sunk beneath them. The little garden house his father had built when Owen was thirteen had lost some roof tiles. They protruded from the barren garden like praying hands. The bright yellow paint on the back fence had paled and was peeling away from the damp wood. The woods drooped over the fence, leaves dripping steadily.

The ground seemed to shift beneath his feet. Owen lifted one shoe and it came away muddy. As he stared into the early morning fog he imagined his father there, laboring furiously over first one area of the yard and then another. Only to repeat these small repairs a few days later.

It took a special person to take good care of a house. A talented and dedicated person. His father had said that many times. Owen wondered if he had it in him. There was so much work to be done here.

After Owen's mother left his father began insisting that they "do more father-son things". And so he had instituted the ritual of the late afternoon swim. His father expected him to be dressed in his swimming trunks by the time he got home from work each day.

It was cold in his bedroom, as it was always cold in his bedroom, which made Owen change quickly into his trunks. But he let his father believe it was an example of the eagerness he insisted on.

"Hurry up, boy! The creek don't like a reluctant swimmer, you know." His father said it each time, and Owen always wondered at his meaning. Maybe it was a joke, but it always made him even colder.

In any case Owen knew it was a mistake to keep his father waiting. As they walked towards the creek bank, his father led the way with a brisk, long-legged stride. When they reached the bank, Owen was to drop his towel immediately and jump into the shiny water. He learned to make the leap into the creek without thinking, resigned to it as one might become resigned to a repetitive bad dream.

Owen leapt, eyes closed, struggling to force his thoughts into a stillness, into the bad dream.

The water was cold. He got some in his mouth. Bitter, and thick. It made him spit and choke.

"That's just from the plants living on the bank . . . give it a bad taste." His father said that every time. And not once had Owen believed him.

It was hard to swim here—however calm the water appeared, it roughened when Owen tried to swim in any particular direction, the small waves pushing against him. The water was heavy on his back. As if someone were sitting on him, trying to push him into the scummy bottom. The surface was oily and burned his eyes. It had taken him a long time to find the right word for it and then he couldn't get it out of his mind: it was an unfriendly place to be.

A hundred times Owen thought of refusing the swim.

"It's important for us to do these things together, son."

"You never spend time with Wes. You should be doing things together!" That was Owen's wife. He agreed with her, and the desperation he heard in her voice pained him. It wasn't that he didn't like Wes. He loved him deeply. And he made attempts to plan activities they could do together—movies and ball games and museums and such. But it always felt so forced. So dangerous.

And now it was all his. The house. The grounds. The bank. The creek. Owen turned and stared at it. Now, the creek was making noise, splashing and sucking, as if it had awakened from a very long sleep. He tried in vain to remember its name, and wondered if it even had a name.

On the morning of the third day back, Owen quickly put away his own gear, then set about on the first repairs. He would wonder for some time why he felt compelled to do this—he wondered even at the time. There was no reason for him to follow in his father's footsteps. He could live a completely different life. And when he woke up that morning he had pretty much decided that was the way it was going to be—he was going to keep the repairs down to a necessary minimum. Shabbiness was one thing that could not get to him. It wouldn't define his life.

Wes, of course, wasn't happy about Owen's decision. "You

promised we'd only be here a little while!" was all he would say.
His son's petulance angered him.

"Just for a little while, Wes. If I do just a few small repairs then
we can get a better price for this place. And I can afford to buy you
some of the things you've always wanted. Now doesn't that make
sense?"

"I don't want you to buy me anything. I just want to get out of
this place. It's cold and wet . . . I hate it!"

It hurt.

But then there were things to do. Several of the fake marble
tiles popped off the wall when he went into the bathroom. He
examined the exposed surfaces, and discovered the old plaster
beaded with water. No doubt the caulking had eroded, letting
the water from the shower seep in. Then he noticed the small
rust stain in the sink, a stain he could swear had not been there
the day before. Then a section of wallpaper peeled loose in the
living-room. And a piece of brick fell down from the fireplace.
He picked it up and it crumbled nearly to dust in his hand. He
examined the rest of the brickwork and found it full of tiny holes,
soft and brittle. As if alternating damp and dry had made it dete-
riorate.

The house was falling apart around him, and he couldn't bear
the thought of that happening so soon after his father's death,
while he was in charge. If nothing else he had to save the house
for his own son's future. Maybe eventually he would put it on the
market and sell the problem to someone else, but he couldn't let
it all disintegrate while he was staying there.

On the living-room shelves were countless books on home
repair. Owen spread one across his lap. The pages smelled musty,
and felt a bit like dough beneath his fingertips. He stared at a rusty
splotch lying on the contents page. When it started to move he
recognized it: a silverfish. He sucked in his revulsion and brushed
the insect away.

The plastic wall tile in the bathroom was easy. He spent about
an hour scraping the old adhesive off the backs of the tiles and the
exposed wall. The wall had dried during the morning and seemed
pretty solid. He found new plastic-tile adhesive in a storage room
in the basement, as well as virtually every other home repair

compound, chemical, tool, and material imaginable. He stood there, adhesive in hand, and tried to calculate the value of such a stock. Probably in the thousands. He spread the backs of the tiles with the adhesive and pressed them firmly into place. Then the joints had to be smoothed.

Owen found himself using the flat end of a toothpick, as if he were sculpting a miniature. An old house like this never forgave shoddy work. Before you knew it, something adjacent would need repair—like an infection spreading. His father must have told him that a hundred times.

Wes spent a great deal of time wandering the grounds and reading. He didn't like sitting on the ground, so he always carried a folding chair with him. Sometimes Owen would discover him behind a bush or some other object, watching Owen make the repairs. Owen thought he seemed content enough.

Rubbing paraffin on all the edges of a sticking kitchen cabinet door seemed to solve that problem immediately. Replacing a door spring with a pneumatic closer from the basement storage room stopped the back screen door from banging. The wobbly legs on the dining-room table were repaired by forcing new glue into the joints. A small hole in one of the walls was filled with gypsum-board joint compound and sanded smooth. Owen discovered a small hole in one of his mother's favorite pewter mugs; he cleaned the metal inside the mug with steel wool, then covered the hole with epoxy mender.

When he returned the epoxy to the basement he discovered that several of the water pipes were sweating, and a puddle had formed on the concrete floor. He stared at the pipes, fascinated by the way moisture just seemed to ooze out of solid metal, then wrapped them with fiberglass tape.

Over the next few days Owen discovered he had a knack for this sort of work, something he never would have imagined. Some repair solutions came to him naturally, unbidden. And for the knottier problems he discovered, by dipping into his father's library, that there were tricks he could use, that the mysteries had discoverable keys. By drilling holes almost through the wood slightly smaller than the nails he was going to use he could prevent the wood from splitting when he nailed two pieces together—

especially useful when working with oak or yellow pine. Coarse sand was required for making good concrete. Cellulose cement made a neater joint than epoxy glue but it broke down under heat. Pyrethrin was a good spray for centipedes, but since they kill many other insects perhaps they'd best be left alone.

The air seemed drier in the house. It had been unexpectedly easy to conquer the dampness. Owen breathed more easily.

Wes spent a great deal of time in Owen's old bedroom, playing with his ship models, taking them apart, reassembling them. And some days he took long walks by himself. But never by the creek.

"Why don't you ever go down to the creek?" Owen had been repairing the porch swing, replacing some of the slats, when Wes walked up behind him. It startled Owen at first; his son had paid a noticeable amount of non-attention to the repair work up until this time. "There's a lot of interesting animals living by the creek, birds and reptiles and things. And it's a lot cooler down there." To his dismay, Owen usually found himself taking up a semi-lecturing tone when speaking to Wes. The canned sentences almost led him to propose that Wes take a swim in the creek. But the suggestion died in a sour taste that filled his mouth.

"I don't like the creek," Wes said. Then, when Owen thought the boy wasn't going to say anymore, "there's something wrong with it."

Owen laid his tools down and turned from the job. "I don't understand what you mean."

"What are we doing here, Dad? You said just a couple of days!"

Owen closed his eyes. He was angry, but he also felt an unaccountable kind of grief. He reached out and touched Wes's tennis shoe. Maybe it was silly—he wanted to hold his son, grab his hand, but the shoe was all he could reach at that moment. "I'm sorry. I know. But I'm real close to settling something, Wes. I can't explain it, but we have to stay just a little while longer. I feel so close now."

He must be babbling like an idiot. He expected his son to look confused or appalled or miffed, but the boy looked almost kindly. "Okay, Dad. But let me help you fix some of this stuff. Maybe then we can get out of here."

Owen nodded.

Owen discovered it relaxed him to make the walk from the house to the creek after a long day repairing the house. He'd sit in an old chair on the bank and nearly fall asleep watching the slight, restless waves. He wanted badly for Wes to join him there, but wasn't about to force him. He could see now why such a ritual might have appealed to his father.

Owen had noticed a peculiar coincidence. The better the repairs proceeded, the nearer some intangible ideal of "finished-ness" the old house approached, the lower the level of the creek against his bank. And the dryer and firmer the ground. If repairs were going exceedingly well, he could hardly see the surface of the water.

Owen spent several more weeks making repairs. He had little time to think about why he was doing them; they just seemed to need doing. But after a while, after long stretches of labor, usually on a weekend when he thought he could rest, things seemed to go all wrong somehow. Concrete and brick he'd repaired three days before crumbled. Chair legs warped, popping their joints. Wallpaper buckled.

The damp was back, undoing Owen's repairs one at a time.

He had grown more and more irritable—he couldn't help himself—but Wes seemed to know enough to stay out of his way. Occasionally he allowed the boy to help out with the small things, the unskilled labor tasks like carrying supplies or bracing beams—but most of the time he refused help. Wes spent more and more time inside Owen's old room, with the shades drawn. Some days they didn't see each other at all. He ate his meals, sandwiches usually, wherever he was working. Wes seemed good at fending for himself.

Once his father had spent most of a week carefully laying flagstones for a patio that was to abut one of numerous flower gardens he had established on the grounds behind the house. By that time his father's anxieties about the house and yard were obvious to Owen. The number of lines webbing his face had increased dramatically, and there was a barely perceptible tremor in his hands. More than once Owen had seen him drop a hammer or screwdriver, then rub his hands violently, as if to work the circulation back into them.

But on this particular day his father seemed worse than usual. He walked around as if on eggshells, as if a cake might fall, or a castle of playing cards topple if he did not move softly enough. He carried the flagstones out to the prepared ground carefully, looking at the ground in front of him before each step. Then he knelt slowly, positioned the stone, then tamped it gently into place with a rubber mallet.

Owen didn't exactly see what happened next, but he heard his father fall and felt the ground shake. And saw, although from a distance, the flagstones sinking into mud. Later he examined the ground there; it had been seriously undermined by the water.

He could have gone to his father that long ago day. He could have comforted him. But could not. Just as Wes could not. They'd always been like that, the two of them. The three of them. They were past changing, past any piecemeal repair.

Owen dreamed about plans for the house—his father's plans, his own plans. If he could only solve the dampness problem, they could have a rec room in the basement. His father had talked about that for years. It would give them more time for each other. Wes would like that. It was important for a father and son to do things together.

Each night Owen would awaken from the dream of a house that demanded no labor, to the sound of the dripping. He'd leap from the bed and roam the house, checking the faucets, the windows, the roof, examining the ground outside. No moisture. And yet when he crawled back into bed he could hear it louder than ever, impossibly loud.

He wondered how Wes could sleep through it all.

He'd remodel the house completely, he thought. He'd put in a den, a children's room. Wes would have his own workshop, his own tools. He'd really like that. Re-shingle the roof, panel the living-room, change the ceiling fixtures, update the wiring. Once the house was unrecognizable perhaps there'd be no more problems.

Owen would walk into the bathroom in the morning and find the faucet running, a continuous silver line as if the metal were leaking into the bottomless pit of the drain. He'd tighten the handle but the leak couldn't be stopped, and he'd stand there watching the metal dissolving, being stolen so quickly by something that lived at the bottom of the drain.

Some nights he'd awaken and wander sleeplessly from room to room. Every faucet in the house would be running in that continuous, echoing, dreamlike way. He'd go back to bed wondering when the porcelain sinks themselves would begin their silent journey into the dimension at the other end of the drain.

He'd build a children's room. A silly thought. But what was a house without children? There was so much work to be done—who had time for a family? Drip . . . drip.

There were hidden leaks in the house. All the good air escaped through the poorly-insulated roof and walls. Some energy projects would be good for next fall. Maybe an insulating blanket around the water heater would help.

He'd wake up in the middle of the night because of the awful subtlety of the noise it made. Drip. He'd pull up the bedclothes and check his toes for cracks in the toenails leaking his life away. His father would be surprised to see how well he'd managed the repairs.

He'd wake up in a heavy sweat, the bedroom impossibly humid, the walls warping inward from the damp. He'd check his damp head, fearing his brain fluid was leaking away.

He had a plan for getting remarried if he ever got out of the house to meet someone. She would be enormously impressed with the improvements he had made. And once she saw his sensitivity demonstrated in his plans for the new children's playroom, she would fall in love with him. They would be married in the living-room, if he could keep it dry long enough.

They would have children. He'd always wanted children.

His bed rotted under his thrashing body. His sheets tore to damp rags in his fists. The wallboard began to decompose, releasing gases into the room that reminded him of swamps and old spring houses. You can smell history in these rooms, he thought, and wondered if he had stumbled across an important discovery.

He woke up with the water in his ears. He stumbled into the bathroom—the liquid oozed from the tap like clear molasses. He went to the kitchen and the water was full-force from that faucet. The "hot" and "cold" handles no longer controlled it. He wandered into the turgid air of the living-room; the walls had begun to sweat.

Where was Wes? Owen scrambled up the stairs and into his old bedroom. The bed was soaked, the sheets falling apart, the models suspended from the ceiling so damp they periodically dropped pieces onto the floor. Like rotting carrion.

But he couldn't find Wes. He fell running back down the stairs. The steps were slick, insubstantial.

Someone was calling for help. A child was lost in the creek, drowning. The child's voice was badly garbled by the fog, each syllable filled with cold and damp. But Owen had momentarily forgotten where the creek was. If anything, the creek surrounded him.

It was quieter outside. The creek kept peace tonight. He could not decide what had made him so anxious.

When his father beckoned from the house for their evening swim, Owen did not hesitate.

HOUSES CREAKING IN THE WIND

He can hear flies striking the window. He can hear flies whispering in the rain. He can hear flies buzzing in the spaces between his
thoughts.

If he can only understand everything in the flies' song, he
thinks, then this house will be transformed, fill with noise and
bright color, and maybe, perhaps, he can say that he is still alive.

Each day he rises earlier in this house on the floor of the desert
valley. Soon he won't need to sleep at all. Nights will become his
mornings.

He has neighbors, but he hasn't spoken to them in years. Their
houses are just like his, so he feels there is no need for words
between them. There is an understanding in the way the wind
moves, and the houses creak.

When he heard about the first son, he was standing here in this
same spot, gazing out these windows, reading the dark before
sleep. The telephone was swift and urgent, and afterwards lay like
a dead animal in his hand. He put it away and would not pick it
up again.

When he heard about the second son he was on the back
porch smoking. His wife came for him, shaking, and he walked
out to meet the men at the door. Out on the side of the road past
their cars he thought he saw the old skull of an animal he himself
had shot as a teenager. The skull still had the light of fear in its
eyes. He smiled as they told him the story of his son's death, and
he knew they would all talk about him later and wonder why.
He smiled because of the joke that had been told on him, but he
did not tell them this because he'd never been good at repeating
jokes.

He was sleeping when they came to tell him about his wife.
They let themselves inside and woke him up. "Another joke?" he
asked, and saw them looking at each other, not knowing what to
make of him. They were different men from the ones who had

come the last time, but they held themselves the same. He was glad to be lying down, because he could no longer hold himself. He thought about sleeping, how the body feels when it sleeps in its own skin. Sometimes we try to sleep in the skins of others, he thought, and we stay awake all night.

There is an understanding in the way the winds move, and the houses creak. He spends all day sweeping the floor clean. Sometimes he pauses to listen for nothing. Then he sweeps the floor again, ridding it even of his footprints.

Each night he waits for the ones vanished to come home. They sit in his chairs, but do not speak. They leave no footprints on his clean floor. He goes out to the porch and his eyes hunt for the skull, but he has not seen it in years. He goes back into his house as if it is he who is just now arriving. Dinner is on the table, and his sons are singing the fly song. Wind blows past the creaking houses and his neighbors all come outside to join in the singing.

He is too happy for words. The house is bright with color again, and the air that moves from room to room is warm as the sun. Outside in the dark yard the neighbors all shout, but here in his warm bright house he opens his mouth to sing and shows each one of his family the song, the flies that have boiled out of his throat, that have gathered on his tongue.

ESCAPE ON A TRAIN

"That town is burning down," Carter says to the stranger sitting across from him.

But the stranger seems not to have heard him. He pulls the spread of newspaper even closer to his face, as if wanting to give his closest scrutiny to some account of murder and mayhem. Or perhaps it's because the train rocks and bucks so severely the stranger has to grip his newspaper all the tighter, drawing it closer to his face. Carter was never very good at physics, but he thinks that's what might occur. He studies the whiteness of the stranger's knuckles against the outside of the paper, trying to gauge by this whiteness just how many foot-pounds of pressure the stranger must be applying. At any moment, Carter expects to see the paper split in half from the forces being applied to each end. But then, luckily, the stranger has selected a tabloid-style paper to read, which Carter imagines must be somewhat sturdier than the larger size. So perhaps the stranger's reading matter is safe after all.

"That town? Outside the window? The one the train is passing? It appears to be burning down."

Still no answer. Carter gazes out the window, wondering at the length of time that has elapsed since the burning town first appeared in the train window, puzzled that the train still has not completely passed it. It makes little sense to him, since the town is small soon to be even smaller) and the train, he is told, moving very fast.

Of course, the train doesn't appear to be moving all that quickly, at least from where he's sitting. He vaguely remembers that there are a number of physical laws specifically concerning moving trains and their relationships to those observers on the train and those observers off the train, say, watching the whole thing—the fire, in this case—from a grassy knoll nearby. But Carter can remember the specifics of none of them. Perhaps there's even a law concerning the relationship of a moving train to the burning town it is attempting to pass—and seemingly unable to pass with any speed—and the observer on the train attempting to interest a stranger into also becoming an observer. He wonders how the concept of "witnessing" figures into this physical equation. Also the concepts of "responsibility" and "guilt".

Outside the train window the small town—just a few buildings isolated out on the prairie where only a train might pass—continues to burn. Carter presses his nose against the glass and imagines he can feel the intense heat on the other side, outside the confines of this swiftly moving train. The small town continues to burn and suddenly he is in pain and when he removes his nose from the glass a small patch of skin from the tip remains, adhering to the hot pane.

Even though the town is some distance away he can observe what is happening there with remarkable detail. An old-fashioned red fire engine is moving between the burning buildings, dragging its ancient canvas hose which is also on fire. Carter thinks the age of the fire equipment would be a problem in any case and now the hose is on fire, and the engine is in fact aiding the spread of the fire by dragging this burning hose through the streets. He wonders if anyone has warned the driver. On closer examination he observes that the man behind the wheel in the open cab, the man in the yellow slicker and black fireman's helmet, is also on fire, his torso and head and upraised arms a long tapering flame like that of a candle.

And yet he knows this is impossible. He knows one cannot possibly see such detail from a moving train. It is that lack of connection, of specific, closely-observed detail, he suspects, which makes travel by rail so attractive in the first place.

Here and there Carter can see open windows like dark mouths and hollow eye sockets within the flaming structures, and burning human beings —women, men, small children—transfixed in these dark openings, their own mouths and eye sockets opening wide with darkness. And it is all impossible, he thinks. Such observations from a moving train are impossible. Such pain must surely be impossible. Suddenly he wishes the train would go faster, much much faster so that it might pull away from the town.

"There are children, children burning up in that town," he insists, staring at the stranger's raised newspaper. On the exposed front page there are articles concerning murder, earthquakes, and arson. The headline reads: FATHER ABANDONS FAMILY: THREE FEARED DEAD. In exasperation, Carter grabs the man's left hand and pulls it down, separating the stranger from his paper. "Can't you see? That town's on fire! People, children are dying!"

The stranger glances out the window, then shrugs. "We're on the train," he says. "There's nothing we can do." Then, amazingly, the stranger grins.

Carter stares at the man. Then he touches the hot glass, pulling it away before his fingers can burn. "Children are burning like cotton! Their faces melting like a cheap plastic doll's!"

The stranger puts his paper full of murder and mayhem aside. "That's very unfortunate," he says. "But we're on the train, you see, moving past the town. The town remains still, an immobile location. It's physically impossible for us to do anything to help those people."

"But they'll die!"

"They're already dead," the stranger says. "There's nothing for us to do. We're on the train, they're on the land, the still, unmoving land. We're removed from them by sheer speed." And again the stranger grins, as if in the pleasure of his explanation.

Carter stares at the man. "And by time, too, I suppose."

The stranger nods. "Precisely."

"Because speed and time are somehow related," Carter continues. "I was never good in physics, but I believe that's true. Time and speed are related. On the train we're removed from them by time, and speed."

"And state of mind," the grinning stranger says. "For the people in the town are wrapped up in their present, workaday lives. We are living on the train, in the future, or towards a future, on a train headed for a destination. Their world could not be more separate from ours."

"So we have no responsibility towards them," Carter says.

"None whatsoever," the stranger replies. "It's simple physics."

It takes a long time for the town to burn to the ground, but not so long, Carter imagines, relative to the average train schedule. The window is still warm to the touch for hours after the town has been reduced to embers.

That night Carter finds it difficult to sleep on the train. The irregular clicking of the rails, the rocking of the sleeping car, the periodic tappings at his window probe into and irritate his sleep. The window tappings are particularly bothersome. Each time he hears them he rises out of the seats which have been converted into a bed and goes to the glass, pressing his face to the glass first on one side and then the other in order to look as far as possible down the length of the train. He sees nothing. He speculates on possible causes: gravel thrown up by the wheels, the slap of branches which have not been trimmed back, grit carried by the wind. The window tappings continue all night long, but he never sees anything. In the morning he discovers hundreds of round, slightly greasy spots on the glass.

There is but one empty seat in the dining car, across from the stranger from the day before.

"May I?" Carter asks, gesturing towards the seat.

"Of course," the stranger replies. "Feeling better than yesterday?"

Carter studies the menu. "Mostly. Some . . . trouble sleeping. That's all, though."

"Glad to hear it." The stranger grins, absentmindedly taps the folded newspaper on the table. Carter wonders if he has already read it, or if he is now feeling anxious to read it. He hopes the man has already read the paper; he doesn't think he could stand it if the man picked up a paper again. He isn't sure why.

Carter can just make out the small headlines showing on the folded portion: MAN KILLS WIFE, CHILDREN, SELF and PLANE FEARED LOST and HUNDREDS DIE IN FIRE. He turns to the train window. Out in a field is an impossible vision: a man in overalls is beating a young boy—his son?—with a piece of timber.

"So, are you married?" The stranger speaks so quietly Carter at first isn't sure the man has actually spoken, or if he's imagined the question.

"Yes . . . yes I am." Outside the train, the man in overalls raises the timber higher with each swing as he beats the boy.

"Children?"

"Two. A boy five, a girl eleven." Is that correct? Suddenly Carter isn't so sure. Outside the train, the little boy's mouth stretches wider and wider in silent agony.

"But they're not traveling with you?"

Carter stares at the man, trying to measure his expression. "Why would you ask me such a question?"

"Just being friendly," the stranger says.

"You think I don't care? You think I'm like those fathers you read about in that damn paper of yours!"

"Just being friendly," the man says again, seemingly unaffected by Carter's outburst.

"You should save your worries for kids like him." Carter gestures towards the violent scene being enacted outside the window.

They both stare at the boy and his father. The boy's mouth now stretches impossibly far in his attempt to adequately express his pain. "Most unfortunate," the stranger says.

"We have to do something," Carter says. "Here we are sitting comfortably in our speeding train, and a child is being beaten. We have to do something."

"But I explained all this yesterday," the stranger says. "We're on the train, removed from that child by time and speed. There's nothing we can do." And again, the stranger grins.

"There must be something we can do," Carter says.

"Nothing. Relax. There's nothing either of us can do."

"That boy'll be destroyed. If not physically, certainly mentally . . ."

"That's his present. We live in the future, on the train. We cannot reach him."

Carter slumps back in his chair. "This was supposed to be relaxing. Like a vacation."

"Then enjoy yourself," the grinning stranger says. "You're riding the most modern of passenger trains. Shattering time and distance. The old life is gone—this is your new life, your destiny."

After the stranger leaves, Carter puts his ear against the glass pane. He can hear the boy's screams fading in the distance. And yet he knows it is impossible to hear such sounds from a moving train.

When night comes he sleeps no better. The rails click and the cars rock, and a tapping that begins at dusk continues through the night. The train passes through open countryside with only a few houses, scattered here and there, but in each house at least one window glows with light. And behind each glowing window Carter knows there is some happiness he cannot share, or perhaps some tragedy he cannot prevent.

A face rises suddenly into the glass, glowing like one of those distant windows. Carter stares hard at this face, but once he realizes that it is his son's face, it disappears, swept away by the wind created by the fast moving train.

"Somebody has to save him," Carter mumbles aloud. But he is on a speeding train, and can do nothing.

Night passes, and then the day, and then night comes around again. He sees the grinning stranger now and then: in the dining car, the lounge, passing through on his way somewhere else. He's afraid to speak to him: afraid of all the questions, the too-easy, yet perfect, excuses. In the landscape outside his train window the impossible occurs: murders are committed, avalanches bury skiers, children are abandoned and ignored, houses burn down. And there is nothing he can do. It is impossible for him to do anything. He has made his escape on the train; their lives could not be more separate. He has left his responsibilities behind on the station platform.

Night passes to day again and the tappings continue at his window. He wonders if they merely want to gain his attention, or if they in fact want to escape their present situation and board the train.

Eventually it seems as if it is the train standing still, and the land, the people enacting their little dramas, rushing past, flooding his senses, leaving him behind.

"You asked about my children," Carter says one morning to the stranger. "Well, I left them behind. Abandoned my wife, and them."

"That's all in the past now," the stranger replies. "You're on this train, now."

"I couldn't support them; I kept losing jobs. I was never a very good father, or husband."

"Look out the window," the stranger says.

In the valley below them a swiftly moving river has improbably left its banks and is pushing houses, cars, livestock, all rapidly down its path. Carter can see the smooth fish-shapes of human bodies tumbling in the flood. The train, of course, is safe, on a bridge high above the valley.

"We can't do anything," Carter says.

"Correct. You have no responsibility. That is another life. You have escaped." The stranger grins so fiercely Carter is surprised the man is able to get the words out.

"It was best that I leave."

"Of course." The stranger thumbs through a week's accumulation of newspapers. Carter can make out only pieces of the headlines: HUNDREDS DIE . . . MAN JUMPS . . . 23 INJURED WHEN . . . CHILD ABUSE ON . . . CANCER UNDER . . . FIGHTING CONTINUES . . . WAR DECLARED BETWEEN . . . ESCAPEE FOUND . . .

"Anyway, I was never very good in emergencies."

"Of course—few of us are," the grinning stranger says. "Few of us are responsible. But you're on the train, now. Its speed is beyond anything you've ever known before. It splits time and space. Its destinations lie in the future, another dimension entirely. Those other people, the ones outside the train, are merely lost messages coded into the winds, and the dry dust which disintegrates as the train pushes through their world. They cannot reach you. They cannot hold you responsible."

"But a witness? Doesn't a witness have some responsibilities?"

"This is the modern era. An era of media, media faster than any train. We are all witnesses. We are born into witnessing."

Carter continues his escape on the train. Rails click and cars rock, his wife and children tap and kiss the window, but he will not look at them. He will not feel guilty. And every day, unthinkably, people die outside his window, towns burn, children starve, planes plough nose-first into the ground alongside the tracks, and all the pleading voices are readily accessible to him. All he has to do is press his ear against the glass. Day rolls over into night and the seemingly endless night turns slowly into day.

Outside his train window he sees his wife and children caught out in an open field, a tornado like a man's anger ripping up the ground around them. Stones are picked up by the fierce winds and hurled like bullets at his family. Branches become spears. Odd bits of debris become flying shrapnel. He watches as his wife covers their children with her own body. He watches as the blouse across her back begins to tear into bloody strips. He watches as his children's clothes are plastered to their bodies by drenching rains. He moves closer to the glass, and he watches.

And as the impossible scene with his family continues, as his unlikely family is tortured and dies, he waits for the stranger to come and sit across from him. He's eager to hear whatever the stranger has to say.

AMONG THE OLD

It was like gazing into mirrors. The silvering must have been inconsistent, for there were variations, but still, each old man had my face.

The park is only a few blocks from my apartment building. I've been going there for years. The community around the park has grown old. The people have grown old.

Yet now there are young people in the park as well. The old are haunted by them. Funny that I should call them "the old", when I'm as wrinkled as the worst, as stooped. As dreamy.

Gottfried wants to know what I've eaten today. He asks me every time I see him.

"Make sure you get the meat," he always says. "But watch your sodium."

I nod and thank him. He's a poor advertisement for a healthy diet. He looks as if he might drop at any second, as if he's not particularly distressed at the prospect.

The old move from bench to bench; they say the young pursue them.

"A boy," Clarkson pants, "he was after my billfold."

"Where is he now?"

Clarkson looks around, befuddled, embarrassed. "I don't know . . . I could swear. He's here I tell you!"

"Of course." I smile. I pat his shoulder.

"He's just like I was at that age . . . reckless, irresponsible. He's capable of anything." Clarkson looks up at me sharply. "You don't believe me!"

"Of course I believe you."

"No, you don't. You look old . . ." He rubs the skin on one of my liver-spotted hands. "But it's a trick. You're not old at all."

The sun in the park warms my scalp, so inadequately insulated by thinning hair. People will forgive anything when it's warm out, even the infirmities of age.

I look down at my hand where Clarkson was rubbing it. I should have stopped him. The skin has stretched out of shape—folds and creases have formed. If you don't want to grow old, don't let people touch you.

My apartment is one room. Sometimes I think it must have been larger once. It shrinks more with every day I grow older. I never go out except to visit this park. Delivery boys bring me life's necessities.

A boy chases a ball that never stops rolling. The boy is me. The old scatter from his path, if "scatter" were a word that could be attributed to the old.

I turn around; a teenager is watching me. A young man behind him. A middle-aged man after that. They are all me; the oldest at last begins to resemble me.

Gottfried harangues a group of young men about proper health habits. They are all him, I think.

"As an old man I cannot remember accurately what it was like to be young," Clarkson says at my shoulder. "But then, as a young man I could not remember what it was like to be old."

I turn to face him. "But I'm only thirty-five," I tell him.

"Look at your hands," he says. I do. The flesh-colored gloves I wear are old and worn. And much too large. They wrinkle at my wrists, and form ridges up the backs of my hands. They wrinkle over every joint in my fingers.

I was young before I began my visits to this park. I had friends, and useful work to do. That was only a few days ago.

Some of the old have captured one of the young hooligans who terrorize the park. He thrashes on the ground, screaming, afraid to look into their wrinkled faces. But many old hands can keep even a violent young man down.

"Look at yourself! Look!" Gottfried insists, holding a mirror up to the young man's face. We all crowd around.

The young man cannot believe what he sees in the mirror: his face, wrinkled and old.

"You were born old," Clarkson says, gently, with a lilt, as if it were a baby's lullaby he was singing. "We all are. And we wear our bodies out chasing the ancient one within."

When the young man struggles to his feet he is old. He begins to argue politics with Clarkson, diet with Gottfried.

It is near dusk when I turn towards the line of trees that borders the south end of the park. The ancient trees turn color even as I watch; they are expert with the properties of light. The ancient grass bides its time; even the mowers don't bother it.

The mountains in the distance wrinkle, and suddenly are old.

In the park the old begin to whisper, a sibilance so compelling I cannot help but join. By nightfall we are one ancient voice.

IN THE TREES

It was a good climbing tree, a good climbing tree for a good boy. And Will's son was a good boy. A wild boy, sure, but a good boy, a beautiful boy. A boy like Will himself could have been, if only he hadn't had to grow up so quickly. The fact was, Will had never been very good at being a boy. He'd never had the knack. At his son's age he'd been cautious and forced, an old man in the soft skin of a boy.

"Go to sleep, son," he said softly, a whisper from the old man he'd always been. He stood in the doorway and gazed at his son's head, small face and soft dark hair barely out of the comforter, sunk to his red ears in the pillow. "You need your rest. You can't understand that now, but take it from me, you'll never have enough rest for what lies ahead."

Will could see past the bed, out the window to where the climbing tree stood, its leaves lighting up with the moonlight. Will took another pull of his beer and wished it were whisky. The climbing tree was a beautiful thing, standing out from the surrounding trees that formed the edge of "the grove"—more like a forest—that spread out from this edge of town seven miles before farmland started breaking it up.

But few of the trees seemed fit for climbing, and none of the others were this close to the house.

"I'm a good boy, aren't I, Dad?" his son spoke sleepily from his bed. But even in the sleepy voice Will could hear the anxiety that had no reason to be there. "I try to be good, don't I?"

"Of course, son. You're a good boy, a fabulous boy."

"Then don't make me go to sleep. I can't sleep."

Will knew this couldn't be true. This was just the boy's natural excitement talking, his anxiety, all the life in him rising to the top that made it hard for him just to lie down and rest, to permit the night to pass without his presence in it. His son sounded sleepier the more he said. He wouldn't be surprised to hear his snores at

any second. He had to go to sleep. Sleep was medicine. And he
had to take his medicine. Had to grow up big and strong. And
bury his old man someday if it came to that.

Will thought about what to say, tried to think about what his
own father would have said, and drank slow and steady from the
can, now lukewarm in his sweaty hand. "Tomorrow's another
day," he finally managed, feebly. "You're young; you have a whole
lifetime ahead. No sense rushing it; that was the mistake I made
when I was a boy. I was always rushing things."

The wind picked up. The longest of the leafy branches
thrashed the window. His son's dark head began to thrash, too,
whipping back and forth across the pillow as if in fever.

"Stay still, son," Will implored, his hands shaking, full of pain.
"That's no good. That's no good at all. You have to get your rest!"

"I can't sleep, Daddy! I just can't!"

Will moved to the side of the bed. It was a kid's bed, low and
small; Will felt like a giant towering over it. "I'll help you sleep,"
he said, his own anxiety bubbling up at his throat. "I'll do anything I can."

Awkwardly Will dropped to his knees beside the bed. He
put the can down on the rug, but it tipped over. Foam erupted
from the opening and dribbled over the edge of the rug on to
the wooden floor. But Will couldn't move his hands off his son's
comforter. He reached over and stroked the good boy's hair, hair
softer than anything in Will's experience. He felt the good boy's
forehead for fever—not sure he would know a fever in a boy this
small. He stroked the shallow rise of comforter that covered his
chest and arms.

"I don't want to go to sleep, Daddy! I'm scared!"

"What are you afraid of?"

"I don't know," the good boy said, thrashing. "I never know."

Will wasn't going to say there was nothing to be afraid of; he
knew better.

Will looked around the room, for something, anything, that
might calm his son down and let him sleep. And let Will sleep
as well, for he knew he couldn't leave the room until a night's
rightful relief for his son was well on its way.

A stuffed tiger, a bear, a red truck, a pillow decorated with tiny golden bells. His son barely looked at the toys as Will piled them up around his tiny, soft, thrashing head. "Had your prayers yet?" Will asked the beautiful, anxious boy, as if it was still more medicine he was talking about, still more magic. Will rubbed his hands together, prayerful-like, now desperate for another drink.

"No! I'm not sleeping!" his beautiful son cried, his tiny head red as blood, the wave of black hair across his forehead suddenly so like the greasy wing of a dead bird. Will made his pained hands into fists, not knowing whether he was going to caress or strike the good boy.

Will put his shaking hands together and prayed for his son to go to sleep.

"I want to climb the tree!" the good son suddenly cried.

And Will, who had never before permitted it, said "Tomorrow. I'll let you climb the tree tomorrow."

Will sat on the floor in his son's dark bedroom, drinking a beer. He watched the beautiful face—no longer bright red, or dark, now pale silver in the moonlight that had slipped through the open window—as his son slept, dreaming the dreams all good boys dreamed, but which Will, who had grown up all too quickly, had forgotten.

Behind and above the headboard of the bed was the open window, and the climbing tree beyond. The moonlight had planted silver flames in its branches. The boy's head was perfectly still. The boy's head no longer thrashed, but the climbing tree continued to thrash in the wind, making the silver flames break and spread, shoot higher up the limbs of the tree.

Will watched his beautiful son's face, relieved at its peace, but could see his nervous, living dreams torturing the bright flaming limbs of the climbing tree.

Again, the beer had grown warm in his hand, but he continued to drink. Tomorrow his wife and daughter would be back from their trip. Maybe she could get their son to sleep. Maybe she could talk him down out of the climbing tree. Will had been crazy to agree to the climb—it wasn't safe, it had never been safe. He'd never let his beautiful boy climb the tree before, no matter how much he'd begged. Now he didn't understand how he could have given in so easily. He'd change his mind and tell the boy, but Will had never been able to break a promise to his son before.

The curtains floated up on either side of his son's window, flapping severely as if tearing loose. Will hugged himself and imagined his small, good son hugging him, protecting him from the chill wind of adult pain.

It was a good tree, an outstanding tree. Will drank and watched his beautiful son play in the uppermost branches of the climbing tree.

His son was better at climbing trees than he had ever been. His son braved things that had terrified the young Will, left him motionless and dumb. And old, so old the other young boys were strangers to him, wild beasts scrapping in the trees. His son was a much better boy than Will had been. His son had all the right talents for being a boy.

He was a wild boy, but a good boy. The boy loved it when the branches almost broke, bent so far they threatened to drop him on his head. The boy laughed at terror; it thrilled him. Like other boys Will had known once upon a time, his sweet boy had no sense about danger.

The boy shook the upper branches and made as if to fly off with the tree, laughing. Will imagined the tree uprooting, then turning somersaults in the darkening, early evening air.

Behind him, the wife said, "Will, it's getting late. It's time to get him in." Will's wife knew about a boy's safety.

But much to his surprise, Will discovered he didn't want his son to come down just yet. As the sky grew darker and the wind increased Will took pride in the way the boy held fast to the uppermost branches, shaking them like some small, fierce animal, dancing among them like some unnatural spirit. That's it, son! That's it, he thought, throwing his head back and permitting the flat beer to gush down his throat. Don't leave the trees for a life down here on the ground. It happens soon enough—you'll understand that someday.

A sudden wind caught Will full in the face: his hair stood up and his eyes were forced closed. Another gust knocked the empty out of his hand. He could almost feel himself up in the tree with his son, just another boy to join that good, wild boy. Will staggered to his feet. The wind took away his lawn chair. He moved forward towards the base of the tree, trying to remember what his clever son had done to begin the climb.

"Daddy, I want to climb, too." Will knew the tug on his pants. He looked down at his little girl, who was using his leg to block the wind.

"You're too small!" Will shouted down. But the wind was dragging his words away.

"You let him!" She began to cry.

Will picked his little girl up in his arms. "Too dangerous," he spoke into her ear.

"Will!" His wife's scream beside him warmed his ear. The wind had grown cold; he could feel ice in the wrinkles of his clothes.

He turned. Her face was white, floating in the cold black air. "It's going to be okay!" Will cried against the wind. "He's a good boy! A great boy! Don't you see? A much better boy than I ever was!"

Will turned back towards the tree, where his son played and laughed, his son's face hot and glorious in the wind, the moon laying shiny streaks into his dark hair. Lightning played in the distant boughs of the forest, moving towards the house. Will started towards the climbing tree, his wife and daughter clinging to him. But he remembered he no longer knew how to climb, and stopped halfway between the house and the tree.

His beautiful son stopped laughing and stared down at Will. Will brought a nervous hand up to his lips, then realized he had no beer. He felt a sudden panic as he knew his son had seen what life was like back on the ground.

Lightning began to ripple the trees. Up in the highest part of the tree, his beautiful son laughed and started climbing higher.

It was a good climbing tree. A wonderful climbing tree. Will had taught his good son not to be afraid to do things. Will had taught him the lessons Will had never known. Will had taught him not to be afraid to live.

"No!" Will cried out to the trees. "Come back! It's not safe!"

But in the trees there were boys laughing and playing, unafraid and with no sense of danger. Dark hair flew as the boys climbed higher, pushing and wrestling in the weak, thin upper branches of the forest. Lightning bleached their hair. Wind and electricity gave them wings.

"Will! Get him back!" his wife screamed.

"He's a good boy, he's a wild boy, he's a beautiful boy!" Will shouted above the wind.

The climbing tree rose up and did a somersault, the kind Will had always been afraid of doing. The forest floated up out of its roots and shouted. And all the boys in the trees laughed so hard they cried, in love with themselves and in love with each other.

And Will's beautiful son was gone, climbing so high, climbing to where Will had always been afraid to go.

OUT LATE IN THE PARK

Once again, Clarence Senior has let the ball get away from him. The other men gasp when it rolls out of the shadowed circle formed by our beloved trees and into the brilliant sunlight baking the sand paths where the beautiful young people stroll. Jacob, one of our oldest, scowls bitterly. I raise an eyebrow in warning— or I believe I do. Facial control has been more difficult these past few months. Often I'm not sure whether my thin line of mouth is smiling or twisted into some shape less agreeable.

As has been typical for him, Jacob ignores me. "He'll spoil it!" he growls through a swallow of phlegm. "He'll spoil it for all of us!"

I raise my hand to stop him, but too late because I can feel the stirrings of the angled things that dwell at the edges of the sun-lit path. It's terrible, worrying that every spat of anger might cause your heart to seize, and then the whole of your body comes tumbling down and there's no more light in you than a dark stone at the bottom of a pond. Finally Jacob recognizes my warning and stops, takes a deep, savored breath as if it's to be his last one. Which it might be, of course. In this park of the world, suddenness is the business of the day.

Clarence Senior, as usual, appears to be somewhat lacking in orientation. He trots playfully after the volleyball. I envy the looseness of his stride, something my own arthritis denies me. But I am pleased that one of our own can still play with such reckless abandon.

"He'll get hit by a car!" George cries nonsensically. "We'll all get hit by cars!" This has been George's signature warning since he first started coming to the park. I assume his family has some tragic history related to the automobile, but of course I do not inquire. Men of our age trust each other well enough not to ask. We all assume tragedy and imagine disaster. Perhaps this makes us less sympathetic— certainly it makes us impatient. And burying the curiosity of our youth has become a measure of the respect we have for one another.

Although, if truth be told, I would say we respect nothing more than the dark, and the half-remembered things that move there.

Now the others are yelling. Of course I have seen this phenomenon before—all of us are quick to panic. It is something that happens to the nerves, I suppose, as the nervous system constantly monitors to determine if the flesh is still alive. Men my age understand the process. There is nothing worse than waking up in the middle of the night to discover that a favorite extremity has died.

"Get him back!" Joseph sobs. He is a weepy thing, old Joseph, more so than the rest of us, even though as a group we are a weepy bunch indeed. "Get him back!" Again, with that disturbing flail of movement-limited arms. Some sort of stroke, I believe. Strokes are as common among our kind as flies on newly harvested meat.

"Just stop it! Stop it!" I complain, unable to bear their old guy whining a second longer. "Can't you just let him play? We have plenty of extra balls—grab a couple and toss them around! Nothing's going to happen to him, or any one of us because of him!"

I do not believe any of this, of course, but it gets their minds off Clarence. He retrieves the ball from a beautiful young woman who has been watching us from the edge of one of those sunny paths. I stare at her for some time, even after Clarence Senior has jogged happily back into our little circle. The other men quickly close around him in case he's been followed.

The young woman is unusual in that she has noticed us. We are not used to being noticed at all, especially by beautiful young women. I wonder if those of us with daughters—Jacob, Samuel, perhaps one or two others— feel the same confused anticipation when a young woman looks at them. I wonder if they suffer from the same temporal dislocation of desire the rest of us experience.

She looks quite familiar. But then all the young women look familiar to me. By the time a man reaches my age he has stockpiled the blueprints of a thousand young women in the caves of his memory, ready for somber perusal during the long, lonely hours before dawn.

The young woman's eyes lock with mine and she slips in a quick smile. My heart speeds as a long stem of black insect leg darts from one corner of her mouth and scratches futilely at her chin before her dark red tongue can usher the leg back inside her mouth.

I look away as if with mere embarrassment, as if some part of her garment had slipped away and revealed more than might be decent. When I look back she is gone, but the ground where she stood appears blackened and torn.

Joseph injures himself again. His eyes are always filling with tears and then he can't see more than a few inches in front of him. He runs into things and then he falls down hard. Clarence Senior is always trying to help by convincing him that he isn't really hurt. "See, no blood!" Clarence Senior shouts with no small measure of delirium. He says this every time, even when there's blood gushing from the wound. Everything is A-OK in Clarence Senior's world, even though Clarence Junior hates him, even though he has the worst nightmares of us all.

"Throw me the ball! Me me me!" George cries, his belly moving independently of his leap. Benjamin, the retired carpenter—perhaps the best coordinated of us all—throws the ball and George drops it. No one laughs or complains— it has always been George's job to drop the ball. He staggers back and forth as he attempts to pick it up, frustrated to tears because his knees will not bend properly. If someday he were to magically acquire competence there would be considerable tension generated in the group, for only by comparison do the rest of us remain competent.

Benjamin shuffles after the ball like some huge, shaggy toy run by remote control. No one knows very much about Benjamin—he started playing with us one day as if he'd always been here. He has never spoken. I get the impression that he simply has nothing to say and will not pretend. A far better way of being in the world, I think. The rest of us speak constantly, fueled more by anxiety than idea.

We toss the ball and drop the ball, we run around things called bases, worshiping at each one briefly before being urged on by the impatient cries of our companions. The bases are old schoolbooks, interestingly shaped stones, and stakes ripped from the hard hearts of trees and driven almost flush into the ground. Who among us would have the power to execute such a pounding? It has always been here, driven ages ago by some comic book hero or other. It would be nice to linger, but our fear is that to stop even briefly, to stop at all, would be to invite the fragments of black into our mouths, into our ears and eyes and anuses, until all motion is stopped forever.

So this tired old group of us, we play and we play and we play, pretending to have fun until, like toddlers run amuck, we collapse into the arms of our mothers at the end of the day.

But, of course, our mothers are not there at the end of the day. Most of us cannot even remember how our mothers died, or how they've otherwise left us. But we think about our mothers often, during these last, long days of play in the park, for we are still the melancholy boys we always were, late for dinner and crying over the day's small, misplaced treasures.

Late in the afternoon Samuel arrives from his job by bright yellow taxi, his favorite mode of transportation. He is the only one of us to continue in a state of gainful employment. He sits down on the graffiti bench ("Peggy loves Frank, but what about God?" "Sing and play all day, but whatever you do don't go past the path at night.") for his daily cry, the rest of us gathering around him for our daily pretense of comfort. "They act like I'm stupid!" he complains. "Like I'm too old to learn anything new!"

We all pat his back and his knee, more fiercely now, agreeing vigorously although we really have no idea what we're agreeing to. We have never been to Samuel's work and most of us haven't worked a regular job in years. Still, we know how it can be out there. Any man knows, past a certain age. The world is something new every day, something you've never seen before, something you feel hopeless to understand. The colors of the world shift their spectrum with each rising of the sun. The mouths of the world mutate the words of the world even as they are formed. "Damn bosses . . . damn wireless whatevers . . . damn computers . . ." We all nod our understanding. Damn whatevers, indeed.

Then there is Willy, standing in his corner of the field waiting for the ball to come to him. He would wait all day if we let him, and more often than not we do, for we enjoy observing his profound patience.

"It's not patience," Jacob declares. "He's just an idiot."

If there is truth in what Jacob says we do not want to know about it. Willy does not appear to suffer the fears that bother the rest of us. Willy has no need for hand-holding. Willy does not appear to need at all. Willy simply stands, and waits, watching for whatever comes next, a ball, or a butterfly, or fragments broken off the shadows and stealing across the lawns.

We try to prevent the ball from coming Willy's way. He would not know what to do with it. He is a watcher, you see.

"He has about a thimbleful of brain," is the way Jacob so delicately puts it. Jacob thinks it is shameful the way I let Willy groom himself: unshaven, hair long and stringy, greasy. Jacob has even brought shampoos and razors to the park from time to time, "To take care of poor Willy. Shameful the way we've let him go like that." As if Willy were an unkempt yard or a dog in need of a trim.

But I always wave Jacob away. Willy is not exactly happy, but he is stable the way he is, and some things should not be tampered with.

Again I see the pretty young woman at the edge of our area, watching. I cannot keep my eyes off her. The beauty of young women is something I truly miss, being able to touch them, to admire them openly. Not that there is no beauty in older women, or that the feelings I'm expressing are primarily sexual. But so much is recalled when I see the newness in them, the untutored look as their eyes open up to the world.

A sudden breeze lifts her hair revealing a sheen of brittle membranes close to the skull. Small nodules like eggs nestle around her ears and above her forehead. Tiny shapes pulse and jerk in the sacs. As one begins to erupt into a flowering of dark, segmented parts, the breeze mercifully drops her hair back over the assemblage.

We are all supposed to be having fun here. Even though sometimes we try a little too hard, laugh a little too hard for comfort. But what are you going to do? Far better than the alternative. That is what everyone says. That is what all the old people say.

At five o'clock we line up and the designated adult checks the

pockets of the others. We stand at lazy attention with our hands
stretching our pockets inside out and sideways so they resemble a
pair of large ears. Clarence Senior always requires some encouragement, Willy has to have his pockets turned inside out for him,
and nine times out of ten George will be hiding something, so we
have to watch him especially carefully to make sure he does not
do anything that is going to get him into trouble. More often than
not I am the designated adult, a fact that I often resent and can be
quite bitter about. In those instances I always have Jacob check
my pockets—I never keep anything in there besides some hard
candy for the others.

By eight o'clock we are well into drowsy, although most of us
will fight sleep with our last breath. We sit up on our bedding and
talk about the day's games and share memories of our mothers,
now and then twisting our heads around to make sure that a particular piece of night remains respectfully in its place.

Jacob and I are always the last to fall asleep. Sometimes I
think it is because we feel a certain paternal responsibility for the
others. Sometimes I think it is because we think our alertness will
protect us from the inevitable.

In the middle of the night they come for Willy. I am somewhat
comforted that he shows no signs of surprise. Surely, this is what
he has always been waiting for. Tonight they come as eight or
nine squirrels and a large black bird with a broken neck. The bird
bothers me most: its head flops and stretches painfully on the
narrow strand of neck flesh as it still manages to grab a bit of
Willy's pants in its beak and pull with the squirrels to drag Willy's
body off into the night. Now and again one of the squirrels will
let go and turn its head, smiling at me so broadly I can see that all
its teeth are missing.

Some people, I believe, are paid for dreaming. But most, I
think, are punished.

In a few days they will come to take another of us. Rabbits,
perhaps, or snakes, or shiny emerald-green beetles, or an old dog
that so resembles one from our childhood we will be convinced it
is the very same one. Soon only Jacob or I will be left.

But that is the worst kind of wish-fulfillment. How do I know I
will be a survivor? At some things the imagination fails.

I know I should not whine about it. It is a natural process that happens to everyone. You can wait for it or you can play with it, you can roll your ball at it or you can run headlong into the cars that seem to be everywhere. But what you cannot do is stop it from coming.

Each morning we awaken to find that life is a bit less under-standable. Each morning we awaken to the disappearance of the known. Each morning we awaken to discover that we have missed the last bus for the life to come.

THE CABINET CHILD

Around the beginning of the last century, on the outskirts of a small southwest Virginia town which no longer exists, a childless woman named Alma lived with her gentleman farmer husband in a large house up on a ridge. The woman was not childless because of any medical condition—her husband simply felt that children were "ill-advised" in their circumstances, that there was no space for children in the twenty-or-so rooms of what he called their modest home.

Not being of a demonstrative inclination, his wife kept her disappointment largely to herself, but it could not have been more obvious if she had screamed it from their many-gabled roof. Sometimes, in fact, she muttered it in dialogue with whoever should pass, and when no one was looking, she pretended to scream. Over the years despair worked its way into her eyes and drifted down into her cheeks, and the weight of her grief kept her bent and shuffling.

Although her husband Jacob was an insensitive man he was not inobservant. After enduring a number of years of his wife's sad display he apparently decided it gave an inappropriate impression of his household's tenor to the outside world and became determined to do something about it. He did not share his thinking with her directly, of course, but after an equal number of years enduring his maddening obstinacy his wife was well acquainted with his opinions and attitudes. Without so much as a knock he came into her bedroom one afternoon as she sat staring out her window and said, "I have decided you need something to cheer yourself up, my dear. John Hand will be bringing his wagon around soon and you may choose anything on it. Let us call it an early Christmas present, why don't we?"

She looked up at him curiously. After having prayed aloud for some sign of his attention, for so many nights, she could scarcely believe her ears. Was this some trick? As little as it was, still he had never offered her such a prize before. She thought at first that somehow he had hurt his face, and then realized what she had taken for a wound was simply a strained and unaccustomed smile. He carried that awkward smile out the door with him, thank God. She did not think she could bear it if such a thing were running around loose in her private quarters.

John Hand was known throughout the region as a fine furniture craftsman who hauled his pieces around in a large gray wagon as roughly made as his furniture was exquisitely constructed. And yet this wagon had not fallen apart in over twenty years of travels up and down wild hollows and over worn mountain ridges with no paved roads. She had not perused his inventory herself, but people both in town and on the outlying farms claimed he carried goods to suit every taste and had a knack for finding the very thing that would please you, that is, if you had any capacity for being pleased at all, which some folk clearly did not.

Alma had twenty rooms full of furniture, the vast majority of it handed down from various branches of Jacob's family. Alma had never known her husband to be very close to his relations, but any time one of them died and there were goods to be divided he was one of the first to call with his respects. And although he was hardly liked by any of those grieving relatives, he always seemed able to talk them into letting him leave with some item he did not rightly deserve.

Sometimes at night she would catch him with his new acquisitions, stroking and talking to them as if they had replaced the family he no longer much cared for. She could not understand what had come over her that she would have married such a greedy man.

Although she needed no furniture, without question Alma was sorely in need of being pleased, which was why she was at the front gate with an apron pocket full of Jacob's money the next time John Hand came trundling down the road in that horse-drawn wagon full of his wares. Even though she waved almost frantically Hand did not appear to acknowledge her, but then stopped abruptly in front of their grand gate. She had seen him in town before but never paid him much attention. When Hand suddenly jumped down and stood peering up at her she was somewhat alarmed by the smallness of the man—he was thin as a pin and painfully bent, the top of his head not even reaching to her shoulders, and she was not a particularly tall woman. The wagon loomed like a great ocean liner behind him, and she could not imagine how this crooked little man had filled it with all this furniture, pieces so jammed together it looked like a puzzle successfully completed.

Then Mr. Hand turned his head rather sideways and presented her with a beatific smile, and completely charmed she felt prepared to go with anything the little man cared to suggest.

"A present from the husband, no?"

"Well, yes, he said I could choose anything."

"But not the present madam most wished for." He said it as if it was undeniable fact, and she did not correct him. Surely he had simply guessed, based on some clues in her appearance?

He gazed at her well past the point of discomfort, and then clambered up the side of the wagon, monkey-like and with surprising speed. The next thing she knew he had landed in front of her, holding a small, polished wood cabinet supported by his disproportionately large palm and the cabinet's four unusually long and thin, spiderish legs. "I must confess it has had a previous owner," he said with a mock sad expression. "She was like you, wanting a child so very much. This was to be in the nursery, to hold its dainty little clothes."

Alma was alarmed for a number of reasons, not the least of which that she'd never told the little man that she had wanted a child. Then she quickly realized what a hurtful insult this was on his part—to give someone never to have children a cabinet to hold its clothes? She turned and made for the gate, averting her head so the vicious little man would not see her streaming tears.

"Wait! Please," he said, and a certain softness in his voice stopped her more firmly than a hand on her shoulder ever could. She turned just as he shoved the small cabinet into her open arms. "You will not be—unfulfilled by this gift, I assure you." And with a quick turn he had leapt back onto the seat and the tired-looking horses were pulling him away. She stood awkwardly, unable to speak, the cabinet clutched to her breast like a stricken child.

In her bedroom she carried the beautifully-polished cabinet with the long, delicate legs to a shadowed corner away from the window, the door, and any other furniture. She did not understand this impulse exactly; she just felt the need to isolate the cabinet, to protect it from any other element in her previous life in this house. Because somehow she already knew that her life after the arrival of this delicate assemblage of different shades of wood would be a very different affair.

Once she had the cabinet positioned as seemed appropriate—based on some criteria whose source was completely mysterious to her—she sat on the edge of her bed and watched it until it was time to go downstairs and help the cook prepare dinner for her husband. Afterwards she came back and sat in the same position, gazing, and singing softly to herself for two, three, four hours at least. Until the sounds in the rest of the house had faded. Until the soft amber glow of the new day appeared in one corner of her window. And until the stirrings inside the cabinet became loud enough for her to hear.

She came unsteadily to her feet and walked across the rug with her heart racing, blood rushing loudly into her ears. She held her breath, and when the small voice flowered on the other side of the shiny cabinet wall, she opened its tiny door.

Twenty years after his wife's death, Jacob entered her bedroom for the third and final time. The first time had been the afternoon he had strode in to announce his well-meant but inadequate gift to her. The second time had been to find her lifeless body sprawled on the rug when she had failed to come down for supper. And now this third visit, for reasons he did not fully understand, except that he had been overcome with a terrible sadness and sense of dislocation these past few weeks, and this dusty bed chamber was the one place he knew he needed to be.

He would have come before—he would have come a thousand times before—if he had not been so afraid he could never make himself leave.

He had left the room exactly as it had been on Alma's last day: the covers pulled back neatly, as if she planned an early return to bed, a robe draped across the back of a cream-upholstered settee, a vanity table bare of cosmetics but displaying an antique brush and comb, a half-dozen leather-bound books on a shelf mounted on the wall by her window. In her closet he knew he would find no more than a few changes of clothes. He didn't bother to look because he knew they betrayed nothing of who she had been. She had lived in this room as he imagined nuns must live, their spare possessions a few bare strokes to portray who they had been.

It pained him that it was with her as it had been with everyone else in his life—some scattered sticks of furniture all he had left to remember them by—where they had sat, what they had touched, what they had held and cared for. He had always made sure that when some member of the family died he got something, any small thing, they had handled and loved, to take back here to watch and listen to. And yet none was haunted, not even by a whisper. He knew—he had watched and listened for those departed loved ones most of his adult life.

His family hadn't wanted him to marry her. No good can come, they said, of a union with one so strange. And though he had loved his family, he had separated from them, aligning himself with her in this grand house away from the staring eyes of the town. It had not been a conventional marriage—she could not abide being touched and permitted him to see her only at certain times of the day, and even then he might not even be present as far as she was concerned, so intent was she on her conversation with the people and things he could not see.

His family virtually abandoned him over his choice, but as a grown man it was his choice to make. He was never sure if his beloved Alma had such choices. Alma had been driven, apparently, by whatever stray winds entered her brain.

The gift she had chosen in lieu of a child (for how could he give his child such a mother, or give his wife such a tender thing to care for?) still sat in its corner in shadow, appearing to lean his way on its insubstantial legs. He perceived a narrow crack in the front surface of the small cabinet, which drew him closer to inspect the damage, but it was only that the small door was ajar, inviting him to secure it further, or to peek inside.

Jacob led himself into the corner with his lantern held before him, and grasping the miniature knob with two trembling fingers pulled it away from the frame, and seeing that the door had a twin, unclasped the other side and spread both doors like wings that might fly away with this beautiful box. He stepped closer then, moving the light across the cabinet's interior like a blazing eye.

The inside was furnished like some doll's house, and it saddened him to see this late evidence of the state of Alma's thinking. Here and there were actual pieces of doll furniture, perhaps kept from her girlhood or "borrowed" from some neighbor child. Then there were pieces—a settee very like the one in this room, a high-backed Queen Anne chair—carved, apparently, from soap, now discolored and furred by years of clinging dust and lint.

Other furniture had been assembled from spools and emery boards, clothespins, a small jewelry box, then what appeared to be half a broken drinking cup cleverly upholstered with a woman's faded black evening glove.

He was surprised to find in one corner a small portrait of himself, finely painted in delicate strokes, and one of Alma set beside it. And underneath, in tiny, almost unreadable script, two words, which he was sure he could not read correctly, but which might have said "Father", "Mother".

He decided he had been hearing the breathing for some time— he just hadn't been sure of its nature, or its source. The past few years he had suffered from a series of respiratory ailments, and had become accustomed to hearing a soft, secondary wheeze, or leak, with each inhalation and exhalation of breath. That could easily have been the origin of the sounds he was hearing.

But he suspected not. With shaking hand he reached into the far corner of the box, where a variety of handkerchiefs and lacy napkins lay piled. He peeled them off slowly, until finally he reached that faint outline beneath a swatch of dress lace, a short thing curled onto itself, faintly moving with a labored rasp.

He could have stopped then, and thought he should, but his hand was moving again with so little direction, and just nudged that bit of cloth, which dropped down a bare quarter inch.

Nothing there, really, except the tiny eyes. Tissue worn to transparency, flesh vanished into the dusty air, and the child's breathing so slight, a parenthesis, a comma. Jacob stared down solemnly at this kind afterthought, shadow of a shadow, a ghost of a chance. Those eyes so innocent, and yet so old, and desperately tired, an intelligence with no reason to be. Dissolving. The weary breathing stopped.

In the family plot, what little family there might be, there by Alma's grave he erected a small stone: "C. Child" in bold but fine lettering. There he buried the cabinet and all it had contained, because what else had there been to bury? Two years later he joined them there, on the other side.

THE FIGURE IN MOTION

The majority of his days he had nothing useful to do. At one time he imagined that was what he'd always wanted. In fact, they had planned their mutual retirement around that simple idea. They would read books. They would go to movies. The staffs of the local parks and museums would know them by their first names. He'd had this vivid image of himself strolling the sidewalks arm-in-arm with the love of his life, making but the slightest, almost immeasurable, ripple of forward motion as they walked together through their remaining days. No one would notice the nearly invisible wake of their passage, but that's what he thought they'd wanted. At some point all motion would stop, and even the memory of them would fade from the world forever. There was a simple dignity in the idea to which he was fully committed.

But then his wife was dying, a terrible disruption so unexpected at first but then gradually inevitable as her illness progressed. During her last few months on the planet he'd attempted to fill himself only with good memories of their life together, a cushion against the crushing loss to come, but he was quickly overpowered by events, and instead was forced to retain a series of images of her passing: her head bowed in burdensome fatigue, sitting shakily upright for a long stare out the window, her face at last too sad for tears, and then that final full day when she insisted on walking by herself across the field of powdered snow.

He'd watched her struggle across that brilliant emptiness, a lone figure changing shape, her shadow altering as sun and clouds moved, lines broken and ragged as she pushed forward into her future, her body so thin and her old dress so tattered she looked as if her skin were shedding while she prowled nervously through the whiteness of that late afternoon.

She left clear marks in the snow, gray holes descending into darkness and a wide scraping across the crystalline surface, making a pattern like angels' wings, which gradually melted, filled and blended, until that world below his window was clean, untroubled, and unoccupied again.

It had surprised him that he wasn't tempted to go help her. But that's not what she wanted—this journey was completely hers to do.

And so through the long years of his retirement without her, it had been these images that had occupied his time. He did manage to read the newspaper and the occasional magazine, to skim volumes of non-fiction, to catch the odd movie, now and then to attend a lecture or museum exhibit, but the main focus of his final years had become memories of her decline, or—when he forced himself to think generously—her radical transformation.

Certainly it must have been some sort of fantastic rationalization that began to let him think of this collection of memories as art.

"I'm too late, aren't I? I knew I would be—traffic was so bad, and I drive so poorly in bad traffic." He knew he was saying too much, but he'd lost the ability to edit his speech some time ago.

"Sorry? Too late for what?" The young woman looked pretty, and amused. Young enough to be his daughter.

He imagined the heat in his face might be presenting itself as a blush. "The tour? The Postmodern Figure?"

"Well, yes. But they just started a tour for one of the local college art classes. You could follow right along. If you stay close I'm sure you could still hear. No one would care, really. I promise I won't turn you in."

He laughed, but only because he thought he was supposed to. He had no idea why some people thought such dialogs humorous—he just recognized that they did. He hurried along, his long winter coat flapping around his knees. He'd be too hot pretty soon, he knew, and then he'd have to decide whether to be uncomfortable wearing it, or awkward carrying it around. His wife had always had a good suggestion or two for such dilemmas, but he'd found that the further he traveled away from her, the tinier his ability to make a simple decision. It was a kind of perspective he'd never heard of, and could find no mention of in the volumes of art history he'd bought since her death.

"After the war the human figure was trivialized in modern art.

It was made to appear insignificant, unreliable, and pitiable. Eventually it all but disappeared from the work of serious artists, as if they thought it beneath their notice, that it had nothing significant to say anymore. Art became dehumanized, less emblematic. As the prime emblem of our daily experience, the figure had to go."

He wanted to protest, to argue with the young guide, but of course she was only doing her job, and, as far as he knew, was completely correct. But he still found it humbling to hear, and was it just his imagination or did some of these students shrink back a bit from her words, become smaller, a bit self-conscious? He himself became more aware of the size of these canvases, many times human size, so that they seemed architectural, part of the walls, which he now realized were of varying heights, many several stories high, making triangles with the sloped ceilings, which swooped down overhead at times, threatening the heads of the patrons with sharp corners and unfriendly windows. He thought those windows were the kinds of windows an angel might use, or some other holy and invisible creature, and considered this an alarmingly odd perception, although perhaps one not so surprising to have in an art museum.

It was at this point, or so he would conclude later, that he first became aware of the figures in the next room of the gallery, beginning to emerge from hiding, just their outlines peeking from the corridor, but when he turned and tried to take their measure, they were gone, and although he stood and waited, they did not reappear.

By the time he gave up looking for them the tour had moved on without him, and he had to hurry to catch up, feeling hot and uncomfortable as he did so, and wishing he had made the decision simply to carry his coat. He was always conscious of perspiring heavily inside his clothing, and, although he bathed regularly, worried about smelling. "Eventually traces of the human figure began to appear in these huge, near-empty canvases. Perhaps not the figure itself, not at first, but the effects of its presence. It was coming out of hiding, it seems, but you might say it was being very cautious about the entire endeavor. The figure became tool and material, and eventually it became battleground."

At the guide's invitation the students spent some time with

these images. Some nodded agreeably with what she had to say, and some had a skeptical air about them, but appeared careful to keep their own figures neutral, betraying no opinion. He dutifully traveled from painting to painting, and sometimes it felt like a journey of years. He had not heard of most of these artists' names, but tried to memorize them so he could look them up later, find out what else they had done, read what they had to say for themselves.

Still, he felt an urge to leave the tour and seek out a Chagall, or a Soutine, one of the Jewish painters he liked so much, or even an expressionist like Robert Beauchamp, whose figures, with their nervousness and agitation, had become almost cartoonish in their attempts to recede and hide inside the paint. As for his own shy figures, he could still feel them lurking nearby, but thought it non-strategic to seek them out.

"There's still some jokiness about the figure's re-emergence, don't you think? A kind of coyness that invites us in. I find that refreshing, don't you? Art needn't be so stuffy. It can look at itself with good humor."

Perhaps he had no sense of humor when it came to art. Perhaps he was too serious about most things and that was his problem. His wife used to complain about his inappropriate joking, but she also understood that impulse of his came out of a belief that the world was a grim and serious place.

He felt a bit of palsy now in his right hand, and stared at it with eyes that did not focus well anymore. Between the two tendencies he was presented with an image of his hand with no clear lines, nothing firm to hold his flesh in. He felt his tears approaching, and stopped them by grabbing the hand firmly with its left partner, which held it decisively but tenderly in check.

He distracted himself from this localized drama by looking at the largest painting in the room. He didn't recognize this part of the gallery and wasn't aware of when the tour might have advanced here. At first he could see no figures in the painting, but then he found the one wavering line suggestive of a hesitant forward motion.

"For years the figure practically vanished from contemporary art."

He continued to stare at the wavering line in the right third of the painting. He didn't care for this kind of scraggly, wiggly art. He never had, except where someone like Beauchamp was concerned, who had this indefinable knack. For the most part, he could never find the emotion in this kind of work. But for some reason he felt this particular painting—in fact he found himself almost moved to tears. He saw more motion in that wavering line in the canvas than in his entire life, as it left its trace in the chaos, as it made its mark.

He looked at the artist's name. Daniel Richter. A German. The name wasn't completely unfamiliar, but it was still one that hadn't been on his radar. As he walked among the other Richter paintings, most of them larger-than-life size, he was impressed by their colors, explosive and alive with blood and neon, living now, and not in some memory of days before, and as more and more of the figures began to appear, coagulating out of the aggressive paint, but still hiding, or attempting to hide, it struck him that so many of the figures weren't much more than outlines, really, and inside those recognizably human outlines floated pools and bursts of color. But it wasn't a portrayal of exterior resemblance on these canvases, but of a peculiar sort of interior, the interior a medical technician might see in an MRI, or the auras of variously colored heat observable by means of some sort of specialized surveillance equipment, or from the cold and inhuman sensory apparatus of a heat-seeking missile now rapidly advancing on its all-too-vulnerable human targets.

For now he did not sense the shy figures he had encountered earlier—perhaps they were wandering the other galleries, reluctant to enter this one, as if worried they might dissolve within the intense colors and the brilliant lights.

But he had no time for this kind of fantastical speculation in any case. He was too busy examining the figures trapped within these paintings, or if not "figures," the evidence that figures had once been there, and now these were the prints their bodies had left behind upon impact with the world, or, looked at another way, their medical records, and the documentation of their trauma.

Of course no one had asked him what he was doing here in the art museum. No one had spoken to him at all. But he had been formulating an answer. He really had no idea where his wife had gone. All too quickly the traces of her outside their small home had been erased. He had no idea where to find her, so he was looking here, examining these paintings for clues. It made no sense, but he was convinced it was the right thing to do.

When he returned home that evening he fixed himself a sandwich and carried it into the living room, and sat with it on the palm of his hand and did not eat it. He could feel it drying out on his weary, outstretched palm, but he could not bring himself to take it into his mouth. Eventually he laid the uneaten sandwich onto a side table alongside several books his wife was never able to finish reading, and sat some more, gazing around the room, trying to find additional traces of where she had been, what she had touched.

He remembered she sometimes sat in this chair and knitted at odd times during the day and night. Sometimes he would awaken in the middle of the night and her side of the bed would be empty. He would come downstairs and discover her sitting here knitting squares, putting together blankets and sweaters and various indecipherable soft objects. She said she just couldn't sleep anymore. She said she had simply lost track of things and now had to figure things out.

After she died he had tried to learn how to knit without any success. He simply could not see how to create patterns, then recognizable objects, out of piles of seemingly limitless string. Instead he had sat here gingerly cupping a ball of yarn in each hand, as if he were holding eggs, as if showing some sort of reverence for the act would bring him understanding. But it never had.

He picked up one of the books she had left behind: *Beloved*, by Toni Morrison. He found the ornate metal bookmark she had inserted a third of the way through the book, a bookmark he had never seen before, but one so special he felt it must have been his wife's way of honoring this particular volume. He remembered that she had talked about this novel, how much she had loved it, how anxious she had been to get to the next page. But he was sorry that he did not remember anything more specific than that about the book itself.

He'd never read much fiction—fiction made him feel uncomfortable. He assumed the main characters were more or less masks of the author. Otherwise, how could the author make the story seem real? Fiction, he thought, must be a very strange sort of autobiography, portraying what the author wanted to happen, dreaded might happen, would happen if the author were of another sex, lived in a different country, had different personality traits, took a different path, job, spouse, etc. How did authors feel when their books were misread? What if people liked the character in your book better than who you were on such and such a particular day? He found such layering disturbing, and all too close to the way most people viewed their own lives.

But she'd loved the book and had wanted to finish it, and so, over the next few days, he finished it for her, reading it aloud despite the weaknesses in his speaking voice. He didn't think he needed to read it aloud so that she might hear it. He'd never believed in such things. Wherever she was he didn't think she was in any position to physically hear anything. He read it aloud so that the words might live in this home they'd shared all their married life.

Across the street from the art museum there was a park where people came to preach, to give speeches, to perform, or to express themselves in any way desired, as long as they didn't ask for money or offend common decency. The city government prided itself on its openness and the privilege was well used. Every day there were crowds.

One afternoon he brought a folding table and a battered old suitcase into the park, and out of the suitcase he retrieved a variety of records, which he laid out on the table for display. All of these records had to do with his wife's life, her long illness, and her death. At one end of the table there were photo albums from her childhood, letters to her parents from camp, a lock of hair from her first haircut. Next to these were laid out their wedding pictures and a variety of snapshots from their marriage: a trip out west, a day at the beach, a picnic in their own front yard when the car wouldn't start. He and his wife appeared together in all of the shots, and when he examined them he became obsessed with trying to remember what friend, neighbor, or stranger had been pressed into service as photographer. For most of the photographs a clear identification of the person taking the picture was impossible, as any normal person might expect. He understood this. But still it troubled him. Had these record makers been purely accidental, or was it possible that some had hung around hoping to be recruited for just such a purpose? Certainly, if these people hadn't been there, there might be no record that his long marriage to this wonderful woman had occurred at all.

At the other end of the table he stacked medical records and some pictures from her final years. He had been the photographer for these, and had taken so many portraits of her during this time that choosing a few representative photos had been a difficult task.

Specific facts having to do with her height and weight, the amount of space she occupied, her exact age to the minute at time of death, were prominently displayed. "This is the space and time she occupied," he repeated again and again when reciting these figures.

There were relatively few visitors to his table that first day, but for those that did come he provided a lengthy narrative concerning his wife, their time together, and her relatively recent death. He was undeterred by the lack of questions—he enjoyed talking about her so much, and it had been such a long time since he'd had the opportunity to talk about her, that the public's lack of interest wasn't about to dissuade him. He returned to the park every day that week and delivered essentially the same presentation.

The following week he decided to add a new element to the performance, not only to make it more interesting for himself, but to draw some of the larger crowds available during warmer weather. Despite his lack of formal dance training, despite his singular ineptitude with anything involving coordinated movement, he positioned himself behind the table and began a series of sweeping, yet precise, gestures, which might have been untrained yoga, untrained martial arts, untrained dance, or the unintentional movements of someone afflicted with a nervous disease. During these movements he delivered the same talk he had the week before, except this time there were more questions from the audience.

He grasped, he moved, he took a large inhalation of air. He faltered, he limped, he ached, he winced. He tried to exemplify how it was to be in the world for the number of years he had walked upon this planet. He tried to show the truth of his body and the solitary nature of his existence, and, without using the exact words, just how much he missed her.

He meditated on his hands as they moved through the air. He tried to make the movements of his performance as natural as possible. He attempted to imitate the everyday movements he made as he went through a normal day: cooking, washing hands, taking medications, holding his face as he wept. He imagined his movements as invisible brush strokes. He imagined himself as Clifford Stills, as Jackson Pollock. He imagined himself as some anonymous figure struggling through the wind and driving rain of his very worst day.

He rarely looked at the figures of his audience as he made his performances. It required too much focus just to imitate everyday natural movements for him to give his audience much more than a passing glance. But every so often he became aware of a slight blurring of the edges of the crowd. Now and then he became aware of the forgotten figures coming out of hiding, their vague outlines filling with heat and color to become targets for his eyes.

His wife had used a dressmaker to make alterations in her careful purchases, so it wasn't too much trouble to ask the woman to make several colored bodysuits fitted to his measurements. The only difficult part of the process was standing before her in T-shirt and shorts so that she could take these exacting measurements. Like a small boy he kept his eyes tightly shut until it was over.

The next week he appeared in the park in a variegated green and brown bodysuit. He thought he looked like a hole in the fabric of the world. He noticed that if he moved his body in certain ways, and at certain speeds, it was difficult for him to find the edge of himself. His sense of a personal outline faded in and out with his every movement, as if made from radio signals from an unreliable transmitter.

He attempted to harness unconscious habits into his performance: nose pickings, butt scratching, spitting.

He was aware that some people were repulsed, and left at the first appearance of some unpleasant bit of personal business. Although it meant the loss of some verisimilitude, he quickly returned to a semblance of politeness.

The following week he added photo manipulation to his performance. He had taken some of those precious photographs of him and his wife together, copied them, and made crude alterations in the copies. In some of the images he had altered her, or scratched her out, leaving a shapeless white defect in her place. In others he had simply folded over the photo in order to essentially erase her from the image entirely. He discovered that the altered photographs made him look ridiculous. He became a mad eccentric holding hands with nothing, speaking to nothing, kissing the nothing that is not there. The outlines in the crowd wavered as their faces began to drain of all color.

As he moved inside his empty body suit he thought he was beginning to resemble them: the figures that were not there. Some days his arms moved so quickly he lost track and could not find them. If he closed his eyes even once he forgot he was even there.

Sometimes people would try to touch him and that was when a museum guard posted near the edge of the crowd warned them away. He had seen the guard there for days but had thought that the man was merely a part of the audience, perhaps out there on his lunch break and wondering why everyone was watching the man who was not there dancing behind a table full of garbage: water-stained photographs and papers so dirty and damaged no one could read them anymore. Of course this put additional weight on his verbal performance to convey exactly who his wife had been. But his voice was failing. Some days he could barely whisper. The crowd sometimes had to edge quite close in order to hear him. "Please do not touch the exhibit," the guard would warn.

Sometimes he would notice the hands of certain audience members: opening and closing as if desperate to hold something. It occurred to him then that perhaps he should add things his wife had held to the table display: knitting needles, books, cooking implements. For didn't the objects she had handled tell an important part of her story? He thought then of adding his own hands to the table display, or at least a casting or a photograph.

On some days if he kept at his performance long enough he became unaware of anything else. His figure became a tangle of moments, lines of force, electrical energy, exhalations, and perspirations. His very presence appeared to fracture the air.

Some days his body became a tired whisper in his ear, which he attempted to ignore. Some days he stood in the audience surrounded by vague figures and shadows of figures, an echo of imitated movements through time, and watched his own performance.

One day he arrived to find the exhibit closed. His table was there, but all his carefully collected documentation was missing. But then he couldn't remember the last time he had seen those documents, and wondered if they might have vanished months ago.

"I'm afraid the exhibit is closed," the guard said.

When he started to reply he realized the guard wasn't talking to him, but to all the figures gathered behind him. They began to shuffle away, the outlines of their forms distorting and flowing across the landscape.

"What am I supposed to do now?" he asked. The guard did not answer.

He began to dance, and could not find his arms, his legs, or his next wandering thought. But even then, his movement did not stop.

AN ENDING

There is nothing more he can say. Perhaps he's told too much already. His daughter used to complain he had an answer for everything, and now he knows she felt bad about saying that for some time, and now he answers to no one, no matter how much they ask. But there is nothing more he can say about that.

Now that he cannot speak, his thoughts are loose in time. No matter how much she asks, he thinks, as if she could ask, as if she were not gone. Just like him, unable to bear witness to the world. Just like him. So does this mean he, too, is dead?

Of course not. Of course not. Not so long as the neurons fire, illuminating the brain, filling the sky with light. Broadcasting the voices.

The songs they sing are measured in broken air and shattered bone. The power of them lies in the stray wind in the high mountains felt and heard by no one. When they cry the earth cries, and the earth cries often. The darkness that is their subject knows no bounds real or imaginary, rubbing at us all.

But she was correct just the same. Once upon a time he did think he had the answers for everything. Now he understands how little he knew. But he cannot tell her.

And if he could speak, what might he say? What would he talk to her about? What message would he bring to the dead to show he understood even a bit of their plight?

He might say no. He might say yes. He might yadda yadda yadda.

He might say there is a new flower growing in the window box. A yellow tulip, his wife's favorite. He might tell his wife he still loves her. He might tell her that he loved her and he loves her and he always will. What better thing might a person say?

The strangest thing about his immobility, he thinks, is how much he moves inside it. His chest rises and falls, ever so slightly, not much more palpable than his thoughts, but still discernible.

Sweat traces his face like the fingertips of blind angels. Fluids and gasses move deep inside him, down in the hidden chambers of the self.

And his eyes move, even though he is rarely aware of it. He sees, but what he sees could be the dream he's having, he has no way of telling. He has no way of telling anyone. His eyes might even be cameras, replacements for the eyes he used to have. Click and click again. Can they do such things? They can do so many things he does not understand. He does not understand.

And the world moves, changes and spins because of something he has done. He is done. The world changes colors and brings forth strange and wonderful creatures who dance and lick and scream, and he knows he is the cause, but he does not know how.

In the other bed his wife stares at him. She may have died but he cannot be sure. Sometimes he thinks a look can last longer than a life. She has stared at him so intently for a very long time. She does not miss a thing. He understands that for a very long time she stared at him with a love beyond anything he had ever experienced before, beyond anything he might imagine, but he suspects the intention of that gray-eyed gaze has changed over the time of their imprisonment to become of another kind of focus and intensity, but he was never quite sure what words might best describe this new state. In his more fanciful speculations, in fact, he imagined that his wife invented a brand new emotion: one that goes beyond love, one that factors the despair of knowing, the knowledge that comes from living with death so close at hand.

He prefers to look not into those hazy gray eyes but at her hairline, at that place where the hair parts above the middle of her forehead, where the combined scents of shampoo and brain heat so often gather, where she smells clean and vital, where her smell is like a taste of the entire of her, where he would live forever if he could.

The phone rings again, a physical tearing of the sour air in the bedroom. His daughter's answering machine picks it up. A loud click followed by another loud click, as if something is snapping. As if the bones of this sorry animal, this answering animal, are breaking, and soon it will answer no more, its sad carcass draped over the nightstand.

Once upon a time it did answer, and so efficiently recorded the details of their daughter's death, which he would not believe at first, because she only went out for some milk, she promised them both (although neither of them could answer) that she'd be right back, and who could die in such a way, on such a small errand?

The voice on the machine had been so crisp, so professionally sympathetic as it delivered the terrible news, who could not believe it?

Now the male voice on the machine asks, "Are you there? Pick up. Pick up. Are you there?" with an urgency that surprises him. Some boyfriend he does not know about? Was that where she was really going when she left here? Did she tell him about her parents, so that maybe he'll think to call the police and send them to her house?

There's always a chance. He used to tell her, from the time she was a little girl, there's always a chance, sweetheart. "Are you there?" Even if he could answer, he does not know what he could say.

His daughter left on her little errand eight days ago.

He knows because of the calendar on the wall just above his daughter's desk. He can barely see it, tucked around the corner there, but it is still clear enough. Kittens above the black, dated squares. He cursed her sweet name for her arrogance, so convinced with her nursing degree that she could take care of them both. No nursing home, no nursing home, Dad. Damn her carelessness. And her driving has always lacked caution, no matter how much he tries to teach her. She thought she knew. She thought she knew. Her father's daughter, she took after him.

No one knows he is here. And no one knows her mother is here. Now the eighth day is passing, slipping like ooze from broken hydraulics, dripping off the edge of the table and out of sight.

And damn her for being dead. She's broken his heart.

And now nothing can be right. There is nothing he can say.

Even when there is so much to say.

His wife's arm hangs limp off the side of the bed. She's been strapped down, but in that last seizure the cloth tears, the arm flopping free, then limp. He'd wanted to be closer then, but all that moved were his desperate tears.

Eight days and some strong smells have faded, some gradually making their presence known. The smell the body makes as fluids give way. The smell of the orange on the sunny table. The stench as the body dies incrementally.

The reek of time, wasted and misused, the days thrown away. The foulness of regret, accumulated until the very end.

His wife was always fussy about matters of toiletry. She had no more odor than a glossy magazine ad. She cared for no variety of incense or perfume, and found even cooking odors somehow rude. She could not be said even to smell fresh. She was cured. She was sealed. She was statuary. Her nose was an anchor for her eyes and nothing more.

Illness, as he would have told her had she just asked, brings indignity. He was the first to fall, robbed of speech and mobility by a blood clot, and he greatly admired the way she put aside her prejudices in order to take care of him. Even changing him when the aide was off duty. She didn't complain, not even involuntarily. She simply did what needed to be done for someone she loved. Could he have done the same for her? He wasn't so sure. At least not with such care, such equanimity.

She'd been bent over him, rearranging his pillow, making it so that it fit perfectly beneath his ears, and he was feeling absurdly grateful, because a crease in the case had been torturing him for hours. Then he detected an ever so faint aroma of urine, and he stared at her in surprise as her expression changed, as if some startling idea suddenly entered her consciousness, and almost immediately he knew it was a stroke—she'd been assaulted by the fairies, and she fell away from him and he couldn't even shout his outrage at the terrible thing. The anger leaked out of him a bit at a time over the following hours, weeks, and months.

What is left of the woman he loved in the nearby bed he cannot know. There is so much he cannot know.

He does not know when the ringing in his ears first began. It seems a recent event but he cannot be sure. He suspects it's the song the brain sings when it dies but of course there is no way for him to know if this is true. Sometimes it is loud and sometimes it is quite soft. Sometimes it is all he can do not to weep when he hears it.

One of the things his wife and he enjoyed most was listening to music together. Now those days are gone, he thinks, or are they? Perhaps even now they are listening to the same tune.

Suddenly there is quiet as if a door has been closed. This is the way. This is the way. When the view becomes unbearable, then shut the door.

He closes his eyes against her death and a loud voice grows, singing from somewhere far below him. It is his own voice he hears, even though his lips do not move.

He has heard, of course, that as the brain dies neurons fire indiscriminately, and what the mind perceives in such circumstances is not to be trusted, is fanciful in its last, desperate attempts to complete a train of notions, and all that is witnessed under these conditions is a product of an electrified imagination.

So what, he thinks. When you are reduced to brain, and the various senses that are accessories to the brain, what more could there be, and certainly, what could be more important than that first trip into insubstantiality where only the imagination can report back, strapped to a shuddering, unhesitant engine of unreason?

So he isn't alarmed to see the great goat stroll through the door, like some new owner surveying the premises purchased for a hard price. The goat gazes at him only briefly, a polite but dismissive look at an eager would-be lover found wanting.

Instead the goat lingers at his wife's side and he is suddenly overcome not only by a bare, numbing grief for her but also by the very reek of her, suddenly more powerful than ever before, like a focused sample of every undrained outhouse and waste pool, every foul abattoir avoided by so-called decent, civilized people. He is terrified, tries to turn away and when he knows the attempt useless, closes his eyes tight as his love for her.

But the goat's huge laughter tears his eyelids open and he has to look at the thing, prancing and dancing over his wife's disastrous bed, now her grave. The goat rises on its hind legs and pounds the ceiling with its split hooves, shaking down plaster and lath, wiring and insulation batts, jangling pipes and a steady and gorgeous fall of fine white powder, continuing long after the goat has settled back onto its haunches, long snout pushed heaven-ward, eyes closed in pleasure over the bath it is receiving.

He surprises himself thinking how oddly beautiful it all seems, the abstract patterns of debris framing the now snow-white animal fur, the blissful yard-long smile spread around the goat's huge head.

Then quickly the goat mounts his dead wife's bed, licks the disaster of her with its long red tongue, and lowers itself, and lowers itself, until it can begin its thrusts effectively, a great back and forth of ripping and damage as it enters his wife's sad rem-nants of flesh, forcing a terrible gasping of air out of her mouth in a hideous parody of orgasm.

After the great goat has done whatever it can, it rises and walks off the bed, dragging remnants of the woman he loved most of his life still stuck to fur, to belly, to genitalia, most of it disinte-grating as the goat strides to the door and out, her skin and hair shattering against the floor like bits of frozen twig and leaf.

A darkness begins to seep from scattered corners of the bedroom. It breaks into wings and the things that wear wings, insects and disasters spat out and eager to escape. Their flight soon fills the room, until he can see nothing else. When their edges fly too close he can feel his skin tearing, but not enough, sweet lord, to bring him release.

In the middle of the world a huge wind begins to turn. In the distance his life shimmers like a beautiful, barely noticed thing, and as he watches the dark shapes rush to surround it: the almost loves and the never agains, their narrow heads brightly plumed with the naive prayers of children.

So he has his release, his ending, his final day. And he's ashamed to say he's grateful not to have suffered what his wife had to suffer. He's grateful to have had some peace at the end, deserved or not it matters little. He's grateful.

What more is there to say at the end, even when he can say nothing? He said all he knew to say a long time ago. Some things can only be said in the language of angels.

Dad? Dad, are you awake? Did you sleep well? Time to get up now. Time for dinner.

He is awake, his eyes wide open, but only now beginning to see. He is so absurdly grateful he begins to weep. No ending here after all. He wasn't ready, he wasn't ready. And somehow the angels knew.

So kind of his daughter to wake him. She's always been a good daughter, a wonderful daughter in fact, and he is grateful. So many fathers have not been as fortunate.

So many fathers have children who leave them, children who stay away even when they are home, children who pretend they have no fathers or mothers, children who have this other life, waiting for their fathers to die.

Dinner, Daddy. Don't let it get cold.

He gazes around the bedroom and again it amazes him how clean she keeps it, how everything seems in its perfect place, how it had no perfect place until she put it there.

The bed he lies on so carefully made, barely disturbed even as he eases from between its crisp white sheets. His wife's bed, equally well made and laden with roses to honor her memory. When did she die? He's not quite sure, because her passing was so peaceful—their daughter has taken such good care of them both he knows she passed with a minimum of fuss and pain.

He had so many fears about this time—how foolish it had been to worry and obsess about what must come to us all. How much better to ease into it without struggle, to see it as simply another stage, no better or worse than any other, just another adventure at the end of your days.

Daddy, please. I don't want you to starve.

Eating always made him feel better, so why not do what made you feel better? Store enough up to last you through the lean times, was the way his father had always put it.

The world had a way of eating at you, so what better way to survive than to have more of you against the world's angry appetite.

"Smells good, sweetheart. Smells wonderful!" He almost laughs, because he's so surprised to hear the sound of his own voice. It seems forever since he's heard the sound of his own voice. But of course it was only this morning, or perhaps last night, certainly no further away than yesterday afternoon. He and his daughter speak every day, after all: long, serious talks about politics and morals and her many dreams. She's always had so much ambition. She takes after him. She takes after him.

Even to the point of sounding like him: his voice, her voice, indistinguishable.

He's just had so many bad dreams of late in which he wasn't able to speak to her, he wasn't allowed to speak to her, and he'd been so hungry for conversation. He is so hungry.

Dad, I'm not telling you again! Dinner!

He's always been late for dinner. He'll get so busy sometimes, there is always so much to do, and a person of ambition can go on and on without replenishment sometimes, building on what he has already done, using the same words, the same thoughts again and again, reusing the dreams he's dreamed a thousand times before.

That line of thinking is making him vaguely uncomfortable. Better to get on to dinner, otherwise he might hurt her feelings. Nothing wrong here. Nothing is wrong.

She's kept the kitchen as spotless as the rest of the house.

Gleaming countertops, crystalline glass, shiny silver of the utensils. The finest linen. But where's the food? He doesn't see any food.

Not that he needs to eat, however hungry he may feel. He's gotten so fat of late, he could lie in bed a year or more and live off all that he contains.

Better not to think of that. Better to keep a positive attitude. He has so many bad dreams. He has so many awful things in his head.

"Sweetheart," he says. "Sweetheart. I don't see the food."

Look down, Daddy, she says from the other side of the wall.

He looks down at his plate but there is nothing. There is nothing to eat. "There's nothing here, sweetheart."

Don't be so helpless, Daddy. Make yourself a meal. Make yourself a meal.

He can feel the sheets gathered around his head. He can hear his wife's body torn asunder and carried out of the world. He can smell the reek and decay of everything he has ever loved. He tries to cover his ears against the screams of this world but he cannot move. He cannot move.

Make yourself a meal, her voice says with finality.

He gazes down at his ponderous belly and fumbles at all the utensils suddenly spilling off the edge of the table: all the sharp edges, all the knives of the world.

The telephone rings. The answering machine picks it up. "Are you there?" the male voice asks. "Pick up. Pick up."

"I'm not here!" he says. "I'm not here!"

Make yourself a meal, she says, and, grabbing the sharpest knife, he does.

TWEMBER

Will observed through the kitchen window of his parent's farmhouse as the towering escarpment, its many strata glittering relative to their contents, moved inescapably through the fields several hundred yards away. He held his breath as it passed over and through fences, barns, tractors, and an abandoned house long shed of paint. Its trespass was apparently without effect, although some of the objects in its wake had appeared to tremble ever so slightly, shining as if washed in a recent, cleansing rain.

"It might be beautiful," his mother said beside him, her palsy magnified by the exertion of standing, "if it weren't so frightening."

"You're pushing yourself." He helped her into one of the old ladder-back kitchen chairs. "You're going to make yourself sick."

"A body needs to see what she's up against." She closed her eyes.

He got back to the window in time to see a single tree in the escarpment's wake sway, shake, and fall over. Between the long spells of disabling interference he had heard television commentators relate how, other than the symptomatic "cosmetic" impact on climate, sometimes nearby objects were affected, possibly even destroyed, when touched by the escarpments, or the walls, or the roaming cliffs—whatever you cared to call the phenomena. These effects were still poorly understood, and "under investigation" and there had been "no official conclusions." Will wondered if there ever would be, but no one would ever again be able to convince him that the consequences of these massive, beautiful, and strange escarpments as they journeyed across the world were merely cosmetic.

His mother insisted that the television be kept on, even late at night, and even though it was no better than a white noise machine most of the time. "We can't afford to miss anything important," she'd said. "It's like when there's a tornado coming— you keep your TV on."

"These aren't like tornadoes, Mom. They can't predict them."

"Well, maybe they'll at least figure out what they are, why they're here."

"They've talked about a hundred theories, two hundred. Time disruption, alien invasion, dimensional shifts at the earth's core. Why are tsunamis here? Does it matter? You still can't stop them." At least the constant static on the TV had helped him sleep better.

"They're getting closer." Tracy had come up behind him. There was a time when she would have put her arms around him at this point, but that affectionate gesture didn't appear to be in his wife's repertoire anymore.

"Maybe. But it's not like they have intelligence," he said, not really wanting to continue their old argument, but unable to simply let it go.

"See how it changes course, just slightly?" she said. "And there's enough tilt from vertical I'm sure that can't just be an optical illusion. It leans toward occupied areas. I've been watch- ing this one off and on all day, whenever it's visible, almost from the time it came out of the ground."

"They don't really come out of the ground." He tried to sound neutral, patient, but he doubted he was succeeding. "They've said it just looks that way. They're forming from the ground up, that's all."

"We don't know that much about them. No one does," she snapped.

"It's not like it's some predator surfacing, like a shark or a snake, prowling for victims." He was unable to soften the tone of his voice.

"You don't know that for sure."

Will watched as the escarpment either flowed out of visual range or dematerialized, it was hard to tell. "No. I guess I don't."

"Some of the people around here are saying that those things sense where there are people living, that they're drawn there, like sharks to bait. They say they learn."

"I don't know." He didn't want to talk about it anymore.

"I hope not." Of course she was entitled to her opinion, and it wasn't that he knew any more than she did. But they used to know how to disagree.

He could hear his father stirring in the bedroom. The old man shuffled out, his eyes wet, unfocused. The way he moved past, Will wasn't sure if he even knew they were there. His father gazed out the window, and not for the first time Will wondered what exactly he was seeing. In the hazy distance another escarpment seemed to be making its appearance, but it might simply be the dust blown up from the ground, meeting the low-lying, streaked clouds. Then his father said "chugchugchugchugchug," and made a whooh whoohing sound, like a train. Then he made his way on out to the porch.

In his bedroom, Jeff began to whimper. Tracy went in to check on him. Will knew he should join her there—he'd barely looked at his son in days, except to say goodnight after the boy was already asleep—but considering how awkward it would be with the three of them he instead grabbed the keys to his dad's pickup and went out looking for the place where the escarpment had passed through and touched that tree.

Will had grown up here in eastern Colorado, gone to school, helped his parents out on the farm. It really hadn't changed that much over the decades, until recently, with that confusion of seasons that frequently followed the passage of escarpments through a region. The actual temperatures might vary only a few degrees from the norm, but the accompanying visual clues were often deceptive and disorienting. Stretches of this past summer had felt almost wintery, what with reduced sunlight, a deadening of plant color, and even the ghostly manifestation of a kind of faux snow which disintegrated into a shower of minute light-reflecting particles when touched.

Those suffering from seasonal affective disorder had had no summer reprieve this year. He'd heard stories that a few of the more sensitive victims had taken to their beds for most of the entire year. Colorado had a reputation for unpredictable weather, but these outbreaks, these "invasions" as some people called them, had taken this tendency toward meteorological unreliability to a new extreme.

Now it was, or at least should have been, September, with autumn on the way but still a few pretty hot days, but there were—or at least there appeared to be—almost no leaves on the trees, and no indications that there ever had been, and a gray-white sky had developed over the past few weeks, an immense amorphous shroud hanging just above the tops of the trees, as if the entire world had gone into storage. Dead of winter, or so he would have thought, if he'd actually lost track of the weeks, which he dare not do. He studied the calendar at least once a day and tried to make what he saw outside conform with memories of seasons past, as if he might will a return to normalcy.

Thankfully there had been few signs as yet of that fake snow. The official word was that the snow-like manifestation was harmless for incidental contact, and safe for children. Will wasn't yet convinced—the very existence of it gave him the creeps, thinking that some sort of metaphysical infection might have infiltrated the very atomic structure of the world, and haunted it.

"Twember," was what his mother called this new mixing of the seasons. "It's all betwixt and between. Pretty soon we're going to have just this one season. It won't matter when you plant, or what, it's all going to look like it died."

He thought he was probably in the correct vicinity now. Parts of the ground had this vaguely rubbed, not quite polished appearance, as if the path had been heated and ever-so-slightly glazed by the friction of the escarpment's passing. The air was charged—it seemed to push back, making his skin tingle and his hair stir. A small tree slightly to one side of the path had been bent the opposite way, several of its branches fresh and shiny as Spring, as if they had been gently renewed, lovingly washed, but the rest with that flat, dead look he'd come to hate.

Spotting a patch of glitter on the ground, Will pulled off onto the shoulder and got out of the truck. As he walked closer he could see how here and there sprays of the shiny stuff must have spewed out of the passing escarpment, suggesting contents escaping under pressure, like plumes of steam. He dropped to one knee and examined the spot: a mix of old coins, buttons, bits of glass, small metal figures, toys, vacation mementos, souvenirs, suggesting the random debris left in the bottom of the miscellanea drawer after the good stuff has been packed away for some major household move—the stuff you threw in the trash or left behind for the next tenants.

The strong scent of persimmons permeated the air. The funny thing was, he had no idea how he knew this. Will didn't think he'd ever seen one, much less smelled it. Was it a flower, or a fruit?

For a few minutes he thought there were no other signs of the escarpment's passing, but then he began to notice things. A reflection a few yards away turned out to be an antique oil lamp. He supposed it was remotely possible such a thing could have been lost or discarded and still remain relatively intact, but this lamp was pristine, with at least an inch of oil still in its reservoir. And a few feet beyond were a pair of women's shoes, covered in white satin, delicate and expensive-looking, set upright on the pale dust as if the owner had stepped out of them but moments before, racing for the party she could not afford to miss.

The old house had been abandoned sometime in the seventies, the structure variously adapted since then to store equipment, hay, even as a makeshift shelter for a small herd of goats. From the outside it looked very much the same, and Will might have passed it by, but then he saw the ornate bedpost through one of the broken windows, and the look of fresh blue paint over part of one exterior wall, and knew that something had occurred here out of the ordinary.

The house hadn't had a door in a decade or more, and still did not, but the framing around the door opening appeared almost new, and was of metal—which it had never been—attached to a ragged border of brick which had incongruously blended in to the edges of the original wood-framed wall. Two enormous, shiny brass hinges stood out from this frame like the flags of some new, insurgent government. The effect was as if a door were about to materialize, or else had almost completed its disappearance.

Once he was past the door frame, the small abandoned house appeared as he might normally expect. Islands of dirt, drifted in through the opening or blown through the missing windows, looked to have eaten through the floorboards, some sprouting prairie grass and gray aster. There were also the scat of some wild animal or other, probably fox or coyote, small pieces of old hay from back when the building had been used for feed storage, and a variety of vulgar graffiti on the ruined walls, none of it appearing to be of recent vintage.

A short hallway led from this front room into the back of the house, and as he passed through Will began to notice a more remarkable sort of misalignment, a clear discrepancy between what was and what should have been.

A broken piece of shelf hung on the wall approximately midway through the brief hallway. It had a couple of small objects on it. On closer inspection he saw that it wasn't broken at all—the edges of the wood actually appeared finely frayed, the threads of what was alternating with the threads of what was not. Along the frayed edge lay approximately one third of an old daguerreotype—although not at all old, it seemed. Shiny-new, glass sealed around the intact edges with rolled copper, laid inside a wood and leather case. A large portion of the entire package bitten off, missing, not torn exactly, or broken, for the missing bite of it too was delicately, wispily frayed, glass fibers floating into empty air as if pulled away. The image under the glass was of a newly-married couple in Victorian-style clothing, their expressions like those under duress: the bride straining out a thin smile, the groom stiffly erect, as if his neck were braced.

A piece of pale gauze covered the opening at the end of the short hall. Now lifting on a cool breeze, the gauze slapped the walls on both sides, the ceiling. Will stepped forward and gently pulled it aside, feeling like an intruder.

A four-poster bed sat diagonally in the ruined room, the incongruous scent of the perfumed linen still strong despite faint traces of an abandoned staleness and animal decay. The bed looked recently slept in, the covers just pulled back, the missing woman —he figured it was probably a woman—having stepped out for a moment. Peering closer, he found a long, copper-colored hair on the pillow. He picked it up gently, holding it like something precious against the fading afternoon light drifting lazily in through the broken window. He wanted to take it with him, but he didn't know exactly why, or how he could, or if he should. So he laid it carefully back down on the pillow, in its approximate original location.

Half a mirror torn lengthwise was propped against a wide gap in the outer wall. Beyond was simply more of the eastern Colorado plains, scrub grass and scattered stone, but somewhat smoother than normal, shinier, and Will surmised that the escarpment had exited the farm house at this point.

He found himself creeping up to the mirror, nervous to look inside. Will never looked at mirrors much, even under normal conditions. He wasn't that old—in his fifties still, and as far as he knew, the same person inside, thinking the same thoughts he'd had at seventeen, eighteen, twenty. But what he saw in the mirror had stopped matching the self-image in his brain some time long ago.

He stopped a couple of feet away, focusing on the ragged edge where the escarpment had cut through and obliterated the present, or the past. More of that floating raggedness, suggesting a kind of yearning for completion, for what was missing. His reluctance to find his reflection made him reel a bit. What if he looked down and it was himself as a teenager looking up, with obvious signs of disappointment on his face?

But it was himself, although perhaps a bit older, paler, as if the color were being leached out and eventually he would disappear. The problem with avoiding your image in the mirror was that when you finally did see it, it was a bit of a shock, really, because of how much you had changed. Who was this old man with his thoughts?

He left the abandoned house and strolled slowly toward the pickup, watching the ground, looking for additional leavings but finding nothing. The empty ground looked like it always did out here, as it probably did in any open, unsettled place, as if it were ageless, unfixed, and yet fundamentally unchangeable. Whatever might be done to it, it would always return to this.

He wanted to describe to Tracy what he'd seen here, but what, exactly, had he seen? Time had passed this way, and left some things behind, then gone on its way. And the world was fundamentally unchanged. His mother might understand better, but Tracy was the one he wanted to tell, even though she might not hear him.

He felt the pressure change inside his ears, and he turned part of the way around, looking, but not seeing. Suddenly the world roared up behind him, passed him, and he shook.

He bent slightly backwards, looking up, terrified he might lose his balance, and having no idea of what the possible consequences might be. The moving escarpment towered high above him, shaking in and out of focus as it passed, and shaking him, seemingly shaking the ground, but clearly this wasn't a physical shaking, clearly this was no earthquake, but a violent vibration of the senses, and the consciousness behind them. Closing his eyes minimized the sensation, but he didn't want to miss anything, so other than a few involuntary blinks he kept them open. He turned his body around as best he could, as quickly, to get a better view.

He could make out the top of the escarpment, at least he could see that it did have a top, an edge indicating that it had stopped its vertical climb, but he could tell little more than that. As his eyes traveled further down he was able to focus on more detail, and taking a few steps back gave him a better perspective.

There were numerous more or less clearly defined strata, each in movement seemingly independent of the others, sometimes in an opposite flow from those adjacent, and sometimes the same but at a different speed. Like a multilayered roulette wheel, he thought, which seemed appropriate.

Trapped in most of these layers were visible figures—some of them blurred, but some of them so clear and vivid that when they were looking in his direction, as if from a wide window in the side of a building, he attempted to gain their attention by waving. None responded in any definitive way, although here and there the possibility that they might have seen him certainly seemed to be there.

The vast majority of these figures appeared to be ordinary people engaged in ordinary activities—fixing or eating dinner, housecleaning, working in offices, factories, on farms—but occasionally he'd see something indicating that an unusual event was occurring or had recently occurred. A man lying on his back, people gathered around, some attending to the fallen figure but most bearing witness. A couple being chased by a crowd. A woman in obvious anguish, screaming in a foreign language. A blurred figure in freefall from a tall building.

The settings for these dramas, suspenseful or otherwise, were most often sketchily drawn: some vague furniture, the outlines of a building, or not indicated at all. The figures sometimes acted their parts on a backdrop of floating abstractions. In a few cases, however, it was like looking out his front door—at random locations a tree branch or a roof eave actually penetrated the outer plane of the escarpment and hung there like a three-dimensional projection in the contemporary air.

It was like a gigantic three-dimensional time-line / cruise ship passing through the eastern Colorado plains, each level representing a different era. It was like a giant fault in time, shifting the temporal balance of the world in an attempt to rectify past mistakes. But there was no compelling reason to believe any of these theories. It was an enormous, fracturing mystery traveling through the world.

And just as suddenly as it had appeared, becoming so dramatically there it sucked up all the available reality of its environment, it was gone, reduced to a series of windy, dust-filled eddies that dissipated within a few seconds. Will shakily examined himself with eyes and hands. Would he lose his mind the way his Jeff had?

If they'd pulled their son out of school when these storms first began he'd be okay right now. That's what they'd been called at first, "storms," because of their sudden evolution, and the occasional accompanying wind, and the original belief that they were an atmospheric phenomenon of some sort, an optical illusion much like sunlight making a rainbow when it passed through moisture-laden cloud, although they couldn't imagine why it was so detailed, or the mechanism of its projection. Tracy had wanted to pull Jeff out until the world better understood what all this was about, and a few other parents, a very few, had already done so. But Will couldn't see the reasoning. If there was a danger how would Jeff be any safer at home? These insubstantial moving walls came out of nowhere, impossible to predict, and as far as anyone knew they weren't harmful. There had been that case of the farmer in Texas, but he'd been old, and practically senile anyway, and it must have been a terrible shock when it passed through his barn.

Tracy inevitably blamed Will, because in Jeff's case it certainly hadn't been harmless, and then Will had compounded things by being late that day. Will was often late. He had always worked at being some sort of success, even though the right combination of jobs and investments had always eluded him. He'd been selling spas and real estate, filling in the gaps with various accounting and IT consulting. Too many clients, too many little puzzle pieces of time, everything overlapping slightly so that at times his life was multidimensional, unfocused, and he was always late to wherever he was scheduled to be.

He'd pulled up to the school twenty minutes late that day to pick up Jeff. Normally it wouldn't have mattered that much—Jeff liked hanging out in the school library using their computers. And if that's where he'd been he would have probably been okay. But that particular afternoon Jeff had decided to hang out on the playground shooting hoops until his dad came to pick him up. And that's where he'd been when the towering wall came through. One of the teachers who'd witnessed the event said later that the wall appeared so suddenly no one had time to move, and it ran over Jeff much like a runaway truck, looking scarily solid, seemingly obliterating everything in its path as it thundered across the concrete and asphalt.

Will had arrived just in time to see that rapidly moving wall vanishing into a dusty brown mist, bending gel-like, quickly losing resolution as it leaned precariously like some old building coming down in an earthquake, but silently—the roar and the shaking were entirely visual, the trauma entirely mental. He had raced into the last of its shimmering eddies and scooped his drooling boy off the ground.

Will drove the pickup back toward his parents' farm more slowly, and with more care than he had when he left. The ambient light of the day had dimmed only slightly, but the canopy of sky appeared even lower than before, only a hundred yards up or so. The landscape looked flattened, stretched out under the pressure of the low-hanging clouds. He could hear rumbles in the distance, and could see the brief glimmer of escarpments appearing, disappearing, surfacing, diving back into the world. Time escaping, time buried and sealed.

Another pickup approached on the narrow gravel road, identical, or almost identical to his. He held his breath, wondering how he would handle it if he encountered a younger or an older version of himself driving the same pickup on the road. Surely that would still be impossible, even during Twember? And if it did occur, might that not shatter the world?

The pickup slowed as it came up alongside him. He stared at the driver. Because it was Lana Sumpter, much as she'd been when she was seventeen years old—her face so new, fresh, and shiny with a soft-lipped smile cradling her words. "Will? Will Cotton? Is that you?"

Both trucks stopped, his head still shook. "I, I'm not sure," he replied. "Probably not the same one. Lana, are any of us the same one?" He was babbling, just like he used to with her. He'd loved her so much his bones used to ache, making his skin seem ill-fitting. He'd never loved anyone that much before, or since.

Lana gazed at him, cheeks slightly flushed. The dark blue of the truck appeared to fade, to lighten, to whiten. Will blinked, then could see the individual bits of faux snow accumulating, layering the truck with a sugary coating, and the white air looking crisp, brittle, about to break. She laughed, but it wasn't really a laugh. It was like words escaping under stress. "I, I guess not, Will. Not these days. Seems like only yesterday I felt too young. Now I feel too old."

Lana's face still flushed, her eyes looking uncomfortable, her smile struggling to remain. And her lips not moving. She wasn't the one speaking.

Will shifted his head a bit to the side and peered past the lovely young girl to the older woman sitting in the shadows on the passenger side. The woman leaned forward, and although the face was somewhat puffy, and makeup had cracked in not the most flattering ways, there was a ghost of a resemblance, and as if a mask of reluctance had been peeled away, Will recognized her with a jolting, almost sickening sensation.

He felt ashamed of himself. He'd never been one to care much about people's appearances, so why did it bother him that he might have passed Lana—at one time the love of his life—on the street and not even recognize her. It was as if he'd been in love with a different person.

"This is my daughter Julie. Julie this is Will, an old friend. We knew each other when we were kids."

"Hi, Julie," he said, and had to take a breath. "You look like your mother."

"Everybody says that," the girl didn't sound as friendly, or as sweet, as Will had first thought.

"Are you out from Denver for awhile?" Lana asked.

"Me and the family. I don't know for how long. I don't know when we should go back, or if."

She nodded, frowned. "A lot of the old crowd came back here. Jimmie, Carol, Suze. I don't know if they wanted to be home at a time like this, if it even still feels like home, or if they thought it'd be better here. It's not really, I don't think. But it's more open out here. Maybe they figure these things will be easier to dodge out in the open." She shook her head.

"I know. But they come up so quickly. Maybe they're not dangerous, but maybe they are."

"I was sorry to hear about your dad," she said. "He didn't run into one of these things, did he?"

"No, he started getting confused, I don't know, at least a year before the first one appeared. I don't see how there could be a connection." She didn't say anything about Jeff, so Will figured she didn't know. Will wasn't about to bring him up. "The doctor prescribed a couple of drugs—they don't seem to help much, but I still make sure he takes them. And for now at least, the pharmacy here still gets them. And the grocery store still gets his favorite chocolate candies. If he didn't get those, well, he'd aggravate us all, I reckon." Will forced a chuckle, and was embarrassed by the fakeness of it.

"Do you think we'll have shortages? My sister does. She says we'll probably see the last supply deliveries any day now. She says why would people continue to do their jobs with all this going on?"

So here they were talking about illnesses and medicines and disasters freely roaming the world threatening everything. Just like old people. Why hadn't they worried about those things when they were younger? Maybe when you were young you really didn't understand what time it was, or how late it could all get to be. "What else are they going to do?" he asked. "It's like the president said—no one knows how long this will last, what it means, or what the final outcome will be, so people need to go on with their lives." It sounded stupid saying it, but he imagined it was still true.

"But that broadcast was three weeks ago. How's your television reception? We have a dish, and we're getting nothing."

"Nothing much at our place either. What does Ray say about all this?" He hoped he had the name right—he hadn't been there when she'd married, only heard about it.

The girl, Julie, looked flushed, and turned her head away. Lana's face fell back into the shadows, and her voice came out shakily. "My Ray died about three months back. COPD. He said it got a lot worse with this new weather, or whatever you want to call it. I don't know, Will—it was already pretty bad."

And again Will felt shame, because along with his sadness for her came this vaguely-formed notion that there might be a new opportunity for him in this. What was wrong with him? He wasn't going to leave his wife and son, so why think about it? He apologized, but of course did not fully explain why, and continued home toward Tracy, his family, and his present.

His eighth grade teacher Mrs. Anderson used to emphasize in her social studies class that even kids from a small town school could become anything they wanted to be if only they applied themselves. "Dream big!" she'd say, "your dreams are the only thing that will limit you." In order to back up her thesis, throughout the school year she would sprinkle in inspirational stories about people from small towns who had "made a difference," who had made it "big."

Halfway in to high school Will, and many of his friends, had concluded that this was all just so much propaganda, the purpose of which was—well—he wasn't sure, maybe to make Mrs. Anderson feel better about teaching in such a small town. But they heard similar messages from other teachers, parents, pretty much anyone who came to speak to their class. Like relatively recent graduates on their way to the army or the peace corps.

Big dreams were great, but they almost always seemed to shrink when you talked to guidance counselors, recruiters, or anyone else charged with evaluating your prospects realistically. There were some important, socially-conscious things you could do with your life, certainly, but not here, and not for much monetary compensation. And these other careers, the ones Mrs. Anderson talked about—the thinkers and writers and scientists and actors—well, all you had to be was somebody else, somebody else entirely, and from some other place.

On the trip back to his parents' farm it was relatively easy for Will to imagine himself, and this land, as something else entirely. The road, the fields, were bleached, as white as he could imagine, and as far as he could see. The whiteness intensified at times to such transparency Will imagined he could almost see to where life both entered the plants and exited them, where time ate through the world and transformed it all into something else. He might have been traveling across Russia before the revolution in his wagon, his buggy, or in middle Europe as it began its entry into the ice age, in nineteenth-century Oklahoma in the dead of winter, the children starving, the wife suffering in their bed, a new baby on the way. And Will couldn't do much more than observe, and try to live, and keep his four wheels on the road, steady toward home.

The farmhouse looked as it had during that long-remembered blizzard the winter he was nine years old, when so many of the cows had died, and a stiffened pheasant stared at him from the front yard, its shining eyes frozen into jewels. A series of flashes drew his own eyes to that distant horizon line in the direction of Denver, and he considered it might be lightning, even though he knew better. Great blocks shifted there, weaving in and out of each other's way as if they had some sort of rudimentary intelligence. They appeared closer by the second, as if that city's buildings themselves were slowly advancing toward him across the eastern plains.

He pulled into the yard at the side of the house and jumped down onto the snow-laden ground, which cracked like layers of candy, allowing a white powdery residue to explode into the air with each of his steps. Of course this wasn't snow—it was nothing like snow. It was like the moments had been snatched from the air and allowed to die, left to litter the ground. He tried to step carefully, but still they fractured with very little force.

Inside the house there was the strong smell of cooking apples. A tree had been propped up in one corner. There were a few decorations on it, and his mother was sitting on the couch singing to herself and stringing popcorn into a garland.

Tracy pushed Jeff into the room and set the wheelchair brake. Their son's moaning stopped and he gazed at the tree. Will looked around for his father, found him in the corner by the front window, staring outside, motionless. Tracy came up to Will and stood there. She didn't smile, but for the first time in a long time she didn't look furious. "What's all this?" he asked.

"Christmas," she replied. "At least according to your mother."

"But it's not Christmas," he said, although truthfully he wasn't completely sure anymore.

"Maybe, maybe not. Is there going to be another Christmas this year, Will? I certainly don't know. Do you?"

He shrugged. "I guess it won't hurt anything. It sure seems to have helped Jeff."

" 'Hold on to the moment.' You used to say that a lot, remember? Why did you stop saying it—was it because of me?"

He shrugged again. "You know I used to like it when you hummed in the bathroom? But the last few years it really annoyed me. That was something I shouldn't have held on to. I mean really, why would that bother me so much?"

"You used to turn the dumbest things into a celebration. Remember when it was Thomas Edison's birthday, and you turned on all the lights in the house?"

"That was before Jeff's—accident. He'd had a really bad day. I ordered pizza and made a pretty bad birthday cake. It cheered him up."

"You wore a lamp on your head, plugged in and turned on. I thought you were going to electrocute yourself! I got so mad."

"You didn't want to be married to a child. I burned my ear pretty badly taking that contraption off."

"Your mother thought this would be a perfect thing, give us all a little something to look forward to. Is that where you got the idea to create all those special holidays? From her?"

"It was my dad," Will replied. "One day he bought my mother an alligator handbag. From that year on we celebrated 'Alligator Handbag Day.' There were special sandwiches. We wore tails made out of newspaper and did a little dance. Actually, my mother didn't always fully appreciate Alligator Handbag Day."

"I can believe that."

There were several moments of awkward silence, then Will said, "This doesn't mean you still love me, does it? I mean, this celebration, this stolen moment, doesn't change anything fundamentally, does it?"

"I don't think I blame you for Jeff anymore. I really don't."

"Things change, moments get away from you, the past pays a visit, and although there's no blame, still nothing is forgiven. It's hard to live here. It always has been," he said.

"Will—" she started to say, but his father drowned her out.

"Whooh whooh!" his father yelled by the window. "Whooh whooh!" The house shook with thunder.

A great striated wall moved past the glass. Will wondered if his healthy son was trapped inside there somewhere, if inside that wall he might find his wife's love again, or some other Will, some other life. He tried to say something to Tracy, but he couldn't even hear himself, so loud everything had suddenly become. He could feel time circling outside the house, circling again, raising its voice and ready to run them down.

ORIGAMI BIRD

Almost at once it became habit. During long days in the file room with no one to talk to, his hands normally unoccupied would snag some scrap of paper or trash and speak what he was unable to find words for. Staring at the scenery his eyes invented out of textured ceiling, out the window where gorgeous creatures reclined in cloud, he would catch his hands pulling and twisting at a candy wrapper, a hen-scratched Post-It, a sheet of lost and yellowing stationery, until at last the first glimmer of bird came through.

He had no inkling of the long traditions of paper folding. He knew far less than his hands knew: of bending, pressing, worrying free the shape poised for flight out of garbage. And when he ran out of garbage he made birds out of the grim chronicles of neglect, disease, and grief salvaged from these long-dead patients' files.

That first paper bird had been a strange thing: wings with the shattered angles of lightning, beak a twisted black tear. Over the years the shapes refined: at times almost delicate in the ways the multiply-creased necks reached up to support the complicated heads, at times unsoundly fantastic as paper stub wings evolved into great wavering flyleaves of actuarial data ready to take the sad facts of a life and journey south over some dark and troubled continent to the nesting grounds along the far edge of where we all came from.

There was no money in what his hands made, of course, but then he had no talent for money, or much else, working only to clothe and feed his small family. Freedom was something fine and good in the antique gold-tooled novels his grandfather had passed his way, which he had sold after a single reading. And he knew he was lucky to live in a country that had so much of it, although he'd never quite been able to grasp the details.

Years later when they cleaned out the old hospital records,

decades of paper and film and what no longer matters, carried the lot to bins and incinerators, they discovered the waste of his hands and heart: birds put away neatly in every folder, birds tucked into envelopes and nested in the gaps of the unused alphabet, birds secreted into record books, birth records, treatment plans, and autopsy reports, birds by the thousands spilling from the boxes the workers carried outside, caught by the wind funneled between the tall buildings, rising with the orderly progress of the flames, set free into air and light, and they all, all of them stopped their lives that day to watch.

FIRESTORM

The flash that covered the city in morning mist was much like
an instant dream.

—Kyoku Kaneyama

*He was not very old, as gods go. He could still remember that brief
instant of his creation, and would remember it for all time. But without
the need for understanding.*

*The winds like silver and black hair for him, fire like speech, uncon-
trolled, the power giving him wings, filling the sky with flame as he rose
into the air. Turning the ground below into fire and light, discoloring
concrete to a reddish tint. Granite surfaces peeled like onion skin. A
pedestrian incinerated, his shadow a bas relief on a stone wall. Wide
cracks in buildings, upturned faces gone white, metallic . . .*

*. . . like his own face, he somehow knew, and the word they were
thinking, the name they were giving him . . . the "flashboom." Pikadon.
The new god . . .*

September 14, 1965 . . .

Tom woke up in his hotel room, feverish, shaking. Again he
had had the dream of burning up in the holocaust, only to rise
phoenix-like and spread the destruction outward, back to his
home in America. In the dream he tried to stop himself, but was
completely out of control. He was surprised at the depth of his
anger toward his country. He was beginning to understand how
profoundly his father had been affected by the war, the division in
loyalties. And, uncomfortably, he was seeing in himself signs of
his father's obsessions.

Tom had come to Japan to do a story on the "New Religions,"
the numerous sects which had sprung up since the defeat. He
knew a major reason he had been selected was his Japanese-
American ancestry. There had been another, more experienced,

Religion reporter on his paper. This bothered him, but he thought the trip to Japan might help him understand some things. It was a religious quest, really. A search for context, for meaning.

Even though his family had been in the States almost a hundred years, he felt some ambivalence about America's role in the war. He dreamed about Hiroshima regularly. More than once he had screamed himself awake, feeling his skin burning from his body. The most disturbing aspect of those dreams, however, was that he was also the pilot of the plane carrying the bomb.

In the dream he prayed before dropping the bomb. The bomb was an offering, a gift to his god. A sacrifice. A return home. He wasn't sure, the dream kept changing.

During the last months of the war Tom, just a boy, had seen a dramatic deterioration in his father's mental condition. He could not understand how his father could change so quickly. It seemed magical, evil. He sometimes imagined his father had been kidnapped and that the FBI had put this impostor in his place to spy on them.

It was a crazy time. There were rumors of hostile warships cruising off the California coast.

His father had been a religious man. But toward the end he was cursing the "white" god, and wouldn't allow his children to go to white churches. He imagined he was under surveillance. Tom remembered his father's shock and outrage when Japanese products and art objects were burned or buried by angry neighbors.

His father clipped pieces out of the newspaper, hateful things, and read them to the family at dinner. "This one says we should be deported! This one that we are liars, barbarians, not to be trusted!" Later Tom heard a violent argument between his parents, and discovered by eavesdropping that his father was taping these articles above his bed.

A Jap's a Jap . . . no way to determine their loyalty. You can't change him by giving him a piece of paper.—Lt. General John L. DeWitt, 1943.

California was zoned, the Japanese-Americans barred completely from Category A zones: San Francisco's waterfront, the area around the LA municipal airport, dams, power plants, pumping stations, military posts.

Earl Warren, California's Attorney General, said that the fact that there had been no sabotage on the Pacific Coast was "a sign that the blow is well-organized and that it is held back until it can be struck with maximum effect." He contended that the fact that Issei and Nisei had not committed sabotage was a sign of their disloyalty.

Dec. 7, 1941—Pearl Harbor. Executive Order 9066.

Germans and Italians were considered separately. It was believed their loyalties could be better judged.

They are cowardly ... they are different from Americans in every conceivable way, and no Japanese ... should have the right to claim American citizenry.—Sen. Tom Stuart, Tennessee.

The rumors of sabotage—setting flaming arrows in sugar-cane fields to direct the Japanese planes, blocking traffic to delay rescue efforts, arson—committed by the Japanese during the attack on Pearl Harbor proved to be totally untrue. FCC investigations discovered no illicit radio signals guiding Japanese submarines off the California coast. But their white California neighbors apparently did not hear of these refutations.

An old Japanese man, a survivor, had promised to lead Tom to the strangest religious group of all, a sect which practiced its rites in secret, so afraid were they of public reaction. The old man claimed he had actually seen this new deity, "a young wind with flaming hair."

"You are here ... seeking this god," the old Japanese man had said to Tom that afternoon, with such certainty it disturbed him.

"Yes," Tom had said distractedly. Then unaccountably had added, "I guess I need a new god."

On September 14, 1965, Nagasawa Shino stood in front of her bedroom mirror, brushing her hair. She planned to visit her cousin Takashi Fujii. He had been a patient in the A Bomb Hospital, Sendamachi, Hiroshima City, for three months suffering from leukemia. The early morning sun flashed through the blinds, filling her mirror with a white light. Kyokujitsu shoten, a gorgeous ascent of the morning sun.

She pulled long black hair away from her forehead, revealing a narrow, bright red, keloid scar. Her hair slipped loose of the brush, fell to her shoulders. Then one by one the strands eased from her scalp and fell like dark streamers to the floor. White patches were spreading on her bald pate. Tiny spots of red, green, and yellow bled like an exotic makeup into the skin of her face. Raised, puffy skin.

She reached frantically for a glass of water on the edge of the basin and it broke under her hand. Her hand rose slowly in front of her face, bleeding from the base of the thumb. It kept bleeding, the blood soon covering her hand, her forearm, creeping up the white silk sleeve of her robe. She knew the bleeding would not stop until her body had been completely emptied.

The spots on her face blended into a brilliant rainbow that flowed down her neck, across her breasts, staining the length of her body.

She remained silent, stared into the mirror growing muddy with her colors, searched out the young, unfocused features of her face hidden within the mirror. Thirty-four, but everyone always said she looked twenty: they often wondered aloud if the bomb had done that to her, kept her young.

Always so many silly rumors, tales of magic. She had always kept the scar hidden under her hair.

Too much light. Too much to be said. The mirror burned, looking rich and jeweled, much like Japan's imperial mirror, the mirror the sun goddess Amaterasu had seen when she was lured out of the cave. Shino even looked like Amaterasu, under the swirling colors, the light of the flashboom, the Atomic bomb. A goddess; she smiled despite herself. Shamefully. She imagined that thousands of people had just disappeared from the streets of the city.

The immense cellar stank of fish and stale grain. Tom leaned back against an old crate in the back of the chamber, breathing in the smell as deeply as he could, thinking of it as the atmosphere breathed by his ancestors, wondering if any of them might have known this cellar. It seemed so familiar, some space from a remembered past, perhaps from before even his father's birth.

He could see now that there had been no reason to hide. The hundred or so Japanese crowded into the room were intent on the service before them, or lost in trance. Many were dressed in his own western-style garb. An older man stood before them, head bowed, apparently praying. There was an altar behind him: a metal bowl on a table surrounded by flowers, and above that a stylized painting of a mushroom cloud.

Tom stared at the painting, mesmerized by the vibrant colors, the boldness and energy of the brushstrokes. He could imagine ground-zero, the leveled field that had once been city, the souls suddenly liberated in the flaming wind.

The bomb had been the climax of a series of humiliations visited upon his father, the memories of which would eventually unhinge him, leaving him saddened and diminished until his death in 1960. They'd taken away his small hardware business. The country he'd loved took him away from the house he'd spent much of his life building, and threw him and his family into a concentration camp in Colorado. Then they'd given him a new name, Nisei.

His god had forsaken him, and sealed this dishonor with a hell on earth.

His father could not believe the bomb; the first reports left him shaking in angry disbelief. Then as the truth became clear the old man fell into a depression from which he would never recover. He could not believe what his own country had done, what God had allowed, what evil power they had created and unleashed upon the world.

As an adolescent Tom had at first been confused and frightened by the changes in his father. Then frustrated, later angry. His father had been weak and silent when he had most needed him. He had let the American government defeat him as devastatingly as the Japanese homeland had been defeated. Tom was ashamed of his father and all the others who had let themselves be humiliated. He made a decision then that he would always be American, American in every way. They had the power. They had the bomb.

The old man was speaking to the congregation. "Pikadon brought a change all over the world; life will never be the same. One can gain power over the everyday problems of life by emulating the power of the great god Pikadon!"

The message was clear and simple. Tom could understand it even with his rough skills in the language. The theme, like that of most of the newer religions, was one of practicality. "Man built the bomb and brought a powerful new deity into being. This only confirms the great power latent in every man. If you meditate on the image of Pikadon, visualize the god within yourself, then you may utilize this power within your everyday life!"

Tom left the gathering secretly during the zadankai, a get-together after the ceremony for discussing specific problems and first-hand encounters with Pikadon. The old man who had told him about the group was speaking when Tom left. "The light, so brilliant. . . ."

Tom knew that soon he would have to visit the hospital.

Takashi Fujii tossed restlessly in his bed in the Atomic Bomb Hospital. The flash of light had moved east to west, as he remembered it, a curtain of pure white fire. It was August 6, 1945. He had been thirty-six, a journeyman welder at the time. His eyes had been giving him trouble, his lungs were congested, so he took the day off from his repair work at the Fukoku Seimei Building and stayed in bed. After the flash there was a burning heat, then a violent rush of air that flattened his wooden home and buried him under planks, clothing, and heavy roof tile. He could not understand; the "all clear" sirens had sounded but minutes ago. At the time his thoughts had returned to his biggest job: work on the domed Industrial Promotion Hall. Welder and rod had worked out of his padded arms like a cripple's hooks; but these were no handicaps. They spewed fire. And in the gathering darkness his fingers, arms, entire body became fire, welding metal and burning the superfluous to ash. Unseen people applauded; his children were proud. In his vision he could see his young cousin Nagasawa Shino approaching his bedside. She was fourteen, beautiful; he was very attracted to her. A bouquet of goosefoot and morning glories rose from her hand and floated down over the bedspread. Only a few flowers, but they covered the entire bed.

This is a race war . . . The white man's civilization has come into conflict with Japanese . . . Damn them! Let us get rid of them now!— Rep. John Rankin of Mississippi.

Religious men, all of them, Tom remembered.

Tom's family was given a week to pay bills, sell or store belongings, say good-bye, close up the house, get rid of the car, and assemble at a nearby center with other frightened, confused Japanese-Americans. He could still recall the intense anger he felt. An old man died while they were waiting. Someone said he had a weak heart, but young Tom knew better.

At first they lived in a converted horse stall at the racetrack. Whitewashed, manure-speckled walls. Spider webs and horse-hair carelessly painted over. April 28 to Oct. 13.

Folded spring cots, boiled potatoes, canned Vienna sausage and two slices of bread. A bag of ticking to be stuffed with straw for a mattress. Hot. The grounds a mud pit in the rain.

Then they were forced to move again. Colorado, they were told. Some place out in the plains. Young Tom dreamed of tornadoes lifting him and his family up, casting them away. He dreamed that the Japanese-Americans had committed some terrible, secret sin, and that a great white god was punishing them. The Japanese nation had better watch out, he had thought, else this god would send tornadoes against them too.

"No Japs wanted here," the signs had said as they evacuated east.

The old man followed Tom out of the meeting hall. Tom watched as he gestured excitedly with both hands, his gray eyes feverish, rheumy. He motioned toward the alley and the dark, unmarked door in the shadows.

"Everything changed . . . so quickly!" the man said. "I had been sleeping, and in the dream, or after waking from the dream, I cannot be sure, I felt such a *power*, such a brilliant light consuming all the world! I'd been dreaming of defeat, defeat I was sure must happen, when this wonderful thing happened! You may think I'm crazy, *addled*, to call such a happening wonderful. But all had to be burned away, all had to be changed, before this new thing could come to be. Flashing eyes, bronze skin I could see him! I've worshiped him since, always!"

Tom held him upright, the old man so overcome by religious fervor his legs had collapsed beneath him. Tom looked again into the alley's dark shadows, and around at the drabness of the neighborhood. It seemed an unlikely setting for a god.

Tom's family was sent to Granada in southeastern Colorado. Eight thousand Nisei there. The family lived in a 16′ by 20′ room, wood sheathing covered with black tarpaper. Furnished by a stove, droplight, steel gray cots and mattresses. Three hundred people packed into the mess hall. Soft alkaline dirt and sagebrush.

His father grew steadily worse. Crazy, said the other boys. Tom got into many fights.

Dust under the loose fitting window sash, dust under the doors, gritty floors, dusty bedding. People weren't meant to live in such a desert. It reminded him of the Jews, when they had been cast out of Egypt. Why should the great white god punish them so? He could not understand. And where was their god? Didn't the Japanese have a god?

Earl Warren said that the release of the Nisei from WRA camps would lead to a situation in which "no one will be able to tell a saboteur from any other Jap."

Tom remembered his father bending over backwards not to offend. Bowing and apologizing to the sadistic young white soldier who had tripped him on the way back from the mess hall.

The American Legion wanted them deported. Tom could still see the windshield stickers: "Remember a Jap is a Jap." The *Denver Post* demanded a 24-hour curfew on "all Japs in Denver." There were rumors of bloodshed at the Tule Lake camp—the papers said it was full of disloyals.

His father was never the same. Tom couldn't really think of his father as a human being anymore. Almost as if he had never existed ... wiped away in the conflagration ... gone instantly from the face of the earth.

Shino's brown suit fit perfectly. Months of exercise had brought her down to her old figure. The spots of seconds ago had disappeared from her face; the mirror had flowed back to normal. She was startled to find a slight smile on her lips, as if the smile belonged to someone else, another woman hiding under her skin.

There was no pleasure in her anticipation of her visit with her cousin; she did not enjoy associating with other hibakusha, the survivors of the bomb. But her cousin was a nice man, and she had no other family left.

She kept her hair combed over the scar and pretended to know little of the bomb horror stories; she didn't want to talk about it. She didn't want people connecting her with the Hiroshima outcasts, those living dead. The bomb people, they all die, some people would say. She wasn't sure this was true, but why argue with common opinion? A dying woman was not meant to be loved; love belonged only to the living. She was hibakusha, and those people, they never recovered.

She had never married. Her body remained fallow; there had been no children, although she knew it was medically possible. At twenty-five she had loved a young man named Keisuke, a lawyer. But his old mother had objected to their marriage, said that she bore the A-bomb disease, that the babies would surely be deformed. After years alone Shino too had this fear, that she might give birth to something other, something never before seen on earth. Males gave birth to strange things through their extremities; she found it difficult now, even to have a man touch her.

She hurried out of the house. She would be late.

As the morning sun rose high over the treetops of Asano Park she remembered the park as it had been that day: the huddling corpses, the silent stares of the living dead, the fire raging in the distance, flame and dark smoke floating over the trees. Everything she had known had suddenly become nothing.

Shino opened her eyes and stared at the two old women huddled over her. She had fainted, and one lady was offering her water from a pink paper cup. The sky was clear again; the smoke had been long ago. It is 1965, she reminded herself. That was so long ago.

The other lady had brushed back Shino's hair and seen the scar; Shino saw her pass a knowing look to her friend.

One evening Tom went to a double feature of old Japanese science fiction films. *Gojira no Gyakushu*, Godzilla's Counter-

attack, and *Uchujin Tokyo ni Arawaru*, Space Men Appear in Tokyo.
He had seen them both as a kid but he found himself reacting
to them quite differently this time. They had been fun then,
although a little scary, and he hadn't seen all that much difference
between Americans and the Japanese based on the evidence of
those two films.

Now he had to wonder what the reaction of the young Japanese must be to these two films. What must they think, watching
the enormous Godzilla, a deliverer of monstrous and bizarre
death and destruction, and who is described as a creature born of
nuclear tests? Surely he must be something from their own childhood nightmares, completely visualized and made concrete.

At least the *Space Men* movie seemed a bit more positive. In
this invaders come to Japan for advice concerning all the nuclear
tests being done on earth. The aliens are worried about them.
Japan's unique knowledge of the bomb becomes a positive thing.
And yet the aliens possess awesome power; Tom wondered if this
was still another example of the Japanese feeling that they had all
been guinea pigs, and that Hiroshima was an "experimental city."

The movies made the bombing seem even larger than before,
mythic. Tom couldn't help thinking they were the stuff of which
religions were made.

The water the women gave her was cool and reminded Shino
of how different it had been twenty years before. There had been
rumors that people were not to give water to the injured, or it
would aggravate their sickness. Such a denial had been difficult
to maintain; it was natural for the victims to request water. Water
was thought to restore life by returning the soul to the body. The
injured had been so polite: "Tasukete kure!" they had said, *Help,
if you please!*

She could not forgive herself for ignoring them so, but she
herself had been injured. She had walked as one in a dream, ignoring their pain. She had passed by the curtains of skin hanging off
their bodies, her hands clasped over her own slashed breasts. She
had been half naked and cowered in shame. Even knowing what
they were, she had walked upon human bowels and brains.

She would be late for her visit with Fujii, but she needed some time to rest. Across the street, they were performing a shinto rite at the grand opening of a new department store. They had done the same when she was a girl. But the military had fooled them into blind support with shinto, the religion and the country become one. How could it ever be the same again? How might she trust either?

She was hibakusha, a person of the bomb. A new deity had been born into the world, a deity born of the loins of little, petty men. But he was greater than they. Man had brought him from the sun at the center of the world for slaughter. He turned and faced her from the street in front of the department store, a slight smile on his lips. Amused by their petty nationalism. Appeared from the crowd, as if he had stepped out of their massed bodies. Flash off his teeth of metal and lightning and suns. He did not speak, but his loud breathing hurt her ears. Bright eyes and dark hair: very handsome.

She thought it strange that he looked only vaguely American; his face seemed to blur in and out of focus. Shaven eyebrows, almond skin. Sometimes he looked like her cousin Fujii.

The god thrilled her; how very handsome he was. *Isamashii,* brave. With him standing there, the breeze from the ocean lifting his long silver and black hair and laying it back against his shoulder, it seemed as if they were the only people really alive: she, the other hibakusha, and this new god. He spoke inside her head, and the power in his voice made her aware of the great responsibility they had; she could feel bombs exploding, giant mushroom clouds of red, yellow, blue and white, like flowers over the globe. People burned with an incandescent flame, then disintegrated into their basic elements, back into the earth to become trees, flowers, the very materials from which the bombs themselves had come. They would all be united; there would be no separation.

The dark-haired god smiled and this movement in his face seemed to harden his features, set lines firmly around his hawk nose, his black steel eyes. A square, mechanical jaw. Lines of sweat down the sides of his face.

A Coca-Cola truck passed, spraying dust in its wake. She realized the opening ceremonies were completed; the people had all left. That day ... sometimes it seemed like yesterday. She had stayed home that day; she had told her mother she was too ill to go to school, but she had lied. Her class of girls had been assigned to clear fire lanes in case the American B-29's dropped incendiary bombs. She admired the way the people had accepted this; many tore down their homes and buildings because they were in the path of a designated fire lane. But all this destruction saddened her; she couldn't bear to help. Her mother left her at home with her sister, who knew she was faking but kept silent. It was just after breakfast, the hibachi stove was still smoldering. At 7:45 her mother left to catch a train downtown. The bomb must have struck when she was still on the train. Shino knew her mother had almost expected it, some disaster like this had worried her for a week, the way the American planes had flown over every day.

The dark-haired god smiled out in the street, people walking by. Shino couldn't remember what year it really was; she breathed noisily. Everything silent, all she could hear was her breathing, the god's breathing. What year was it? She imagined herself a girl again, at the side of the dark-haired god. He smiled and embraced her, searing her breasts with his flaming hands. She did not cry out in pain.

Tom thought that Hiroshima looked much like any busy port city, although perhaps the setting was lovelier than most; the seven fingers of the Ohta river supported it, and it was ringed by low mountains. There still seemed to be much of the small, provincial town here in the people and their lifestyles. Certainly nothing to suggest the dramatic event which had once occurred here.

But the castle, shipyards, and municipal buildings had been rebuilt. The Aioi Bridge, target site of the *Enola Gay*, once more spanned the Ohta river. So many Tom talked to still expressed surprise that things could get better so soon.

The new downtown seemed western with its wide streets and attractive store-fronts, arcaded shopping areas. The new pride of the city was their baseball stadium and their team the Hiroshima Carps.

But he was aware of something else here, whose presence

betrayed itself in an accumulation of small clues: a bit of fused metal, a warped post. Imprinted in the steps of Sumitomo Bank was the shadow of a man who had sought refuge that day twenty years before.

The god drifted in the pollution staining the rooftops, the pollution defiling the wind, the sea. All the old gods of sea and air, defeated so easily by people.

By people's creations, which they themselves could not even control.

The god sensed without thinking the great stupidity of people, their lack of control.

The god disdained the attempts of the followers of his own religion to influence him, seek his favors.

The new god Pikadon knowing something like incompleteness even in his instincts of stone. . . .

Anger.

Tom spent the day in the Peace Park. The skeleton of the Industrial Exhibition Hall dome made an eerie backdrop. The park was full of children, and Tom thought how all that he had become obsessed with had happened long before any of them were born. He wondered what their parents must tell them.

He wandered around the Cenotaph, the official Atomic Bomb monument, where the names of those who perished, and continue to perish, are inscribed. Some had told him that the souls of the dead reside there. Tom stared at the sculpture, feeling like a survivor himself, drawn in to their horror, guilty. Many hibakusha, he knew, resented the nine story office building which had been built behind the park, as they thought it profaned this sacred place. There were conservatives in Hiroshima, however, who even wanted to tear the "Atomic Dome" down. Times change. People forget.

There is another statue in the Peace Park, an oval granite pedestal, symbolizing Mt. Horis, the fabled mountain of paradise. Atop this stands the image of Sedaho, a child who died. She holds a golden crane in her outstretched arms. Beneath her are tangles of colorful paper leis that people have left her, each lei consisting of a thousand paper cranes.

A crane can live a thousand years. If you fold a thousand paper cranes they will protect you from illness. At the base of her statue —"This is our cry, this is our prayer: peace in the world."

Tom spent a long time in the Peace Memorial Museum. A regular art gallery, he thought. First the "Atomic Sculptures," twisted metal, tile, warped stones, fused coins and convoluted bottles, a bicycle wrenched into a tangled snarl, a shattered clock stopped at 8:10, a middle school boy's uniform that had turned to rags from the gamma rays of the bomb, rows of life-sized dummies modeling the remnants of clothing, a face black with ash, skin hanging from swollen faces. . . .

The paintings, the photos: victims packing the barracks and warehouses, all that death in a moment, eyeballs melted across a cheek, peeling skin, gutted torsos. . . .

There was a mechanical fountain in front of the peace museum. The Fountain of Prayers, offering fresh water to those who had died begging for it so long ago. Too late.

A few hundred yards downstream from the dome Tom discovered the Kanawa floating restaurant whose specialty was fine Hiroshima oysters. But he could not eat. He kept seeing the restaurant patrons as corpses, the people in the street as corpses, their stiffened forms accusing him, their eyes singling him out.

Tom looked into the stream and saw himself: his hair burned away, his skin melting like tallow, and he began to weep. Even his own eyes accused him.

And the all-seeing eyes of an unknown deity, whose face Tom saw a moment in the water, but which disappeared with a passing ripple.

Shino had this fantasy. At last she has a baby, her own. A miracle! But the umbilical cord is rotten, and the skin peels off the face like decayed cloth. . . .

For a long time Tom was reluctant to visit the A Bomb hospital itself. He knew that most members of the cult visited there, seeking recruits. It was an essential part of the story. But he was afraid.

So he spent much of his time researching the hospital before making his first appointment there, with one Takashi Fujii. In the meantime Tom made many notes:

The A Bomb Hospital

A Bomb hospital completed 1956—120 beds—each admission disturbs the survivor community. Each death creates a new wave of hysteria. Local newspapers keep a faithful obituary list.

People suddenly dying—a bomb ticking within them. Severe anemia—need periodic blood transfusions. Depressed areas of the city often called Atomic Slums.

A reporter found all these abnormal children, all micro-cephalic with small heads and mental retardation. Mothers three or four months pregnant and within two miles of the hypocenter. Others, twenty-four years old, mental age of three, size of a ten-year-old. The Mushroom Club—first the cloud, then they're all growing like mushrooms in the shade.

176 leukemia victims since the hospital's founding in 1956. Coming down suddenly with leukemia twenty years after, with no previous signs.

Failure to marry—many of those who are still living cannot find happiness.

Tom had made a long list of questions for Takashi Fujii, yet still he did not know what he could say to the man.

The young reporter ... Tom ... that was his name ... had come to visit. He was a young American, but with a Japanese face. His curiosity irritated Fujii. He did not like to be thought of as someone odd. He was just a man, a strong man, like many others. But he admired Americans as a whole; he had to admit that. They had brought the bomb, and the bomb was a big thing. It had been like a new beauty in the world, a terrifying beauty that had changed everything. And he really did enjoy talking about the bomb; he had little else to do.

The young American turned on his tape recorder, and, after some fidgeting with his bed covers, Fujii began to speak:

"I was in the midst of a well-deserved vacation. There had been some repair work needed on the steel substructure of the

Fukoku Seimei Building, and the owners knew I was the man for the job. But I did need a rest, so I told them they would have to wait. Of course, they held up the work just for me. They knew I was the right man. Unfortunate that I didn't get a chance to finish the job." Fujii twisted in the bed, a wide smile stretching his nose.

"I had been lying in bed, drinking some fine Suntory whiskey. Then I was buried under my home. Much later I woke up, blood running from my nose. Much as it did recently, when I first discovered I had been stricken with leukemia. Ah, the bomb gets us all in the end. It hides in your body for years sometimes before it strikes. But I am a brave man; I don't complain.

"When I got out from under the house I saw many terrible things. The city, it was gone, smashed like a nest of insects. People ran about like beetles, pulling possessions, their fellows, out of the wreckage. The great atomic bomb had done this; Hiroshima was a great religious experiment for man.

"The great dome of the Industrial Promotion Hall was but a skeleton. Hiroshima Castle had been flattened. The entire western sector was a desert. A reddish brown powder over everything. The Fukoku Seimei Building had only been 380 meters from the center of the blast; I certainly would have died if I had gone there.

"I saw many beautiful women naked, running around with skin hanging from their limbs. Sabishii! Sad! I helped bandage many of the half-clothed women. There was much shame; they would crouch and try to hide themselves, but they were in so much pain; they needed my help. The bomb had left terrible burns—they call them keloid—on their bodies. One old lady's face had grown together so that with the puffy red tissue I could not tell if she was facing me, or if her back was turned. There were many young girls from the secondary schools who had been out clearing fire lanes, most naked and terribly scarred and frightened. They reminded me of my young cousin Shino. I felt very sorry for them; I helped them with much affection. It was a terrible time.

"But sometimes, I would think that the bomb had left them with beautiful—perhaps that isn't the word—fascinating, yes fascinating, markings. Red, and yellow, and blue green, and black

stars and circles. Some so beautiful. The scars were like orna-
ments. I try to remember them, the women, as beautiful. I forget
the disfigurement.

"The bomb was so large; I feel it has made me somewhat
larger, stronger. For the first time, man had made a god, a god
not . . . limited, like himself, but something part of everything,
the dream that fills . . . everything. If I try, I can see him as a man.
Multicolored flames in his scalp; a bronze, naked body. He sleeps
curled inside us, in our hearts, just waiting to be released through
our working hands, fingers, genitals. I was never confused as to
what this new weapon truly was. I knew it immediately. It was of
man's interior, the Atomic Bomb."

Tom shut off the tape recorder and stared at Fujii's beaming,
almost gleeful face.

"Everything collapsed," Fujii said. "My Buddhist neighbors,
they thought that they were really in hell. They fell to their knees
in prayer. Imagine! They really thought the world was ending . . .
that it had become hell!"

He paused, and looked at Tom sadly. "I sometimes think
it does no good for people to believe in a religion. If these
Buddhists had not believed . . . they would not have been so
mortally terrified. They would have seen this as an occurrence of
war, not a sudden arrival of hell. Ours was an experimental city,
nothing more.

"I could have done more. I must tell you, I know that now,"
Fujii said with tears in his eyes. Tom looked down, suddenly
embarrassed. "Most of us, we acted selfishly. We were too frightened, our minds too full of this flash, this fire, to help each other.
So we left people alone . . . left them to die. We shamed ourselves
before whatever god there might be. I too, I admit it, feel a great
shame. I did a terrible thing."

*The dark-haired god of the gleaming skin, Pikadon, rested within
a silver layer in the clouds covering the islands of Japan. He had just
exhaled 1945, and breathing in 1965 left 1985 and beyond a mere exhalation away.*

Hurricane force winds gathered in his hair indistinguishable from whiffs of cloud. Fire settled into the corners of his imagined mouth like small red droplets of spit. He looked into the heads of his followers and imagined himself with silver and black hair flowing out into the horizon line, scarlet wings lifting him up into the sun, his bronze form scintillating with hot vapor.

The god snatched a bird from the air and blackened it, swallowed it, cast it back through his anus. Concrete is discolored. Human souls turn to flaming wind. He is enraged, frustrated.

Below, the Japanese islands appeared in the gaps of morning mist, divine children of the deities Izagagi and Izanami, along with the waterfalls, trees, and mountains. The fire god had been last, and killed his mother Izanami with burning fever.

A new fire god had come, and his rage could turn the islands back into the original oily ocean mass.

Takashi Fujii stared past his cousin, out the window to the parking lot. His cousin seemed strangely quiet. But of course she had said very little to him the last ten years, although they had lived in the same house.

Shino thought about some of her dreams of the night before. Dreams of white faces, keloid flowers on her body, the walking dead, undiscovered atomic bombs constantly overhead or embedded deep inside her belly.

Shino remembered the way the red ashes rose out of the flattened rubble and took form as more survivors. Walking dead. No way to tell their fronts from their backs, arms dangling from elbows held out like wings. Ghosts wandering aimlessly. They couldn't bear to touch themselves. They walked very slowly, like ghosts. She had thought she had recognized an old friend. *Oh, my god*, she thought, *it is Okino!*

Shino had left her sister alone in the house. After a few hours, her sister had died. It made her feel very guilty: she had not stayed with her long. Shino's sister's wounds had oozed much pus and dark blood. She smelled so bad Shino couldn't stand to be near her.

She sometimes dreamed her sister would return some day from the realm of the dead to accuse her. She had failed her. She no longer found solace in the old religions; they had died when all those thousands of believers had died. They were religions for the dead. For memories. For ghosts.

It was a shame; he had never married. Neither had Shino; their family line would soon die out. Family was very important to Fujii; he didn't want the name to die. The family maintained one's immortality; this was man's central purpose in life.

Fujii thought much of religion these hours. Never particularly devout, but he was a strong patriot and nationalist. He believed in science, technology, little else. Shortly after the war he had become interested in various machine age cults, religions based on the glories of technology. But that had been long ago; Japan needed a new religion, an object to unite behind.

He glanced over at Shino. "I truly did not know what it was. Remember, I used to believe it had been a *Molotoffano banakago*, a Molotov Flower Basket? I did not know it could do these things."

"He is a god. He burns up the sky," she replied quietly.

Shino thought of how the day was much like an earlier September, when green had crept over the rubble and along what had been barren riverbanks. Spanish bayonets, clotbur, and sesame had covered the ruins. It had been beautiful, and even the tiny hemorrhages the size of rice grains on her face and hands did not bother her. Insects had filled the air, rising in clouds over the city.

Fujii thought of the bodies and their final cremations. The people had not been able to dispose of the bodies properly earlier, and many corpses were already rotting. They burned with a smell like frying sardines; blue phosphorescent flames rose into the air. As a child he had been told they were the spirits of the departing dead, fireballs, and he imagined he saw some of his neighbors' and friends' faces in the smoke.

Tom drove through the city streets lost in thought, the cyclic changes from skyscrapers and other technological monuments to slums and ancient architecture having a mesmerizing effect on him, almost convincing him that he was time traveling, surveying the lives of his ancestors and his progeny. A strange smell seemed to permeate the air, the smoke giving him a sense of great buoyancy. He decided to return to the church and talk to the old man about what he had seen, what the others had seen. He had a hundred questions.

First Street, Hell. That was what the survivors had called the city.

In the dream he had returned to Japan, land of his ancestors, to find god. No religion had ever answered his doubts before, none were identifiable within the context of the sometimes terrible and sometimes beautiful landscapes he saw inside himself. Every time, however the dream might begin, it always ended with the firestorm. With hell.

Violent inrushing winds ... the air in his lungs seeming to combust spontaneously; he roared through the city like a part of the firestorm himself, aware of the moans of the burning, the asphyxiated in their shelters, but so caught up in his own fiery power he could not stop, for he was part of the flaming god himself, and the daily drama of frustration and loss undergone by people so similar to what he used to be ... they were far removed from him. ...

... the glorious flames spreading, Tom leapt into the air with them, spreading the destruction back to America like a contagion. ...

... and the vengeance was a terrible one. Tom stood in his glorious cloak of flame, a few miles from each epicenter, one bombing after another, as eyelids ran, sealing the beautiful vision of himself forever within the eyes of all witnesses. Clothes melted into skin, bodies flew as if the law of gravity had been momentarily rescinded. The air filled with flames, brighter than any sun, brighter than anything an ancient god might concoct.

... as refugees wandered the streets in broken bodies wailing that God had forsaken them, but Tom was there, Tom in his God's form, welcoming all into his congregation.

... as stomach walls were ruptured, as eyeballs turned liquid and ran on cheeks like egg white. ...

... as metal ran into glass ran into cloth ran into flesh and bone and brain and the end of all desire and the end of all thought ...

Tom smiled and took it all inside himself. The world had become truly one, flowing and intermingling, one within fire, one within God.

And all doubt, all loneliness was answered.

Fujii could almost smell the burning bodies of his friends and neighbors, the sweet perfume of their liberated souls, free of the body's gross control. He knew a man who talked of a new religion, a religion based on the bomb. Perhaps when he left the hospital. . . .

At last, Shino was seeing her lover again, the beautiful bronze face in the clouds, the endless streamers of silver and black hair reaching out toward the ends of the world. The god's beckoning wing. . . .

The smoke rose above the city of Hiroshima and spread to the surrounding islands, and out to cover the world. Tom watched the smoke mix into the clouds. The god Pikadon gathered the rising spirits within his scarlet wings. And his wings covered the world.

WHEN WE MOVED ON

We tried to prepare the kids a year or so ahead. They might be adults to the rest of the world, but to us they were still a blur of squeals that smelled like candy.

"What do you mean move? You've lived here forever!" Our oldest daughter's face mapped her dismay. Elaine was now older than we had been when we found our place off the beaten path of the world, but if she had started to cry I'm sure I would have caved. I hoped she had forgotten that when she was a little girl I'd told her we'd stay in this house until the end.

"Forever ends, child," her mother said. "It's one of the last things we learn. These walls are quickly growing thin—it's time to go."

"What do you mean? I don't see anything wrong—"

I reached over, patted her knee and pointed. "That's because the house is so full there's little wall to be seen. But look there, between that sparkling tapestry of spider eggs and my hat collection. That's about a square foot of unadorned wall. Look there."

She did, and as I had so many times before, I joined her in the looking. I was pleased, at least, that this semi-transparent spot worn into our membrane of home provided clear evidence: through layers of wall board like greenish glass, through diaphanous plaster and thinnest lathe, we could see several local children walking to school, and one Billie Perkins honored us with a full-faced grin and a finger mining his nose for hidden treasure.

"Is that Cheryl Perkins' boy?" she asked. "I haven't seen her in years." She sounded wistful. It always bruised me a bit to hear her sounding wistful. I've always been a sloppy mess where my children are concerned.

"You should call her, honey," her mother said, on her way into the kitchen for our bowls of soup. My wife never tells you what's in the soups she serves—she doesn't want to spoil the surprise. Some days it's like dipping into a liquid Cracker Jack box.

Elaine had gone to the thin patch and was now poking it with her finger. "Can they see us from out there?" Her finger went in part way and stuck. She made a small embarrassed cry and pulled it out. A sigh of shimmering green light puffed out in front of her, then fell like rain on the floor.

I handed her a cloth napkin and she busily wiped at the slowly spreading stain. "They just see a slight variation in color," I replied. "It's more obvious at night, when a haze of light from the house leaks through."

She smiled. "I've noticed that on visits. I just thought it was the house sparkling. It's always been." She stopped.

"A jewel?"

"Yes. That's not silly of me? I always thought of it as the 'jewel on the hill,' so when it seemed to sparkle lately, to look even more beautiful than ever, I thought nothing of it."

Of course she has been using this phrase since she was a little girl, but I said "What an interesting comparison! I'd never thought of it that way before. But I like that, 'The Jewel on the Hill.' We could paint a sign, put it up on the wall."

"Oh, Daddy! Where would you find the room?"

This was, of course, the point of the conversation, the fulcrum about which our future lives were to turn. A painting can become too crowded in its composition, a brain too full of trivia, and a house can certainly accumulate too many plans, follies, acquisitions, vocations, avocations, heart-felt avowals, and memories so fervently gripped they lose their binding thread.

All about us floated a constellation of materials dreamed and lived, attached to walls and door and window frames, layered onto shelves and flooding glass-fronted cabinets, suspended from or glued to the ceilings, protruding here and there into the room as if eager for a snag. There were my collections, of course: the hats, the ties, the jars of curiosities, monstrosities, and mere unreliabilities, the magazines barely read then saved for later, and later, all the volumes of fact and fiction, and the photographs of fictive relatives gathered from stores thrift and antique or as part of the purchase of a brand new frame, bells and belts and pistols and thimbles, children's drawings and drawings of children drawing the drawings, colored candles and colored bottles and colors inexplicably attached to nothing at all, my wife's favorite recipes pasted on the walls at levels relative to their deliciousness (the best ones so high up she couldn't read them clearly enough to make those wonderful dishes anymore), and everywhere, and I mean everywhere, the notes of a lifetime reminding our children to eat that lunchtime sandwich as well as the cookie, don't forget piano practice, remember we love you, and please take out the trash. Our notes to each other were simpler and less directive: thinking of you, thinking of you, have a great day.

In one corner of the living room you could see where I had sat reading a year of my sister's unmailed letters found in a shoebox after her death, each one spiked to the wall after reading, feeling like nails tearing through my own flesh. And near the windows kites and paper birds poised for escape through sashes left carelessly ajar. An historical collection of our children's toys lay piled against the baseboards, ready for the sorting and elimination we'd never quite managed, and floating above, tied to strings were particularly prized bits of homework, particularly cherished letters from camp, gliding and tangling with the varied progress of the day. And the authors of those works, our precious children, preserved in photos at nearly every age, arranged around the ceiling light fixtures like jittering moths, filling with their own illumination as the ceilings thinned to allow the daylight in. Gathered together I thought each child's history in photos could have been portraits of a single family whose resemblances were uncanny and disturbing.

There were trophies mounted or settled onto shelves for bowling, swimming, and spelling, most candy bars sold and fewest absent days. And the countless numbers of awards for participation, for happy or complaining our children always did participate.

Some of the collections, such as the spider eggs or selected, desiccated moth wings I couldn't remember for sure if their preservation had been intentional. Others, like the gatherings of cracks in corners or those scattered arrays of torn fabrics were no doubt accidental, but possessed of beauty in any case and so needed to stay.

These were the moments of a lifetime, the celebrations and the missteps, and I wondered now if our children ever had any idea what they both stepped in and out of on their average day in our home.

"What's going to become of it all?" our daughter exclaimed. She moved through the downstairs rooms unconsciously pirouetting, glancing around. She'd seen it all before, lived with all but the most recent of it, but blindness comes easy. I could see her eyes trying to remember. "You can't just throw it away!" she cried, when a rain of doll's heads from a decayed net overhead set off her squeals and giggles.

"You kids can have whatever you like," my wife replied from the passage to the kitchen. "But thrown out, left behind, or simply forgotten, things do have a way of becoming gone. Which is what is about to happen to your lunches, if the two of you don't come with me right now!"

Within the sea of salt and pepper shakers (armies of cartoon characters and national caricatures with holes in their heads) that covered our kitchen table my wife had created tiny islands for our soup bowls and milk glasses. I had the urge to sweep that collection of shakers off onto the floor, just to show how done with this never-ending tide of things I'd become, but I knew that wasn't what Elaine needed to see at that moment. She stared at the red surface of her soup as if waiting for some mystery to emerge.

"Sweetheart, we just don't need all this anymore."

"You seemed to need it before," she said to all the staring shaker heads.

"It's hard to explain such a change," I said, "but you collect and you collect and then one day you say to yourself 'this is all too much.' You can't let anything else in, so you don't have much choice but to try to clear the decks."

"I just don't want things to change," she said softly.

"Oh, yes, you do," her mother said, patting her hand. "You most certainly do. Everything has an expiration date. It just isn't always a precise date, or printed on the package. And you would hate the alternative."

I'd been distracted by all the calendars on the kitchen walls, each displaying a different month and year, and for just that moment not sure which one was the current one, the one with the little box reserved for right now.

Elaine looked at her mother with an expression that wasn't exactly anger, but something very close. "Then why bother, Mom? When it all just has to be gotten rid of, in the end?"

"Who can know?" My wife smiled, dipping into her soup, then frowned suddenly as if she'd discovered something unfortunate. "To fill the time, I suppose. To exercise—" She turned suddenly to me. "Or is it 'exorcise'?" Without waiting for an answer she turned again to her soup, lifted the bowl, and sipped. Done, she smiled shyly at our daughter with a pink mustache and continued, "our creativity. To fill the space, to put our mark down, and then to erase it. That's what we human beings do. That's all we know how to do."

"Human beings?" Elaine laughed. "You know, I always thought you two were wizards, superheroes, magical beings, something like that. Not like anybody else's parents. Not like anybody else at all. All of us kids did."

My wife closed her eyes and sighed. "I think we did, too."

Over the next few weeks we had the rest of our children over to reveal something of our intentions, although I'm quite sure a number of unintentions were exposed as well. They brought along numerous grandchildren, some who had so transformed since their last visits it was as if a brand-new person had entered the room, fresh creatures whose habits and behaviors we had yet to learn about. The older children stood around awkwardly, as if they were reluctant guests at some high school dance, snickering at the old folks' sense of décor, and sense of what was important, but every now and then you would see them touch something on the wall and gasp, or read a letter pasted there and stand transfixed.

The younger grandchildren were content to straddle our laps, constructing tiny bird's nests in my wife's gray hair, warrens for invisible rabbits in the multidimensional tangles of my beard. They seemed completely oblivious to their parents' discomfort with the conversation.

"So where will you go?" asked oldest son Jack, whom we'd named after the fairytale, although we'd never told him so.

"We're still looking at places," his mother said. "Our needs will be pretty simple. As simple as you could imagine, really."

I looked out at the crowd of them. Did we really have all these children? When had it happened? I suspected a few strangers had sneaked in.

"Won't you need some help with the moving, and afterwards?" Wilhelmina asked.

"Help should always be appreciated, remember that children," I said. A few of them laughed, which was the response I had wanted. But then very few of our children have understood my sense of humor.

"What your father meant to say was that moving help won't be necessary," my wife said, interrupting. "As we said, we're taking very little with us, so please grab anything you'd care to have. As for us, we think a simple life will be a nice change."

Annie, always our politest child, raised her hand.

"Annie, honey, you're thirty years old. You don't need to raise your hand anymore," I told her.

"So what are you really telling us? Are we going to see you again?"

"Well, of course you are," I said. "Maybe not as often, or precisely when you want to, but you will see us. We'll still be around, and just as before, just as now, you'll always be our children."

We didn't set a day, because rarely do you know when the right day will come along. We'd been looking for little signs for years, it seemed, but you never really know what little signs to look for.

Then one day I was awakened early, sat up straight with eyes wide open, which I almost never do, looking around, listening intently for whatever might have awakened me.

The first thing I noticed was the oddness of the light in the room. It had a vaguely autumnal feel even though it was the end of winter, which wasn't as surprising as it might normally have been, what with the unusually warm temperatures we'd been having for this time of year.

The second thing was the smell: orange-ish or lemon-ish, but gone a little too far, like when the rot begins to set in.

The third thing was the absence of my wife from our bed.

Even though she always woke up before me, she always stayed in bed in order to ease my own transition from my always complicated dreams to standing up, attempting to move around.

I dressed quickly and found her downstairs in the dining room. "Look," she said. And I did.

Every bit of our lives along the walls, hanging from the ceiling, spilt out onto the floors, had turned the exact same golden sepia shade, as if it had all been sprayed with some kind of preservative. "Look," she repeated. "You can see it all beginning to wrinkle."

I'd actually thought that effect to be some distortion in my vision, for I had noticed it, too.

"You know what you want to take?" she asked.

"It's all been ready for months," I said. "I'll be at the door in less than a minute."

I ran up the stairs, hearing the rapidly drying wooden steps crack and pop beneath my shoes. When I jerked open the closet door it seemed as if I was opening the door to the outside, on a crisp fall day, Mr. Hopkins down the street is burning his leaves, and you can smell apples cooking from some anonymous kitchen. I brushed the fallen leaves from the small canvas bag I had filled with a notebook, a pencil, some crackers (which are the best food for any occasion), and extra socks. I looked up at the clothes rod, the rusted metal, and nothing left hanging there but a tangle of brittle vines and the old baseball jacket I wore in high school. It hardly fit, but I pulled it on anyway, picked up the bag, and ran.

She stood by the front door smiling, wrapped in an old knit sweater-coat with multi-colored squares on a chocolate-colored background. "My mother knitted it for me in high school. It was all I could find intact, but I've always wanted to wear it again."

"Something to drink?" I asked.

"Two bottles of water. Did you get what you needed?"

"Everything I need," I replied. And we left that house where we'd lived almost forty years, raised children and more or less kept our peace, for the final time. Out on the street we felt the wind coming up, and turned back around.

What began as a few scattered bits leaving the roof, caught by the wind and drifting over the neighbor's trees, gathered into a tide that reduced the roof to nothing, leaving the chimney exposed, until the chimney fell into itself, leaving a chimney-shaped hole in the sky. We held onto each other, then, as the walls appeared to detach themselves at the corners, flap like birds in pain, then twist and flutter, shaking, as the dry house chaff scattered, making a cloud so thick we couldn't really see what was going on inside it, including what was happening to all our possessions, and then the cloud thinned, and the tiny bits drifted down, disappearing into the shrubbery which once hugged the sides of our home, and now hugged nothing.

We held hands for miles and for some parts of days thereafter, until our arthritic hands cramped, and we couldn't hold on any more no matter how hard we tried. We drank the water and ate the crackers and I wrote nothing down, and after weeks of writing nothing I simply tore the sheets out of the notebook one by one and started pressing them against ground, and stone, the rough bark on trees, the back of a dog's head, the unanchored sky one rainy afternoon. Some of that caused a mark to be made, much did not, but to me that was a satisfactory record of where we had been, and who we had been.

Eventually, our fingers no longer touched, and we lost the eyes we'd used to gaze at one another, and the tongues for telling each other, and the lips for tasting each other.

But we are not nothing. She is that faint smell in the air, that nonsensical whisper. I am the dust that settles into your clothes, that keeps your footprints as you wander across the world.

THE COMPANY YOU KEEP

Richard lived alone in an apartment above a decrepit carriage house off an alley in the oldest part of the city. He believed that once upon a time rich people had occupied the neighborhood —that's why there were so many large houses (now divided and re-divided) and oversize utility buildings, like his carriage house. These had been people whose faces and reputations were known, even written about. People who might sneak out in disguise from time to time for a brief vacation in anonymity, that place where he—and most people he knew—lived all their lives.

Of course, the rich all picked up and drifted away at the first smell of shabbiness, not even waiting until that shabbiness made its actual appearance. Now he survived as best he could, the end recipient of a progression of hand-me-downs.

He'd been in the carriage house at least twenty years. When he attempted to recollect his move-in day more precisely, he became irretrievably lost in the lies and self-deceptions of memory. Surely, it couldn't have been that long ago. Surely, it had. Surrounded as it was by taller buildings with thicker walls, and a shadowing backdrop of huge trees preserved through some rich woman's personal campaign, it was quieter here than a room so close to the heart of the city's commerce had any right to be.

"People will judge you by your companions," Richard's father once said, responding to one of the countless confessions Richard had made concerning some trouble he and various friends had gotten themselves into. "You become known by the company you keep."

Good advice, he thought now. Very perceptive. But unbeknown to his father, somewhat off the point, as all of Richard's confessions had been lies. There had been no trouble. No legal entanglements due to bad influences, no youthful misadventures with peers less conscientious than he, despite dozens of such tales told and retold.

Richard would much rather have his father think he chose his companions poorly than know that Richard had no companions at all.

Not that he lied out of shame. He simply didn't want to have to explain himself to his father. Although he'd always desired friends, he wasn't sure what friendship might mean for him. He'd imagined the state of friendship as one in which your friend understood you, supporting your dreams, empathizing with your failures and imperfections. Someone always on your side. But he'd seldom seen such friendship in the relationships of others. And over the years his idea of a friend seemed increasingly improbable, a creature more at home among unicorns and banshees. Loneliness, on the other hand, was something he could always bank on, a predictable destination at the end of every workday when solitude became total, but more than that, an attitude he might carry with him into the office, out to restaurants, even into one of the increasingly rare social gatherings he might feel duty-bound to attend. He had come to carry that loneliness around with him much the way a monk carried bliss.

It would be difficult to say precisely when he discovered that his particular brand of solitude might not be as simple as all that. But certainly it solidified the day he met the pale man on the corner by the library.

Richard had been returning some long-overdue travel guides. He'd been in a hurry—he didn't like to linger in or near the library. Something about the enforced quiet, and all that wealth of information at your disposal if you knew the right questions to ask. But of course Richard never knew the right questions to ask.

Although there'd been no particular reason to isolate this one man among the many who gathered there that day, there had been something about the posture—something vaguely anticipatory about the man's stance—that filled Richard with a sudden, peculiarly overwhelming, and inexplicable empathy for this lone figure awash in the torrents of flesh, bone, leather, and cloth that flooded the sidewalks of this inhospitable concrete sprawl.

For a brief moment the man had turned to face him, and Richard had been struck immediately by the paleness of the face; then a look as of recognition vaguely distorted the sheet-white features, and the man turned away with a kind of desperate speed, stumbled, and almost fell.

Richard might have forgotten all about the incident, despite the strong impression of the man's seemingly bloodless complexion, when several other people in that vicinity made the same stumbling move.

Nothing remarkable or similar about these individuals in any way, both men and women, a variety of races, dress, and facial types—and yet for some reason they had stumbled almost identically.

But stranger still had been Richard's reaction. He felt as if he knew them, although surely he'd never seen them before. They were like him. They were meant for greater things they did not understand. They possessed capacities unrecognized, even to themselves. They had lived their lives as solitary warriors, and now at last their army had begun to form.

He had no idea why he should think such things. His life had not altered appreciably in years. He had seen no signs of change, had heard no call. No one approached him in the street, and at work he was still known by his last name and the relative coordinates of his cubicle walls.

When he was a boy he'd imagined himself imbued with superpowers. The drawback had always been that he didn't know what those powers might entail. But he had faith that they would reveal themselves at the appropriate time: A child would fall from a window and he would suddenly find himself flying up to catch her. Some disaster would occur—a factory explosion, a collapsed parking garage, a hospital on fire—requiring his unusual strength and courage. Everyone would be surprised by his transformation, but no one more so than he.

Richard was due for a two-o'clock appointment up on the sixth floor. He found himself at the elevator in the lobby at a quarter till. He'd developed this habit of referring to himself in the third person. Found himself was a deliberate choice of words —often lately he would catch himself that way, find himself in some location or situation with no clear memory of what came immediately before.

It was a small group gathered before the elevator, staring at the downward progress of numbers over the doors as if in suspense over the outcome. Normally he would fix his own eyes on that fascinating numeric display, but in recent weeks his habit had become to examine the members of any group he might find himself in, looking for some vague confirmation of questions he had no language for, seeking some signal or sign, some indication that he had at last landed in the right place and time.

There was nothing remarkable about any of these people: four men and three women dressed in gray, black, and brown business attire. The one Hispanic woman who'd attempted to add color with an orange scarf looked uncomfortable in it, as if the attempt might strangle her. One of the men was taller than the others by a few inches. He appeared to stoop further the longer they waited, as if attempting to reduce himself before anyone noticed.

They barely left room for the exiting passengers as they rushed into the opening doors, but those they jostled betrayed no discomfort at this, nor did Richard's group appear aware that they might have created some discomfort.

Once inside, they fit closely together. The elevator seemed to ascend slowly, as if hauling weight well beyond its posted limits. Richard watched as the man in front of him placed a hand on his right hip, sending a narrow elbow against the Hispanic woman, who in return leaned away and placed her own right hand on her own right hip.

The man beside her did the same. And the man beside him, all around to Richard, who, so embarrassed he found it difficult to breathe, did the same.

The man ahead of him put one foot forward and the others, including Richard, did the same.

A very slight shuffle to the right and a step back. Richard struggled to maintain his composure, did the step just the same, feeling as if he'd been kidnapped. By the time they reached the sixth floor, he felt barely capable of exiting. He turned quickly to see what might be in their faces, but they'd fallen back into their still, stuffed positions. He entered the offices of the insurance company sweaty and disheveled. And sorry to have left the elevator behind.

He was told he was ten minutes late and would have to wait an

hour for the next appointment. The clock above the reception-
ist's desk pointed to two o'clock exactly, but he did not object.
The reception area was full. He found a solitary chair against the
wall, mostly hidden by a large potted plant. He had to remove a
large pile of magazines from the seat in order to sit down. Not
seeing any place to put these, he pulled them into his lap, hugging
them and hunching over to keep them from falling.

A few feet away a fat man raised his right hand slowly and
placed it on the front part of his head, immediately above the
hairline, pressing down with obvious strain, as if trying to keep
one particular train of thought from jumping track.

On the other side of the reception area, almost behind the
desk, Richard saw another man—well-groomed, hair slicked
back—do the same.

A younger man with his face buried in a financial magazine
raised his hand slowly, palm up and wavering like a snake's head,
then brought it over in a stretch-like motion, finally settling it
somewhat surreptitiously onto the same region of his head.

Richard's vision filled with the nervous flapping of shadows
like dozens of birds exhausted from their long journey. He closed
his eyes, looking for his place of quiet solitude, and, unable to
find it, opened them again. The men still held their heads in the
same way, as if waiting.

Richard searched a last time for a place to put down the magazines, and, failing that, raised his hand high and slapped it over the
same region of his head. The magazines crashed to the floor and
spread in a wave over the shoes of the people sitting nearest him.
Everyone in the room glanced his way except for the three men
with hands on their heads, who now lowered their hands without
a glance in his direction. He felt his face burning, got up, and left
the office.

Out on the sidewalk and everyone appeared to be walking his
way. As he pushed through them they raised arms and elbows,
overlapping one against the other as if to prevent his flight. On
the next street corner a small group stood off to themselves,
wrists raised at exactly the same angle as they stared at watches
that were missing, pale bands of skin left as evidence.

He felt only a whisper of guilt about stealing a car. Richard maneuvered the stolen car through streets full of chatting, focused people, people with important appointments to go to, places to see, definite things to do, conversations to have, parties to attend, shadows to scatter, loneliness to bury in a cascade of forced laughter. He at last felt the growing anxiety of someone with a destination. And he would not permit a crowd of other people, those people, the people whose full lives had always put the lie to the so-called life he had cobbled together on his own, to delay him in any way, make him late for the meeting he had waited for all his life.

It saddened him that the truth of it had never been clear to him before, that people like him, people who had endured a solitary desperation all their lives, required no words for their secret communications, that their private handshakes demanded no actual exchange of touch, that their meeting places were spontaneous and secret even unto themselves, that, like the early Christian churches in a world of persecution, they met wherever and whenever more than one of them came together in one place.

Richard looked out the driver's-side window into another car that had pulled alongside. He wagged his head to the left, veered the stolen car to the left, and that other driver did the same. And another car beside that one, as a result driving up onto the sidewalk, plowing over the crowds there, striking the front wall of a department store, exploding into flame.

Richard grimly focused again on the road to his destination, hoping that none of the people he had recently recognized were out on the sidewalk just then, and sparing a good thought for the brave and devoted driver who had no doubt lost his life in service to the cause.

But of course we are legion, he thought. When one of us dies there is always another to take his or her place. We always thought we were alone, and our gratitude at discovering our belonging knows no bounds.

The building ahead of him looked little different from the rest, which was appropriate. No crowds pushed inside as if this were some concert hall or sporting event, and that, too, was appropriate. Because no matter how many of them there might be they would never be a crowd, not in the way these successful and ful-filled unenlightened ones made a crowd.

Richard was pleased to see that no one lingered around the entrance to the building. No one paid it any particular attention, and that was as expected, and wonderfully, joyfully, appropriate.

He stopped the car a few feet from the entrance and aban-doned it there. Going in he glanced at the sky, the way the roof-line pierced it so nicely, demanding respect.

A few gathered before the elevators, joining him as he made his way through the doors, repeating his gesture of rubbing at his left eye (let it not offend), scratching at his neckline (let it bare itself before thee), pulling at his trousers (my legs belong to you).

They were on the rooftop, waiting, although they did not appear to be waiting. They did not appear even to be aware that others were up on this rooftop with them. They stared at the sky. They stared at the streets below and at the horizon of stone and steel containers stretching in all directions. His company. His associates. They did not look at each other.

But they were here together. Richard understood that the way of silence, the way of solitude, was their way. There was no plan or determination. None was needed.

Well after it began, Richard realized there were fewer of them. Then fewer still. Then he saw a few slip over the edges, like birds sucked one by one into a rising tide of wind.

He was proud that when his own urge arrived he did not hes-itate, but floated across the border between gravity and release without a second thought.

They descended like huge, mad fowl, their mouths open in anger or weeping. There were a few hundred or more, and it was said that the way they twisted as they fell to their deaths, the way they swept their arms and legs out viciously in their final few feet of air, they seemed to be trying to kill as many in the crowds below them as they could.

2 PM: THE REAL ESTATE AGENT ARRIVES

In the back yard, after the family moved away: blue chipped food bowl, worn-out dog collar, torn little boy shorts, dinosaur T-shirt, rope, rusty can, child's mask lined with sand. In the corner the faint outline of a grave, dog leash lying like half a set of parentheses. Then you remember. The family had no pets.

THE CARVING

She'd told her friends how they'd met, how after a week's courtship they'd married.

True in part but there'd been no courtship. She'd fallen for this man, for the strength and sureness of his hands, and she'd asked him to marry her. And because he was the man he was, needing an ordered place where art might happen, he'd said yes. Two years later the baby was born, and she'd set out to make this strange artist love his only child.

Out on the deck his exacting hands sent into wood chisels as sharp as dread. Flakes rose into bright air and fluttered the long descent to the rocks below. He did not mark the wood, did not reduce it with machinery before his preliminary cuts. Outlines, he said, were no use for freeing the true shapes within.

Their boy always played near his father's working, even when the man's careless indifference brought him pain. For the boy knew that the carver could not keep his hands off the thing he had made, the thing he had freed from unfeeling matter, and in this way the boy got his hugs and impromptu dances and a quick toss in the air that made him believe in wings.

A steady thok as steel parted wood a hundred years old. She imagined their son sitting patiently, watching those steady hands, waiting for his toss.

Her friends said he was too self-absorbed, that life with such a man would leave her empty and desperate for talk. But she knew what her son knew: there could be no greater love than that which the artist bore for the thing he had freed from the world.

Such unshakable focus, she thought, opening the door that led out onto the deck and her husband's working. The steady rhythm of hammer and hand uplifted her in just the hearing, so that she, too, felt winged and freed from a mundane world. She looked for her son, expecting him there waiting for his little toss, but her son was not there.

Her husband sat hunched over his work. For a moment she was furious about his lack of care. Where was their son? Then following the flight of chips, white and red and trailing, over the railing's edge and down onto the rocks, she saw the fallen form, the exquisite work so carelessly tossed aside, the delicate shape spread and broken, their son.

She turned to the master carver, her mouth working at an uncontrolled sentence. And saw him with the hammer, the bloody chisel, the glistening hand slowly freed, dropping away from the ragged wrist.

This man, her husband, looked up, eyes dark knots in the rough bole of face. "I could not hold him," he gasped. "Wind or his own imagination. Once loose, I could not keep him here."

And then he looked away, back straining into the work of removing the tool that had failed him.

JESSE

Jesse says he figures it's about time we did another one.

He uses "we" like we're Siamese twins or something, like we both decide what's going to happen and then it happens. Like we just do it, two bodies with one mind like in some weird movie. But it's Jesse that does it, all of it, each and every time. I'm just along for the ride. It's not my fault what Jesse does. I can't stop him—nobody could.

"Why?" I ask, and I feel bad that my voice has to shake, but I can't help it. "Why is it time, Jesse?"

"'Cause I'm afraid you're forgetting too many things, John. You're forgetting how we do it, and how they look."

We again. Like Jesse doesn't do a thing by himself. But Jesse does everything by himself. "I don't forget," I say.

"Oh, but I think you do. I know you do. It's time all right." Then he gets up from his nest in the sour straw and starts toward the barn door. And even though I haven't forgotten how they look, and how we do it, how he does it—how could anybody forget something like that?—I get up out of the straw and follow.

When Jesse called me up that day I didn't take him all that seriously. Jesse was always calling me up and saying crazy things.

"Come on over," he said. "I gotta show you something."

I laughed at him. "You're in enough trouble," I said. "Your parents grounded you, remember? Two weeks at least, you told me."

"My parents are dead," he said, in his serious voice. But I had heard his serious voice a thousand times, and I knew what it meant.

I laughed. "Sure, Jesse. Deader than a flat frog on the highway, right?"

"No, deader than your dick, dickhead." He was always saying that. I laughed again. "Come on over. I swear it'll be okay."

"Okay. My mom has to go to the store. She can drop me off and pick me up later."

"No. Don't come with your mom. Take your bike."

"Christ, Jesse. It's five miles!"

"You've done it before. Take your bike or don't come at all."

"Okay. Be there when I get there." He made me mad all the time. All he had to do was tell me to do something and I'd do it. When I first knew him I did things he said because I felt sorry for him. His big brother had died when a tractor rolled over on him. I wasn't there but people said it was pretty awful. I heard my dad tell my mom that there must have been a dozen men around but none of them could do a thing. Jesse's brother had been awake the whole time, begging them to get the tractor off, that he could feel his heart getting ready to stop, that he knew it was going to stop any second. Dad said the blood was seeping out from under the tractor, all around his body, and Jesse's brother was looking at it like he just couldn't believe it. And Jesse was there watching the whole thing, Dad said. They couldn't get him to go away.

It gave me the creeps, what Jesse's brother had said. 'Cause I've always been afraid my heart was just going to stop someday, for no good reason. And to feel your heart getting ready to stop, that would be horrible.

Because of all that I felt real bad for Jesse, so for awhile there he would ask me to do something, anything, and I'd do it for him. I'd steal somebody's lunch or pull down a little kid's pants or walk across the creek on a little skinny board, all kinds of stupid crap. But after awhile I just did it because he said. He didn't make you want to feel bad for him. I wasn't even sure that he cared that his brother was dead. Once I asked him if he still felt bad about it and he just said that his brother picked on him all the time. That's all he would say about it. Jesse was always weird like that.

I hadn't ridden my bike in over a year—I wasn't sure I still could. I thought sixteen-year-olds were too old to ride bikes—guys were getting their licenses and were willing to walk or get rides with older friends until that day happened. And I was big for my age, a lot bigger than Jesse. I felt stupid. But I rode my bike the five miles anyway, just because Jesse told me to.

By the time I got to his farm I was so tired and mad I just threw the bike down in the gravel driveway. I didn't care if I broke it—I wasn't going to ride it home no matter what. Jesse came to the screen door with a smirk on his face. "Took you long enough," he said. "I didn't think you were coming."

"I'm here, all right? What'd you want to show me that was so damn important?"

He pulled me down the hall. He was so excited and it was happening so fast I was having a real bad feeling even before I saw them. He stopped in front of the door to his parents' bedroom and knocked it open with his fist. The sound made me jump. Then when I looked inside there were his parents on the floor, sleeping.

A short laugh came out of me like a bark. They looked silly: his mom's dress pulled up above her knees and his dad's mouth hanging open like he was drunk. They had their arms folded over their bellies. I never saw people sleeping that way before. The sheets and blankets and pillows had been pulled off the bed and were arranged around them and underneath them like a nest. His mom had never been a good housekeeper—Jesse told me the place always looked and stank like a garbage dump—but I'd never thought it was this bad, that they had to sleep on the floor.

The room was full of all these big candles, the scented kind. There must have been forty or fifty of them. And big melted patches where there must have been lots more, but they'd burned down and been replaced. There was a box full of them by the dresser, all ready to go. They also had a couple of those weird-looking incense burners going. It made me want to laugh. There were more different smells in that room than I'd smelled my whole life. And all of them so sweet they made my eyes water.

But under the sweet there was something else—when a breeze sneaked through and flickered the candles I thought I could smell it—like when we got back from vacation that summer and the freezer broke down while we were away. Mom made dad move us to a motel for awhile. Something like that, but it was having a hard time digging itself out of all that sweetness.

"Candles cost a fortune," Jesse said. "All the money in my dad's wallet plus the coins my mom kept in a fruit jar. She didn't even think I knew about that. But they look pretty neat, huh?"

I took a step into the room and looked at his dad's mouth. Then his mom's mouth. They hung open like they were about to swallow a fly or sing or something. I almost laughed again, but I couldn't. Their mouths looked a little like my dad's mouth, the way he lets it hang open when he falls asleep on the couch watching TV. But different. Their mouths were soft and loose, their lips dark, all dry and cracked, but even though they were holding their mouths open so long no saliva came dripping out. And there was gray and blue under their eyes. There were dark blotches on Jesse's mom's face. They were so still, like they were playing a game on me. Without even thinking about it I pushed on his dad's leg with my foot. It was like pushing against a board. His dad rocked a little, but he was so tight his big arms didn't even wiggle. Jesse always said his old man was "too tight." I really did start to laugh, thinking about that, but it was like my breath exploded instead. I didn't even know I had been holding it. "Jesus . . ." I could feel my chest shake all by itself.

Jesse looked at me almost like he was surprised, like I'd done something wrong. "I told you, didn't I? Don't be a baby." He sat down on the floor and started playing with his dad's leg, pushing on it and trying to lift up the knee. "Last night they both started getting stiff. It really happens, you know? It's not just something in the movies. You know why it happens, John?" He looked up at me, but he was still poking the leg with his fist, like he was trying to make his dad do something, slap him or something. Any second I figured his dad would reach over and grab Jesse by the hair and pull him down onto the floor beside them.

I shook my head. I was thinking no no no, but I couldn't quite get that out.

Jesse hit his dad on the thigh hard as he could. It sounded like an overstuffed leather chair. It didn't give at all. "Hell, I don't know either. Maybe it's the body fighting off being dead, even after you're dead, you know? It gets all mad and stiff on you." He laughed but it didn't sound much like Jesse's laugh. "I guess it don't know it's dead. It don't know shit once the brain is dead. But if I was going to die I guess I'd fight real hard." Jesse looked at his mom and dad and made a twisted face like he was smelling them for the first time. "Bunch of pussies . . ."

He grabbed the arm his dad had folded against his chest and tried to pull it away. His dad held on but then the arm bent a little. The fat shoulders shook when Jesse let go and his dad fell back. The head hit the pillow and left a greasy red smear.

"The old man here started loosening up top a few hours ago, in the same order he got stiff in." Jesse reached over and pinched his dad's left cheek.

"Christ, Jesse!" I ran back into the hall and fell on the floor. I could hardly breathe. Then I started crying, really bawling, and I could breathe again.

After awhile I could feel Jesse patting me on the back. "You never saw dead people before, huh, Johnny?"

I just shook my head. "I'm s-sorry, Jesse. I'm s-so sorry."

"They were old," he said. "It's okay. Really."

I looked up at him. I didn't understand. It felt like he wasn't even speaking English. But he just looked at me, then looked back into his parents' bedroom, and didn't say anything more. Finally I knew I had to say something. "How did it happen?"

He looked at me like I was being the one hard to understand. "I told you. They were old."

I thought about the red smear his dad's head made on the pillow, but I couldn't get myself to understand it. "But, Jesse . . . at the same time?"

He shook his head. "What's wrong with you, John? My dad died first. I guess that made my mom so sad she died a few minutes later. You've heard of that. First one old person dies, then the person they're married to dies just a short time after?"

"Yeah . . ."

"Their hearts just stopped beating." I looked up at him. I could feel my own heart vibrating in my chest, so hard it hurt my ribs. "I put them together like that. They were my parents. I figured they'd like that."

He had that right, I guess. After all, they were his parents. Maybe he didn't always get along with them, but they were his parents. He could look at them after they were dead.

I made myself look at them. It was a lot easier the second time. A whole lot easier. I felt a little funny about that. Even without his dad's blood on the pillow they were a lot different from sleeping people. There was just no movement at all, and hardly any color but the blue, and they both looked cool, but not a damp kind of cool because they looked so dry, and their eyelids weren't shut all the way, and you could see a little sliver of white where the lids weren't all the way closed. I made myself get as close to their eyes as I could, maybe to make sure one final time they weren't pretending. The sliver of white was dull, like on a fish. Like something thick and milky had grown over their eyes. They looked like dummies some department store had thrown out in the garbage. There wasn't anything alive about them at all.

"When did they die?"

Jesse was looking at them, too. Closely, like they were the strangest things anyone had ever seen. "It's been at least a day, I guess. Almost two."

Jesse said we shouldn't call the police just yet. They were his parents, weren't they? Didn't he have the right to be with them for awhile? I couldn't argue with that. I guessed Jesse had all kinds of rights when it was his parents. But it still felt weird, him being with their dead bodies almost two whole days. I helped him light some more candles when he said the air wasn't sweet enough anymore. I felt a little better helping him do that, like we were having a funeral for them. All those sweet-smelling candles and incense felt real religious. Then I felt bad about thinking he was being weird earlier, like I was being prejudiced or something. But it was there just the same. I quit looking at his mom and dad, except when Jesse told me to. And after a couple of hours of me just standing out in the hallway, or fussing with the candles, trying not to look at them, Jesse started insisting.

"You gotta look at them, John."

"I did. You saw me. I looked at them."

"No, I mean really look at them. You haven't seen everything there is to see."

I looked at him instead. Real hard. I could hardly believe he was saying this. "Why? I'm sorry they're dead. But why do I have to look at them?"

"Because I want you to."

"Jesse . . ."

". . . and besides, you should know about these things. Your mom and dad don't want you to know about things like this but I guess it's about the most important thing to know about there is. Everybody gets scared of dying, and just about everybody is scared of the dead. You remember that movie *Zombie* we rented? That's what it was all about. Now we've got two dead bodies here. You're my friend, and I want to help you out. I want to share something with you."

"Christ, Jesse. They're your parents."

"What, you think I don't know that? Who else should I learn about this stuff from anyway? If they were still alive, they'd be supposed to teach me. What's wrong with it? And don't just tell me because it's 'weird.' People say something's weird because it makes them nervous. Just because it bothers them they don't want you to do it. So what do we care, anyway? Nobody else is gonna know about this."

Jesse could argue better than anybody, and I never knew what to think about anything for sure. Before I knew it he had me back in the bedroom, leaning over the bodies. It was a little better—I guess I was getting used to them. At least I didn't feel ready to throw up like I did a while ago. That surprised me. It surprised me even more when he took my hand and put it on his mom's —his dead mom's—arm, and I didn't jerk it away.

"Jesus ..." I guess I'd expected it to be still stiff, but it had gotten soft again, as soft as anything I'd ever felt, like I could just dig my fingers into her arm like butter. It was cool, but not what I expected. And dry.

"See the spots?" Jesse said behind me. "Like somebody's been painting her. Like for one of those freak shows. Oh, she'd hate it if she knew. She'd think she looked like a whore!"

I saw them all right. Patches of blue-green low down on his dad's belly. Before I could stop him he raised his mom's skirt and showed me that the marks on her were worse: more of the blue-green and little patches of greenish red, all of it swimming together around her big white panties. I was embarrassed, but I kept staring. That's the way I'd always imagined seeing my first panties on a woman: when she was asleep or—to tell the truth— when she was dead. I used to dream about dead women in their panties and bras, dead women naked with their parts hanging out, and I'd felt ashamed about it, but here it was happening for the real and for some reason I was having a hard time feeling too ashamed. I hadn't done it; I hadn't killed her.

"Look," he said. I followed his hand as it moved up his mother's belly. I tensed as he pulled her dress up further, back over her head so that I couldn't see her mouth anymore, her mouth hanging open like she was screaming, but no sound coming out. "I know you always wanted to see one of these up close. Admit it, John." His hand rested on the right cup of her bra. Now I felt real bad, and ashamed, like I had helped him kill her. Her white, loose skin spilled out of the top and bottom of the cup like big gobs of dough. With a jerk of his hand Jesse pulled his mother's bra off. The skin was loose and it all had swollen so much it was beginning to tear. I knew it was going to break like an old fruit any second. "She's gotten bigger since the thing happened," he said. I started to choke. "Come on, John. You always wanted to see this stuff. You wanted to see it, and you wanted to see it dead."

I turned away and walked back into the hall when he started to laugh. His mom was an it now. His dad was a thing. But Jesse knew me so well. He knew about the dreams and he knew what would get to me, what I always thought about, even though I'd never told him. It made me wonder if all guys my age think about being dead that way, wanting to see it and touch it, wanting something real like that, even though it was so awful. I used to dream about finding my own parents dead, and what they would look like, but never once did I imagine I would do that to them. Not like Jesse. I knew now what Jesse had done to his parents. No question about that anymore. But I was all mixed up about what I felt about it. Because, even though it was awful, I still wanted to look, and touch. Wasn't that almost as bad?

"Here." Jesse grabbed my arm and turned me around. He led me back over to his mother's body. "You don't have to look. You can close your eyes. Let me just take your hand." But I wanted to look. He took me over to her side. There was a big blister there, full of stuff. Jesse put my hand on it. "Feel weird, huh?" He didn't look crazy; he looked like some kind of young scientist or something from some dumb TV show. I nodded. "Hey, look at her mouth!" I did. In her big loose mouth I could see pieces of food that had come up. A little dark bug crawled up out of her hair. This is what it's like, what it's really like, I thought. I thought about those rock stars I used to like all made up like they were dead, those horror movies I used to watch with Jesse, and all those stoner kids I used to know getting high every chance they had and telling me it don't matter anyway and everything was just a drag with their eyes half shut and their mouths hanging open and their skin getting whiter every day. All of them, they don't know shit about it, I thought. This is what it's really like.

Jesse left me by his mom and started going to the candles one at a time, snuffing them out. A filmy gray smoke started to fill the bedroom. I could already smell the mix of sweet and sharp smells starting to go away, and underneath that the other truly awful smell creeping in.

Jesse turned to me while the last few candles were still lit. That bad smell was almost all over me now, but I just sat there, holding my breath and waiting for it. He almost grinned but didn't quite make it. "I guess you're ready to take a hit off all this now," he said. I just stared at him. And then I let my clean breath go.

And now Jesse says he figures it's about time we did another one.

We took off from his house with the one bike and Jesse's pack but we had to walk most of the time because Jesse figured we'd better go cross-country, over the fences and through the trees where nobody could see us. He didn't think they'd find the bodies anytime soon but my parents would report me missing after awhile. It was hell getting the bike through all that stuff but Jesse said we might need it later so we best take it. The scariest part was when we had to cross a couple of creeks and wading through water up over my belt carrying that bike made me sure I was going to drown. But I thought maybe I even deserved it for what I'd seen, what I'd done, and what I didn't do. I thought about what a body must look like after it drowned—I'd heard they swole up something awful, and I thought about Jesse showing off my body after I'd died, letting people poke it and smell it, and then I didn't want to die anymore.

Once Jesse suggested that maybe we should build a raft and float downriver like Tom Sawyer and Huckleberry Finn. I'd read the two books and he'd seen one of the movies. I thought it was a great idea but then we couldn't figure out how to do it. Jesse bitched about how they don't teach you important stuff like that in school, and used to, dads taught you stuff like raft-building but they didn't anymore. He said his dad should have taught him stuff like that but he was always too busy.

"Probably," I said, watching Jesse closer all the time because he seemed to be getting frustrated with everything.

I thought a lot about Tom and Huck that first day and how they came back into town just in time to see their own funeral. I wondered if every kid dreamed about doing that. I wondered if my parents found out about what I did in Jesse's house what they would say about me at my funeral.

We slept the first night under the trees. Or tried to. Jesse walked around a lot in the dark and I couldn't sleep much from watching him. The next morning he was nervous and agitated and first thing he did he found an old dog and beat it over the head with a hammer. I didn't know he had the hammer but it was in his pack and I pretty much guessed what he'd used it for before. He didn't even tell me he was going to do it, he just saw the dog and as soon as he saw it he did it. We both stood there and looked at the body and touched it and kicked it and I didn't feel a damn thing and I don't think Jesse did either because he was still real nervous.

Later that morning the farmer picked us up in his truck.

"Going far?" he asked us from the window and I wanted to tell him to keep driving mister but I didn't. He was old and had a nice face and was probably somebody's father and some kid's grandfather but I couldn't say a thing with Jesse standing there.

"Meadville," Jesse said, smiling. I'd seen that fakey smile on Jesse's face before, when he talked to adults, when he talked to his own parents. "We're gonna help out on my uncle's farm." Jesse smiled and smiled and my throat and my chest and my head started filling up with that awful smell again. The old man looked at me and all I could do was look at him and nod. He let Jesse into the cab of the truck and told me I'd better ride with my bike in the back. The old man smiled at me a real smile, like I was a good boy.

The breeze was cool in the back of the truck and the bed rocked so on the gravelly side road we were on I started falling asleep, but every time I was getting ready to conk out we'd hit a bump or something and my head would snap up. But I still think I must have slept a little because somewhere in there I started to dream. I dreamed that I was riding along in the back of a pickup truck my grandfather was driving. He'd been singing the whole way and I'd been enjoying his singing but then it wasn't singing anymore it was screaming and a monster was in the front seat with him, Death was in the front seat with him, beating him over the head with a hammer. Then the truck jerked to a stop and I looked through the cab window where Death was hammering the brains out of my grandfather and coating the glass with gray and brown and red. My grandfather scratched at the glass like I should do something but I couldn't because it was just a dream. Then Death turned to me and grinned while he was still swinging the hammer and fighting with my grandfather and it was my face grinning and speckled with brains and blood.

I turned around to try to get out of the dream, to watch the trees whizz by while the truck was rocking me to sleep, but the land was dark and the trees were tall bodies all swollen in their dying and their heavy heads hanging down and their loose mouths falling open. And the wind through the trees was the breath of the dead—that awful smell I thought we'd left back at Jesse's house.

Later I kissed my grandfather goodbye and helped Jesse bury him under one of those tall trees that smelled so bad.

And now Jesse says he figures it's about time we did another one. He grins and says he's lost the smell. But I can smell it all the time—I smell, taste, and breathe that smell.

Outside Meadville Jesse washed up and stole a shirt and pants off a clothesline. From there we took turns walking and riding the bike to a mall where Jesse did some panhandling. We used the money to buy shakes and burgers. While we were eating Jesse said that panhandling wasn't wrong if you had to do it to get something to eat. I couldn't watch Jesse eat—the food kept coming up out of his mouth. My two burgers smelled so bad I tried to hold my breath while I ate them but that made me choke. But I still ate them. I was hungry.

We walked around the mall for a long time. Other people did

the same thing, staring, but never buying anything. It reminded me of one of those zombie pictures. I tried not to touch anybody because they smelled so bad and they held their mouths open so that you could see all their teeth.

Finally Jesse picked out two girls and dragged me over to them. I couldn't get too close because of their smell, but the younger one seemed to like me. She had a nice smile. I looked at Jesse's face. He was grinning at them and then at me. His complexion had gotten real bad since we'd started traveling—there'd been more and more zits on his face every day. Now they were huge. One burst open and a long skinny white worm crawled out. I looked at the girls—they didn't seem to notice.

"His parents are putting him up for adoption so we ran away. I'm trying to hide him until they change their minds." Jesse's breath stank.

The girls looked at me. "Really?" the older one said. Her face had tiny cracks in it. I looked down at my feet.

Both of the girls said "I'm sorry" about the same time, then they got quiet like they were embarrassed. But I still didn't look up. I watched their sandaled feet and the black bugs crawling between their toes.

The older one could drive so they hid us in the back seat of their car and drove to the end of the drive that led to the farm-house where their family lived. We were supposed to go on to the barn and the girls would bring us out some food later. We never told them about my bike and I kept thinking about it and what people would say when they found it. Even though I never used the bike anymore I was a little sorry about having lost it.

I also thought about those girls and how nice they were and how the younger one seemed to like me, even though they smelled so bad. I wondered why girls like that were always so nice to guys like us, guys with a story to tell, and I thought about how dumb it was.

After we were in the barn for a couple of hours the girls—they were sisters, if I didn't mention it before—brought us some food. The younger one talked to me a long time while I ate but I don't remember anything she said. The older one talked to Jesse the same way and I heard her say "You're a good person to be helping your friend like this." She leaned over and kissed Jesse on his cheek even though the zits were tearing his face apart. Her shirt rode up on the side and Jesse put his dirty hand there. I saw the blisters rise up out of her skin and break open and the smell was worse than ever in the barn but no one else seemed to notice.

I finished eating and leaned back into the dirty straw. I liked the younger sister but I hoped she wouldn't kiss me the same way. I couldn't stand the idea of her open, loose mouth touching my skin. Underneath the straw I saw that there were hunks of gray flesh, pieces of arms and legs and things inside you I didn't know the name for. But I covered them over with more straw when nobody was looking, and I didn't say anything.

And now Jesse says he figures it's about time we did another one. He thinks I've forgotten. But I haven't.

I've been thinking about the two sisters all night and how much they trust us and how good they've been to us. And I've been thinking how they remind me of the Wilks sisters in *Huckleberry Finn* and how Huck felt so ornery and low down because he was letting the duke and king rob them of their money after the sisters had been so nice to him. Sometimes I guess you don't know how to behave until you've read it in a book or seen it on TV.

So he gets up from his nest in the sour straw and starts toward the barn door. And I get up out of the straw and follow. Only last night I took the hammer, and now I beat him in the head until his head comes apart, and all the stink comes out and covers me so bad I know I'll never get it off. He always said he'd fight really hard if he knew he was dying, but his body doesn't fight back hardly at all. Maybe he didn't know.

I hear the noises in the farmhouse and now there are voices and flashlights coming. I scrape my fingers through the straw to find all the pieces of Jesse's head to make him look a little better for these people. I lie down in the straw beside him and close my eyes, leaving just a sliver of milky white under each lid to show them. I drop my mouth open and stop my saliva. I imagine the blue-green colors that will come and paint my body. I imagine the blisters and the insects and the terrible smell my breath has become. But mostly I try to imagine how I'm going to explain to these strangers why I'm enjoying this.

PREPARATIONS FOR THE GAME

It's the day of the big game. He has a date, oh, a beautiful young date. A member of a leading sorority on campus, auburn hair, perfume behind the ears and down her cleavage, a lure for his young red alcoholic nose. Could there ever be better times?

Certainly not. Not when he has such a beautiful date, his first date in months, and not when they're doubling with the president of his fraternity, who just happens to be seeing his beautiful date's best friend.

Things are looking up for him, oh, certainly.

They pull up in front of his apartment. I'll just be a minute, he says cheerily. Just a change of clothes. His pennant. His flask. Once out of the car, he gazes back in at their fixed smiles. The fraternity president scratches his wool pants. The beautiful date's best friend rubs at her cheekbones distractedly. He reaches into the car and pulls his beautiful date's hand from her fur muff. And grasps rods of bone, well-articulated, carpals and metacarpals.

But no. Just the effect of thin winter air against skin. He looks down at her small, narrow hand, with its pale white flesh. So delicate.

It's going to be a great game, he calls, jogging up the apartment building steps.

In his apartment he rummages through piles of clothing. What to wear? He picks up his checkered gray slacks, throws them behind the couch. He picks up the dark blue monogrammed sweater-shirt, tosses it on top of the refrigerator. He stumbles through piles of books, garbage, unmatted prints with curling edges. What to wear?

He is aware of a skeletal hand curled around the front doorknob. Without looking around he tells her, I haven't the time. I'll be late for the game.

It suddenly occurs to him it's the first time anyone has ever visited his apartment.

But still he tells her, I just haven't the time, I mustn't be late for the game. She slides around the doorframe, her short red shift tight over her emaciated figure, her thin hands twisted into tight fists.

It suddenly occurs to him she may be out to spoil his good time.

He turns around, pretending that she isn't there. He picks up a Nehru jacket, casts it away. He picks up his bright red turtleneck, and drops it on the coffee table. I haven't time, I haven't time, he pleads softly, then silently to himself.

She steps toward him, her eyes two dark stones. He clumsily avoids her, almost tripping over a pile of shoes.

She swings the edge of a cupped hand toward his face. He steps quickly once to his right, his eyes averted, still seeking something to wear to the game. Her blow misses.

What does she want from him? Why doesn't she leave him alone?

Now he is forced to look at her. He's cornered at one end of the small breakfast bar. I'll be late for the game, he repeats, almost crying. Her black hair is filthy, plastered to her skull.

He sidesteps past his television set. Something metallic shines in her moving hand. She smashes the screen. I'll be late, he whimpers. She steps closer. He senses just a hint of corrupted flesh beneath her rough, bluish lips.

The blood is rising into her cheeks and eyes, suffusing them with a light pink color. She swings her hands back and forth, in slow motion.

And still, he attempts to ignore her. He puts on his heavy coat, the dark brown with contrasting tan pattern. He slips his bright orange scarf around his neck, still walking away from her, adjusting the thick folds so that they cut across his neck at the most aesthetically pleasing angle, and still she follows him, swings her hands at him, misses him, and again he stumbles, slightly, before catching himself. His steps become quicker. He attempts to make his movements unpredictable.

He says it rapidly to himself, a magic formula, a prayer. I can't be late for the game. I just can't.

Again, from the corner of his eye he can see she is approaching. He walks briskly, still seeking his spectator's wardrobe, falters briefly, his gaze distracted. She steps around the low couch, directly behind him now, reaching for his coat. Mustn't be late, mustn't be late, he mutters to himself, suddenly deciding to forego the proper dress, to leave now. For wouldn't it be a graver offense, to make the president of his fraternity late for the game, not to mention his beautiful young date and her best friend?

He hurriedly, almost running, makes it to the door, jerking it open as she makes a final, determined lunge. He hears the faint knock of her knuckles or perhaps, cheekbones rasping the door panel as he runs down the stairs pulling at his ill-fitting pants, tucking in his shirt, running fidgety hands over his improper clothing.

At the curb he halts in dismay. The car is gone with the president and the two pretty girls inside. The stadium is miles away; he'll never make it in time. What will they all think of him? He sits down on the curb, the sound of footsteps on the staircase growing louder behind him.

He has been unable to leave his apartment for weeks. He sleeps days at a time, his moments awake so brief they seem like dreams to him. Dinner comes at 2:00 A.M., breakfast twelve hours later. He throws the garbage into a cardboard box under the sink.

One twilight he remembers that he has a date set up for that day. They are all going to the big game. He, his beautiful young date, her best friend, and the president of his fraternity who he had never really talked to and probably still wouldn't have gotten to know if their beautiful young dates hadn't been such good friends. What time is it? He's going to be late. The phone is ringing. His parents again? While not quite deciding not to answer it, he fails to answer by default.

He rummages through piles of clothing, attempting to find the one proper outfit for his venture outside, to the game.

He needs to go to the bathroom, but not wanting to walk the ten yards or so down to the restroom in the hall, he walks over to his sink and begins urinating there.

He is aware of a skeletal hand curled around the front doorknob.

Without looking around he tells her, I haven't the time. I'll be late for the game.

It occurs to him it's the first time anyone has ever visited his apartment.

But still he tells her, I just haven't the time. I mustn't be late for the game.

She slides around the door frame, her short red shift tight over her emaciated figure, her thin hands twisted into tight fists.

It occurs to him that he's seen her before, at one of his fraternity's dances. She danced with Bob, Tom. Perhaps she even danced with the president. It occurs to him that maybe even he danced with her that night.

He can't remember her name.

She approaches him slowly, her arms outstretched. He stumbles backwards over the couch. The phone is ringing again. I can't be late for the game, he pleads with her.

The phone stops ringing. Outside a horn is blaring. It must be his fraternity president, his beautiful date, her best friend. He lunges toward the door, forgetting his good clothes. I can't be late for the game, he cries it now. He can hear her quickening steps behind him.

At the curb he halts, looking about in confusion. The car is gone. He'll never make it in time. He suddenly realizes that he is naked; his legs startle him with their chalky whiteness. What will they all think of him? He hears her footsteps behind him. Looking down, he discovers that his feet are bare, bleeding from all the broken glass in the street.

He races down the street. He figures that if he can just find the proper bus, he can make it to the game on time. I mustn't be late, he mutters, then grows self-conscious and worried, thinking some passerby might have heard him talking to himself, and think him strange.

His heavy coat tails, the dark brown with contrasting tan pattern, flap in the wind. His bright orange scarf hangs loosely around his neck, untying itself with his exertions. His hands grab at the material, trying to maintain his neat appearance.

Occasionally he looks around to see if she is following. Small dogs growl at his feet.

Ahead of him, he thinks he sees the back entrance to the bus station, a tall whitewashed building with a blue roof. But he can't remember which bus it was that traveled the route to the stadium.

He races up the back stairs, seeking information. He pushes open a steel door at the second floor, turns left, and jerks open a wooden door.

And he is back in his own apartment once again, the unmade bed, the scattered clothing, the sweet ripe smell of garbage under the sink. She has been waiting for him, his small boy scout hatchet clutched tightly in her hand. I can't be late, he starts to whine, then stops. He can't hear his own voice. She walks toward him now, the hatchet slightly raised.

He finds it difficult to move. What is her name?

He sits in the restaurant across from his apartment, sipping his morning coffee. The big game is today, and he waits now for the president to arrive with his late model Chevy, and their two beautiful young dates. He doesn't know the president well, but hopes that will soon change. He is wearing his very best clothing: his brown heavy coat with the tan pattern, his orange scarf, his dark alligator shoes with the small tassels. They'll be here in an hour, he thinks with satisfaction, preparing to eat a leisurely pre-game breakfast.

But then he looks up at the clock; hours have passed, the game already started, half over by now he thinks. He rushes out of the restaurant, looking frantically up and down the street. No sign of cars. He suddenly thinks of all the times he's been forgotten, the times left at the playground, the school parties missed. But they must have come by, waited for hours he thinks, and somehow he didn't know they were out there. They finally had no choice but to leave; they couldn't be late for the game. He walks across the street and climbs the narrow stairs to his third floor apartment. Opening the door he sees her sitting stiffly on his couch, hands clenched in her lap.

Her black hair is filthy, plastered to her skull. He senses just a hint of corrupted flesh beneath her rough, bluish lips.

He thinks he recognizes her. The president had brought her to the house initiation night. After the blindfolded bobbing for peeled bananas in a tub of pudding, after the nose-to-anus farting matches, the hard licks with the paddle and the naphtha poured on the groin, they'd been led one by one into her room. She'd been pale and silent, her high cheekbones flushed in the dim light, and they'd each fucked her, a minute or two apiece.

Her nose had been running the whole time, he remembers.

She rises from the sofa and approaches him. Livid scars criss-cross her wrists and forearms.

He gazes about his room, looking for a nice outfit to wear to the game, pretending she isn't there. His eyes rest on a pile of soiled, stained underwear by the couch. He can't smell them, but imagines their corpse-like scent, like a pile of dead white sewer rats. He is suddenly anxious that she might have seen them. He stares at her in intense agitation as she reaches her arms out for him. He is filled with acute embarrassment for himself.

After blocks of strenuous running, he finally makes it to the bus, leaping to the first step just before the driver closes the doors. The driver pays no attention as he drops his coins into the metal box. He momentarily wonders if he could have gotten away without paying, so intent is the driver on some scene ahead.

He strides to the middle of the bus, slightly out of breath, grabbing a seat near the side doors so he can hurry out when they reach the stadium.

The bus contains a half dozen passengers, all of them old, quiet, and somewhat unattractive. One old man has a large purple birthmark covering the side of his face; wart-like growths, also deep purple, spot the area under his right eye. He suddenly realizes he can't hear the sounds of the traffic outside.

When the bus pulls to his stop he leaps out the door, and momentarily the illusion of soundlessness follows him into the street outside. When the traffic noise returns, he is staring up at a white-washed building with blue tile roof, his apartment house.

He begins climbing the stairs to his apartment on the tenth floor.

Three of his fraternity brothers pick him up at the restaurant across the street from his apartment building. He's just had a leisurely breakfast of coffee, cereal and eggs, the waitress was pretty and smiled a lot, and he is now ready to have a wonderful time at today's big game.

When he gets into the car, the late model Chevy, his three brothers compliment him on his choice in clothing, the heavy brown coat with tan pattern, the orange scarf. They joke a bit, slap each other's shoulders, and pull rapidly out of their parking space.

His brothers ask him if he'd like a little sip from their flask. He replies no, thank you, I have my own. But as he reaches into his back pocket he discovers it missing, dropped out somewhere in the scramble to be on time, no doubt, so yes, he would care for a small slug.

He raises the flask high over his mouth and pours the warm yellow liquor. Some splashes on his bright orange scarf. He feels panicky, has an urge to wipe it off before it stains the beautiful material, but for some reason seems unable to. He drinks, endlessly it seems. He drinks.

The brothers sing old fraternity and college songs, between various versions swapping stories of fraternity life. Rush. Initiation night and all the fun they had. How all the girls are dazzled by a fraternity jacket. The dumb pledge who almost suffocated when a five-foot mock grave collapsed on him. Chug-a-lugging "Purple Jesuses": Vodka, rum, grapes, oranges, and lemon juice. The night they caught a pig, beat it, kicked it, dragged it across the parking lot, hung it up by the snout, and then finally drowned it in the bathtub.

He remembers his old pledge buddy, a fat kid no one else liked. They had driven him ten miles up into the mountains the day before initiation. He hadn't seen him since.

The brothers are taking a new road to the stadium, one he's sure he's never seen before. It meanders out into the country, through patches of wood and around fields and small farms. He has a moment of uneasiness, worried that perhaps they plan to leave him out here, that he'll never make it to the game on time.

As the car rounds a wide bend in a wooded section, it slows.

The brothers stop the car and the driver races the engine. They stare into the clearing a hundred feet ahead and slightly below them.

On a stump beside the road there is a body, lying face up, the back and rump resting on the flat cross-section. Its red shift is tattered and water-spotted.

The driver yells at the top of his lungs, the other two brothers chorusing. They sound like coyotes. The car lurches forward, bearing down on the stump. The brother at the front passenger window pulls a small pistol out of the glove compartment.

As the car suddenly swerves around the stump the brother puts two bullets into the body's torso.

He can see that there are dozens of other bullet holes and torn places in the body's skin. He also notices that it might have been a man, or a woman with short hair. Certainly sexless by now, however.

As the car speeds out of the woods, his brothers laughing and hollering, he looks back at the clearing. He can see another car approaching in the distance. He thinks the body is stirring, about to rise, and his legs tighten up at this thought. He knows that if he were standing by the stump, and if the body did rise, he would not be able to move his legs. He would be unable to run away. But then he realizes this is all just his imagination, that it's the wind rustling the few remaining rags on the corpse, that no, it isn't going to rise.

He sees a gun appear at the window of the distant car, preparing to put more bullets into the body. A road sign, he thinks.

He figures it's no more than fifteen minutes to kickoff.

Outside the stadium he stumbles and falls in the gravel. He's going to miss the kickoff, and he was so close. He'd been lucky to catch the bus; he'd flagged it down, in fact. He is worried about the woman back in his apartment, probably even now looking at all his scattered clothing, his unkempt rooms. He is worried about his torn brown pants, his scuffed alligator shoes. He worries about the fact of the corpse back on the stump, the fact that he will no doubt miss the kickoff.

He runs into his parents as he nears the stadium entrance.

They look so old. His old father, his shriveled lips unable to catch the moisture dripping from his mouth as he speaks, pleads with him, wondering why he hasn't answered their phone calls. His aged mother nods, distracted, singing to herself.

His father grabs him by the arm, pulling him closer conspiratorially, whispering hoarsely, Your mother . . . she hasn't been the same, and Don't go in there. First time I had it . . . down by one of the old sorority houses. She pulled me back into the bushes . . . unzipped me, stuck it up there herself . . . was awful, like a big old frying pan in there . . .

He pulls away from the old man and pushes past his mother, seeking the stadium entrance. He sees nothing but a smooth limestone wall. Where is it? He's going to be late.

His beautiful young date is in there waiting for him, her bony fingers encircling a paper cup full of beer.

As he enters the stadium it's a few minutes to halftime. It has been a long walk. The crowd seems strangely silent, as if they were watching an engrossing chess match.

But he's forgotten his tickets, now he knows this, and knows too that he will therefore be unable to watch the game. He searches the crowd for his fraternity president, their beautiful dates, his beautiful date, but it's impossible in this crowd. Everyone looks the same, dressed in grays, blacks, dark blues, their faces pale, hair cropped short. When they try to cheer the players out on the field, no sound comes out.

An usher touches his arm from behind and he begins formulating an excuse for not having a ticket but the usher says nothing, instead leads him to a seat a dozen rows down, on the aisle.

He is sitting next to a family of spectators. They all have light brown hair, the father, the mother, the daughter and son, and perfect smiles, displayed to each other, not to him, in their mutual pride. They clap in unison to approve some play on the field, though strangely, he seems unable to see, to get the field into proper focus. Their clapping makes no sense.

He looks around a bit. Rows of spectators, stacked at an angle, back and upwards, as far as he can see. But except for the family sitting next to him, he can discern no movement, not even a nervous tic. He again looks at the family beside him, and is drawn to their smooth, tucked-in lips. And their light blue pallor.

Discomfited, he stands up and starts down the aisle toward the field, still unable to get the players into focus. No one attempts to stop him. He reaches the retaining wall above the sidelines, climbs on top, and jumps down, the thud of his feet in the grass the only sound he can hear.

When he reaches the center of the field he turns around. There's no one on the field. The stands seem empty. A slight breeze begins to rustle the grass.

He attempts to reenter the stadium through the tunnel leading to the players' dressing rooms. The light here is dim.

Mummified corpses line the walls, sprawl over dressing tables and tile shower floors. The bodies have lost most of their flesh and only thin strands of hair remain. They still wear their scarlet jerseys, though most of the color has leached away. Bones in white or sporty gold togs peer out of open lockers.

Entering the stadium he discovers to his relief that the game hasn't yet started. All seems well. No corpses, parents, or strange women to trouble him. He pulls his ticket out of his unwrinkled pants pocket and makes his way to a seat on the fifty-yard line. His friends are all there and are overjoyed to see him.

The fraternity president slaps him on the back and says, "Great to have you here. Wouldn't be the same without you. And say . . . after the game, I'd like to talk to you about your maybe becoming our new pledge master."

His fraternity brothers pass on their congratulations from their seats further down the aisle.

The crowd suddenly leaps to its feet to cheer the upcoming kickoff. He is thrilled by the motion, color, and sound. His fraternity brothers are slapping each other on the back, stamping feet, shouting, and bussing their pretty dates on the cheeks. Popcorn and empty cups fly through the air. Frisbees are tossed from section to section.

He turns to greet his beautiful young date with an embrace. She opens her mouth widely. He notes the blueness of her throat. She grins and shows her perfect white teeth.

Later he climbs the steps for popcorn and soft drinks for the girls. He wonders if he might not just marry his date someday; she seems so much like him. The day is going so well now, and he wonders if maybe it's time for him to finally settle down, maybe have a family.

He is slowly aware of two arms, clothed in tatters of red, coming around his sides from behind as if to embrace him. The hands are thin, almost bone.

Everything is suddenly quiet again.

LITTLE CRUELTIES

He had changed. Sometimes he didn't recognize himself. His voice sounded wrong—the timbre was unfamiliar, the vocabulary wasn't his, the opinions were unrecognizable. And he did things he could not have imagined.

Again and again, Paul came back to the incident with the chicks. It had been only a little thing, a small cruelty. Something he could never feel proud of, certainly, but not an act that deserved such intense shame. Ten years ago, for Christ's sake. Joey had been only five. He couldn't have taken care of the chicks, anyway. He wasn't old enough. He was old enough for resentment, however. He'd always been old enough for that.

It had been their last Easter in the old house. Joey had wanted chicks. Paul had explained very carefully how they had no place to keep pets like that in the city—their yard was too small, and he didn't want animals smelling up the basement or the garage. They had a nice old urban home; they didn't live on a farm, for Christ's sake. And he was too little to take proper care of them anyway. Mom or Dad would end up taking care of them and that wasn't very fair, now was it?

Joey had cried so much that weekend that Eve had finally given in, going out the Saturday before Easter and coming back with the three yellow chicks. Paul hadn't even known about it until Joey'd brought the basket in for him to see, all excited and thanking him profusely, climbing up on his lap—basket and chicks tipping precariously—to kiss him sloppily on the cheek.

Paul had been furious, but he couldn't say no. Joey was too excited. Besides, Paul couldn't let himself be the bad guy.

It snowed in April that year. Freakishly late, and heavy. The yard and the hill behind the house were white ice. The chicks were sick, losing feathers, near death. Joey had failed to take care of them, just as Paul had predicted. He didn't take any pleasure in that; it was just simple fact.

They were suffering. Paul felt terrible about it—it was his responsibility. He was Joey's father, after all. He had to do the right thing. He got up at dawn, dressed warmly, and sneaked into Joey's bedroom to get the chicks. They were so sick, he would take pains to remember, that they barely made any noise when he picked up the box. Joey was dead to the world, the covers twisted tightly around his legs. Paul stopped for a moment, set the chicks down, and freed his son.

He walked up the slight hill in his heavy winter boots, the ice-covered snow crackling with each step. The chicks began to shiver, but remained silent. When he reached the top of the hill he found he couldn't go any farther, and he also couldn't see himself setting the chicks gently down into the snow. It was a failure of nerve. He'd wanted to do the right thing. He suddenly tossed the box over to the other side and turned away. A cat, maybe a dog, would take care of them.

On his way back into the house he thought about fraternity pranks he'd heard about in college. Pig embryos left in a sorority house. Dead dogs mailed to opposing football coaches. A snow-ball of frozen chicks. But he'd wanted to do the right thing.

It was ridiculous to think that the death of chicks might diminish him somehow.

Paul told Joey that the chicks had died during the night and that he'd disposed of them. The boy cried most of the next day. "I wanted to bury 'em," he'd said between sniffles. "They were mine."

"It's too cold outside. The ground's frozen."

"Then how did you do it?"

Paul couldn't look him directly in the eyes. "I'm a grown-up man. I can shovel better than you can."

"I don't think I believe you. You buried 'em? Good?" His son moved closer. Paul never failed to be surprised, almost appalled, by the directness of the little boy.

"Yes, I . . . I buried them." From the way Joey nodded, Paul knew he'd believed that, at least at the moment. But the doubt was still obviously latent in his son.

Paul was up at dawn the next day, raking gloved fingers through the top layers of snow that still covered the shaded hill.

Every few minutes he found a clump of wet mud and leaves, or dog shit masquerading as one of the rancid little corpses, but the dead chicks eluded him. He thought maybe he'd been lucky and a neighborhood animal had in fact eaten them or dragged them away.

He gave up when he saw Joey's bedroom light come on. In a few minutes the child would be down in the family room for his morning cartoons.

Later Paul would think that all these actions were not normal for him. If he'd just had time to think about it, plan it out, then maybe he would have behaved better. As it was, he could not recognize himself. He could not fully accept the things he was doing.

Two days after the thaw, he saw Joey playing with the desiccated chick corpses in the back yard, passing them from hand to hand like lumps of gray modeling clay. Paul had to restrain himself from going out and stopping it, from explaining how dead things bore germs, how dead things might make a little boy sick.

Joey had to know what his father had done. But they never talked about it; neither of them could even bring it up. Paul had just wanted to do the right thing.

What Joey would never understand, what none of them seemed to understand, was how much it pained Paul to hurt his son. It happened too often, he knew, and always in such little ways, but it wasn't as if he wanted the hurt to happen. He just couldn't stop the little cruelties from happening to Joey (even when he seemed to be so much a part of them), any more than he could stop the little cruelties from happening to himself. Sometimes Paul didn't understand the situation, and so Joey was punished unnecessarily. Sometimes Paul did something—like take a particular toy away from his son, or deny him a trip to a neighbor's house, or devise a particular kind of punishment—that was meant to help the child grow up. But sometimes it backfired, and on reminiscence it appeared to be a cruel thing. But Paul had tried to do the right thing—he'd done the best he could. That was the way of things; that was the way the world usually worked. For Christ's sake—he loved his son.

In any case, the city was no place for animals.

Sometimes he imagined he heard his son crying in the night.

Little cruelties. It was the small malevolences, the tiny hate-fulnesses, the lesser portions of ruthlessness which had always made Paul's life in the city seem a little sour, and which finally led him to move his family out of the old house on Parker Street.

Joey hadn't wanted to go—all his friends were there, friends he'd be starting first grade with. Paul tried to be reasonable, but how many close friends could a six-year-old have, anyway?

Eve hadn't liked the idea either, but was willing to go along with whatever Paul thought was right.

Paul had no doubts.

He didn't know what it was about the city that made people act the way they did—whether it was because of overcrowding (he thought often of those experiments in which mice were packed into a confined space), or lack of contact with the ground (you spent 99 percent of your time on concrete or asphalt), or the deterioration in municipal services (on how many mornings was the first thing he smelled garbage?), or some sort of degeneration of the species. But every day he saw more and more tense people, more and more crazy people.

He saw people trapped in the middle of traffic jams, going berserk when someone cut in front of them—ramming the other car repeatedly with their own, getting out and trying to drag the other driver out through a window.

He had neighbors who couldn't keep a sprinkler head, or a hose, or even a trash can for more than a few months at a time, before it was stolen or destroyed. Security lights didn't make any difference, and small nightly destructions had become so commonplace you didn't bother to distinguish the sounds.

Every day someone was insulted. Saying it made it sound banal, but Paul had become convinced that the little insults people had to endure each day—the "We can't do it, it's not procedure," delivered by a minor government official, the "How many other stores have you stuck?" from some anonymous bill collector on the phone, the "You have to do something about your weight," from an employer—were dragging people down gradually to the level of the animals. People stepped on you, and there really wasn't a lot you could do without getting yourself into a great deal of trouble.

Paul himself felt slighted a dozen different ways each week. No one seemed capable of seeing that he was hurt by their remarks. He did his best—surely that was worth a great deal in the scheme of things. And yet every encounter hid a potential insult.

Little cruelties. He didn't discuss them aloud with anyone—more often than not, putting his complaints into words made them sound faintly ridiculous. Occasionally he was moved to write a letter to the editor concerning the latest such lapse in human compassion: the woman who got rid of the cookies molding in her cookie jar by passing them out to kids on Halloween, the man who was charged for leaving a puppy tied to a tree for two days in the pouring rain, the neighbor's little girl who sneaked into her best friend's closet and tore up all her dresses when she wouldn't lend her doll. These people never murdered anybody. These were little crimes, little cruelties. But as these unkind examples accumulated Paul began to see them as monstrous in their implications. His letters were eloquent, but he rarely mailed them.

The little cruelties were the worst. They made each day a series of subliminal defeats. Trying to stop them seemed futile—they were too much a part of life in the city. He could never decide if it was the city changing the people, or the people changing the city.

Sometimes he thought he could hear his son crying in the night. It had been like that for a very long time—the faintest echo of a wail, or a howl, as if the boy had shrunk back to embryonic size or smaller and was being tortured in some other world. He used to check on his son, climb down the two flights of stairs to his room, where he always slept soundly, where the covers had been knocked awry with his feet, and Paul was compelled to fix them, tuck his beautiful boy in, kiss him lovingly somewhere in the nimbus of down that covered his face, awed still again by the sweet smell of him. After a few years he finally stopped the checking—he now knew it probably wasn't his son who'd cried out, and there no longer was any excuse for the nocturnal visitation.

Sometimes he thought he could hear his son crying in the

night. But he knew that could not be. Particularly now, when Joey no longer lived there. He wondered how many times it had happened that you heard a distressed voice in the night—someone crying or screaming, someone asking for help—but you did nothing, because that sort of thing happens all the time in the city, and you didn't know if the person crying was drunk or stoned or just crazy. And there was always the possibility that there might be danger for you there, even from a phone call, because they always seemed to know who had complained. And in any case you'd give it away by your actions—standing by the windows and holding the curtains apart, to see what the police were going to do.

But Paul still believed it was a bad thing not to call—people might die if you didn't. People died all the time because of inaction, because of all the small neglects.

The day they moved into their new house didn't go smoothly. Paul made a mistake arranging for the truck and had to pay double for a replacement. Eve complained that she didn't have adequate time to pack, and spent the last few days cramming unsorted clothing, papers, and junk into cartons and garbage bags. And at the last minute she discovered a whole new series of complaints.

"I'm going to lose my friends, my Wednesday-afternoon bridge club, and the good fresh meat from Kelsey's butcher. Not to mention Jimmy the flower vendor—he's been giving me free cut flowers at the end of every weekday for over five years now!" She looked up from her packing and glared at him. "What are you giving up, Paul?"

Paul couldn't stand to be in the same room with her when she was like that. He headed for the door. "It's for our safety, for Christ's sake! I'm just trying to fulfill my responsibility, but I guess you just can't see that."

Joey had been alternatingly crying and sullen. Some of his friends had come by to see him, but he'd refused to come downstairs, even when Paul got angry with him about it. They just didn't understand what he was trying to do for them.

Christ, they thought he was being thoughtless. They thought

he didn't care about their feelings. They thought he was being cruel.

The new house was meant to protect his family. He'd spent years trying to find just such a place. It wasn't actually outside the city, but in a small community called Globeville, which had been segmented and virtually torn apart when two crossing interstates were built over it. Most of the commuters who passed over it every day didn't even know it existed.

The day they drove to the new house Eve had seemed increasingly anxious. Paul found the Globeville neighborhood quaint, and appealingly isolated. Eve thought it looked like a slum.

"Half the stores are boarded up!"

"We can still do our shopping in the city, if you like." She was going to spoil their first day with an argument. She was always starting the arguments. He never could see any reason to argue.

"I haven't seen a single restaurant or grocery store that isn't out of business."

"There's a pretty good Mexican restaurant down here, and a couple of bars. And a grocery store, just a little smaller than Kelsey's, but I'm sure they stock enough for most of our needs."

"So where is everybody, Dad?" It was the first thing Joey had said since he got into the car.

"They're mostly old people. People who have lived here all their lives, even some who were here before they built the interstate—that's one of the best things about the neighborhood. I guess old people don't always get outside that often." But Paul himself was vaguely disturbed by the almost empty streets.

Somehow the neighborhood seemed shabbier to him with Joey and Eve in the car. A large percentage of the houses hadn't been repainted in years. A number of the empty buildings served as warehouses for downtown businesses who wanted storage facilities midway to the suburbs. There were delivery trucks parked along the streets, but very few cars. Most of the cars he could see were in the yards, up on blocks and overgrown with weeds, rusting to a dirty cinnamon color. For a moment Paul wondered if it might be the city air settling here.

But it could be seen as peaceful. Certainly he could see it that way. Despite the fact that the highways were almost on top of them, the combination of trees and elevated roadway kept the neighborhood relatively quiet.

"It is . . . nice, Paul." There was hesitation in her voice. Paul looked up. A slight hill on their left. They'd arrived.

The Victorian house was in great shape. Paul had checked it out with the realtor several times. Most of the exterior wood-work—the gleaming white frills and gingerbread—was intact, as if immune to the acidic pollution which had taken its toll on old houses in other parts of the city. The red brick walls and gray stone foundations were firm and showed no signs of crumbling or even discoloration. Perhaps his favorite features were the two round towers—like sentry turrets—that rose from the second story, one at each corner. And for all that sense of age, the house had a modern kitchen and a good heating plant. The house was going to keep the city available to them when they needed it, and yet still provide a sanctuary.

An evolution was afoot; human beings were being trans-formed within the concrete womb of the city, into what he didn't even want to speculate. The evidence was all around them, the cruelties accumulating into a disease of harshness spreading throughout every metropolitan area.

But Eve and Joey—they just didn't want to see it. He probably should have moved them all to the country.

"The neighborhood's terrible!" Eve's complaints became a familiar litany. "There isn't any crime, but it's so dirty here, Paul. I clean the house top to bottom and it needs dusting again almost the very next day!"

"It's an old house, Eve. You get dust in old houses. But at least it's not like the pollution we had to live with before. Admit it. Wasn't that a lot worse?"

"There's nothing to do here!"

Maybe if he had it all to do over again he'd move them to the country, but he'd felt the need to monitor the progress of the city's disease, and Globeville provided him the perfect vantage point. . . .

Now, he would sometimes gaze out his bedroom window and see Joey digging up the back yard, straightening up occasionally to examine the balls of dirt in his hands. But Joey and Eve had been gone for years, Eve long before Joey, and in any case Joey would be at least sixteen now, and this was a younger Joey excavating his lawn, silently examining the moist dirt and drier clay, looking for dead Easter chicks.

Sometimes he did not recognize himself. His sadness belonged to someone else.

Eve left less than a year after they'd moved into the Globeville house. He supposed it was inevitable—she missed her friends and she could see nothing in Paul's theories, which even he knew were becoming a bit of an obsession.

What he could not understand was the way she left Joey behind. He was just a child, her child. He gathered she had said goodbye to the boy, but Joey never would tell him what she'd said.

He changed. Sometimes he could not recognize himself. Raising his son on his own was far different from what he'd imagined it would be. Paul never knew how to act. He didn't know how to convince his son that his intentions were good, whatever mistakes he might make.

He could not convince his son to love him.

Sometimes he hid his son's toys. Sometimes he took Joey's homework out of his Road Runner notebook and threw it away. Sometimes he slipped down to the basement and threw the circuit breakers, and the little boy who was terrified of the dark was forced to struggle through rooms of shadow and sudden night.

Sometimes he heard his son cry out faintly in the darkness and he did not come.

"Your son is bullying the other children." The voice on the phone was distant, unreliable. He should never have allowed Joey to attend school in the city.

"No, not my son. You must be mistaken."

"He curses the teachers. He writes vile things on the walls. He defaces school property."

"No, no. It's the school. It's you people. I should be educating him here, in our own home."

"He's cruel to . . ."

"What's wrong is you people! I've seen the way you let the children hang around outside the school, smoking and laughing, acting like little adults for Christ's sake! Not like children at all. You've robbed them of their childhoods. No wonder they think they can say whatever they please."

He slammed the phone down, shaking. He could hear Joey moving around downstairs.

He wondered if Eve had sensed that Joey too had become infected by the cruelty.

He wondered if Eve ever suspected what had really happened to the chicks.

He had gone downstairs to talk to Joey. Maybe he was going to talk to Joey about the chicks. Maybe he was just going to discuss the boy's behavior in school. He would never be quite sure.

When he walked into the kitchen Joey was sitting cross-legged on the floor. He had two oblong lumps of clay, passing them from hand to hand. He looked serene, contented. He made no sounds, but Paul could almost hear the gentle hum the boy's mind must have made. Paul looked past his son, and saw that the floor was dirty. Gray and white animal fur adhered to the green tile. A sticky substance stained the floor and the lower part of the pale yellow cabinets. He looked back at his son. Now he could see the faint pinkness in the clay lumps, the edges of red, the small gaping mouths with sharp teeth. For several days there had been a poster on the telephone pole outside their house announcing two lost kittens. The lettering was crude, done with crayon, and above the lettering there was a crayon illustration of the two missing pets—one of them gray and one of them white.

Joey stared at him, as if waiting. Paul's lips moved silently, as if by themselves. He turned and went back up the stairs.

That night Paul heard things in the darkness, small cries and whispers. He imagined someone somewhere was in need of help. But he did not leave his bed.

The next morning Joey was gone.

Today, on foot and on his way back from the grocery store, he had seen Joey, or someone who looked like Joey, standing across the street from the Globeville house, watching it. He'd run to catch the teenager but the grocery sacks were too bulky and he didn't want to drop them.

Joey had been gone several years now. Paul couldn't even be

sure he was still alive. The police were of no help—in fact, for a time they seemed to suspect that Paul had actually done something to Joey. As if he were a murderer. That had been a cruel suspicion, and by it Paul knew they'd been infected the same as everyone else. Finally they concluded that Joey had run away to, or been kidnapped by, his mother. They weren't optimistic about ever finding him.

Paul couldn't see it. Eve had abandoned Joey, so why would he leave his father? It wasn't as if his father were a murderer, a thief, a fiend. He knew his son must be dead. Someone had taken the boy from his bed, and the cruelties had just gotten out of hand. They had a way of doing that, cruelties did, as if they had a life of their own.

And yet the boy was outside, in the night, digging up his father's yard.

It was a cruel thing.

Even chicks had their place in the scheme of things. Their deaths could change how you lived within the world.

Eventually, Paul began seeing Joey, or someone who looked like Joey, nearly every afternoon. Passing in front of the Globeville house, but on the other side of the street, like a shy lover.

At night, the boy excavated his yard.

During the day, Paul could see the changes that had occurred to brick and wood, the subtle disintegrations so like plant blight, or cancer.

Paul made sure his windows and doors were locked at night. Sometimes he would wake up and watch the ceiling over his bed, where the shadows of windblown tree limbs and thick power lines tangled over a dim yellow oval of glare. He thought he could hear the sound of narrow hands sliding repeatedly into soft earth, like a dying fish flapping on a sodden wooden plank.

"It's not as if I tried to hurt anyone," he'd whisper to the dark.

He'd hear his own voice crying softly in the distance, and no one bothered to investigate.

He'd seen no one on the street in front of his house for days, but he hadn't been out, and the weather was breezy. Mostly old people, retired people lived here, and the air might have been too much for them.

Despite the breeze the pollution was bad, which was a little hard to figure. Black, cottony lines of smoke floated low over the buildings—a chimney must be working somewhere, he thought. The sunsets were soiled shades of magenta, orange, red, and bruise-colored. During Indian summer the clouds started to bleed after four o'clock.

The gutters were lined with trash, but then that had happened before. A jurisdiction problem between municipal sanitation departments. There appeared to be more cracks in the pavement out front than he remembered, but these back streets got short shrift on road repair.

Stray slivers of noxious pollution rubbed the brick edges of his house. Red decay powdered the gray-green bushes planted near the house's exterior walls. Occasionally he'd open a window but then shortly would close it because of the smell. Periods of still air trapped the stench in his neighborhood.

Eve had insisted that the house needed cleaning every other day. He had never much seen the point. He kept the garbage in airtight bags on the back porch, and someday he would haul it all out. He kept the door to the back porch closed, except when he needed to add another bag to the pile.

He watched a many-legged insect—he couldn't remember the name—leave a thin trail up the dining room wall.

Dead insects filled the windowsills. Some nights the house grew stuffy and he ached to open the windows, but he was afraid.

Weeds grew over the curb and softened the borders of the street.

The guttering along the eaves rusted. One of the exit pipes turned brown and fell into the yard. Then he never saw it again. The grass swallowed it. The grass swallowed the walk and he became afraid of stepping into the yard.

The pipes made cracking noises in the night. He secretly hoped the pipes would break and separate completely—they linked him to the city's sewer system.

Graffiti grew along the walls of his beautiful, strong house like a vine, flowing with the grain of the brick, then separating, multiplying, seeking any empty space.

One night his garage roof fell under its own weight, crushing his car, but the gas tank had been empty anyway.

Toward the end of the month it rained for several days. When it was over he stood out on his front porch. Water had flooded the gutters. The sewer vomited. Yolky and cinnamon-colored liquids oozed out of the sewer grates and stained the pavement. A grayish human corpse lay face down with its skull against the opposite curb, the viscous water nudging it rhythmically. Paul had the urge to go down and touch it, pick up the lifeless arm and the head, play with it, pass the disease from hand to hand. Sores spotted his lawn. Paul went back in and secured the door.

He could never decide if it was the city changing the people, or the people changing the city.

Joey dug up his back yard. Great piles of earth lay sprawled, decayed while they slept. They cried softly in the distance, but no one called the police.

Paul wandered the darkened rooms of his sanctuary, the dried bodies of insects crackling under his old socks. Sometimes he would try to open a window, brushing leaves and wallpaper chips and brittle insect hulls from the window ledge, but the window fell apart when he lifted.

He watched Joey painting huge green, white, blue graffiti in the middle of the street. Somebody should have stopped him, but no one left their quiet, worn houses. He watched Joey breaking the windows of the house next door.

"It's not as if I were . . ." he tried to say.

Paul mourned the day and cried in his sleep. He bruised his cruel hands against the walls, and scratched at his cruel face with the broken fingernails.

All the next day Paul waited by his empty body while Joey called from the distant tunnel he had dug for himself underground, that snaked its way under the yard and curled in on itself deep under the house.

No one knew him, or recognized his absence, or the minute reduction of cruelties in the world once he had disappeared.

Around him the concrete rotted, the city pavements grew rancid.

THE MEN AND WOMEN OF RIVENDALE

The thing he would remember most about his days, his weeks at the Rivendale resort—had it really been weeks?—was not the enormous lobby and dining room, nor the elaborately carved mahogany woodwork framing the library, nor even the men and women of Rivendale themselves, with their bright eyes and pale, almost hairless, heads and hands. The thing he would remember most was the room he and Cathy stayed in, the way she looked when she curled up in bed, her bald head rising weakly over her shoulders, the way the dark brocade curtains hung so heavily, trapping dust and light in their intricate folds.

Frank thought he had spent days staring into those folds. He had only two places to look in that room: at the cancer-ridden sack his wife had become, her giant eyes, her grotesque, baby-like face, so stripped of age since she had begun her decline. Or at the curtains, constantly adrift with shadows. They were of a dark, burgundy-colored material, and he never knew if they had darkened with dust and age or if they were meant to be just that shade. If he examined the curtains at close range he could make out the tiny leaf and shell patterns embroidered over the entire surface. From a distance, when he sat in the chair or lay on the bed, they looked like hundreds of tiny, hungry mouths.

Cathy had told him little about the place before they came—that it was a resort in Pennsylvania, in the countryside south of Erie, and that it used to have hot springs. He hadn't asked, but he wondered what happened to the spring water when it left such a place. As if somebody somewhere had turned a tap. It didn't make any sense to him; natural things shouldn't work that way.

Her ancestors, the family Rivendale, had run the place when it was still a resort. Now many, perhaps all of her relatives lived in the Rivendale Resort Hotel, or in cottages spotted around the sprawling grounds. Probably several dozen cottages in all. It had been quite a jolt when Frank walked into the place, stumbling over the entrance rug with their luggage wedged under his arms, and saw all these Rivendales sitting around the fireplace in the lobby. It wasn't as if they were clones, or anything like that. But there was this uneasy sort of family resemblance. Something about the flesh tones, the shape of the hands, the perpetually arched eyebrows, the sharp angle at which they held their heads, the irregular pink splotches on their cheeks. It gave him a little chill. After a few days at Rivendale he recognized part of the reason for that chill: the cancer had molded Cathy into a fuzzy copy of a Rivendale.

Frank remembered her as another woman entirely: her hair had been long and honey-brown, and there had been real color in her cheeks. She had been lively, her movements strong and fluid, an incredibly sleek, beautiful woman who could have been a model, though such a public display would have appalled her and, he knew without asking, would have disgraced the Rivendale name.

Cathy had told him that filling up with cancer was like roasting under a hot sun sometimes. The dusty rooms and dark chambers of Rivendale cooled her. They would stay at Rivendale as long as possible, she had said. She could hide from nurses and doctors there.

She wouldn't have surgery. She was a Rivendale; it didn't fit. She washed herself in radiation, and, after Frank met these other Rivendales with their scrubbed and antiseptic flesh, the thought came to him: she'd over-bathed.

She never looked or smelled bad, as he'd expected. The distortions the growing cancer made within the skin that covered it were more subtle than that. Sometimes she complained of her legs suddenly weakening. Sometimes she would scream in the middle of the night. He'd look at her pale form and try to see through her translucent flesh, find the cancer feeding and thriving there.

One result of her treatments was that Cathy's belly blew up. She looked at least six months pregnant, maybe more. It had never occurred to either of them to have children. They'd always had too much to do; a child didn't have a place in the schedule. Sometimes now Frank dreamed he was wheeling her into the delivery room, running, trying to get her to the doctors before her terrible labor ceased. A tall doctor in a brilliant white mask always met him at the wide swinging doors. The doctor took Cathy away from him but blocked Frank from seeing what kind of child they delivered from her heaving, discolored belly.

Nine months after the cancer was diagnosed, the invitation from the Rivendales was delivered. Cathy, who'd barely mentioned her family in all the years they'd been married, welcomed it with a grim excitement he'd never seen in her before. Frank discovered the invitation in the trash later that afternoon. "Come to Rivendale" was all it said.

One of the uncles greeted her at the desk, although "greeted" was probably the wrong word. He checked her in, as if this were still a resort. Even gave her a room key with the resort tag still attached, although now the leather was cracked and the silver lettering hard to read. Only a few of the relatives had bothered to look up from their reading, their mouths twitching as if they were attempting speech after years of muteness. But no one spoke; no one welcomed them. As far as Frank could tell, no one in the crowded, quiet lobby was speaking to anyone else.

They'd gone up to their room immediately; the trip had exhausted Cathy. Then Frank spent his first of many evenings sitting up in the old chair, staring at Cathy curled up on the bed, and staring at the curtains breathing the breeze from the window, the indecipherable embroidered patterns shifting restlessly.

The next morning they were awakened by a bell ringing downstairs. The sound was so soft Frank at first thought it was a dream, wind-chimes tinkling outside. But Cathy was up immediately, and dressing. Frank did the same, suddenly not wanting to initiate any action by himself. When another bell rang Cathy opened the door and started downstairs, and Frank followed her.

Two places were set for them at one of the long, linen-draped tables. "Cathy" and "Frank," the place cards read. He wondered briefly if there might be someone else staying here by those names, so surprised he was to see his name written on the card in floral script. But Cathy took her chair immediately, and he sat down beside her.

There was a silent toast. When the uncle who had met them at the desk tapped his glass of apple wine lightly with a fork, the rest raised their glasses silently to the air, and then a beat later tipped them back to drink. Cathy drank in time with the others, and that simple bit of coordination and exaggerated manners made Frank uneasy. He remained one step behind all the others, watching them over the lip of his glass. They didn't seem aware of each other, but they were almost, though not quite, synchronized.

He glanced at Cathy; her cheek had grown pale and taut as she drank. She wasn't eating real food anymore, only a special formula she took like medicine to sustain her. Although her skin was almost baby-smooth now, the lack of fat had left wrinkles that deepened as she moved. Death lines.

After breakfast they lingered by the enormous dining room window. Cathy watched as the Rivendales drifted across the front lawn in twos and threes. Their movements were slow and languid, like ancient fish in shallow, sun-drenched waters.

"Shouldn't we introduce ourselves around?" Frank said softly. "I mean, we were invited by someone. How do these people even know who we are?"

"Oh, they know, Frank. Hush now; the Rivendales have always had their own way of doing things. Someone will come to us in time. Meanwhile, we enjoy ourselves."

"Sure."

They took a long walk around the grounds. The pool was closed and covered with canvas. The shuffleboard courts were cracked, the cracks pulled further apart by grass and tree roots. And the tennis courts . . . the tennis courts were his first inkling that perhaps he should be trying to convince her of the need to return home.

The tennis courts at Rivendale were built atop a slight, tree-shaded rise behind the main building. He heard the yowling and screeching as they climbed the rise, so loud that he couldn't make out any individual voices. It frightened him so that he grabbed Cathy by the arm and started back down. But she seemed unperturbed by the noise and shrugged away from him, continuing to walk toward the trees, her pace unchanging.

"Cathy . . . I don't think . . ." But she was oblivious to him.

So Frank followed her, reluctantly. As they neared the fenced enclosure the howling increased, and Frank knew that it wasn't people in there making all the noise, but animals, though he had never heard animal sounds quite like those.

As they passed the last tree Frank stopped, unable to proceed. Cathy walked right up to the fence. She pressed close to the wire, but not so close the outstretched paws could touch her.

The tennis courts had become a gigantic cage holding hundreds of cats. An old man stood on a ladder above the wire fence, dumping buckets of feed onto the snarling mass inside. Mesh with glass insulators attached—electrified, Frank thought—stretched across the top of the fence.

The old man turned to Frank and stared. He had the arched eyebrows, the pale skin and blotched cheeks. He smiled at Frank, and the shape of the lips seemed to match the shape of the eyebrows. A smile shaped like moth wings, or a bite-pattern in pale cheese, the teeth gleaming snow-white inside.

Cathy spent most of each day in the expansive Rivendale library, checking titles most of the time, but occasionally sitting down to read from a rare and privately-bound old volume. Every few hours one of the uncles, or cousins, would come in and speak to her in a low voice, nod, and leave. The longer he was here the more difficult it became to tell the Rivendales apart, other than male from female. The younger ones mirrored the older ones, and they were all very close in height, weight, and build.

When Cathy wasn't in the library she sat quietly in the parlor or dining room, or up in their own room catnapping or staring up at the ornate ceiling. She would say every day, almost ritualistically, that he was more than welcome to be with her, but he could see nothing here that he might participate in. Sitting in the parlor or dining room was made almost unbearable by the presence of the family, arranged mummy-like around the rooms. Sometimes he would pick up a volume in the library, but invariably discovered it was some sort of laborious tome on trellis and ornate gardening, French architecture, museum catalogs. Or sometimes an old leather-bound novel that read no better. It was impossible to peruse the books without thinking that whatever Cathy was studying must be far more interesting, but on the days he went he never could find the books she had been looking at, as if they had been kept somewhere special, out of his reach. And for some reason he hesitated to ask after them, or to look over his wife's shoulder as she read. As if he was afraid to.

This growing climate of awkwardness and fear angered Frank so that his neck muscles were always stiff, his head always aching. It was worse because it wasn't entirely unexpected. His relationship with Cathy had been going in this direction for some time. Until he'd met Cathy, he'd almost always been bored. As a child, always needing to be entertained. As an adult, constantly changing lovers and houses and jobs. Now it was happening again, and it frightened him.

The increasing boredom that was beginning to permeate his stay at Rivendale, in fact, had begun to impress on him how completely, utterly bored he had been in his married life. He'd almost forgotten, so preoccupied he'd become with her disease. When Cathy's cancer had first begun, and started to spread, that boredom had dissipated. Perversely, the cancer had brought something new and near-dramatic into their life together. He'd felt bad at first: Cathy, in her baldness, in her body that seemed, impossibly, both emaciated and swollen, had suddenly become sensuous to him again. He wanted to make love to her almost all the time. After the first few times, he had stopped the attempts, afraid to ask her. But as she approached death, his desire increased.

Sometimes Frank sat out on the broad resort lawn, his lounge chair positioned under a low-hanging tree only twenty or so feet away from the library window. He'd watch her as she sat at one of the enormous oak tables, poring over the books, consulting with various elderly Rivendales who drifted in and out of that room in a seemingly endless stream. He'd heard one phrase outside the library, when the Rivendales didn't know he was near, or perhaps he had dreamed his eavesdropping while lying abed late one morning, or fallen asleep midafternoon in his hiding place under the tree. "Family histories."

The pale face with the near-hairless pate that floated as if suspended in that library window bore no resemblance to the Cathy he had known, with her dark eyes and nervous gestures and narrow mouth quick to twist ugly and vituperative. They'd discovered it was so much easier to become excited by anger, rage, and all the small cruelties possible in married life, than by love. They'd had a bad fight on their very first date. He found himself asking her out again in the very heat of the argument. She'd stared at him wide-eyed and breathless for some time, and then grudgingly accepted.

Throughout the following weeks their fights grew worse. Once he'd slapped her, something he would never have imagined himself doing, and she'd fallen sobbing into his arms. They made love for hours. It became a delirious pattern. The screams, the cries, the ineffectual hitting, and then the sweet tickle and swallow of a lust that dragged them red-eyed through the night.

Marriage was a great institution. It gave you the opportunity to experience both sadism and masochism within the privacy and safety of your own home.

"What do you want from me, you bastard?" Cathy's teeth flashed, pinkly ... her lipstick was running, he thought. Frank held her head down against the mattress, watching her tongue flicking back and forth over her teeth. He was trapped.

Her leg came up and knocked him off the bed. He tried to roll away but before he could move she had straddled him, pinning him to the floor. "Off! Get off!" He couldn't catch his breath. He suddenly realized her forearm was wedged between his neck and the floor, cutting off the air. His vision blurred quickly and the pressure began to build in his face.

"Frank ..."

He could barely hear her. He thought he might actually die this time. It was another bad joke; he almost laughed. She was the one who was always talking about dying; she could be damned melodramatic about it. She was the one with the death wish.

He opened his eyes and stared up at her. She was fumbling with his shirt, pulling it loose, ripping the buttons off. Maybe she was trying to save him.

Then he got a better look at her: the feverish eyes, the slackening jaw line, tongue flicking, eyes glazed. Now she was tugging frantically at his belt. It all seemed very familiar and ritualized. He searched her eyes and did not think she even saw him.

"Frank . . ."

He woke with a start and stared across the lawn at the library window. Cathy's pale face stared back at him, surrounded by her even paler brethren, their mouths moving soundlessly, fish-like. He thought he could hear the soft clinking of breaking glass, or hundreds of tiny mouths trying their teeth.

The thing he would remember most was the room, and the Rivendales watching. They had a peculiar way of watching; they were very polite about it, for if nothing else they were gentlemen and ladies, these Rivendales. Theirs was an ancient etiquette, developed through practice and interaction with human beings of all eras and climes. Long before he met Cathy they had known him, followed him, for they had intimate knowledge of his type. Or so he imagined.

Each afternoon there was one who especially drew Frank's attention: an old one, his eyebrows fraying away with the heat like tattered moth wings. He walked the same path each day, wearing it down into a seamless pavement, and only by a slight pause at a particular point on the path did Frank know the old man Rivendale was watching him. Listening to him. And that old one's habitual, everyday patterns were what made Frank wonder if the world might be full of Rivendales, assigned to watch, and recruit.

He was beginning—with excitement—to recognize them, to guess at what they were. They would always feed, and feed viciously, but their hunger was so great they would never be filled, no matter how many lives they emptied, no matter how many dying relationships they so intimately observed. Like an internal cancer, their bland surfaces concealed an inner, parasitic excitement. They could not generate their own. They couldn't even generate their own kind; they had to infect others in order to multiply.

Frank had always imagined their type to be feral, with impossibly long teeth, and foul, blood-tainted breath. But they had manners, promising a better life, and a cold excitement one need not work for.

He was, after all, one of them. A Rivendale by habit, if not by blood. The thought terrified.

The thing he would remember most was the room, and the way she looked curled up in bed, her bald head rising weakly over her shoulders.

"I have to leave, Cathy. This is crazy."

He'd been packing for fifteen minutes, hoping she'd say something. But the only sounds in the room were those of the shirts and pants being pulled from drawers and collapsed haphazardly into his suitcase. And the sound the breeze from the window made, pushing out the heavy brocade curtains, making the tiny leaf and shell pattern breathe, sigh, the tiny mouths chatter.

And the sound of her last gasp, her last breath trying to escape the confines of the room, escape the family home before their mouths caught her and fed.

"Cathy . . ." Shadows moved behind the bed. It bothered him he couldn't see her eyes. "There was no love anyway . . . you understand what I'm saying?" Tiny red eyes flickered in the darkness. Dozens of pairs. "The fighting is the only thing that kept us together; it kept the boredom away. And I haven't felt like fighting you for some time." The quiet plucked at his nerves. "Cathy?"

He stopped putting his things into the suitcase. He let several pairs of socks fall to the floor. There were tiny red eyes fading into the shadows. And mouths. There was no other excitement out there for him; he couldn't do it on his own. No other defense against the awesome, all-encompassing boredom. The Rivendales had judged him well.

Cathy shifted in the bed. He could see the shadow of her terrible swollen belly as it pushed against the dusty sheets and raised the heavy covers. He could see the paleness of her skin. He could see her teeth. But he could not hear her breathe. He lifted his knee and began the long climb across the bedspread, his hands shaking, yet anxious to give themselves up for her.

He would remember the bite marks in the cool night air, the mouths in the dark brocade. He would remember his last moment of panic just before he gave himself up to this new excitement. The thing he would remember most was the room.

HUNGRY

Mama?

Vivian Sparks took her hands out of the soapy water and stared into the frosted kitchen window. There was a face in the ice and fog, but she wasn't sure which of her dead children it was. Amy or Henry, maybe—they'd had the smallest heads, like early potatoes, and about that same color. Those hadn't been their real names, of course. Ray always felt it was wrong to name a stillborn, so they didn't get a name writ down on paper, but still she had named every one of them in her heart: Amy, Henry, Becky, Sue Ann, and Patricia, after her mother. Patricia had been the smallest, not even full-made really, like part of her had been left behind in the dark somewhere. Ray had wanted Patricia took right away and buried on the back hill, he'd been so mad about the way she came out. But the midwife had helped Vivian bathe the poor little thing and wrap her up, and she'd looked so much like a dead kitten or a calf that it made it a whole lot worse than the others, so dark and wet and wrinkled that Vivian almost regretted not letting Ray do what he'd wanted.

Mama . . .

But it wasn't the dead ones, not this time. A mother knows the voice of her child, and Vivian Sparks felt ashamed to have denied it. It felt bad, always hearing the dead ones and never expecting the one she'd have given up anything for, no matter what Ray said. Ray wouldn't have let her adopt him, if it hadn't been for those stillborns, but she would have done it on her own if she had to, even if she'd had ten other children to care for. It was her own darling Jimmie Lee out there in the cold foggy morning. It had to be.

Vivian opened the back door and looked out onto the bare dirt yard that led uphill to the lopsided gray barn. Ray's lantern flickered in there where he was checking on the cows. She couldn't see much else because of the dark, and the fog. It was still trying

real hard to be Spring here in late March—she'd caught a whiff of
lilac breeze yesterday afternoon—but it worried her that the hard
frost was going to put an end to that early flowering before she'd
see any blossoms. That was always a bad sign when the lilacs
came out too soon and the ice killed the hope of them.

"Mama, it's me."

Vivian reached up and touched her throat, trying to help a
good swallow along. Suddenly her throat felt as if it were full of
food, and she just couldn't get it all down. Ray said it was because
of Jimmie Lee, her problem with eating, said it had been like that
for her ever since Jimmie Lee came into their lives. "You don't
eat right no more. I guess you can't," he said over and over, the
way he repeated something to death when he had a mad feeling
about it. "Can't say that I even blame you—it's understandable.
Watchin' him go at it, it'd put anybody off their food. That's why
I never watched."

She guessed there was truth in what he said, but she didn't like
to think about it that way. What she liked to think was that it was
all her feelings for Jimmie Lee coming up into her throat when
she'd looked at him, or now when she thought about him, all the
sadness and the love that made it hard for her to breathe, much
less eat. And the memory of him touching her on her throat,
gazing at her mouth the night before he left home to join that
awful show. That was another reason for her to be touching her
throat now, in that same place.

"Mama, I come back to visit."

Vivian could hardly speak. Maybe the love in her throat was
so big it was closing up her windpipe. "Come on, come ... on,
honey. Been a long time."

Past the east fence she could see the darkness gray a little and
move away. She started to walk over but a simple yet awful sound
—a young man clearing his throat—stopped her. She clutched
the huge lump in her throat. It was warm, as if it might burn her
fingers.

"Mama, I ate something off the road a while back. I just gotta
get rid of it, then I'll come up where you can see me."

She turned her back to him even though it would have been
much too dark to see what he was about to do. But after watch-

ing him a thousand times when he was little she felt like he was a grown boy now, and deserved some show of respect, and she wasn't sure but maybe this was one way to do it. At the same time she knew her turning away wasn't all being the good mama, either. She didn't want to see it anymore. She didn't feel like she should have to.

Back in the darkness there was a sound like damp skin stretching, splitting, some awful coughs and gurglings like her son's throat was turning itself inside out (dear God it's got worse!) and then a loud, mushy thump.

A few minutes later she could hear him walking up behind her. "I'm sorry, mama." His voice was hoarse, like he'd been crying. He used to cry all the time when he was little, complaining all the time about being so hungry, and never getting full no matter how much she fed him, how much Ray let her feed him, or how ever much Jimmie Lee ate on his own to try to fill that awful hunger. His nose would run and his eyes would look all raw and scraped and he'd stop trying to keep himself clean. Vivian took a handkerchief out of her front apron pocket now and turned around to give it to him.

"Thanks, mama. I'll get good and clean for you, just for you." The young man standing in front of her, saying just what he used to say to her when he was a little boy and had made himself such an awful mess, was taller, surely, and had little scraggly patches of beard here and there where once had been unnaturally pink skin, but other than that he still seemed the pale, skinny little boy who had left her years ago. His chin was covered with thick, soupy slobber which he wiped off with the handkerchief. She didn't mind—that had always been her job, to provide the handkerchiefs, the towels, waiting patiently while he cleaned himself up, directing him now and then to a missed spot or two. Ray had never been able to stand even that little bit of clean up; he'd always just left the room.

"My goodness!" She made herself sound impressed, although what she was really feeling was relieved, and desperate to hug him to her. "My handsome older son."

Jimmie Lee grinned then, showing teeth even worse than she remembered. She could see that at least he'd been able to get some dental work done, but it looked like the fillings and braces had been filed, points added here and there to make him look more like a silly machine, some big city kitchen gadget of some kind. She wondered if it really helped him get the food down or if it was all just for some sideshow or movie work he'd been doing. He'd written her once about one of the movies—"Flesh Eaters From Beyond Mars," or some such silliness. He'd said in the letter that the movie people liked him because he saved them money on special effects, but she'd never really understood what any of that was about.

Other than the metal in his mouth her sweet boy hadn't changed much. Certainly he couldn't weigh much more now than when he'd left her: his body straight up and down like a sleeve with no hips or shoulders to speak of, but his neck about twice as wide as it should be, and faintly ringed, like a snake's belly. Set atop that stout neck was the largest jaw she'd ever seen—it hung out like the birdbath on top the pedestal she had out in the front flowerbed. His mouth was wider than normal, she guessed, but had never seemed as big as it should be for that size jaw. His lips were almost blue, and cracked, and there were a bunch more splits in the skin at the corners of his mouth. Because of all the stretching his skin had to do there hair growth had always been spotty. She'd tried to get him to use lotions and oils, but like most children he just forgot all the time. So she'd always rub some into his face every night, being especially careful around the mouth and chin. She wondered if he knew somebody now who cared enough to do that for him.

His eyes were the wide eyes of a lost child's, but then they always had been. Jimmie Lee now was just a larger version of the poor baby that had been born in a backwoods barn and just left there eighteen years before. No one else had wanted the funny looking child but Vivian had known from the very first moment she saw him that this was her son, and would be forever. Even Ray, for all his puffin' and embarrassment about the boy, had resented it when one of the neighbors suggested that maybe they shouldn't keep him. This was his son, even though sometimes he sorely couldn't stand being around him.

And then Jimmie Lee had gone out into the world, maybe to

find his "real" mother, or maybe to find whatever it was he was hungry for. She didn't know, and was afraid then, and was afraid now, to ask. All she'd had to remember him by was this awful swelling in her throat every time she thought of him, and every time she struggled to eat or drink something. But nobody'd ever told her that life was fair to mothers.

"Did you ever find her, son?"

"Who, mama?"

"Why, the one who gave birth to you. The one who just left you here all them years ago." She tried to keep the bitterness out of her voice, but the vein went too wide and deep to hide.

His throat gurgled and a raw smell escaped. She started to turn away, but he held out his hand to stop her. "It's okay, mama. I still got it under control. I'm a lot more careful about how and when I eat now. Something I learned on the road, having to be around other people." He looked at her. She waited. "I never found her, mama. Guess I didn't try much after the beginning. I guess I was a little afraid of what she'd look like."

"You stayin' long?"

"I can't. I finally figured out it's best I be around folks who don't know me so well. But I just had to see you again, and smell you, and listen to you talk. I had to."

Her throat filled and she had to force it back down so that she could speak again. "You best get inside now, have something to . . ." She looked away from his nervous, hungry face, to where he'd come from in the dark beyond the fence, now turning gray so fast she could see a little bit of what he'd left there: great big mounds of meat still steaming in the cold, their hides partly dissolved away, large hunks of their manes missing, the meat turned to something like jelly, their teeth protruding from lipless mouths. A couple of Winn Gibson's prize mares, she suspected. Well, she guessed Ray was just going to have to deal with Winnie on that one, like he had all those times before. She sighed. "Guess you'd best just get inside . . ."

Jimmie Lee held up the brightly-colored, tattered poster beside his face. "It don't look much like me, I reckon, but the owner said they had to exaggerate a little bit to draw a crowd. He said people expected it like that, so that it wasn't lyin' exactly. They called me the Snake Boy." The poster showed a giant snake with her son's lost baby eyes on it, its huge mouth gaped open and an elephant disappearing inside. Lined up into the distance were chickens, bears, and a horse with a huge belly, all with worried looks on their faces.

"That's very nice, son," Vivian said quietly.

"But I only stayed there a few months. I didn't much like people lookin' at me like that, you know, mama?"

"I know, sweetheart."

"It was like the way people used to stare at me around here, only worse. Worse 'cause they were strangers, I guess. I never did like strangers watchin' me while I was eatin'."

"It certainly is impolite," she said. "People shouldn't stare at other people while they're eating. You can hardly digest your food that way." She raised her hand to her throat.

"So that's why I left the show. I did odd jobs after that, until I got to do those movies I wrote you about. And once for a few months I had me a dandy of a job in one of those meatpacking plants. It was late at night, and I had the place all to myself. It was great."

"I'm sure it was, Jimmie Lee."

"But the owner of the sideshow, he really could entertain you. That was a good part of it, mama—it weren't all bad. He'd crack all these jokes when he introduced me, and then he'd make more of 'em while I did my 'act,' but all I did was sit up on that stage and eat. But he'd say these things and all the people would laugh and I reckon that's a real good thing. He was real funny, mama, you shoulda seen. You'd a laughed till you cried, I bet."

"I bet I would that, honey."

"We had ourselves enough show 'round here to last us a lifetime, I reckon."

Vivian clutched at her apron. She hadn't heard him come in. She twisted in her chair in time to see Ray throw down his old coat and go stomping off to the bathroom to wash up.

"I guess daddy still don't want me around here." Jimmy Lee sat still with his legs spread, long nervous hands dangling and twisting between his knees.

"Your daddy just gets tired, honey. We all get tired now and then."

She could hear her husband splashing in the water, then hands slapping it onto his face. Jimmie Lee's eyes were large and white in the dimly lit room. When he was small his eyes always looked like that. Before they discovered the hunger he had, Ray used to joke that Jimmie Lee's eyes were bigger than his mouth. "I get tired, too," Jimmie Lee said. "And mama, I still get so hungry."

Vivian couldn't move. She stared at her son with tears in her eyes. "I love you, honey. I just keep loving you and loving you."

"I know, mama. But it's like the love goes inside me and gets lost and then it just isn't there anymore. Like I eat the love, mama. And then I'm still hungry."

Ray came back into the room and flopped down into his recliner. He sighed and looked directly at Jimmie Lee. "Well, son, you're lookin' . . . better. Better than the last time I seen you. That's good to see. You doin' a job now? You find yourself somethin' you can do?"

Jimmie Lee leaned forward and tried to smile. But the cracks in his lips and around his mouth bent and twisted the smile. Vivian started crying softly to herself and Ray looked at her with what she thought was an unusual sadness on the face of this man she'd known almost all her life. Then Jimmie Lee must have known something was wrong, because it looked as if he were trying to pull the smile back in, and it just made it worse.

"I left that show, papa. I know that'll please you. Made a couple of movies. And I did some real work, too, like at a packing plant, and once I spent almost a year at this junkyard outside Charlotte . . ."

"Junkyard? You learn the junk business? Now that can be a good trade for a young man. There's always goin' to be junk lyin' around."

Jimmie Lee looked down at his feet. "Well, papa, there was pieces the man couldn't sell, and they were just sittin' around his yard, takin' up too much space he said, and he couldn't get rid of them . . ."

His father interrupted. "You're talkin' about the eatin' now, and I ain't gonna talk about the eatin'."

"But, papa, eatin' metal junk, especially cars, why that's become almost like a regular thing in some places. They put it in the papers, and sometimes it even gets on the T.V. Some fella'll eat a big Buick, or an old Ford Mustang . . ."

His father leaned forward out of his recliner and stared hard at Jimmie Lee. "We don't talk about the eatin' in this house. Look how you've gone and upset your mother."

Vivian sat rock-still in her chair, her eyes closed and mouth open, crying without sound.

"Vivian, why don't you go on out to the hen house and get the boy some fresh eggs? The boy always liked fresh eggs."

She stared at him, her eyes sharp and red. "Wh-what?"

"Papa, I don't need eggs . . ."

"Sure you do. Vivian, go get the boy some eggs. He used to eat a dozen of 'em at a time, from what I remember. Shell and all. But at least it was real food. Go on now."

Vivian stood stiffly, and left the room. She went out through the back door and around the side toward the hen house. But when she passed near the open window of the living room she stopped, because she could hear her husband and her son talking inside. And she knew what they would be talking about—she knew what Ray would be saying to Jimmie Lee. She crept closer, and stood just under the lilac bush by the window, where she could see their faces, and the feelings painted there.

Ray started talking low and firm. "Now it's good to see you, I mean that, son. I know I ain't always been as soft as I should of when you were at home, but I been thinkin' about you every day since you left us. You been sorely missed—you sure have—and not just by your mama." He leaned back and sighed. "But your mama's sick, boy, real sick, and I just don't know if she can stand watchin' what you go through, havin' it be like it was before."

"Mama? What's wrong with her? Tell me . . ."

"Well, she never did eat all that well, and I reckon we all know the reason for that." Jimmie Lee looked down at his stomach and away. Vivian held her throat and struggled not to make a sound. "But that don't matter so much now. It weakened her, and she's had pneumonia so many times over the years she damn near coughed her lungs out. But she's got the cancer now, and it's clean through her, Doc Jennings says, and she can't have long to go."

Jimmie Lee's face was sheened with sweat. That's what he did, instead of crying. His body never had let him cry.

"Even less, I reckon, if you stay around, son."

Jimmie Lee stood up. "I understand, papa. I appreciate you levelin' with me."

"You're a good son, Jimmie Lee."

Vivian rushed down to the hen house and grabbed what she could, then ran back into the house and into the living room, out of breath, a scarf full of eggs hugged to her bosom. Jimmie Lee was still standing, but had already started for the door. She looked at her husband, then at Jimmie Lee. "You're leavin'," she said flatly. The eggs tumbled out of her arms and splattered across the braided rug.

"I gotta check some things out down at the pasture," his father said, getting up. He pulled on his sweater, started to leave, then walked over to Jimmie Lee and gave him a quick hug.

After her husband left the house Vivian still stood there among the broken eggs, looking at Jimmie Lee as if she were memorizing him, or trying to puzzle him out. Jimmie Lee bent over and started picking up the eggshells. "Leave those alone," she said softly. He straightened back up and looked down at her, his thin lips twitching, the scars around his mouth wrinkling like worms moving across his face. "He told you, didn't he?" she said. "He told you all of it."

Jimmie Lee nodded. "I better go, mama."

"You come here, baby." She held out her arms to him and when he wouldn't come any closer she walked over to him and attached her frail body to his. "You're not leavin' me this time."

"Mama, please. I gotta go."

"No, sir."

"Mama, I'm hungry." And he tried to push her body away.

She pressed closer, and raised her hand to his lips. "I know, baby." And pulled his thin, cracked lips apart with her fingers. And put her fingers inside her baby's mouth, and then put her hand inside, then both hands. As if out of his control, his huge jaw dislocated, his pliant facial muscles stretched. He tried to pull back, to make his mouth let go of her, but she wouldn't have any of that. "No, child. Just take it, child." His mouth wouldn't let go, and as her head disappeared inside him he heard her say again, "I'm not leaving you."

For the first time in his life, what he ate, all that he ate, became nourishment, and remained inside him.

MIRI

They spread the blanket over the cool grass and took their places. The puppet stage was broad and brightly lit, with a colorful and elaborate jungle set. Rick framed his children inside the LCD screen on the back of his camera as they settled in front of him: Jay Jay who was too old for this sort of thing but would enjoy it anyway, and seven-year-old Molly, worrisomely thin, completely entranced, her large eyes riveted on the stage as oversized heads with garishly painted faces danced, their mouths magnified into exaggerated smiles, frowns, and fiercely insistent madness.

The colors began to fade from the faces—the painted ones, and his children's—he took his eyes away from the camera and blinked. The world had become a dramatic arrangement of blacks and whites. Molly raised her stark face and stared at him, her eyes a smolder of shadow. Where is she? he thought, and looked around. He thought he caught a glimpse—there by a tree, a pale sliver of arm, a fall of black hair, lips a smear of charcoal. He could feel the breath go out of him. Not here. But he couldn't be sure. He closed his eyes, tried to stop the rising tide of apprehension, opened them, and found that all the colors had been restored to the world with sickening suddenness.

He quickly took a dozen or so more shots, his finger dancing on the shutter button. Elaine patted his hand and took the camera away. "Enough already," she whispered into his ear. He tried not to be annoyed, to no avail. She had no idea what she was talking about. It didn't matter how many pictures he took—it would never be enough.

Between the kids lay the pizza box with their ragged leftovers. Jay Jay would finish it if they let him. Molly would sneak a guilty glance but would not touch it. Rick had no idea what to do to help her; next week he would make more calls.

"You're a wonderful dad, and a really good person," Elaine whispered, and kissed that place above his ear where his hairline had dramatically begun to recede. Especially in this early evening light she was lovely—she still managed to put a hitch into his breath.

He smiled and mouthed thanks, even though such naked compliments embarrassed him. He'd finally learned it was bad form, and unattractive, to argue with them. So even though he was thinking he just had a few simple ideas, like always giving your kids something to look forward to, he said nothing. In any case it would be hypocritical. Because he also would not be confessing that he wasn't the good person she thought he was. Or telling her how often he wished he didn't have kids—it had never been his dream, and sometimes spending an entire day with them and their constant need left him drained, stupid, and angry. He was ashamed of himself—perhaps that was why he sometimes made himself so patient.

An unreal ceiling of stars hung low over the lake, the park, the puppet stage, and all these families sitting out on their assorted colorful blankets. Elaine pulled closer to him, mistakenly saying "I love that you still love the stars."

But he didn't. These stars were a lie. This close to the center of the city you couldn't see the stars because of the electric lights. And the dark between them had a slightly streaked appearance, as if the brush strokes were showing. Somehow this sky had been faked—he just didn't know how. But he knew by whom.

Was he lying when he allowed Elaine to mistake his silence or his distraction, for something sweet and good? If so he was a consistent and successful liar.

His gaze drifted. Off to his left an elderly couple standing on their blanket looked a bit too textured, too still. At the moment he decided they were cutouts the vague suggestion of a slim female form moved slowly in behind them, looking much the cutout herself, a black silhouette with a painted white face, a dancing paper doll. She turned her head toward him, graceful as a ballerina, presenting one dark eye painted against a background of china white, framed expressionistically by black strokes of hair, black crescent cheekbones, before she turned sideways and vanished.

"I'll be right back," he whispered to Elaine. "Bathroom." He climbed absently to his feet, feeling as if his world were being snatched out from under him. If I could just get my hands on that greedy, hungry bitch.

The kids didn't even notice him leave, their eyes full of the fakery on stage. He quickly averted his glance—the color in their faces, the patterns in their shirts, were beginning to fade.

He moved through the maze of blankets quickly, vaguely registering the perfectly outfitted manikin couples with rudimentary features, their arms and legs bent in broken approximations of humanity. Near the outer edge of the crowd he bumped into a stiff tree-coat of a figure with a gray beard glued to the lower part of its oval head. He pardoned himself as it crashed to the ground, scattering paper plates and plastic foods onto the silent shapes of a seated family.

He passed into the well-mannered trees, which grew in geometric patches around the park. He could see her fluttering rapidly ahead of him, alternating shadow side and sunny side like a leaf twirling in the breeze off the water. She peeked back over her shoulder, her cheek making a dark-edged blade. She laughed as sharply, with no happiness in it. Something was whipping his knees—he looked down and the flesh below his shorts had torn on underbrush that hadn't been here before, that had been allowed to grow and threaten. He started to run and the trees grayed and spread themselves into the patchy walls of an ill-kept hallway—inside the residential hotel he'd lived in his last few years of college. Dim sepia lighting made everything feel under pressure, as if the hall were a tube traveling through deep water.

Wearily he found his door and stepped into a room stinking of his own sweat. He slumped into a collapsed chair leaking stuffing. He thought to watch some television, but couldn't bring himself to get up and turn the set on. Gravity pushed him deeper into the cushion, adhering his hands to the chair's palm-stained arms.

The knock on the door was soft, more like a rubbing. "Ricky? Are you home?"

He twisted his head slightly, unable to lift it away from the thickly-padded back. He watched as the doorknob rattled in its collar. He willed the latch to hold.

"Ricky, it's Miri," she said unnecessarily. "We don't have to do anything, I swear. We could just talk, okay?" Her voice was like a needy child's asking for help. How did she do that? "Ricky, I just need to be with somebody tonight. Please."

She knew he was there, but he didn't know how. He'd watched his building and the street outside long before he came in—she'd been nowhere in sight.

"Are you too tired, Ricky? Is that it? Is that why you can't come to the door?"

Of course he was tired. That had been the idea, hadn't it? Everything was so incessant about her—you couldn't listen without being sucked in. She wanted him too tired to walk away from her. He closed his eyes, could feel her rubbing against the door.

He woke up in his living room, the TV muted, the picture flickering in a jumpy, agitated way. It looked like one of those old black and white Val Lewton films, *Cat People* perhaps, the last thing he'd want to watch in his state of mind. He was desperate to go to bed, but he couldn't move his arms or legs. He stared at his right arm and insisted, but he might have been gazing at a stick for all the good it did. He blinked his grainy eyes because at least he could still move them. After a few moments he was able to jerk his head forward—and his body followed up and out of the chair. He almost fell over but righted himself, staggering drunkenly down to their bedroom.

He couldn't see Elaine in the greasy darkness, but she whispered from the bed. "I know it's the job, wearing you out, but the kids were asking about you. They were disappointed you didn't come say goodnight—they wanted to talk more about the puppet show. Go and check on them—at least tomorrow you can tell them you did that."

He felt like lashing out, or weeping in frustration. Instead he turned and stumbled back out into the hall. He could have lied to her, but he went down to Jay Jay's room.

The boy in the bed slept like a drunk with one foot on the floor. He looked like every boy, but he didn't look anything like his son. What his son actually looked like, Rick had no idea.

Molly had kicked all the covers off, and lay there like a sweaty, sick animal, her hair matted and stiff, her mouth open exposing a few teeth. She seemed too thin to be a child—he watched as her ribs made deep grooves in the thin membrane of her flesh with each ragged breath. How was he expected to save such a creature? He walked over and picked her sheet off the floor, tucked her in and, when she curled into a sigh, kissed her goodnight.

When he climbed into bed Elaine was asleep. He avoided looking at her, not wanting to see whatever it was he might see. He must have looked at his wife's face tens of thousands of times over the years of their marriage. If you added it all up—months certainly—of distracted or irritated or loving or passion-addled gazes. And yet there were times, such as after the 3 A.M. half-asleep trudge to the bathroom, when he imagined that if he were to return to their bedroom and find Elaine dead, it wouldn't be long before he'd forget her lovely face entirely.

He sometimes loved his family like someone grieving, afraid he would forget what they'd looked like. An obsession with picture-taking helped keep the fear at bay, but only temporarily. As a graphic designer he worked with images every day. He knew what he was talking about. It didn't matter how many snap-shots he kept—we don't remember people because of a single recognizable image. In his way, he'd conducted his own private study. We remember people because of a daily changing gestalt —because of their ability to constantly look different than them-selves. The changing set of the mouth, the tone of the skin, the engagement of the eyes. The weight lost and the weight gained. The changing tides of joy and stress and fatigue. That's what keeps people alive in our imaginations. Interrupt that flow, and a light leaves them. That's what Miri had done, was doing, to him. She was draining the light that illumined his day. Sometime during the night he turned over and made the error of opening his eyes, and saw her face where Elaine's used to be.

"Rick, you're gonna have to redo these." Matthew stood over him, a sheaf of papers in hand, looking embarrassed. They'd started in college together, back when Rick had been the better artist. Now Matthew was the supervisor, and neither of them had ever been comfortable with it.

"Just tell me what I did wrong this time—I'll fix it."

"It's this new character, the Goth girl. The client will never approve this—it's the wrong demographic for a mainstream theater chain."

"I didn't—" But seeing the art, he realized he had. The female in each of the movie date scenes was dark-haired and hollow-eyed, depressed-looking. And starved.

"She looks like that woman you dated in college."

"We didn't date," Rick snapped.

"Okay, went out with."

"We never even went out. I'm not sure what you'd call what we did together.'

"I just remember what a disaster she was for you, this freaky Goth chick—"

"Matt, I don't think they even had Goths back then. She was just this poor depressed, suicidal young woman."

He smirked. "That was always your type, if I recall. Broody, skinny chicks."

Now his old friend had him confused with someone else. There had never been enough women for Rick to have had a type. "Her name was Miriam, but she always went by Miri. And do you actually still use that word 'chick'? Do you understand how disrespectful that is?"

"Just when I'm talking about the old days. No offense."

"None taken. I'll have the new designs for you end of the week."

Rick spread the drawings out over his desk and adjusted his lamp for a better look. He never seemed to have enough light anymore. There was an Elvira-like quality to the figures, or like that woman in the old Charles Addams panel cartoons, but Miri had had small, flattened breasts. It embarrassed him that he should remember such a thing.

In college all he ever wanted to do was paint. But it had really been an obsession with color—brushing it, smearing it, finding its light and shape and what was revealed when two colors came against each other on the canvas. He'd come home after class and paint late into the night, sometimes eating with his brush in the other hand. Each day was pretty much the same, except Saturday when he could paint all day. Then Sunday he'd sleep all day before restarting the cycle on Monday.

Women were not a part of that life. Not that he wasn't interested. If he wanted anything more than to be a good painter it
was to have the companionship and devotion of a woman. He
simply didn't know how to make that happen—he didn't even
know how to imagine it. To ask a woman for a date was out of
the question because that meant being judged and compared and
having to worry if he would ever be good enough and unable to
imagine being good enough. He'd had enough of that insanity
growing up.

At least he was sensitive enough to recognize the dangers of
wanting something so badly and believing it forever unobtain-
able. He wasn't about to let it make him resentful—he wasn't
going to be one of those lonely guys who hated women. The
problem was his, after all.

He was aware a female had moved into the residential hotel,
because of conversations overheard and certain scents and things
found in the shared bathroom or the trash. Then came the night
he was at the window, painting, and just happened to glance
down at the sidewalk as she was glancing up.

Her face was like that Ezra Pound poem: a petal on a wet black
bough. Now detached from its nourishment, now destined for
decay.

A few minutes later there was a faint, strengthless knocking on
his door. At first he ignored it out of habit. Although it didn't get
louder it remained insistent, so eventually he wiped the paint off
his hands and went to answer.

Her slight figure was made more so by a subtle forward slump.
She gazed up at him with large eyes. "I'm your neighbor," she
said, "could I come inside for a few minutes?"

He was reluctant—in fact he glanced too obviously at his
unfinished painting—but it never occurred to him to say no.
She glided in, the scarf hanging from her neck imbued with a
perfume he'd smelled before in the hall. Her dress was slip-like,
and purple, and might have been silk, and was most definitely
feminine. Ribbons of her dull black hair appeared in the cracks
among multiple scarves covering her head. She sat down on a
chair right by his easel, as if she expected him to paint her.

"You're an artist," she said.

"Well, I want to be. I don't think I'm good enough yet, but maybe I will be."

"I'll let you paint me sometime." He stumbled for a reply and couldn't find one. "I have no talents. For anything. But it makes me feel better to be around men who do."

She didn't say anything more for awhile, and he just stood there, not knowing what to do. But he kept thinking about options, and finally said, "Can I get you something to eat?"

There was a slight shift in her expression, a strained quality in the skin around the mouth and nose. "I don't eat in front of other people," she finally said. "I can't—it doesn't matter how hungry I am. And I'm always hungry."

"I'm sorry—I was just trying to be a good host."

She looked at him with what he thought might be amusement, but the expression seemed uncomfortable on her lips. "I imagine you apologize a lot, don't you?"

His face warmed. "Yes. I guess I really do."

"I'd like to watch you paint, if that's okay."

"Well, I guess. It'll probably be a little boring. Sometimes I do a section, and then I just stare at the canvas for awhile, feeling my way through the whole, making adjustments, or just being scared I'll mess it up."

"I'd like to watch. I'm not easily bored."

And so she sat a couple of hours as if frozen in place, watching him. He might have thought she was sleeping if not for the uncomfortably infrequent blinking. Now and then he would glance at her, and although she was looking at him, he wasn't sure somehow that she was seeing him. And his dual focus on her and on his painting was rapidly fatiguing him. He appreciated her silence, however—he might not have been able to work at all if she'd said anything. It occurred to him she smelled differently. Under the perfume was a kind of staleness—or gaminess for lack of a better word. Like a fur brought out of storage and warming up quickly. Finally it was he who spoke.

"You're great company." It was the first time he'd ever said such a thing. "But I'm feeling so tired, I don't know why, but I think I might just fall over. I'm sorry—I usually can work a lot longer."

"You should lie down." She stood and led him to the bed in the other room of the small apartment. So quickly there hardly seemed a transition. Despite her slightness she forced him down into a reclining position. And without a word lay down beside him, close against him like a child. But even if she had said something, even if she had asked, he would not have said no. And of course he didn't stop her when she first removed his clothes, then threw off her own. It was all such a stupid cliché, he would think later, and again and again, for the six months or so their relationship lasted, and for years afterward. All the bad jokes about how men could not really be seduced, because they were always ready to have sex with anyone, with anything—it was just part of their nature. They couldn't help themselves. It embarrassed him, he felt ashamed. He'd never thought it was true, and now look at how he was behaving.

For there was this other sad truth. Men who never expected to be loved, who'd never even felt much like men, had a hard time saying no when the opportunity arrived, because when would it ever come again?

At least he had never been able to fool himself into believing that she actually enjoyed what they were doing. Most of the time she lay there with her eyes closed, as if pretending to be asleep or in some drug-induced semi-consciousness. He was never quite sure if he was hurting her, the way her body rose off the bed as if slapped or stabbed, her back arching, breath coming out in explosions from her as-if wounded lungs, eyes occasionally snapping open to stare from the bottom of some vast and empty place. Certainly there couldn't be any passion in her for it, as dry as she was, her pubic hair like a bit of thrown-out carpet, so that at some point every time they did it he lost his ability to maintain the illusion, so much it was like fucking a pile of garbage, artfully arranged layers of gristle and skin, tried to escape, but like that moment in the horror movies when the skeleton reaches up and embraces you, she always pulled her bony arms around him, squeezing so hard he could feel her flailing heart right through the fragile web of her rib cage, as they continued to rock and bump the tender hangings of their flesh until bruised and bloody.

"Daddy! I said I saw a monkey at the zoo today!" Across from him at the dinner table, Molly looked furious.

"I know, honey," he said. "I heard you."

"No you didn't! You weren't paying attention! "

He looked at Elaine, maybe for support, or maybe just for confirmation that he had screwed up. She offered neither, was carefully studying the food on her plate. "Honey, I'm sorry. Sometimes I don't sleep too well, and the next day I have a hard time focusing, so by the time I get home from work I'm really very tired. But I'm going to listen really closely to you, okay? Please tell me all about it."

Apparently she was willing, because she began again, telling a long story about monkeys, and thrown food, and how Brian got on the bus and started throwing pieces of his lunch like he was the monkey, and what the bus driver said, and what their teacher said, and how lunch was pretty sick-looking, so she couldn't eat anything again anyway, except for a little bit of a juice box, and some crackers. And the entire time she was telling this story a tiny pulse by her left eye kept beating, like the recording light on a video camera, but he still kept his eyes on her, and he made himself hear every tedious word, and he let the pictures of what she was telling him make a movie in his brain, so that he felt right there.

Even though at the corners of his eyes his view of the dining room, and his daughter speaking at the center of it, was breaking down into discordance, into a swarm of tiny black and white pixels, and even though Miri's face was at one edge of the dining room window, peering in, before her silhouette coiled and fell away.

So that by the end of his daughter's little story he had closed his eyes by necessity, and spoke to her as if in prayer. "That's a really nice story, sweetheart, and thanks so much for telling it. But you know you really must eat. Why, tonight you've hardly touched anything on your plate. That little piece of meat hung up in the edge of your mouth—I can't tell if it's even food. But you have to keep your strength up; you're really going to need every bit of strength you can find."

The rest of the evening was awkward, with Elaine pleading

with him to see a doctor. "You're not here with me anymore," she was saying, or was that Miri, and that was the problem, wasn't it? He no longer knew when or with who he was. It was all he could do to keep his eyes in the same day and place for more than a few minutes at a time.

By the end Rick had known Miriam for six months or so. He'd told Matt about her, but then had been reluctant to share more than a very few of the actual details. He just wanted someone to know, in case—but he didn't understand in case of what. Matt ran into them once, when Rick had tried to drive her to a restaurant. He'd been so stupid about it—he should have been driving her to a hospital instead. She'd lost enough fat in her face by then that when she reacted to anything he couldn't quite tell what the emotion was—everything looked like a grimace on her. When she walked she was constantly clicking her teeth together and there was a disturbing wobble in her gait. He knew she must eat—how could she not? But it could not be much, and she had to be doing it in secret because he'd never actually seen her put anything into her mouth except a little bit of water.

When she breathed sometimes it was as if she were attempting to devour the space around her—her entire frame shook with the effort. When he first experienced this he tried to touch her, pull her in to comfort a distress he simply could not understand. But soon he learned to keep his distance, after getting close enough he felt he might dissolve from the force of what was happening to her.

He hadn't told her they were going to a restaurant. He said he just wanted to get out of that building where they spent virtually all of their time. Finally she stumbled into his car and caved into the passenger seat. He drove slowly, telling her it was time they both tried new things.

"What, you're breaking up with me?" A thin crimson line of inflammation separated her eyes from their tightly wrinkled sockets.

"No, that's not what I meant at all. I mean try new things together, as a couple. Go places, do things."

"You have the only new thing I need, lover." Her leer ended with a crusted tongue swiped over cracked lips.

"It doesn't feel healthy staying in the way we do. Maybe it's okay for you, but it doesn't work for me."

He pulled up in front of a little Italian place. It wasn't very popular—the flavors were a bit coarse—but the food was always filling.

"No," she said, and closed her eyes. She was wearing so much eye makeup that it looked as if her eyelids had caved in.

"All I'm asking is that you give it a try. If you don't like it, okay. No problem. We'll just go home."

She slapped his face then, and it felt as if she'd hit him with a piece of wood. She continued hitting him with those hands of so little padding, spitting the word "lover!" at him, as if it were some kind of curse.

He had no idea what to do. He'd never been struck by a woman before. He couldn't remember the last time he'd been in a physical fight with anyone. And now she was screaming, the angular gape of her mouth like an attacking bird's.

"Hey! Hey!" The car door was open, and someone was pulling her away from him. Miri was beside herself, struggling, kicking. Rick was leaning back as far as possible to avoid her sharp-pointed shoes. Over her shoulder he saw Matt's face, grimly determined, as he jerked her out of the car.

She spat at both of them, walking back toward her apartment with one shoe missing, her clothes twisted around on her coat-hanger frame.

"I should go get her, try to coax her back into the car," Rick said, out of breath.

"Glad you finally introduced us," Matt was bent over, wheezing.

Of course she had apologized in her own way, showing up at Rick's door the next night, naked, crying and incoherent. He got her inside before anyone else could see. And then she would not leave for weeks, sleeping in his bed, watching him eat or stand before his easel unable to paint. Most of the time he slept on the floor, but sometimes he had to have something softer, and lay on the bed trying to ignore her mouth and hands all over him, in that fluttering way of hers, until she stopped and lay cold against him.

*

"I'm glad you were able to join us today." Matt stood at Rick's office door, looking unhappy. "Were you really sick, or did you get Elaine to call in and lie for you every day?"

Rick was unable to do anything but stare as Matt's words rushed by him. He'd been in the office for only five minutes or so and already he was feeling disoriented. Papers were stacked all over his desk, and message notes were attached around his monitor, even to his lamp base. He never left things like this.

Finally, he looked up at his old friend. "I have no idea what you're talking about."

"You haven't been here in four days! I can't keep coming up with excuses for you with the partners."

"Four days?"

Matt stared at him. It made him uncomfortable, so he started sifting through the piles of papers. But these were piles of print on paper, black on white, black and white. Before he could turn away he was seeing the shadows of her eyes, the angles of her mouth in the smile that wasn't a smile. "Maybe you are sick," Matt said behind him.

"You said Elaine called in every day?"

"Right after the office opened, once before I even got in."

"Elaine never lies. That's one of the best things about her. I don't think she even knows how," Rick said absently, looking around the office, finding more phone messages. Some appeared to be in his handwriting.

"Well, I know. Of course. Look, I didn't mean—"

"Are you sure it wasn't someone who just pretended to be Elaine?"

But then someone was softly knocking, or rubbing, on the door outside. And Rick couldn't bring himself to speak anymore.

"Ricky?" she had said. "Are you home?"

But he couldn't get out of his so well-cushioned chair. The doorknob rattled in its collar. He willed the latch to hold.

"Ricky, we don't have to do anything," she said in her child's voice, muffled by the door.

"Ricky, I just need—are you too tired, Ricky? I just need—"

After a few weeks she had stopped. Later he heard she'd killed

herself, but he never saw a word about it in the papers. One afternoon a truck came and took away all the stuff in her apartment.
A white-haired man came by, knocking on each door. But Rick
hadn't answered when the old man knocked on his. Later one
of the other tenants would tell Rick the white-haired man had
claimed to be her uncle.

The next week was when the color-blindness had come over
him like some sort of virus, intermittently, then all at once. One
of the doctors he saw said it appeared to be a hysterical reaction
of some sort. Whatever the source, or the reason, he stopped
painting, and she mostly left him alone for a long time after that,
reappearing now and then to monochrome the world for awhile,
or to take a day or two, or to eat one of his new memories and
leave one of the tired old ones in its place.

And now it had looked as if he was going to be happy, or at
least the possibility was there, and she couldn't just leave that be.

The bedroom was completely black, except for a few bright
white reflections of window pane. And the side of Elaine's face,
as she slept on her back. Lovely and glowing and ghostly.

The children were out there asleep in their own beds, or
should be. At least he hadn't heard them in hours. He prayed they
were. Sleeping.

But it was all so black, and white, and something was rubbing
at the door.

UNDERGROUND

They had started in April to excavate the block across from Tom's apartment building. Now it was September, and because of work stoppages and other delays there was still the largest hole Tom had ever seen right in the middle of the city, and right in the middle of his life. The library research company he worked for had its offices in a building at the north edge of this giant, muddy hole. Certainly it was a rare moment when he'd noticed any dry earth around the site. September's rainfall had been the heaviest on record. He'd read in the papers that the construction company had had some trouble with slides at the site. Two workers had been killed. Experts had been called in from more rainy climates to offer their recommendations.

He often considered whether Willie would live long enough to see the new complex. Willie had always been an avid fan of new construction, especially projects this complicated. Staring out the window into the squarish crater filled Tom with doubt. He wasn't sure he believed there was enough steel, stone and concrete in the state to fill such a hole. Construction projects were often as unpredictable as a ravaging disease. The holes in Willie's immune system would not be easy to fill, either. As the complex was beginning a dramatic rise out of the raw wound of ground, Willie was slowly, inexorably, being sucked back into it.

The height of the dirt walls at the site impressed him. When the digging had first begun, he'd walked close to the site each day, spending time at the various peepholes cut into the temporary roofed walkways around its perimeter. He'd been surprised at the fecundity of the earth; even at a depth of a hundred feet or more it was rich and moist like cake.

Topsoil was supposedly only a few feet deep, but here he could see roots and animal holes and insect tracks and all the dark strata of decades of decay meant to feed generations of new life that went far deeper than that. Impossibly deep, he thought. The living feeding off the dead. After a week, the machines were still uncovering small animal skeletons and black compost. After two weeks of this grave robbing Tom stopped visiting, trotting through the walkways briskly as he went from apartment to job and back again.

A park over a portion of the site had now vanished into the cavity. Four or five cast statues—a general on a horse, a standing man with his hand on a book—had been lifted out of the way and temporarily stored in a blocked-off portion of street that once ran alongside the park. There were also a couple of old stone statues in the lot, badly weathered and veined heavily with black. From his office window they looked like bystanders, gone to the edge of the pit to see what lay inside.

He had a poor understanding of what was required for such constructions; he had no idea why they would need to dig a hole so large. He tried to imagine how many years of the city's history they had ripped away. How many skeletons of cats and dogs, family pets buried in the back yard? On the news they'd reported the discovery of a human skull within the last week, thought to be over a century old. Foul play was not suspected. They thought it might have drifted down from the cemetery a half-mile away. Tom tried to imagine such a thing, dead bodies drifting underground, swimming slowly through what most of us liked to think of as too solid ground.

But they weren't bodies anymore, exactly. Separate bones, the flesh gone to earth. Now it seemed as if the buried skeletons had discarded their old suits of flesh and slipped on the entire world as their new bodies. The world's movements had become the movements of the ancient dead, its dance their dance, its seasons their dreams of birth, death, and renewal. So maybe he himself was just a reflection of some dead man's forgotten desire.

Willie would have liked that conceit, Tom thought. He might have laughed at the elaborateness of it, but it still would have meant something to him. Now Willie had good reason to appreciate such an image. Tom liked to imagine Willie alive, doing the things they'd always done together, making plans, watching the city change even if most of the time they thought it was for the worse. But Willie wasn't going to be a watcher anymore. Willie was about to become part of the rest of the world.

The basement of Willie's house had been crumbling for decades. Tom had warned him against buying the place, sure that someday the entire structure would collapse, but Willie had just shrugged, saying that he loved the upstairs too much not to have it, the cool and the old world charm of it, and in the meantime continued a practice begun by the previous owners: filling the basement cavity with whatever clean fill dirt he could find, packing it down, adding occasional large rocks for more mass. Now it was the structure of Willie himself that was collapsing, and the basement was almost full with a half-dozen or more varieties of earth.

Tom struggled with his key in Willie's front door, the lock out of true, the door itself beginning to list noticeably to the right. *The ground's coming up to get you, Willie,* he thought, and grimaced as the key began to bend just before the door popped open. He glanced at the key once, ran his finger along the warp of it, turned and tossed it out into the front yard. He wouldn't be needing it after today. The yard was almost barren—Willie had let it go after he was diagnosed, and refused to let Tom, or anyone else, do anything with it. Damp red clods of earth heavy with worms showed through vague whiskers of grayish grass, the dirt loose and clumpy as if it had frothed up above the roots and stems, leaving only the tallest plants exposed. The flower beds were a sea of jagged, dark stalks.

He stepped inside onto a discolored patch of carpet. Dirt followed him in, clouds of it forming in the bright light. There used to be a dark green awning over the front door, but somewhere along the line it had disappeared. He looked down at the filthy rug, troubled by all the dirt. He stepped back out onto the single step that was meant to raise a visitor to the level of the door. It was as if it had dropped several inches during last month's heavy rains, leaving only a vague lip above the ground. But Tom knew that couldn't be—if that had been the case the step up to the door would have been far steeper than before. He stared at the threshold. Willie's entire front yard appeared to have risen. The

seemingly solid ground rubbed at the bottom of Willie's front
door. Trails of dark brown earth had crept up over the worn oak
threshold until parts of it were submerged. *Oh, Willie, you didn't
stand a chance*, he thought, and stepped quickly back inside, away
from this determined stretch of ground. He pushed the door
shut firmly, forcing a cloud of earthy smell up into his face.

"Is that you, Mr. Davison?" John, Willie's last lover and now
Willie's nurse, stood in glaring light at the top of the stairs. He'd
always called him *Mr. Davison*, and Tom had always felt vaguely
insulted by the formality. Tom fumbled with the living room light
switch, but the overhead bulb was dead. The room was shrouded
in black. As Tom made his way up the stairs into the light it felt as
if the dark had taken on the weight of earth, pulling him back,
seducing him with the impulse to lie down, to sink, to fall back
and close his eyes. "Mr. Davison, there's not much time." John
reached out and grabbed Tom's hand as if to reel him in. The
gesture made Tom uncomfortable, but he permitted John to help
him up the remaining steps.

Willie's bedroom door was half-open. Tom stopped with the
impulse to knock, then, suddenly angry, pushed the door the
rest of the way, slamming it against the edge of Willie's bed. He
had never been expected to knock before; he wasn't going to end
things knocking.

"We're not doing well today, I'm afraid," John said behind
him. Tom turned and, without thinking, searched John's face for
evidence of sores. John gestured toward the bed, at the bundle
of bedding where Willie was supposed to be. He looked down at
the edge of the door pressing against the mattress and frowned
slightly. Tom felt defensive, as he usually did in John's presence,
but he didn't want to say anything in front of Willie. Instead he
looked away with deliberation, his eyes searching the bed for his
old friend as if there were some question as to his whereabouts.

The dark shadows on the sheets looked like great splotches of
dirt, or even excrement. Tom was suddenly filled with rage and
started to turn back to John and let him know about it when the
cloud cover outside the window changed, and he realized those
splotches were actually shadows after all.

"John . . . leave us alone . . . now." The voice under the sheets was so low Tom could barely recognize it as Willie's. The throat sounded full. Tom thought of the darkness downstairs, and imagined the loose, gray earth rising up the staircase, eventually filling the mouth of the second floor hall. John looked at Tom with a vaguely troubled expression, then left without protest.

"I feel bad . . . I can't make him . . . at ease. He's scared . . . you know? But I'm glad he's here. Come . . . come closer." It was an eerie feeling, hearing that vaguely recognizable voice coming from beneath the bedclothes, as if Willie were already dead and buried and it was his voice haunting the bed. Tom walked slowly to the head of the bed. "Un . . . uncover me, will you?" Tom leaned over and pulled away the sheet which had been tucked tightly under the shoulders. Appalled, he felt as if he were unwrapping a mummy.

Willie looked up at him, his face a mask of sweat, his skin pocked with sores, his eyes dark as if too much makeup had been applied. ("That's the worst thing, really," he once said. "I'm starting to look like some old drag queen.") Tom thought Willie's flesh looked unstable, as if it might fall off the skull at any moment. He imagined a plate full of such flesh, a grave full of it. "He doesn't mean to, but . . . he keeps . . . covering me . . . a little too much. So he won't . . . have to see." Willie grinned hideously.

"Jesus, Willie. That's horrible. Don't let him."

Willie grinned again. "You don't . . . understand us. Not really."

Tom felt like turning away, but the grin fascinated him. He realized again it was as if Willie was already dead. It was as if a rock had suddenly smiled at him, as if a patch of bare ground had opened up and grinned at him. The thought worked cruelly through him—after all, Willie was his best friend, he loved Willie—but it refused to be ignored: Willie was well on his way to compost.

"Don't let . . . them bury me." Tom looked at him in shock, as if his old friend had been reading his mind. Again Willie smiled. Or was it the same smile, and now his face was frozen that way, the words squeezing past the yellowed bars of his teeth? "Make sure . . . I'm cremated."

Tom shook his head. *No, I won't let them,* or *No, I can't do that* . . . He wasn't sure which he intended by the gesture. Willie's face seemed to be dissolving right in front of him. But his friend wanted help with his last wish, and didn't he *owe* him that, even though his friend was already dead? "Why cremation, Willie? Why do you want that?"

The grin fell away so suddenly Tom thought of magic tricks, Willie wearing a tall dark hat and waving a wand. "I don't want this body . . . even hidden under dirt. This isn't *me*! . . . want it . . . *burned* away. Let . . . the rest of me . . . inside . . . fly *away*, Tom. Fly away."

"Okay, Willie. Okay."

"Don't . . . let them. They'll . . . bury me."

"I promise."

It was almost over when John came back into the room. Maybe it already *was* over. Maybe it had been over months ago. Tom felt as if he had no understanding here, and in that had let his best friend down. Willie had fallen back, unconscious. John went to the side of the bed and grabbed Willie's hand. *He really loves him*, Tom thought, the first nice thing he'd ever thought about John, but he couldn't watch, didn't even think he should watch. So he left.

Dirt now covered the entire length of the threshold. Dirt formed a wide, shallow pool over several square feet of the carpet in front of the door. As he stepped into the front yard, dark earth slopped over his shoes and stained his socks. He had a sense of the entire house sinking behind him. He was sure that if he came back to this site in a few weeks he'd find only a barren splotch of ground.

It was at that point that Tom realized he had no intention of keeping his promise to his old friend. What was he supposed to do, drag the body away in the night? John was Willie's lover, and what was Tom? A coward of a friend who had been too embarrassed to let other friends know that Willie was gay.

He turned around in the yard, feeling the need to go back up those stairs and tell Willie that he wouldn't be keeping his promise, that he was too embarrassed, that he was too frightened, when he again saw the dirt on the carpet, the way it moved, the way it spread. Like a fluid. Liquid ground covering the floor slowly, soon to ascend the stairs in its quest for Willie. And certainly there could be no way of fighting such hungry ground.

Tom left the yard quickly, intending never to be back.

At Willie's funeral Tom said nothing as they lowered him into the ground. The day of the funeral was unusually hot for that time of year. Early in the afternoon a temperature inversion dropped a lid over the city, compressing the air as the cars continued to move over the dusty streets and the heavy machinery continued to chew away at the rich body of the earth. By the time of the late afternoon funeral a thick stew swirled over the tops of the buildings, drifting slowly down into the streets where it forced itself into open windows, cars, and raw, desperate throats.

At the gravesite John's eyes met Tom's briefly as John dropped the first handful of rich, crumbling dirt over the lid. *Don't let them bury me*.

"But the dead have no say in such things, Willie," Tom thought. "After the ground takes you back it's the living that get to decide."

Never before had he felt such shame. For having been embarrassed. For being one of the living who continue to make decisions for the dead, even if only by default.

A month after Willie's funeral the work still continued on the giant hole in the middle of Tom's world. He couldn't understand why it was taking so long. The papers mentioned continued delays, but work was obviously taking place—there were simply no indications of impending completion. What disturbed him most was the fact that the hole appeared less uniform, more unfinished, as the work progressed. The excavation had lost its squareness, and now appeared as if something rotted had been removed, as if corruption were distorting the edges of this gigantic earthen wound. Digging had spread past the original wooden walkways and barriers, and some of the bordering buildings appeared in danger of being undermined. Some barriers had actually fallen into the hole, where they were mulched to the point of being indistinguishable from the remaining soil.

During slow periods at work Tom researched the decomposition rates of flowers, mahogany coffins, and a human body short on fat and muscle following a long, debilitating disease.

The temperature inversion recurred several times during

that month. Some afternoons the air felt abrasive, and tasted of soil. Other days unusually high winds blew dirt out of the excavation and across the windows of the neighboring buildings. From inside his office the windows appeared smeared with urine and feces. One afternoon the office was evacuated because of an air pollution alert. Tom refused to leave, instead choosing to surround himself with piles of crumbling antique volumes—research whose purpose he'd quite forgotten—while he coughed into a dirty handkerchief.

He'd never intended to go back. But in the will John and Tom had been jointly delegated the task of sorting through Willie's belongings. John had told him this briefly, curtly over the phone. They'd agreed on a day, then John hung up.

Yellow signs had been plastered to the outside walls of Willie's house. The property had been condemned. Tom was hardly surprised—the front door frame had shifted with the loose ground until it could no longer be completely closed. Someone had fixed a metal bar across the door, secured by a hefty padlock. This contraption now hung loosely beside the wide open door. Boxes containing a variety of junk were stacked high on either side. The front room contained an inch or more of dirt tattooed with a riot of footprints, but a clean, narrow patch had been swept to make a corridor to the bottom of the staircase.

He tried the light switch again but with no luck. Vivaldi's *Four Seasons* drifted down to him. Tom took the stairs carefully, his steps creating dark, musty clouds around his feet.

"You're late. I've already done about half of it." John turned from the bed where he'd been folding some of Willie's sweaters. "I hope that's okay."

"Sure, I . . . I'm sorry," Tom said awkwardly. John kept looking at him, his hands resting on the pile of sweaters. *What does he want me to say?* "You would know best where everything should go, anyway."

John nodded, as if that had been the correct answer. "I appreciate that. I guess I do know who Willie would have liked to have his things, and what should go to Goodwill. I loved Willie, do you know that? I really did."

"I know. I loved him, too."

John sighed, and continued folding the sweaters. "But it isn't the same, is it?"

Tom didn't reply. John sent him for boxes and he got them. Together they packed the boxes—John told Tom whose name to put on each box. Together they dismantled the bookcases and sorted through the books. John thought Tom should take a number of those for himself, and Tom accepted the idea. Now and then Tom would be aware of an increased amount of dust in the air—clouds of it would drift past the yellowed window panes. He thought John didn't notice until he stopped once and said, "We'll have to hurry. In a couple of days they won't be letting anyone back into the place. And the floorboards are creaking more than they used to. I think that's probably not a good sign."

"He should have moved a long time ago," Tom said, throwing a bundle of old clothes into the Goodwill pile. They appeared streaked with blood, or feces. But that couldn't be—he knew that sort of thing would have been washed, or burned. Maybe it was just plain old mud, as if they'd been used to dam a flood.

"I was telling him all the time he should move in with me. But he wanted to stay independent. Sometimes you see someone close to you doing something, or living a certain way that you know isn't good for them, but what do you do? Even if you know you know better, they have to make their own decisions, right?"

Tom dropped the clothes and rubbed his hands briskly against his jeans. "Unless they're dead."

John turned his head, a puzzled set to his lips. "Beg your pardon?"

"I say unless they're dead. They can't make their own decisions if they're dead, and even if they've already made them those of us still living can just pretend we never heard, and do what we want."

"What are you talking about?" John rubbed his scalp in irritation. Tom had seen the gesture before, when Willie was being particularly stubborn about something.

"He wanted to be cremated, John. And you went ahead and buried him, you and your friends. Because that's what *you* wanted."

"Where'd you get that idea? Willie never said . . ."

"He would have told you—you were his lover. You were *responsible* for the arrangements. He must've just told me because he wasn't sure you would do it. But I was a coward, I admit it. I couldn't deal with it—I couldn't deal with you and Willie's other friends. But you should have done what he asked for, John. Christ, it was his last . . . 'Don't let them bury me,' he said."

"You stupid fool." John stared at the bed, and the piles of clothes. Tom could see red dust drifting out of the empty sleeves and pant legs. "It wasn't in the will. He told *you* because he wanted to spare me. In him I saw not only the one person who'd ever loved me dissolving into nothing, but I saw myself and all our gay friends. Disappearing like everyone had always wanted us to. He told *you* so that you could *tell me*. He trusted you to carry the message."

Nothing more was said until all of Willie's things were packed and sorted. Tom found the enormous size of the pile going to Goodwill vaguely upsetting. But he trusted John's judgment. John knew that Tom was a fool, and John was correct.

"It goes too fast," John said finally. "A lifetime of things and they can haul it all away in hours. I'm afraid of disappearing like that. Like Willie."

"I'm afraid, too," Tom said.

Over the next few weeks Tom immersed himself in scatter-shot, seemingly aimless research. When the secretary asked which client to bill his hours to, Tom gave Willie's name.

His hands shook as he ran them through a large volume on the meat industry, counting off the steps involved in butchering cattle in a meat packing operation. He made notes and compared these steps with the standard operating procedures used by pathologists during an autopsy and morticians during an embalming.

He buried himself in the pictures in a book called *Techniques of Forensic Investigation*. They made his head feel as if it was about to split (gunshot wound? ax?) but he persisted, wondering if these techniques and procedures might have some sort of theological significance. (The rate of discorporation is inversely proportional to our impatience to arrive in heaven, all our sins tattooed onto our naked backs.)

He dug up the geological surveys for his part of the city, for the emptiness next door. He carefully examined the figures concerning the composition of the soil, looking for something of Willie there, and, finally, something of himself.

The next day he was in bed, quite unable to climb up out of the gritty darkness.

Don't let them bury me.

Poe would have understood such a request. Back then, Tom thought, many people might have been buried alive. Or embalmed alive—he supposed that still came first. Filling your body full of inert chemical was the logical preparation for your own eternity of inertness. Without advanced medical procedures, how could they have been sure? Maybe in a hundred years, Tom thought, we'll discover how many we're still burying alive today. We, the living. Always making decisions for the dead. But was there really such a clear distinction between us and them? A breath of wind, a drip of moisture, a vague presence of heat—not much more than that, certainly. Walking dirt and dancing clay.

Under his feet, under his building, the dead were swimming vast distances underground, endlessly seeking rest.

He was out of bed now, but he had not been back to work. He could not bring himself to go out. Outside his apartment, the giant hole in the earth grew bigger every day, a grave that swallowed larger and larger chunks of his world.

It's coming to get me, too, Willie.

A portion of the neighboring streets had buckled and collapsed. The city had rented out the parking lot of his apartment building and moved the homeless statues from the park as a precaution. The workers had conducted this operation in haste, however—nobody liked working too close to "the hole"—resulting in considerable damage. Several of the metal statues had massive splits, arms and legs had separated, and one of the stone statues had been reduced almost to powder. They lay on the pavement below his apartment window, a jumble of disinterred body parts, the dark, rich soil still clinging to their secret surfaces.

Several days of alternating intense heat and wind served to loosen the dirt that was now omnipresent in the neighborhood. It had spread out from the massive hole, dark and reddish as blood, to creep down the streets and alleys, filter into the cracks and mortar that held the walls together, staining stone, metal, and glass with its rich color.

Tom was reminded of childhood days spent in the sandbox his father had built in their back yard: four walls of rough timber holding back a foot-deep mound of sand whose look of sparkling cleanliness seemed impossible, given its constant use. He and his brother Rick would play in the sandbox for hours, even on days when the sun was so intense the crystalline specks in the sand sparked like bits of broken glass and by late afternoon had begun to burn them, and then the grit of it irritated the oval patches of burn that had formed above their waist bands and on the backs of their legs.

Tom remembered that sand as having remarkable powers of adherence; he'd find traces of it in his clothes, in his bed, drifting in narrow ridges through his toy box for days afterward. Sometimes there'd be enough of it pressed into his pajamas and bed clothes that his dreams that night would be about endless days at the beach, lying half-buried with the crabs creeping up on his small face. He'd never quite understood the reason for the terror in those dreams, since he'd always loved burying himself in the sand. Rick, too. Sometimes they'd be "tree men," the larger part of themselves rooted deep inside the sandbox, only their small, growing heads exposed. Tom and Rick had seen their dad dig up roots out of the back yard—the roots had gone all soft and crumbly like they'd become part of the ground. Rick told him that would happen to them, too, if they stayed buried too long. That's what happened to dead people, he'd said; they fell apart and fell apart until they *were* the ground.

Rick died in Viet Nam. Later Tom found out from his dad that they'd sent back only part of the body. The rest was part of that big overseas sand box.

By the time Tom had decided he couldn't take another day of staring out his apartment windows at the ever-widening hole—now wide enough that he was beginning to think the hole surrounded his building, making an eventual trip outside compulsory if he was to accurately evaluate his current living conditions—a renewed vigor of excavations in combination with high winds solved the problem: his windows became so caked with red-brown dirt he could no longer see out of them.

The building owners no longer provided window washing—there would be no point until the project had been completed. Tom also suspected it would be difficult to get anyone willing to wash windows with that kind of emptiness yawning below them, like working over the edge of the Grand Canyon. On the other side of the glass he could hear the thick rumble of machinery as it chewed still deeper into the earth—he wondered if they had changed the plans to permit more stories underground. Tornado or perhaps hurricane protection?

Or maybe the workers were simply feeling the kind of frustration he'd been experiencing all along: the project seemed simply to refuse to get done. Now they were expending all their energies in a day and night marathon of desperation, attempting to finish off the hole before it could turn and swallow them, bulldozers, backhoes, and all.

Don't let them bury me.

One morning Tom awakened to no gas or electricity, no phone. Only a trickle of water from the faucet to refresh him, to keep the dust out of his eyes and off his hot face. He didn't bother to check with the super. He strongly suspected that in their rush to completion the workers had accidentally severed the service lines leading into the building. He was tempted for the first time in days to go down to the front door and out to the parking lot to see how things were progressing next door (and to check on the condition of the statues, whose broken images had filled his dreams many times of late), but he resisted. He could wait until all power was restored by the professionals.

That night in his dreams Tom was in an elevator rocketing deep into the earth's core. He woke up suddenly with his eyes burning, his mouth tasting of sand.

The windows had become so filled with dirt that almost no light got through. His mouth was sick with its own taste of dirt and dry flesh. He spent hours staring at his dirt-packed windows, imagining that he was looking into a kind of aquarium, the dead swimming slowly through the dirt on the other side of the glass. But because the dead had been there so long, and because there were so many of them, they had become so like the medium they swam in, so much a part of the dirt that he could not tell the difference between the two.

Don't let them bury me.

Finally he had no choice but to take that elevator trip he had dreamed of. Several days of minimal food had left him weak. As he staggered down the corridor to the elevator he imagined himself falling into his own shadow, but there was no light to cast a shadow. Confused, he thought he might be the shadow cast by a self who was always behind him, whom he could not see even if he turned around quickly.

He sank into the cool, earthy darkness of the elevator, pressed the button for the lobby, and let it drag him down.

He must have fallen asleep, because he could clearly see the elevator taking him down through millions of years of strata. When he woke he could hardly breathe because of the pressure. His lungs felt on the verge of collapse. The elevator coughed him out at the bottom of the run.

Down here the walls were mud. And flesh. Mud becoming flesh and flesh becoming mud. Willie and anyone else Tom had ever loved was a whisper lost somewhere within the movements of the ground.

He could smell body odor and the mingled scents of cooking, the blossoming odors of human beings working and meeting and loving, millions of such smells buried deep underground.

He suddenly realized he was naked—he'd left his apartment without bothering to put his clothes on. But the mud had smeared so thickly across his chest and thighs he actually felt modest.

He wanted to tell them he loved them all. He wanted to say things he'd never been able to say before. He wanted to speak to the mud and have the mud speak back.

When he'd been in his sand box with his brother the sand had been like love to him, warm and caressing, insinuating itself so quickly into every part of him.

And yet here, as he began to speak of his regrets and the mud began to melt and the dark earth pushed into his throat to meet the words, he knew there was no love here. He had gone past love completely, to something far more elemental.

Tom tried desperately to hold on to his body, the soft bleeding slide of his own flesh, but his body was gone.

VINTAGE DOMESTIC

She used to tell him that they'd have the house forever. One day their children would live there. When Jack grew too old to walk, or to feed himself, she would take care of him in this house. She would feed him right from her own mouth, with a kiss. He'd always counted on her keeping this promise.

But as her condition worsened, as the changes accelerated, he realized that this was a promise she could not keep. The roles were to be reversed, and it was to be he who fed his lifetime lover with a kiss full of raw meat and blood. Sweet, domestic vintage.

Early in their marriage his wife had told him that there was this history of depression in her family. That's the way members of the family always talked about it: the sadness, the melancholy, the long slow condition. Before he understood what this meant he hadn't taken it that seriously, because at the time she never seemed depressed. Once their two oldest reached the teen years, however, she became sad, and slow to move, her eyes dark stones in the clay mask of her face, and she stopped telling him about her family's history of depression. When he asked her about the old story, she acted as if she didn't know what he was talking about.

At some point during her rapid deterioration someone had labeled his family "possibly dysfunctional." Follow-up visits from teachers and social workers had removed "possibly" from his family's thickening file. Studies and follow-up studies had been completed, detailed reports and addenda analyzing his children's behavior and the family dynamics. He had fought them all the way, and perhaps they had tired of the issue, because they finally gave up on their investigations. His family had weathered their accusations. He had protected his wife and children, fulfilled his obligations. Finally people left them alone, but they could not see that something sacred was occurring in this house.

The house grew old quickly. But not as quickly as his wife and children.

*

"You're so damned cheerful all the time," she said to him. "It makes me sick."

At one time that might have been a joke. Looking into her gray eyes at this moment, he knew it was not. "I'm maintaining," he said. "That's all." He thought maybe her vision was failing her. He was sure it had been months since he'd last smiled. He bent over her with the tea, and then passed her a cracker. She stretched her neck and tried to catch his lips in her teeth. He expected a laugh but it didn't come.

"You love me?" she asked, her voice flat and dusty. He put the cracker in his mouth and let her take it from his lips. He could hear his teenage daughters in the next room moaning from the bed. They'd been there two months already, maybe more.

She reached up with a brittle touch across his cheek. "They take after me, you know?" And then she did smile, then opened her mouth around a dry cough of a laugh.

Downstairs their seven-year-old son made loud motorcycle noises with moist lips and tongue. Thank God he takes after his father, he thought, and would have laughed if he could. Beneath him his sweet wife moaned, her lips cracked and peeling. A white tongue flickered like the corner of a starched handkerchief.

He bit down hard into the tender scar on the inside of his mouth. He ground one tooth, two, through the tentative pain. When he tasted salt he began to suck, mixing the salt and iron taste with saliva that had become remarkable in its quantity, until the frothy red cocktail was formed.

He bent over her lips with this beverage kiss and allowed her tongue to meet his, her razor teeth still held back in supplication. In this way he fed her when she could no longer feed herself, when she could not move, when she could not hunt, when in their house tall curtains of dust floated gently around them.

"The girls," she said, once her handkerchief tongue was soaked and her pale lips glistened pinkly.

But still he could not go into his daughters' bedroom, and had to listen to them moan their hunger like pale and hairless, motherless rats.

"Tell me again, Jack," his wife whispered wetly from the bed. "Tell me again how wonderful life is." These were among the last words she would ever use with him.

The young man at the front door wore the blue uniform of the delivery service. Overripe brown sacks filled each of his arms, blending into his fat cheeks as if part of them. He smiled all the time. Jack smiled a hungry smile back.

"Your groceries, sir." Behind him were the stirrings of dry skin against cloth, insect legs, and pleadings too starved and faint to be heard clearly.

As the young man handed the sacks over to him, Jack's fingertips brushed the pale backs of the man's hands. He imagined he could feel the heat there, the youthful coursing through veins, feeding pale tissues, and warming otherwise cold meat.

Sometimes he took his daughters hunting, if they were strong enough, but so far he had been able to limit them to slugs, worms, insects, small animals. He wondered how long he could hold them to that when the stores kept sending them tender young delivery boys. He wondered how long it would be before his daughters were as immobile as his wife, and begged him to bring them something more. Somewhere behind him there was a tiny gasp, the rising pressure of tears which could not fall.

Some evenings he would sit up talking to his family long into the night. They did not always respond precisely to his confessions of loneliness, of dreams which did not include them, and he wondered if it was because of the doors that separated them from him.

Sometimes he would go to the closet doors and open them. Where his wife stood, folded back against the wall with the coats and robes. Where his daughters leaned one against the other like ancient, lesbian mops. Kiss us, the dry whisper came from somewhere within the pale flaps of their faces. Jack still loved them desperately, but he could not do what they asked.

His youngest, his only son, had taken to his bed.

Jack brought his daughters mice and roaches he had killed

himself. They sucked on them like sugar candy until most of the color was gone, and then they spat them out.

Months ago they had stopped having their periods. The last few times had been pale pink and runny, and Jack had cried for them, and then cleaned them up with old burlap sacks.

His son disappeared from his bed one evening. Jack found him standing in the closet, his eyes full of moths, his hands stiffened into hooks.

Later his son would disappear from time to time, sometimes showing up in one of the other closets, clutching at mother or sisters, sometimes curled up inside the empty toy box (the boy had no more use for toys, having his own body to play with—sometimes he'd chew a finger into odd shapes).

Jack continued to feed his wife from his own mouth. Sometimes his mouth was so raw he could not tear any more skin off the insides. Then he'd bite through a rat or a bird himself, holding its rank warmth in his cheeks until he could deliver the meal. She returned his kisses greedily, always wanting more than he could provide. But he had spoiled her. She would not feed any other way.

His son became a good hunter, and sometimes Jack would hear him feeding on the other side of the closet door. Pets began disappearing from the neighborhood, and Jack stopped answering the door even for delivery boys.

His daughters became despondent and refused to eat. When he opened their closet door they tried to disguise themselves as abandoned brooms. Finally Jack had to hold them one at a time, forcing his blood smeared tongue past their splintered lips into the dry cisterns of their mouths so that they might leech nourishment. Once he'd overcome their initial resistance they scraped his tongue clean, then threatened to carve it down to the root, but Jack always knew the exact moment to pull out.

Sometimes he wondered if they still considered him a good father, an adequate husband. He tried singing his children lullabies, reciting poetry to his wife. They nodded their full heads of dust in the gale of his breath, but said nothing.

When the food delivery boys no longer came he saved a portion of his kills for himself. And whenever possible he swallowed his own bloody wet kisses, and tried to remember the feel of his wife's hands on his face, back when her skin was soft and her breath was sweet.

In the houses around him, he knew a hundred hearts beat, desperately chasing life's apprehensions through a racecourse of veins. He tried to ignore the hunger brought on by such thinking. He tried to picture his neighbors' faces, but could not.

His family became so light he could carry them about the house without effort. If he hadn't heard their close whispers, he might have thought them a few old towels thrown across his shoulder. Sometimes he would set them down and forget them, later rushing around in panic to find where they'd been mislaid. The lighter, the thinner they became, the more blood they seemed to require. When his mouth became too sore to chew he would apply razor blades to the scar tissue, slicing through new white skin into the thicker layers beneath, finally into muscle so that the blood would fill his mouth to spilling before he could get his mouth completely over theirs. Blood stained their thin chests with a rough crimson bib.

And still they grew thinner, their bones growing fibrous, pulpy before beginning to dissolve altogether. He made long rips in his forearms, his thighs, his calves, and held his wife and children up to drink there. The blood soaked through the tissues of their flesh, through the translucent fibers of their hair, washing through their skin until in the dusty shadows of the house they looked vaguely tanned.

But almost as quickly they were pale again, and thin as a distant memory.

He took to slicing off hunks of thigh muscle, severing fingertips, toes. His family ate for months off the bloody bits, their small rat teeth nibbling listlessly. They had ceased using words of any kind long ago, so they could not express their thanks. But Jack didn't mind. This was the family he'd always dreamed of. The look of appreciation in their colorless eyes was thanks enough.

At first he tore his clothes to rags to staunch the blood, but even the rags eventually fell apart. One day seeing his son sucking up the last bit of red from a torn twist of cloth he decided to forego the last vestiges of his modesty and throw the ragged clothes away. After that time he would walk about the dreary old house naked, wearing only the paper-thin bodies of his family wrapped around him, their mouths fixed tightly to his oozing wounds.

This went on for months, wearing his family constantly, their feeding so regular and persistent it seemed to alter the very rhythm of his heart. He would wake up in the middle of the night to the soft sucking noise their lips and teeth made against his flesh. He would awaken a few hours later and the first thing he would see was the stupored look in their eyes as they gazed up at him in adoration. He was pleased to see that such constant nourishment fattened them and brought color to their skin so that eventually they fell off his body from the sheer weight of them. Wriggling about his feet at first, they eventually decided to explore the house on their own. Obviously, they felt far healthier than before.

Again they did not thank him, but what did a good husband and father need of thanks?

They soon grew thin again, soft, transparent.

After a year he had not seen them again. Although occasionally he might swear to a face hidden within the upholstery, an eye rolling past a furniture leg, a dry mouth praying silently among the house plants filmed in a dark, furry dust.

After five years even the garbled whispering had stopped. He continued to watch over the house, intent on his obligation. And after preparing a blood kiss in the pale vacancy of his mouth, he was content to drink it himself.

GRANDFATHER WOLF

Her grandfather sat in the big red chair in the living room, staring out the double windows at the back lawn where her father had put in tennis courts, a playground for her, and a workshop where he could make furniture whenever he wanted to. The chair was one of those old ones, with elaborate designs in gold thread, a high back and wings. She thought it made her grandfather, especially with his long white hair, look like a king, or maybe a wizard.

Her grandfather had not spoken to anyone since arriving, except for the maid who had brought him a copper-colored drink in a tall crystal glass. He had smiled at the maid, but he hadn't smiled at anyone else since then. Abigail's mother told her she should go speak to him—after all he was her grandfather, and she'd never met him before. Even though they all—her father and mother, her two younger brothers—now lived in his house, grandfather himself had been away for many years. No one ever explained why, and she had never asked. Perhaps another girl might have asked, but she was just that way. No one in her family ever asked anything.

"But you mustn't bother him," her mother warned, grasping Abigail's forearms tightly and speaking directly into her face, "and if he becomes angry with you, you must leave the room immediately."

How could Abigail know she was bothering him before it was too late? This was the sort of caution she'd received before when dealing with adults, and their dire warnings never helped her know how to behave. But there was obviously something more important about this particular warning, something in her mother's eyes and in her voice. Abigail just couldn't tell what it was. Instead of frightening her, her mother's warning led her to believe that her grandfather must be a very important adult indeed, which made her all the more eager to meet him.

As she'd been taught to do for parties, Abigail grabbed a plate full of cookies off the serving table and carried it to her grandfather with the intent of offering him one. She didn't know if this was appropriate for a family gathering or not, or if her grandfather even had a sweet tooth (What a strange expression—surely an entire mouth full of "sweet teeth" was what was required!), but at least it gave her an excuse, and something to hold between herself and this old man she'd never met before.

She stood in front of him, staring—he appeared to be asleep. His face was long, and serious, and outlined in whiskers the color of shiny steel pots. He had a wide mouth he kept cracked slightly open, providing just a glimpse of the mystery of his teeth. His lips were like velvet pillows, full and ripe and much more like a girl's than a man's, she thought, although she understood that was an opinion she best keep to herself.

His eyebrows were like fat spaniels, wiggling very slightly as they struggled to hold his wrinkled lids down.

"Grandfather, can I interest you in a cookie or two, perhaps?" She used her sweeter, politer voice, the one designed for important visitors and foreign dignitaries.

She wasn't sure if he'd heard her, but the top of one of his ears appeared to bulge slightly upward, like an ocean wave drawn by the moon. Then one big nostril twitched, followed by the other. His eyes crept out from behind their lids, shifted, and found her at the end of his long nose. "I never eat sweets, child," he said and looked away, closing his eyes again. So he didn't want a cookie. She understood that. But he could still talk to her. She stood there awhile, waiting. Finally he spoke again, his eyes still closed. "Was there something else?"

There was everything else, but she didn't know how to say that, so she asked, "How did you know I was still here? With your eyes closed?"

"Do not take this the wrong way, but I could smell you," he replied, eyes still shut.

"I took a bath this morning, before the party. Mother made me."

"That would not help. Nothing personal, you understand. Predator and prey, that sort of thing. It is, what you call, nature. And nature cannot be dissuaded."

She didn't understand what he was talking about, so she just said what she knew. "You're my grandpa, you know?"

He opened his eyes immediately, stared at her, studied her up and down, and then loudly sniffed the air. "Yes. Of course I am. What was your name?"

"I have the same one I always had, Grandpa. It's Abigail."

"After your great-grandmother."

"I—think so." Abigail thought the air smelled kind of funny, like it did when their last dog had puppies, or how it smelled in the attic that time when she found a box some mice had eaten through and there had been three or four little mice still inside the box, sleeping in a mound of chewed paper.

"You sound like her as well, just a bit. You're a bit precocious for your age, aren't you? How old are you?"

"Thirteen. Daddy says I'm precocious, too. That's a compliment, isn't it? At least when Daddy says it, it sounds like a compliment. I'm not so sure about you." Her grandfather made a snuffling sound. She guessed that was supposed to be a laugh. "Great-grandmother, she was your mother?"

Once again he sniffed the air loudly before he answered. "Yes, child. I take after her in some ways. I think you take after her in some ways. But you're not much like your father, or your mother, are you?"

"I don't know. My mother and I don't always get along, but I still love her."

"Child, I didn't mean it as an insult. Simple observation. Family members have many differences. Sometimes you have more in common with an earlier generation than a previous one."

"If you say so." She was beginning to feel bored, and unsure of exactly what he was saying, she wanted to leave.

"Turn your head slightly to the left, please."

She did as she was told, although she didn't like it. She wondered if he was checking to see if she'd done a good job washing her face.

"You do have Jackson's—your father's—eyes. But everything else—your nose, the curve of jaw, that mouth—those are definitely all your great-grandmother Abigail's. How interesting."

Abigail didn't understand what was so interesting about it.

Weren't people in the same family supposed to look like each other? She wasn't sure what she wanted from her grandfather, if anything. Perhaps she just wanted to know more about her family, why they were the way they were, and why her grandfather had always stayed away. But she decided she wasn't going to learn anything from this strange old man. She started to go— his eyes were closed again so obviously he wouldn't even notice —when she saw the sketchpad and the pencil on the table by his chair.

"Do you draw, Grandpa?"

He opened his eyes again. "I sketch, yes. It relaxes me."

"Daddy is an artist—did you know? Except he says his canvas is wood."

"Is he? Then I assume these are his handiwork? They weren't here when I kept up the place." Her grandfather gestured at the carvings around the doors and windows, the fronts of the bookcases, even the rims and legs of the tables: deer and bears and many dogs and people running, carrying torches, carrying guns, something leaping although you could never quite tell what it was.

Abigail nodded. "He made them when I was little."

"Very . . . impressive."

"I like to draw, too," she said. "Daddy says I inherited his talent. Maybe I inherited your talent as well." And so happy she was at discovering something in common between them, she boldly picked up the sketchpad and started flipping through it.

After she looked at a couple of the drawings it occurred to her that perhaps she'd been too forward. But her grandfather had made no attempt at stopping her, although that slightly dirty, slightly moist, hairy smell was even more intense in the room. "Wow, Grandpa! You're a much better draw-er than I am!"

"I've had practice, child," he said softly.

The drawings were a mix of pencil and charcoal. Many of them were of birds—robins, cranes, blue jays, doves—and so real Abigail thought she could see the flicker in their eyes, the rapid pulse in their throats. She put her longish nose close to the paper and could swear she smelled the smell of bird.

But there were other animals as well—a rabbit peeking out

from behind a clump of grass, its nose swelling ever so slightly, a deer leaping between two trees—she was sure she saw its ribcage move. A slow-moving turtle, a fish dissolving into a wave, a dog with its ears suddenly alert.

And the last picture, the only human in the bunch, a little girl, a toddler, standing by the corner of a house, looking straight out from the paper, her eyes so, so wide. Abigail recognized her as a child who lived on the next street.

"Could you show me how to draw the way you do, Grandpa?"

"I suppose I could show you, oh, a few tricks. Pick up that pencil, please, and turn to a fresh page."

Even though she was eager, Abigail turned the page of the sketchpad carefully so as not to tear or smudge it. She gripped the pencil tightly. "Tell me what to do, Grandpa."

"First you have to hold the pencil properly, my dear, so that you may use your entire arm when you make your marks. Grasp it further back, the way you might hold a paint brush, and not so tightly."

But Abigail could not manage to position her fingers properly —they felt like sticks attached to her hand, and she dropped the pencil several times. Finally in frustration she hopped up onto her grandfather's lap and snuggled her back up against him. It was a little kid thing to do, she knew, but he was her grandfather, and she really wanted to learn this. She held out her pencil. "Show me," she said.

Her grandfather said nothing for a moment, although she could hear his mouth making a creaking, wheezing sound as if he were having difficulty breathing. She started to turn and ask him if he was okay when his right hand came around and slowly enveloped hers, manipulating her fingers and molding her grip. His hand was long—it looked almost as long as her entire arm —and she could feel the strength of it, all kinds of hard muscles inside as if it were full of steel wires and rods. He guided her at first like she was a helpless puppet, making spheres and cones and long cylinders, but before she knew it she was connecting those shapes on her own, making long graceful curves that transformed cones and spheres and cubes and cylinders into hummingbird beaks and giraffe necks and gorilla torsos. "Help

me make a rhinoceros," she said, and they did. "Help me make a
hippo," she demanded, and soon a wet-backed hippo gazed out
at her from a gleaming pool of pencil marks. "Now let's make a
wolf," she cried, and her grandfather's long hand stopped, hover-
ing patiently over the paper.

"Child, I will not draw a wolf," he murmured into her ear.

"Why not?" She held her breath.

"Because they are wretched and miserable and a plague upon
the countryside, and cantankerous as they grow old, intolerant
and most untrustworthy. I will not draw one."

"That's okay, Grandpa. How about a dog?"

"Dogs are fine animals, and loyal to a fault, I am told."

So together they drew dogs and cats and all the pets in the
neighborhood. Abigail lost track of the time as they filled the
sketchbook with every kind of animal she had ever seen or
imagined, except wolves. Her grandfather nodded in and out
of sleep with some bit of encouragement or instruction before
another untroubled, gentle doze.

She was only vaguely aware of the dimming light and the first
cooking smells drifting in from the kitchen when she heard the
sound of tongue on lips behind her, and again caught that stench
of animal life. "Do the smells make you hungry, Grandpa?"

But he did not answer. Instead she felt his electric shudder,
and as she teetered from his lap she grabbed hold of his arms on
either side of her. She felt his skin ripple, then something prickly
against her palms and the undersides of her fingers. She looked
down at her hands as wire-like hair sprouted and grew around
them.

"Away," he said, in the midst of a gargling noise. "Away, girl!
Now!"

She sprang from his lap at the same moment he might have
tumbled her, and turning around she saw him crouched in the
windowsill, pushing out the double windows, leaping out into
the yard where he became a painful red blur skidding across her
vision, disappearing behind her father's workshop.

Late that night she was vaguely aware of the commotion, the
electricity of frantic activity as her family moved about the grand
old house, but she was far too deep in sleep to investigate, and

much too enthralled by her dreams of animals leaping out of pages, of penciled torsos heaving in fright or flight.

The next time Abigail saw her grandfather it was in that same living room, except the red chair was gone now, and an old-fashioned wooden wheelchair sat in its place. Her grandfather sat there, tied to the chair at his waist. Her mother had assured her it was for his safety, so that he wouldn't fall out when he fell asleep, and for no other reason.

The bright white bandages were thick on the stubs of his arms where his hands used to be, and even thicker around his ankles. Abigail thought they looked like those swami hats like people from India wear. One of the ones around his ankles had a little different shape. She'd overheard her daddy say that that was because Grandpa still had some of his foot left on that side.

Abigail carried the sketch pad over to her grandfather. She was very pleased with herself—she'd filled many more pages with drawings of animals. But she didn't want to smile in front of her grandfather, not just yet.

"I'm sorry, Grandpa."

He raised his head as if it weighed three times as much as it had before. "No worries, child. It had to be done. At least now I can stay awhile, get to know my grandchildren better, perhaps help you further your drawing studies."

"But Grandpa, you can't . . . hold my hand and help me."

"Oh, I think you're well beyond that stage. You can sit at my —you can sit in front of my chair and we'll chat. I'll look over your shoulder and provide suggestions from time to time. Now, will you show me what you've been drawing?"

"Sure!" She plopped down, folding her legs daintily beneath her.

"No drawings of wolves?"

"No wolves. But lots of dogs and cats, and squirrels. A big old hoot owl. A raccoon. A few snakes."

"Child, have you been walking in the woods?"

"A little, I guess. See my raccoon?"

The old wooden wheelchair creaked as he leaned over. She could feel his breath on her shoulders. She could smell the dank leaves in it, the rotting hearts of fallen trunks, the scattering corpses of small animals beneath running feet.

"It is very—detailed. Surprisingly so." He sniffed the air above her loudly. "Have you seen many raccoons, child?"

"A few. Look at my squirrel."

The squirrel was bent oddly, the head folded over so comically, Abigail had to stop herself from giggling. Its flattened head half-covered the large hole in its belly.

"Skillfully done, child. Very skillfully done. Child, have you been running in the woods?" He sniffed loudly again.

"Sometimes. Not too often, I don't think. See my rabbits? The way I have them all on their sides pointing in the same direction, lined up in a row? Aren't they cute?"

"Quite precious, my child. Your great-grandmother did something very similar, or so I was told."

She said no more then, turning the pages of the sketchbook slowly, showing her grandfather each new drawing, each carefully arranged final pose. Finally, without turning, she asked, "Grandpa, do you think your teeth could ever reach me now?"

"Oh, I hardly think so. I'm sure you could easily outrun me."

"I'm the best runner in my entire school. And I can jump farther than anyone I know."

"Oh, I'm sure you can."

"Did it hurt very much, Grandpa? When you lost your hands and feet?"

"The pain was—exquisite, child. As it should have been."

"I can't figure out how you did it. I've been thinking and thinking about my daddy's table saw, and I just can't figure out how you got all four."

Her grandfather made a sound behind her then. It sounded like a shudder, but she thought it was really a laugh. "I did the hands first, clasped together, with one quick sweeping movement of the arms. You have to use your entire arm, remember? It's easier that way. Then I leapt with all my might . . ."

"I'm a good leaper," Abigail said.

"I'm sure you are. I leapt straight up onto the table, directly down on the spinning blade. But I was slightly off balance, you see, and I fell off before the blade had eaten through the rest of the one foot."

Abigail was quiet for a time, then she asked, "May I draw a picture of all that? I can see things much more clearly if I can draw pictures of them."

"Yes, you may. But you must promise never to show them to anyone, especially not to other members of the family."

"I'm not a stupid little girl, Grandpa. I know better than that."

"I apologize."

"That's okay." Abigail stared out the window. "Grandpa, do you think if the time ever comes for me, I can do what needs to be done?"

"I cannot answer that for you, my child."

"I think I can. Daddy says I know how to do the right thing. I think I can do what needs to be done. I think I could even jump on a saw blade, if I needed to."

"Very well," her grandfather replied. "Very well."

And that's the last they ever spoke of it. They spent the rest of that day talking about art, and growing up, and changes, and the secrets that lay hidden beneath the muddy, leaf-trodden pathways of the forests beyond.

THE BEREAVEMENT PHOTOGRAPHER

"So, have you been doing this a while now?"

"A few years."

"Sorry for asking, and tell me if I'm out of line, but you can't possibly be making a full-time living doing this can you?"

I actually almost say, "It's a hobby," which would be disastrous. But I don't. I look at the fellow: sandy-haired, a beard whose final length appears to be forever undecided. He looks terrible in the suit—either long outgrown or borrowed for the occasion. And it is an occasion—a grim occasion but an occasion none the less. He watches me as I set up, without a glance for his child. The young wife fusses with her to make ready for this picture, this family portrait.

I'm used to this. Who could blame him.

"I'm a volunteer. They reimburse me for film and lab costs. It's a way . . . of being of service."

He glances down, gazes at his wife rearranging the baby in her arms, glances away again, with no place to look.

Me, I have only one place to look. I peer through the lens, musing on composition issues, the light, the shadows, the angles of their arms. "Could you move her a little to the left?" The husband and father stares at me, puzzled, then bends to move his wife's chair. She blushes.

"No, sorry. You, ma'am." I straighten up behind the camera. "Could you move the baby a little to the left?" Notice how I said "the" baby, not "your." I try to avoid upsetting words. These are family portraits, after all. Just like all families have. Most parents don't want to be crying. I have folders full of photographs of mothers and fathers wailing, faces split in the middle. Believe me, they don't want to keep those. Sometimes I have taken roll after roll until there is sufficient calm for me to make the picture that will go into some leather-bound matte, slipped into some nondescript manila folder, or, if they're so inclined, up on the living room mantel in a place of honor, there, oh so much there, for the whole world to see.

I've been doing this for years. But still I find that hard to imagine.

I feel bad that I haven't found the right words for this father, the words that will soothe, or at least minimize his discomfort and embarrassment. But sometimes there are just no right words. At least I can't always find them.

"I'll be taking the shot in a few minutes," I say. "Just make yourself comfortable. This isn't going to be flash flash flash and me telling you to smile each time. The most important thing is to try to make yourselves comfortable. Try to relax and ease into this shared moment."

This shared moment. Whatever words I say to my subjects, I always include these. Even though I've never been sure they were accurate, or fair. The moment is shared in that it happens to both of them. But most of the time, I think, the experience is so personal and large it will soon split the marriage apart if they're not careful.

I've seen it happen so much. I've seen so much.

"Okay, then," I say in warning and again I move behind the camera, almost as if I expect it to protect me from what is to come. As I peer into the electronic viewfinder, so like a small computer screen, so distancing in that same way, I see the mother's smile, and it is miraculous in its authenticity. I've seen it before in my portraits, this miraculous mother's smile, and it never fails to surprise me.

And I see the father at last look down upon his dead baby girl and reach out two fingers, so large against the plump, pale arm, and he lets them linger, a brief time but longer than I would have expected, and I realize this touch is for the first, and last, time.

I again shift my focus to the light, to the shadows and the play of shadows, and ready myself to shoot. The father attempts a dignified smile, but of course goes too broadly with it. The mother holds the child a bit too tightly. And I trigger the camera once, then twice, the baby looking as if she were merely sleeping. The baby looking. Then I take a shot for the photographer, a shot I will never show the parents, an image to add to the growing collection I keep hidden in a file drawer at home, the one in which the baby opens its eyes and fixes its gaze upon me.

I should explain, I suppose, that I've never had much talent for photography. I have the interest, sometimes I've had the enthusiasm, but I've never had the eye. I got this volunteer position because my next door neighbor is a nurse, and she used to see me in my back yard with camera and tripod shooting birds, trash, leaves, whatever happened to land in front of me. Inconsequential subjects, but I was afraid I'd screw up a more significant one, which would have broken my heart, maybe even have prevented me from ever taking another photograph. I didn't want to risk that.

Not that I wanted to risk taking such an important photograph in a family's life, either. But Liz had talked about how temporary this was, how they just needed someone to man the camera now, and every time I tried to tell her I really wasn't that good at it, she said I didn't have to be—the families just wanted the photograph—having it was the idea and they wouldn't care how good it was, technically.

But I told her no anyway. Even unpaid, I would have felt like an impostor. Not only was I not that good as a photographer, but I wasn't that good with kids.

Maybe that sounds terrible under the circumstances. It seemed to me at the time that the appropriate person for this kind of sensitive task would be someone with a strong empathy and dedication to and involvement with children. And I didn't have that. Of course I used to be a child, and my sister Janice and I had pretty good parents, but I don't remember childhood as being a particularly happy time. I could hardly wait for it to be over so I could be out on my own. And I can't say that I've ever enjoyed children. I've never particularly liked spending time with them. My nephews are okay—I've taken them to ballgames and movies and such and I think they're great kids now that they're older. When they were little I didn't know what to say to them and, frankly, they scared me a little. They seemed so needy and fragile and that was pretty much the extent of their personalities.

As far as other kids go, I'd have to say I've basically ignored them. Their concerns are not my concerns. Most of the time I haven't even been aware they were there.

That weekend I was in the city park taking bad pictures. I tried shooting couples, failing—everything looked fuzzy and poorly-framed. Composition was eccentric at best, whatever I tried. A number of families were barbecuing. I noticed one small group in particular: really young parents, kids themselves, with a huge, dish-shaped barbecue looking hundreds of years old.

Suddenly there was an explosion of shouts, barking, shapes racing through the crowd. Then several large dogs burst from the wall of people to my right, followed by a half dozen teenage boys, red-faced, barking like hyenas, and all of them converging on that young family.

I shouted a warning, but too late. One of the dogs knocked the unwieldy barbecue over, and several others a few feet away. The little kids started screaming, the mother and father running toward them, but the air was full of thick, white, choking smoke. The mother grabbed up two of their kids and folded them into her. But the little one, "Jose!" the young father screamed. "Jose!"

I could not breathe in the smoke, but I could not close my eyes. And almost as if to protect my eyes I raised my camera in front of my face and started taking pictures of the turmoil and the panic, the father gesturing as if mad, and I'm wondering how could this be, all this over some kids and their pets, but these poor people, their lives changing forever. And then the little boy appears out of the smoke like some apparition from the mists, some ghost back to rejoin his family because the taking of him had been a mistake, arms reaching up for his daddy, crying and sobbing and the father sobbing as well.

It was at that moment I decided to say yes to my neighbor, and became the hospital's bereavement photographer. Even before I saw the photographs I had taken: the looks on the young couple's faces on their rapid descent into despair, and that small boy appearing out of the clouds like a tragedy retrieved from the fierce and unforgiving eddies of time.

"Oh, Johnny, those poor people!" Janice is my older sister, my confessor, and, I'm a little embarrassed to say, my barometer as to what's normal or abnormal, what's okay and what's not okay.

The day after I'd made that decision to volunteer my photographic services (Would I have changed my mind if she'd responded negatively? I still don't know.) she had a barbecue of her own. I was invited, of course. With no family or even regular girlfriend, I usually ate at her house three, four times a week. Tom didn't seem to mind, but of course you never really know when you visit married couples. They might have been fighting for hours before you got there, but when they open the front door they're like a glossy advertisement for the connubial life.

"Sounds like pretty sad work to me," Tom said morosely.

"Tom!"

"I'm not criticizing him, Janice. It just sounds like it'd be pretty grim stuff, and he's not even being paid to do it."

"Well, I wouldn't be doing it every day," I said, somewhat off the point. I just wanted them both to believe that, contrary to appearances, I lead a pretty balanced life. Despite the fact that I had no girlfriend, spent most of my spare time at their house, and obsessively took photographs even I didn't think were very good.

Janice snorted. "Don't listen to him, Johnny. It's a noble way to spend your time. We should all do at least one activity like that."

The subject mercifully disappeared into a conversational salad of new movies, music, old friends recently seen, what my twin nephews were doing (now fifteen, athletic, and a deadly combination with an alarmingly broad age range of females), and, of course, the pregnancy.

"You should have one of your own, sometime," Janice said, smiling and rubbing her belly as if it were silk.

"Wrong equipment, sis."

"I meant with a girl."

"Oh, duh, I didn't understand."

"You guys." Tom, an only child, didn't get it.

"Actually I think I would, even have it myself, if it made me half as happy as you look every time you're pregnant."

"Every time? Two times, little brother."

"Could be more," Tom said, and ducked when she tossed the ketchup squeeze-bottle at his head.

I looked around. The angle of the light had changed, deepening some colors, brightening others. There had always been an intensity and vividness about my sister's life. It was almost unnatural the way the environment shifted its spectrum to suit her. The bright blue stucco house, the grass green as Astroturf, the red- and white-checkered cloth over the redwood table, laden with matching yellow plates and cups and a rainbow of food. A few feet away the tanned blond boys passing the football through the jeweled spray from the sprinkler. Unexpectedly, the sight made me hold my breath. My beautiful nephews. I could have been a better uncle. But perhaps for the first time, their connection to me seemed sharp and undeniable, and it didn't seem to matter that I didn't understand them most of the time.

All of it like one of those Kodachrome photographs from the sixties: colors so intensely unrealistic, so vividly assaultive, they dazzled the eyes.

The job was meant to be only temporary. That actually increased my stress over the whole affair, because I felt I didn't have that much time to figure out how to do things right. I'd spend a long time with the camera, framing the shot, then suddenly I'd feel everything was wrong, that I'd be leaving this family with nothing to remember their dead child by. So I'd compulsively start all over again adjusting, readjusting, my fingers shaking and sliding off the controls.

Invariably I'd take too long and the family's understandable nervousness would increase ten-fold. They'd suddenly be anxious to let go of this child or they would slip over some invisible line and would act as if they might hold onto this child forever. The mothers, mostly. The fathers would usually just be irritated, but most of them started out irritated, angry. They were being asked or pressured into doing something they weren't really sure they could do.

Liz could see what was happening. She let me struggle a little at first, scoping out the boundaries of my difficulty, and then she finally stepped in, talking to these parents, letting them know what to expect, helping me set up, letting me know what to expect, by example teaching me what to say, what to look out for, how to pace things so the experience wasn't too much, wasn't too little.

Despite all my worries, I never took a bad picture for any of these people. Oh, some shots were better than others, certainly, but I don't think I ever took a really bad shot. As morbid as it sounds, I had found my subject.

And my subject had found me.

Taking pictures of dead children—well, as I've said the work generated the expected tension in both the families and the photographer. I'd spend so much time trying to get a pose that looked natural. Sometimes I'd be working so hard to make everything look just right I'd forget why these people were looking so sad and I'd catch myself hoping that the baby would wake up and look at the camera.

And when one of them finally did, I went on with what I was doing and took the shot without a thought about what had just occurred.

Then minutes later—I stood up and looked over the camera at the couple and their tiny, tiny baby. Dead baby—I could not have imagined a creature so small who looked so like a miniature human being could have survived our comparatively brutal, everyday air.

The couple looked at me uneasily. Finally the man said, "Are we done here? Something wrong?"

Everything's wrong, I wanted to say. Your baby is dead. How much wronger could things possibly get?

"No," I said. "No." And I looked closely at this child, hoping to see that it was sleeping, but immediately knew it was not.

Dead children, at least the really small ones, have an unformed, stylized quality even though there may be nothing missing anatomically. Their tiny bodies recall some unusual piece of art, perhaps of an animal that's never been seen before, some part-human, part-bird thing, or some new breed of feral pig or rodent. They are like remnants of the long, involved dream you just had, mysteriously conveyed to our waking world. They are like hope petrified and now you have no idea where to put the thing.

That was what sat perched against the young mother's swollen breasts, a sad reminder of her fullness craving release.

Of course I decided almost immediately that what I was sure

I had seen hadn't even happened at all. One of the things that occurs when you spend a great deal of time staring into a camera lens is that stationary things appear to move, moving things freeze, and a variety of other optical illusions may occur. Things appear, disappear, change color and shape. Of course you don't have to use a camera to see this—stare at almost anything in the real world long enough and these kinds of phenomena occur. That's true enough, isn't it? I mean, it isn't just me, right?

The great photographers are great because they see things differently from the rest of us. So from our perspective they see things that aren't there. I've long had this notion, not quite a theory, that the world changes when a great photographer looks through the lens.

As I said before, I'm not a great photographer. But when I took those first rolls home and developed them I think I got just a glimpse of what the great photographer sees. In three of the shots the baby's eyes were open, looking at me.

I admit that upon occasion I do fall prey to a certain suggestibility. I'm wound pretty tightly at times. I get somewhat anxious in the darkroom. I'm interested in shadows in an aesthetic sense, but I'm also uncomfortable with them. Unexpected sounds can make me jump out of my skin. I don't care for scary movies. And I'll believe almost anything that comes out of the mouth of a well-spoken man or woman.

So I wasn't about to let myself believe what the pictures were telling me. Not without a fight.

"Liz, did you ever notice the babies' eyes? How sometimes they're . . . open just a little?"

I don't know if I expected her to ask me if I'd been drinking, or suggest that I get more sleep, or maybe just stare at me with that evaluating look I'd seen her give some of the patients. But I didn't expect the calmness, the matter-of-factness. "Sometimes the eyes don't close all the way. When they get to the embalmer, sometimes he'll sew the lids down, or glue them maybe. Whatever seems necessary for the viewing. Occasionally I'll warn the parents, if I think it will upset them. Why, has it been bothering you, or is it just something you noticed?"

Relieved, I almost told her what I'd been thinking, what I'd been imagining, but I didn't. "I just noticed," I said.

So for a while I refocused myself on just taking the pictures, trying to relax the couples (or in some cases, single moms, and in one very complicated case, a single dad, who seemed angry about the whole thing, and frowned during the picture, but still insisted that the picture with his son was something he had to have. Liz was obviously nervous about that one, and hung around outside the room while I hurried the session.) My composition got better; the pictures improved.

Sometimes there would be something different about a baby: a certain slant to the shoulders, a small hand frozen in a gesture, an ambiguous expressiveness in the face that tugged at my imagination, but I withheld any response. I knew that if I brought any of these details to Liz's attention she would give me some simple, calm, rational answer, and I would feel that I was only making myself suspect in her eyes.

Yet I felt almost guilty not to be paying more notice to these small details, as if I were ignoring the appeals of some damaged or frightened child. And what did I know of these things? I'd never been a parent, never hoped to be a parent. I knew nothing, really, of children. I had learned a little about grieving parents: how they held their dead babies, how they looked at the camera, how they held themselves.

And I could see clearly, now, the way the eyelids sometimes loosened a bit, sliding up to expose crescent-shaped slivers of grayish eyeball. I'd seen this look in people who were napping —there was nothing unusual about it. But I still didn't like seeing this in the babies. For in the babies it didn't look like napping at all—it looked like additional evidence of their premature deaths.

I had become more relaxed in my volunteer work. I didn't expect any surprises and no surprises occurred. And yet still I would occasionally take those special pictures out of their folders and examine them. And it did not escape my notice that the babies in the pictures, the ones who appeared to be staring at me, had eyes which remained wide open, with an aspect of deliberate, and unmistakable intention.

*

This vocation of bereavement photography is hardly a new one. From the earliest days of photography you will find pictures of dead people staring at the camera, sometimes with the surgeon's or embalmer's stitches all too visible around the scalp or chest. The adults are in their best clothing, sometimes slouched in a chair, sometimes propped up in bed, a Bible underneath one hand. Sometimes the women are holding flowers.

Many, of course, appear to be sleeping, caught by the sneaky photographer as they nap the afternoon away. Others look terrified: eyes wide and impossibly white, the enlarged dots of their pupils fixing you in a mean, unforgiving gaze.

These gazes are artificial, of course: the eyes painted on to the closed, dead lids. They look, I think, like stills from some badly animated cartoon.

In those days portraiture was quite a bit more formal, and sittings a special occasion. Few families owned cameras of their own, and you might have only two or three photographs taken of yourself over the course of a lifetime. Sometimes a grieving relative's only chance for a photographic record of a beloved's life was after the beloved was dead.

This was particularly true in the case of children. Infant mortality in the days of our great-grandparents was so high that without the photographic proof people might not ever know you'd ever been a parent. You dressed them up as angels and paid the man good money to take their ever-lasting portraits, money you doubtless could not spare. You put those portraits up on the mantel or in an honored place on the parlor wall, and you showed them to friends and neighbors, even salesmen come to call. And you alternately preened and choked with grief when they commented "how precious," "how handsome," and "how terribly, terribly sad."

The issue returned with the Wilson child.

Did I mention before that most of the children I photographed were stillborns? Of course that would make sense as there would be no opportunities for school pictures or family portraits or any of the other usual domestic photo opportunities. The need for my services was greater.

But occasionally an older child of one or two years would be signed up for the service, accompanied by parents who were always a bit ashamed for not having engaged in that normal, parental obsession of incessant snapshots and home movies.

I have to say I was glad this particular age group didn't come up too often. It was awful enough to take pictures of parents devastated by the loss of a dream—a child who might have been anything, whose likes and dislikes, the sound of the voice, were completely unknown. Worse was the child who had developed a personality, however roughly formed, who liked toy trucks and hated green beans, who smelled of a dozen different things, whose eyes had focus.

The Wilsons were older than the usual couples I saw. She was in her early forties; he had to be on the far side of fifty. They had a small chicken farm twenty miles outside the city. Mrs. Wilson smelled of flour and of make-up carelessly and too thickly applied. In fact I think make-up was a rare accessory for her. She had pupils like little dark peas, washed up in cup of milk. There was something wrong with her hip; she shuffled and bobbed across the room to the metal chair I'd set up for her. The nice chair was being cleaned, and the appointment had been hastily arranged. I felt bad about that. I knew nothing about her, but I would have liked to have photographed her in the finest hotel in the city.

This reaction was all silliness on my part, of course. She wouldn't have cared—she was barely aware of her surroundings. Her eyes were focused on another piece of furniture in the room: a gurney bearing a small swaddled bundle, an elderly nurse stationed nearby as if to prevent its theft or escape.

Mr. Wilson also came to me in layers. Floating above it all was the stink of chickens, of years of too much labor with too little reward. Under that was a face like sheared-off slabs of rock, and eyes scorched from too little crying, no matter what. Unlike Mrs. Wilson, there appeared to be nothing wrong with his body, but he shuffled across the floor just the same, a rising tide of anger impeding forward progress. He stopped dutifully by the rigid metal chair, gripping the back with narrow, grease-stained fingers, a little too tightly because he thought no one would notice. He watched as his wife made her way painfully over to the gurney and stood there patting and stroking—not the sunken little bundle, but the sheets surrounding it.

He didn't move another step. He knew his place.

The nurse asked if they'd like to "get situated," and then she'd bring them their son. I couldn't imagine what she meant—it sounded as if they were moving into a new place, or starting a new job. They appeared to understand her better, however. Mrs. Wilson dropped into the chair and held on to her knees. Mr. Wilson straightened up as if to verify the height listed on his driver's license.

The nurse carried the package over, whispering comforting things into its open top. She unwrapped the child and fussed with him in mock-complaint, trying to position him in his mother's lap so that the large dent in the side of his head wouldn't show. She almost managed it by laying the dent against his mother's chest and twisting his pelvis a little. She pretended not to notice the mother's profound shudder.

Then the nurse quickly backed away from the house of cards she'd just constructed, holding her breath as if even that might trigger collapse. She retreated to the back of the room, with a gesture toward the family as if presenting some magic trick or religious tableau.

The couple stared straight ahead, slightly above me at the dark wall behind. I didn't bother telling them to look at or reposition the child. They were done with me and what I represented.

All that was left for me to do was to gaze at the child and snap the shutter.

Even slumped inwards like that, he was actually a pretty sturdy kid. Broad-faced with chubby arms and legs. The head a little large, and I wondered briefly if there had been a spreading due to impact and I shook slightly, a bit disgusted with myself. This couple's beautiful little boy.

But the head wasn't quite right, and the composition was made worse by the couple's hunched forward, intense stares. I moved the camera and tripod a little to the left, while gazing through the viewfinder, ready to stop moving when things looked right.

The little boy opened his eyes, the pupils following me.

I looked up from the viewfinder. The eyes remained closed.

Back with my eye to the lens and the boy's eyes were following me again, as I moved further left, then back right again. It was probably just the position of his head and the slump of the shoulders, but he looked angry. He looked furious.

Finally I stopped. The eyes closed. But as I started to press the button they opened again. Bore down on me. Impatient, waiting.

I took shot after shot that afternoon. Most of them were unusable. What was he so angry about? It was as if he didn't want his picture taken with these people and he was blaming me for it.

After that day the children opened their eyes for me now and then, although certainly not during the majority of these sessions. I don't believe I'd still be doing this work today if it had happened with every child. Most of the time my volunteer work consisted of calming the parents without actually counseling them—I don't have the temperament or training for it. Positioning them, feeling out what they would be comfortable with, and finally taking the shot. That's what it's all about really, taking the shot.

The children who opened their eyes to me hampered that work, since obviously I couldn't send those poor couples home with that kind of photograph. Increasingly they seemed angry with me, and increasingly I was irritated with them for the obstacle they had become.

"Okay . . . uh, could you move her to the left just a bit? There, that's good. That's perfect."

And she is. This child, this Amy, my flesh, my blood, my niece. Tom grips Janice's shoulders a little too firmly. I can see the small wince of discomfort playing with the corners of my sister's mouth. I look at Tom, he looks back at me, relaxes his hands. He looks so pale—I think if I don't take this family portrait soon he might faint. The twin boys stand to each side of him, beautiful and sullen, yet they pull in closer to his body for his support and theirs.

Janice looks up at me, her little brother, not sure what she should do. I offer her a smile; she takes it, attempts to make it her own, and almost succeeds.

Then I look through the lens. I look at Amy, and she's otherworldly, beautiful as her mother. And then she opens her eyes, giving me that stare I've seen a hundred times before, but it's different this time, because this is Amy, this is one of my own. I see the anger coming slowly into her eyes, but I smile at her anyway. I make a kiss with my mouth, and I hope she understands it is just for her. And I take the shot, this one for me, and she closes her eyes again, and I take the other shot for them.

INVISIBLE

Over the past few months something painful and awkward had come into the light. Ray was never quite able to define it, and of course did not feel he could check out this perception with anyone else. It would be an odd thing to say, and he knew he had a reputation for saying odd things, although no one had actually told him so.

There were days he could barely stand to open his eyes. Something in the atmosphere, perhaps, that stung the cornea. Every object he looked at was outlined in bright white light. A brilliance he was not supposed to see, a visibility not meant for him. These haloing strokes appeared hesitant, as if part of an unsure painting.

It was the kind of light he imagined you would see at the end of the world: a sad, quiet fading of form and color, as if all earthly materials were dissolving from a mass failure of conviction.

Although he did not expect confirmation of his anxieties, or really want one, Ray listened to the hourly radio weather reports, noting the announcer's tone when he spoke words such as "overcast," "upper atmosphere," and "visibility." There was anxiety in the slight, random trembling of the otherwise smooth voice. Did the weatherman hold something back? The answers were all there, he suspected, floating through the air, hiding in the aftertaste of water, momentarily visible in the bright, painful regions of reflected sun, if one only knew the right way to see, to taste, to hear.

He called his wife two or three times during the day to see how she was feeling, thinking she might be sensing something similar, but he was unable to ask her directly. At some point they'd stopped authenticating each other's sadder perceptions about their places in the universe.

At least in the office there were few windows, and the predictable lines of the cubicles were comfortably familiar. Weather ceased to be a factor once he arrived at work.

Anyone up for lunch? Ray had waited an hour or so for someone to make the invitation. He normally timed his work so he could be available any time between noon and one.

He stood up in his cubicle. Several other heads popped up out of the maze of short, upholstered partitions, like prairie dogs out of their holes. The others waved to the speaker—Marty, a lead programmer—and grabbed their coats. After an awkward pause with Marty staring straight at him, Ray tentatively raised a hand and waved as well. Marty's expression didn't change. He couldn't have missed Ray's intention.

Ray saved his work, jotted down some notes, stood and slipped on his coat. He got to the elevators just as the doors were closing. His coworkers stared out at him without recognition. No one tried to stop the doors. He waved again, said, "Hey!" He ran down four flights to the lobby. He almost ran over a woman on the second floor landing. He stopped to apologize but could see the distaste in her eyes (or was it pity?). Out of breath, he reached the outside doors. He watched as they pulled away, all of them jammed into Marty's green Ford. How did they get out there so quickly? Again he waved as the car swung past the entrance and out the driveway. A woman from another office scooted by him and out the door. It suddenly embarrassed him that she'd seen him with his hand up, waving to no one, greeting nothing as if nothing might wave back, and he lowered it.

He went back upstairs to his cubicle, hoping no one had seen him return. He went back to work on the day's projects, not thinking to remove his coat. From time to time hunger pains stroked his belly like nervous fingers. He had a lunch in the office refrigerator—he always had a lunch in the office refrigerator—but he didn't bother to go get it.

The sky outside went from a misty white to a deep blue, then to grays and oranges, as if painted on an enormous turning disk. He did not learn this from looking out the window but saw it reflected in his computer screen. Days passed in this awkwardly glimpsed view of the world. He could feel his hands on the keyboard begin the painful petrifaction that must surely lead to transparency. At some point Marty and the others wandered past as they returned from lunch, louder than usual. Marty eventually brought some papers by for Ray to look at. There was no mention of the missed lunch. Ray thought perhaps his intentions had been misunderstood. They were all well-meaning people here. The world was full of well-meaning people. It wasn't their fault he didn't know how to conduct himself.

At the end of the day he took the stairs down to the parking lot, leaving fifteen minutes early. He did this every day. It was unlikely he'd be fired for such an offense, but he somewhat enjoyed imagining the possibility. Perhaps an announcement would be made. Perhaps he would be forced to exit through the reception area carrying his box of meager belongings as other employees stood and watched. Would any of them wish him well in his future endeavors?

Outside the air shimmered with possibility. He did his best to ignore it.

Traffic was again heavy and slow, the cars unable to maneuver beyond the occasional lane change. There was a quality of anger in the way people sped up and slowed down, changed lanes, slipped into the breakdown lane in order to make an illegal pass on the left. The anger made Ray feel as if some explosion was imminent, some volcanic eruption of blame he might drown in.

But he didn't mind the traffic per se—it gave him the opportunity to gaze into the interiors of the other cars, to see what the people were doing when they thought no one was looking, observe the little things (singing, grooming, picking their noses) they did to divert tedium, follow the chase of expressions across their faces, all of them no doubt feeling safe and assured of their invisibility.

His was simply one more can awash in a sea of metal. He was content to wait until the tide brought him home.

Janice didn't turn around when Ray walked into the kitchen. "It's almost ready," she said. "We have to be there by six-thirty. We can't be late."

"If we're late, she might think we're not coming. We can't let that happen."

"No, we can't." She dealt slices of tomato rapidly into the stew. "So, what did you do for lunch today? Did you go out with anybody?"

She always tried to sound casual about it. She always failed.

"No." He started to make up a satisfactory reason, then gave up. "I worked through." He looked over her shoulder into the bubbling liquid, always fascinated by the way carrots and meat, potatoes, peas, and corn blended simply through constant collision. He pulled back when he remembered how much she hated him looking over her shoulder when she cooked. "How did you do today?"

She dropped a handful of peas into the pot. She filled a pan with water, slid it onto the burner, took two eggs from the fridge. "No one noticed my new hair. A hundred and twenty dollars. If it had been anybody else, they'd say something. Even if they didn't like it."

She stood there with her back still turned, eggs in hand. Ray reached to touch her arm but stopped an inch or so away. "I'm sorry, honey. I don't know why that happens."

"It's always the same conversation, isn't it?" she said. "It's like talking about the weather for us."

"It shouldn't happen that way," he said, not knowing what else to say. When she didn't respond, he started to go upstairs to change.

"But what I hate most is that it's all just too damn silly!"

He paused in the doorway. "It's not silly if it's hurting you." She was crying, still with her back to him. The right thing to do would be to put his arms around her. But he couldn't bring himself to do it. He didn't want to talk about this. He didn't want to say that he, too, felt it was silly and stupid and he felt small and petty every time his own feelings were similarly hurt. And he didn't want to say that he was angry with her for not being better at this than he was. She'd always been the more socially adept of the two of them—if she couldn't solve this, what hope did he have?

"There are people without homes," she said, "people who

have lost everything. There are people whose every day is a desperate gesture, and here I am crying because some silly women at the office where I work didn't notice my new hairdo!"

"I know. But it's more than that."

"It's more than that. It's the lunches. It's the conversations. It's all the moments you're not invited in."

"It's feeling like whatever you say, they're not hearing you. That no matter how much you wave your arms and jump up and down, they're not seeing you. You feel stupid and crazy and paranoid, because you know it doesn't make much sense—it has to be something you're doing, but you never can find a good enough reason in the things you're doing to explain it."

"And when you . . . when we die, no one but our daughter is going to remember we were ever here."

"I just can't believe that," he said.

"Really? You don't believe that?"

"I can't accept it," he said.

The high-school parking lot was full and then some. It was all senior kids in the show, and for many of these parents it would be their final opportunity to see their children as children, even though so few of them looked like children anymore.

"I never imagined her this way," he said.

"What way?"

"Grown up. It's ridiculous, but I never imagined this day would actually come."

"Wouldn't it be sad if it never came, Ray?"

"Oh, of course. But still, it feels as if she just went out to play one day, and never came back."

They ended up in the overflow parking by a rundown grocery. They crossed the street nervously, watching the traffic. Visibility was poor. Wet streets and black, shiny pavement, multicolored lights drifting in the wind.

Ray kept glancing at the front entrance as he pushed forward. Around them the headlights and car reflections floated randomly, like glowing insects looking for somewhere solid to land.

The lobby was packed with parents and their children, leaving little room for movement. Molly would already be on stage, waiting nervously behind the curtain. Janice wanted to rush into the auditorium, always afraid they'd be left without a seat, but Ray held back. Like Janice he hated crowds, but he needed to take in this part of it one final time. He would never experience this again. No more opportunities to act like other parents, in front of other parents.

These were families he had seen at dozens of events over the years, not that he really knew any of them. Some looked so pleased they actually glowed. But most had the anxious look of someone who has forgotten, and forgotten what they have forgotten.

He couldn't focus on any single group or conversation for more than a few seconds. He closed his eyes against the growing insect buzz, opened them again to clusters of colored dots vibrating asynchronously. If he were only a little smarter, he might understand what was going on here.

A man a few feet away exclaimed "Hey there!" and started toward him. Ray recognized him as a neighbor from a few blocks away—the daughter had been in Molly's classes for years. Ray felt his face grow warm as the neighbor—Tom? Was his name Tom? —held out his hand. Deep in his pants pocket Ray's hand itched, sweaty, as he began to pull it out.

"Quite the special evening, don't you think?" said Tom, if that was his name.

Ray had his hand out and managed a smile. Tom looked somewhat startled, nodded curtly, then brushed past to shake the hand of a man behind Ray. Ray wiggled his fingers as if stretching them, then stuck his hand back into his pocket.

Janice tugged at his sleeve. "Let's just go inside," she said, strain in her voice. But Ray didn't think he could move.

The lights blinked twice, and he was thinking there might be a power outage when he realized, of course, they were signaling the curtain. The crowd pushed forward and he felt himself dragged along, Janice's hand clutched in his.

When the curtain rose and the music started—an impressive storm of violins and horns—they craned their necks looking for Molly. The bandleader tended to move her for almost every performance. Ray always had the fear that she would be left out, that she'd be depressed that evening and hide out in the bathroom (she could be surprisingly dramatic for an offspring of such parents), or that she'd be miscued, misplaced. He was always prepared to defend her with his anger, for it was one thing to ignore him, or to ignore Janice, but it was beyond bearing for the daughter they both adored to be ignored, to have her feelings hurt.

But there she was! Second row back, close to the end, her black bangs whipping as she vigorously sawed with the bow. He could feel Janice settle back with relief. He sighed and started to lean back himself when he heard the high cry of a violin and looked up, already knowing it was Molly, playing the first solo part of the night, her eyes streaming. Leaning so far forward he could breathe the warmth of the woman's head in front of him, Ray felt himself beginning to cry and buried his face in his hands as his daughter's violin made that sweet, lonely sound floating high into the rafters and beyond.

He barely heard the rest of the concert, but it sounded impressively professional. Not that he was qualified to judge, but it had none of the rough, slightly off-key flavor he had expected. Nothing to impress the way Molly's moment in the spotlight had, but quite good, surely, none the less. He and Janice decided to sit through the break, not wanting to wade into that crowd scene again. He watched the audience: some still on the edges of their seats, some leaning back in bored, awkward semblances of relaxation. A few with heads bowed, touching each other, as if praying.

Did any of these people realize they were being watched? In their private moments did they imagine they, too, were invisible?

He glanced back up at the stage. Molly was staring at him. He felt a rush of embarrassment, hoping she didn't think he had been ignoring her performance. She looked smaller, younger, and it made him think of when it seemed she had been mostly his and not this almost-adult traveling at the speed of light out of his world. Claire didn't invite me to her sleepover and I'm, like, her third-best friend! The way she had looked up at him that night, surrounded and embraced by toys she'd soon find babyish, he had thought she was demanding some explanation. It was as if she'd suddenly discovered she'd inherited his leprosy—why hadn't he told her before?

"These things happen, sweetheart." Of course they do, especially in this family. "I'm sure she didn't mean to hurt your feelings." Because she wasn't aware of you or your feelings. "Sometimes you just have to be the organizer, the party-thrower, and invite her." It had been good advice, but he had prayed she wouldn't follow it. What would he say to her when they ignored her invitations?

In fact, Molly did not follow his advice, and he never heard another word from her on the subject. Perhaps she understood better than her parents. A child prodigy in the realm of invisibility. If she had friends after that, if she was invited places, she didn't share that information.

After the concert they made their way backstage to congratulate her, even though the seeming aggressiveness of the crowd agitated him. Janice pressed herself as close to the walls as possible, her cheekbone practically rubbing the brick. Finally they stood huddled together backstage as rivers of people flowed around them, spinning off into laughing, celebratory groups. Ray scanned the room for Molly, thinking that of course none of this should be any cause for anxiety, but he felt a rising tide of nervousness, beginning with an itchiness in the bottoms of his feet, tightening his calves and creating small but intense shooting pains in his knees. He held his head up stiffly and gulped for air. The room grew suddenly gray, the people moving around him outlined in ice and silver. He held one hand out, the skin ragged around the outlines, fading.

"Daddy?"

Molly stepped out of the bright light and into his reach. She carried her violin folded into her arms like a baby. Her eyes were wide, frightened, but they did not blink, did not avert from him even for a second as she looked at him, looked at him.

He pulled her to him and the three stood close together, not hugging—none of them good about hugging in public—but making sure they maintained contact as the world spun and jerked and solidified in its slow return to the real.

Molly hardly spoke on the way home, turning away their compliments with uninviting syllables, grunts, and nods, even refusing her father's proposition of hot dogs and sundaes at a neighborhood shop. She retired early, but they could hear her playing her romantic classical CDs softly, rearranging furniture, "doing her inventory" as Janice called it, packing for college and the life to come. She'd been packing for more than a month, trying to decide what bits of her old life to bring forward. The plan was she would leave in three weeks for a summer job at a music camp in upstate New York, and from there to school in the city. They had argued for months over whether they would drive her—it felt wrong not to be there with her for the big transition. It seemed all terribly too grown-up and recklessly premature to Ray, who already missed her to the point of physical pain. But something about Molly's determination that she do this alone finally persuaded him, and Janice reluctantly went along. Now Janice refused to speak about it.

The most difficult part of it all was that he was almost thrilled she was leaving. He imagined her going north, being absorbed into the life of the city and coming out of it a success, a famous person who had escaped the sick anonymity passed down from her unfortunate parents. In his imagination she became a fabulous, soaring star, and even as his heart was breaking in anticipation of her absence, his lost, invisible voice inside was saying go, go, go, don't look back.

Even with that sense of hope, however, they could not escape what their lives had become. An hour later Ray and Janice were ready for bed. They lay down together in loose-fitting pajamas, pushing off the bedclothes lest they bind and constrict. They both could feel the pain approaching, as if from a long distance gathering speed, its mouth open and the night wind whistling through the narrow gaps between its needle-like teeth.

They clasped hands as their spasms began, Janice's rocking her body almost off the bed. She clutched his hand until he cried out, which triggered even worse convulsions in the both of them, bodies snapping at the ends of whipping arms, mouths pulled back in fish-expression grimaces, tears and sweat burning across their faces and softening the roots of their hair. He willed his body to stay together, to remain solid, begged it to stop its flow across the bed and onto the floor, as every skin cell fought against transparency and his mind battled evaporation.

They bit their lips until they bled, clamping their mouths to prevent the escape of their cries. They had decided long ago that Molly must not know, that if she weren't told she might even escape this. And if she were to overhear, what could they say to her? For how do you explain the terrible pain of invisibility?

A month later Molly was gone as planned. Another week and she'd still not called to check in. It bothered them both, but perhaps Janice the most. Now and then he would catch her visiting in Molly's room, but she would not speak of any of it.

Eventually Janice quit her job without notice. She'd been there fifteen years, but she said she'd "never felt welcome."

"Never? Not even in the beginning?" Ray couldn't quite believe it. He was a little angry with her—they needed the money, and she hardly seemed ready for job hunting.

"In the beginning I pretended. I don't know why, but now I can't pretend anymore. I go in and I shut my office door and I cry all day."

"All day?" He wanted to be sympathetic, but he was too shocked. He'd believed she'd been happy until the last few years. She hadn't been like him—she'd seemed to have friends, she talked as if there'd been a camaraderie at work, her opinions were respected. He'd always suspected that the invisibility she'd felt these few years had been something she'd contracted from him. "I'm so sorry . . . I had no idea."

She collapsed in his arms. He wanted to tell her he understood, that he knew how she felt.

Finally, a few days later, Ray decided to call the place Molly worked. At first the person on the other end claimed never to have heard of her. Ray sat down on the edge of the couch, holding the phone to his chest. Then someone else came on who knew her, then finally it was her voice, distant yet energetic, interested in a way he'd never heard in her before, and yes she was all right, she'd just been busy, yes she would write, but she was just so busy.

Ray didn't tell her that her mother had quit her job. He said they were doing wonderfully; they had so many things to do they couldn't fit them all in. He went so far as to make up the name of a couple they'd recently met, with similar interests, and the events they had attended together.

Molly responded with a few stories of social events of her own. He had no idea if she was telling the truth, but he decided to believe her, and she did sound convincing. She sounded as if her parents had no further place in her life. Although this brought a note of genuine sadness into everything he said to her after that, he still cheered her on, and actually hoped, God help him, that she stayed as far away from them as possible, for her sake.

He told Janice about the call, making it seem that he and Molly had talked far longer than they actually had. She nodded as if disinterested, but he could see the wetness of her eyes, the stiffness in her features. She wouldn't talk about it.

That night the spasms were more violent and painful than ever before. Janice's sweeping arms broke a bedside lamp, and he spent half the night comforting her and bandaging her wounds.

At work Ray made himself say hello to everyone in his office every morning. It was part of a plan to make himself present. Never mind that he had tried similar tactics before. He used to keep a journal of such attempts: times he'd said hello with no response, times he had been ignored in conversations, obviously excluded from invitations. Stores where he had been unable to get sales assistance, restaurants where the waiters ignored him even when he waved menus in their faces, times cars had almost struck him in pedestrian crosswalks, days in which he'd had absolutely no human contact before the daily escape home to Janice and Molly.

Now he pulled this journal out of his desk and threw it into the trash, determined once again that these things wouldn't happen to him again or, if they did, he would ignore them. He would be his own company, if need be. The best of companions.

That afternoon the building had a fire drill. He walked out with the other employees, offering up his own jokes to match theirs. He couldn't be sure whose jokes were being laughed at, and whose ignored. Too much noise and confusion. But he at least felt like part of the group.

Out in the parking lot the group of employees separated into two groups, one on either side of him. He looked around: he was at the exact center, the point of separation, standing with neither group. He turned to the group on his left, listening to the general conversation, seeking an opening. Finally he offered up some comment about the hot pavement. He could almost see his words slide by their faces, catching on nothing, drifting beyond the group. He turned to the group on his right, wondering aloud how long the drill was supposed to last. The group appeared to stare up into the hot sun, preferring to blind themselves rather than to acknowledge him. When the all-clear sounded, the other employees returned to work upstairs. But Ray climbed into his car and went home.

Another month passed and he noticed Janice seemed to have less and less to say to him when he called home. Then there was a period of days in which she didn't answer the phone at all. After work he would walk into the house to confront her, and her excuse would be she must not have heard the phone ringing, she'd been out working in the yard (their yard, layered as it was with gravel and wood chips, seemed to have little to work on), or she'd been out shopping (but what did she buy?).

Then there came the morning Ray called home every ten minutes with no response.

A few minutes after his last call he found himself loitering outside his boss's office door, coughing, trying to look as ill as possible. He felt like a kid. He winced dramatically as he walked through the door, then looked up to see his boss hadn't noticed. Of course.

Ray cleared his throat. No answer. "Excuse me, Jim?" Jim appeared to be hypnotized by whatever he had up on the screen. "I'm feeling really ill. I have to leave!" He practically shouted it.

His boss looked up in surprise, said, "Sure, do what you have to do," and turned back to his computer.

At first he couldn't find Janice. She wasn't in the kitchen, and the living room TV was cold. He called her name from the bottom of the stairs, but there was no answer. He went outside and walked around the yard looking for signs of her supposed gardening activities. The yard looked as sad and neglected as he'd expected. He felt compelled to look into the shrubs, pull back weeds and search the ground for her body. He found some of Molly's old toys: a yellowing Barbie and a toy ice-cream truck. They must have been hiding out there at least a decade. He looked up at the house. It appeared abandoned. The roof was badly in need of repair. How long had it been deteriorating? He looked at his hands, half expecting them to be an old man's hands. Had he been asleep? How many years had he lost?

Finally, in their bedroom, he found her.

She writhed in pain, an insect pinned alive to the bed. Her arms and legs wriggled, her mouth opened and closed silently. He'd never imagined she did this alone—this was something they'd always shared.

He looked more closely. Some distortion of the body. Then he realized she had no hands, no feet.

Ray called in sick the rest of the week and stayed home with Janice. The week after, with her no better, he applied for two weeks of sick leave. On the phone his boss again seemed nonchalant. Do what you have to do. As if Ray really had a choice. Did his boss even know Ray was married? Ray didn't think the man had ever asked. Ray wore a ring, but it was pale yellow, blending into his skin. Invisible if you weren't really looking.

He saw no evidence, however, that his remaining home did her any good. During her better times she would lie there, staring at the ceiling, her skin glowing with the gray of fish in shimmering pools. Now and then one piece or another of her would fade into shadow, or bleach to the color of the surrounding sheet, making of her body an archipelago as she slept. These bits would fade back into visibility as she awakened, and sometimes she would be reinvigorated, getting up and walking around, fixing herself something to eat.

At her worst she shuddered and convulsed, gripping the sides of the bed with hands that weren't there, the skin on her arms and legs flickering in and out of existence like quick bursts of lightning. Despite his growing horror at touching her, he would lie down next to her and embrace her, hold her tightly as if to anchor her to the world. The irony was that he rarely convulsed himself during this period and had not been aware of his own painful invisibility for some time.

"I'm taking you to the doctor," he said one morning. "It's ridiculous that we've waited this long."

"You can't," she said from under the covers. She'd pulled them up over her head, so that all he could sense of her was her frail voice, a few rounded shapes, stick-figure limbs beneath the quilt. If he went over and pulled the covers back, would he see anything?

"Why can't we try?"

"He won't believe you."

"Maybe there have been other cases, and they're not letting on because it would cause a panic. Besides, he'll see the spasms, he'll see what happens to your body, your skin."

"Do you really think he'll see anything? Do you think he'll notice anything at all?"

Of course not. But he would not say it. "We have to do something. I have to do something."

"Stay with me. That's doing something."

And he did.

One night he awakened to her coughing. He lay watching her, her naked back glowing, pulsing with each cough. There was a pearly green aura he thought strangely beautiful, and he felt guilty that he could think it beautiful. She sighed. The coughs grew softer, the color shifts more subtle, a gauzy, greenish cream. She seemed to recede from him into the other side of the bed. Cough. Into the wall.

And then he was looking at the bare wall, the empty plain of bed beneath it. He held perfectly still. And waited. He gave it time, gave her time to come back to him. Waited an hour. Then waited two hours. And then began to cry. And then began to sob.

He did not leave the house for several weeks. This was a conscious decision. Not out of grief. He wasn't even sure he was grieving. His reasons were investigative. Experimental. Since she had vanished so suddenly, couldn't she reappear suddenly as well? He could be sitting at breakfast, and she might suddenly be sitting in the chair across from him, sipping her coffee and

reading the morning paper. Or perhaps she'd show up at the
front door, knocking, since she hadn't had her keys when she
disappeared. Or perhaps he'd wake up one morning and she'd be
lying in bed beside him, her face nuzzled against his arm, because
their bed was the last place he'd seen her.

Ray worried that if he wasn't in the house when she arrived,
Janice might panic. It made perfect sense to him that she would
arrive back in this world in a state of some confusion. He couldn't
let her go through that alone.

He didn't bother to call work. It certainly didn't surprise him
that they didn't call him. He imagined going to work as usual,
then disappearing out of his cubicle leaving a half-eaten sandwich behind. How long would it take them to realize something
was amiss?

But it seemed less funny after four weeks with no one calling.
The automatic deposit of his paychecks continued uninter-
rupted.

Each day he spent an hour or so sitting in different chairs in different rooms. He saw things he had never noticed before: a small
truck in the background of a painting, a birthmark on the ear of
an anonymous relative in one of the photographs in the living
room, a paperback book he'd thought lost under one side of the
couch. He developed a new appreciation for the pleasant home
he and Janice had created together.

After that first month he considered whether he should come
up with a story to explain her absence to the curious. For the first
time he realized how suspicious the circumstances of her disappearance might look to the police. He thought it fortunate that
Janice had quit her job. She had no living relatives that he was
aware of, and no friends out of her past (had there even been any?)
ever bothered to call. Wouldn't the neighbors be a bit curious,
wouldn't they notice that now he lived alone? Of course not.

Molly had to be told eventually. The next time she called he
would offer some sort of explanation. He owed her that. But
what if she never called? Should he track her down, introduce this
sad twist of physics into the life of the one human being he still
held dear?

Ray could not bear the idea that his daughter might never look into his face again, making him feel, at last, recognized. But it seemed as inevitable as his wife's fade from the world.

Four years later Ray was walking past a church a few blocks from home. It had become his habit each night to walk the nearby neighborhoods, not returning home until sometime after midnight. Each house window was like a dimly-lit television, the people inside moving about with unexplained purpose behind partially drawn shades and curtains. The noises could just as easily be sobs or laughter, and he had no responsibility for knowing which was which.

Sometimes he attended nighttime lectures at this church, sitting near the back to observe. The lectures were usually non-religious or at least nondenominational. Usually on a social issue "Of Concern To Us All," or a recounting of some overseas trip or expedition. Never anything he hadn't heard a hundred times before.

"Spontaneous Human Invisibility," it said on the church activities sign. "8 PM Wednesday." It was five after the hour. The lights inside appeared dim, and he thought for a moment the lecture must have been canceled. A woman his age, graying hair pulled back, a pale brown, unflattering knee length dress, appeared suddenly out of the shadows and turned into the church, disappearing through the doors. Without thinking he hurried after her.

"In every case the person was physically present, but according to reliable witnesses of good reputation and standing in the community, the person could not be seen or heard."

The man at the podium wore a stiff white shirt, striped tie, black pants. Black shoes that gleamed with a high-gloss, plastic-like finish. He reminded Ray of a Jehovah's Witness who had once come to his door, except the fellow at the altar wasn't smiling.

Perhaps eight or nine people sat in the front rows and an equal number on the sides. He could see movement in the unlit overflow seating sections off to either side behind rows of pillars: a fluttering as of birds trapped in shadow, a jerky nod, a gleam of cuff link or teeth. It seemed odd that people would sit in the dark, unless they were embarrassed or didn't want their attendance noted.

Then there was the lady he'd followed in here, sitting a few rows ahead of him. Particularly noticeable in that she was the only person in the room smiling.

"Besides these third-party witnesses, we have limited testimony from the victims themselves, limited apparently because of embarrassment, or because they could not believe anyone would listen to their stories."

Ray felt movement nearby, saw three men sitting a few feet away, listening intently. They must have arrived after him, but he hadn't seen them come in.

"We have the story of Martha, who stopped going into grocery stores because not once in six years had a clerk answered any of her questions."

A nodding to Ray's immediate left. More late arrivals, but he hadn't felt or heard them sit down.

"And what are we to make of Lisa, a gorgeous woman from all accounts, who hasn't been asked out on a date since she was sixteen?"

A stirring in seats all around him, as if the air was charging with emotion.

"These are active, living people, who through no fault of their own have found themselves sadly, spontaneously invisible, often at the very moment they needed to be seen the most. Missed by their children, ignored by their spouses, underappreciated in the arenas of commerce, I contend these are members of the most persecuted of minorities, in part because it is a minority whose existence has gone for the most part unperceived."

These remarks were greeted with thunderous applause. Ray glanced around: every pew, every seat was filled. He stared at some of the faces and saw nothing remarkable about any of them. Nondescript. Forgettable. The lady who'd led him here got up and headed briskly toward the door. He scrambled to follow her.

He passed close to one of the dark overflow areas. The faces staring out at him were gray, with even grayer eyes. They filled every inch of space, a wallpaper of monotone swatches.

When Ray got outside he discovered to his dismay that the woman was already more than a block ahead of him. Her shadow hinged like a stick insect as she made the corner.

STEVE RASNIC TEM

"Hey!" he shouted. "Hey!" And ran after her.

He followed her for several blocks, never making much progress. He shouted and screamed until his lungs were on fire, at first thinking the local residents would be disturbed. Infuriated, they would call the police.

No, he thought. No, they won't.

And so he shouted and screamed some more. He yelled at the top of his lungs. There were no words in what he was screaming, only fragmented syllables his anguished mouth abused.

At the end of the street the sky had lightened, yellow rays spreading through lines of perspective, stringing the distant houses together with trails of fire. He could see the woman had stopped: a charred spot in his retina, the edges of his vision in flames.

He arrived breathless and on the verge of fainting, awed by the observation that the sun had arrived with him. All around him the world lightened, then bleached, became day, and then became something beyond. White and borderless and a pain in his heart. He was amazed to find she was looking directly into his face.

"You see me," he whispered. Then, "But am I still alone?"

It seemed as if he'd never seen pity until he'd seen it in her face. Looking at him, looking at him, she nodded sadly for him and everyone else waking up in solitary beds at the edge of nonexistence.

And the world was silver. Then pewter as it cooled. He waited, and waited, then, finding enough shadow to make a road, he followed it to his house and the rest of his days there. Alone.

And to any eyes that might pry on that place, occasionally, and only occasionally, visible.

BETWEEN THE PILINGS

The dark blue neon scribble was so faint he had to stare awhile to determine if it said VACANCY or not. Finally Whitcomb decided to take a chance. He went up to the battered screen door beneath the water-damaged sign: Between the Pilings, and in smaller letters Innsmouth Beach, and in even smaller letters, an afterthought, worn almost to illegibility, Accommodations.

A light was on inside over a small counter, no brighter than a nightlight, really, and he couldn't tell if the hunched shape beneath it was a person or the back of a chair. But the door was unlocked, so he went inside.

He didn't see the clerk. Indeed it was just a counter with a battered surface and the rounded top of a chair behind. He gazed around the shabby, antiqued room. The lichen green wallpaper appeared to be dotted with tiny pale flowers, but they were so faded they might have been random stains. The armchairs and the couch might have originally been of high quality, but were now so scraped and worn it was hard to believe a business would countenance their use. The rug sparkled, but he determined it was from the grains of sand worked into its fibers. There might have been a central pattern, but the design was thoroughly obscured in grime.

Because of the numerous faded rectangles on the walls, he decided a number of pictures had been taken down. He had vague memories that it had been a fairly full gallery of past patrons displayed here. He didn't remember this room being so dilapidated. But he'd been barely eight years old when last he'd been here, so how could he know? He'd had no standards. He'd been happy just to be alive, to swim and play and watch television. And to eat cake. Oh, how he'd loved his cakes, the strawberry ones his mother used to make, the slices delivered to him on sparkling white plates, with a kiss on the cheek.

"Room?"

The word was so low-pitched and faint it might have come from the floor. Whitcomb looked more closely at the counter, the door behind it. The bluish glow coming from somewhere below the counter's edge. Had someone just come through the door? But he still didn't see them. He moved closer, peering over the edge.

He didn't believe in staring at people with disabilities—people all had differences, and we were all better off for it, in his opinion. But because he couldn't quite grasp the young man's malady, Whitcomb's gaze was fully engaged in staring.

The body on the wide chair was relatively short, fat and lop-sided, and he thought, collapsed as if the spine or a portion of the spine had been removed, allowing the rest of the young man to fall down in a clump because now there was too much flesh for the available height. The head was pushed forward by the swollen neck so that it was easier for the young man to look at the small computer screen in front of him than to look at Whitcomb above him. His too-fleshy fingers flapped against the keys. His skin was pale and oily, and poorly washed. Whitcomb thought of a giant frog that had once frightened him as a boy.

"Yes. I would like to rent a room. For three days, perhaps four."

"That'll be two days in advance then," the young man said, still without looking up. "Forty-five dollars on the counter please."

Whitcomb put his money down. The clerk used a pole with a hook on it to transfer keys from a pegboard to the counter, all without taking his eyes off the screen. "Number eight. You been here before?"

"A long time ago. I was a child."

"Won't have changed much, 'cept the beach is a tad closer. You have to leave your car parked up here on the street. Nobody'll bother it—Innsmouth isn't like other places. There's some steps at the end of the building. You take those down under the board-walk and out to the beach. The rooms are built around the timber pilings."

"I remember that part. It's unusual."

"It's why we have the name. Number eight is near the middle. But you'll have to wait up here a bit while the maid sweeps it out."

"Sweeps it out?"

"We have a sand problem."

Whitcomb didn't remember a sand problem, nor was he exactly sure what that phrase meant. But children often didn't notice the things adults classified as disastrous. The opposite, Whitcomb thought, was also true.

He looked for a place to sit. The couch looked like it might sink and fold itself around him, and the seats of all the chairs were thoroughly, darkly stained. He picked the least objectionable one, closed his eyes and sat down. It made a squishing sound, as of rotting fruit.

The room was silent for a time except for the flap-clicking of the keys on the other side of the counter and the occasional sigh or struggle of breath from the clerk. Whitcomb could see out the dingy front window and down the street: spare of street lamps or even the usual illuminations leaked from windows or car headlights. Still, a bit of parchment glow made the shadows deeper, and fuzzy-edged, and sometimes runny as darkness flowed from door to door, from one side of the street to the other. Feet and fingers and faces turned away. It was probably just him and his softly dying memories, but they might have been real. Had it been this way when he was a child? But everything was some bright adventure in a child's eyes, especially on vacation. His mother had hated it, he remembered that much, right up until the end.

That summer his mother had wanted to return to the Southern seacoast where she'd been raised, to the extensive sands of Myrtle Beach or at least Virginia Beach so that their son could have "a proper beach experience," but his father insisted they had to stay in New England—they couldn't afford to travel farther than that. His father had won—as he did all arguments in which money was involved. At that point Mother wanted nothing more to do with the planning.

He hated those old men who babbled all the time, who had to fill up every silence with their voices, but there was so much to talk about, and no one to talk to.

"The billboards on the highway going in? I remember them as being so much brighter. That first one, Visit Historic Innsmouth, with a collage of quaint Victorian buildings. You can barely make out the details now."

The clerk said nothing. But even when Whitcomb had been a child and saw that billboard for the first time, the colors had seemed off, shaded into dirty grays. Far more bothersome had been the cartoon character who was supposedly speaking those words. Whitcomb had guessed it was meant to be a fish. But the eyes were wrong, the pupils appearing fixed and dilated. Perhaps he was editing it in the remembering, but he recalled them as the eyes of a dead human being. On this trip that figure was missing completely, that side of the billboard scratched out.

"The second billboard, well, there's not much of an image left at all, is there? I remember this lovely picture of the Innsmouth pier with a wide shot of the ocean. Now everything is so heavily graffitied—loops and swirls and all kinds of nastiness emerging from the waves."

"I've never been to the highway," the clerk murmured. "I've never seen them."

"Oh, sorry." Whitcomb thought perhaps he'd been rude to the young man, insensitive to his disability, whatever its specifics. He would not ask him, then, about the final billboard, now completely blank. Worse than blank, actually—scoured down to gray, flaking wood. He couldn't imagine how the damage had occurred—even a hurricane wouldn't have created such complete erasure.

He tried to remember what it had looked like before, but he had never understood what it had been intended to depict. It had been in the process of being changed at the time, he thought, newer strips pasted over older ones, or perhaps the newer bits torn off to reveal what lay underneath: the legs of a sun-bathing beauty married to a beached sea lion or something similar, a chaos of torn and frayed buildings collapsing over them.

He felt a cold draft and glanced at the front door. He saw no obvious gap at the bottom, but there was sand there, fingers of it flowing his way as if blown. Suddenly the door banged open, and a squat gray woman stood there holding the largest broom he had ever seen, the thick shaft of it filling her hand. "The Mister's room is ready!" she proclaimed, and glared at him. He came quickly off the chair and squeezed past her, dashing to his car to retrieve a small suitcase.

The trip down the stairs was long, and Whitcomb was glad not to have a steamer trunk to drag. It was also dark and the railing minimal, so he took the steps slowly. In fact, it was so deeply in shadow in places the only illumination was a sliver of moonlight reflected off the damp edges of scattered timbers.

He remembered negotiating these steps as a child. Of course it had been daylight and mid-summer then. He remembered alternating areas of sunlight so bright it glazed the gray boards a brilliant white between shadows so dark he disappeared stepping into them. His mother behind him had been hysterical, sure he would kill himself flying down those rickety stairs.

Now at the bottom Whitcomb was confused. He remembered how it had been when he was eight: a broad strip of grass with a fountain and a bordering walk that shimmered from all the sea shells embedded in the concrete, and beyond that the gleaming white beach. It would never look as good as it had on that first glimpse, and over the years he would wonder if his imagination had simply embellished it, because every day after that while they were there it had appeared a bit grayer, a bit shabbier.

Now there was no grass at all—he had stepped off into sand. And a few feet away were the piles of rubble, broken concrete and other rubbish. And, looking around him, he didn't see the rooms. Certainly the few closest to the staircase were gone, leaving only hollow dark cavities filled with more sand.

He started walking parallel to the pilings, peering into the darkness for some sign of the old motel and finding none. It was hard to fathom how the young man up in that office at street level could believe he could get away with such a blatant con, taking money for rooms which no longer existed, but Whitcomb had his own eyes and the memory of what had once been here. He even ventured into the deeper shadows beneath the boardwalk thinking the rooms might have been set back further into the seaside structure than he remembered, but the area was wiped clean.

Then he passed one of the thicker pilings and there was what was left of the old motel: a short stretch of rooms with battered screen doors and a single window each. He remembered the walls as a bright coral red, but these were a pale salmon color, repaired here and there with gray cement like disease spots or patches of dead skin.

A small light glowed above each door along with a number. The first he saw was number six. He paused in front of eight before trying the key.

He remembered following his father into the room all those years ago. He had no idea which number it had been—it hadn't been important to him and they had all looked the same. There had been a bright multicolored oval rug inside, some blonde furniture, and one large bed. He'd gazed at that bed in dismay until he'd seen the rollaway they'd rented just for him. He'd sat on that bed and bounced, declaring it perfect.

His mother had come in slowly, her face drawn. She was rubbing her arms. "This sand, the wind blows it everywhere. It's burning my arms."

"It's just ordinary sand, dear," Whitcomb's father had said. "You probably just have a sunburn."

"We've barely arrived, how could I—"

"The drive in, all those miles. You had your window rolled down, remember? And your arm resting on the frame? I told you you should have put on sunblock when the trip began."

"I'm wearing long sleeves." She'd said it crossly. She hadn't wanted to come here at all.

"Light-weight fabric. You can practically see your arms through the cloth. It doesn't take much, a hot day like this."

His father had never thought his mother intelligent. That was why he'd always been explaining things to her, trying to explain why she shouldn't feel upset, why she shouldn't be disappointed or angry. Everything was always fine, the way his father had explained things, even when Whitcomb didn't understand the explanations.

Obviously his mother didn't understand them either, because as far as Whitcomb could remember, they had never helped. He'd resented that sometimes. She could have at least pretended to be happy. She could have been a good sport. Part of being happy, as he remembered from his childhood, was being able to pretend.

Whitcomb felt strangely hesitant to enter number eight. He was afraid to be disappointed in what he found inside. Sand as white, as pure-looking as snow, had drifted out of the shadow-land fronting the ocean and up to the concrete step in front of each door. It required only the dim light above each number to bring out the sand's unusual brilliance, its eerie luminescence. He looked down at his feet—of course, he was standing in it. There was no grass or sidewalk anymore. From above it looked oddly liquid, milk-like, rising and falling around his shoes—nothing like sand at all.

But he was tired, and he was drunk with memory. He fixed his eyes on the door and stepped forward. It was late, and the world was always a different place in the morning.

The key made a scraping sound as it went into the keyhole. It felt like there might be debris inside. He turned the key and tiny particles drifted out of the hole and down to the threshold, joining the fingers of sand that had already blown onto the recently-swept step. He pushed the door open.

It was dark and chilly in the room, as if instead of going inside he'd actually gone out. He reached for a light switch and found it, coated in grit, so was not optimistic about the maid's cleaning job. But when the lights came on he was pleasantly surprised.

The room brought back vividly the one from decades before. The furniture was the same or of a similar style, blonde wood with clean lines, typical of the fifties. There was even a rollaway, although the mattress was grayish, the frame spotted with rust. But the floor was clean, and the rug, although it wasn't the colorful one from years before. The colors were more muted, as were the colors throughout, he realized, shaded toward graying pastels. The blonde wood duller. The ceiling white less white. But there was a comfort in all that. After all, if it had been exactly the same he might have been terrified.

But that was all quite enough. Whitcomb thought he could not bear to be awake any longer. He dressed into his pajamas quickly, turned off the light, and slipped into bed. The sheets didn't feel crisp, but at least they weren't sandy. He didn't bother to set the alarm clock—he hadn't even noticed if there was one. He was content with awakening whenever.

He had no idea how long he had slept when he first awakened. It was still dark out, according to his window, but he hadn't

STEVE RASNIC TEM

slept through the night in years, so that wasn't surprising. Wind scratched and occasionally beat on the door. He thought it might be raining because he could hear the spray against the glass. Surely the ocean was too far away for it to be the advance spray of a wave, but he could not bring himself to check. Better not to know if he was about to drown.

He leaned over the side of the bed to get a good view of the door—white had eased through the bottom, a few threads of it. Sand. But perhaps he'd just tracked that in when he first came inside.

His mother had complained of the sand, the way it burned, the whole time they had been here. Whitcomb hadn't understood —he'd loved it, couldn't get enough of it, the way it squeezed between the toes. It frightened him that she should have such a strong reaction. For years afterward he would think of her when he met anyone with allergies or peculiar sensitivities. Some people lived in an unfriendly world. Certainly, no one lived in his world, and he was uncomfortable whenever he ventured out of it.

"You're supposed to drive your life, not let your life drive you." Jane had shared that bit of insight the last time she'd consented to see him. "Do something spontaneous for once!" It was goodbye advice, but at least she had been sincere. She might have liked him more if he'd managed to be someone else.

He might have pretended to her that his return visit to Innsmouth was a spontaneous act, but of course it was not—it had been coming for years. He'd just been gathering his nerve.

Over the years he'd tried to remember every detail of that vacation when he'd been eight, and although he'd recreated much of it, a great many moments were still missing. It angered him, the way the bits wore off, and he could not decide if it was the mind's normal decay or the old realities themselves which were going away. Something about the process seemed deliberate, as if the universe didn't want him to remember everything.

Something collapsed against the door, weeping, and he discovered sympathetic tears in his eyes. He did not feel sorry for himself—he'd made his choices, but he realized not everyone had a choice. Eventually all the bits of a life wore off, and for some even the memories went away. His father had gone on with his life, using drink to wipe the memory. But Whitcomb would remember his mother until the end.

He must have dozed off, because when he opened his eyes again the window was burning up with sun. He dressed himself in the sweats he'd bought for the occasion—he'd never owned a pair before. The door refused to open. He supposed the dampness had made it swell. He kept pulling until it came loose with a pop sound. A rain of grit poured from the jamb.

He stepped out into an intense scouring of sky and sand, so much blue and white he had to close his eyes, opening them slowly again using his hand as a shield. The beach looked ravaged, a churning of tiny white dunes and pitted places, black timbers and rocks showing ragged edges as if chewed. Streamers of rotting seaweed laced the beach, gulls landing to snatch tidbits, swiftly leaving as if the sand were too hot or corrosive to touch. Large amounts of fish flesh lay in partially digested chunks, the reek of it so foul his nose refused to process the smell. He gagged and turned to go back inside, but, deciding he would not be so easily defeated, struck off down the line of pilings again, thinking he would see what remained here from his memories.

There appeared to be no one else about, and given the unpleasant state of the shore here he supposed that should come as no surprise. In bright daylight he had a good look at what was left of the motel—eight units, with the last two missing numbers and doors. He couldn't imagine who might rent such lodgings, unless they were beyond desperate or ignorant like himself. Perhaps they did all their renting after dark, when the extent of the damage could not be seen. He was curious if he had neighbors, but wouldn't go out of his way to meet them.

The place hadn't been that busy when he'd been here before, when things were painted, in good repair, and at the height of summer. At best there had been five or six other family groupings, and a few isolated stragglers, tall figures in rain gear with large hats pulled down over their features, strolling the beach. And not all the family members made use of the beach—some, like his mother, made only rare forays past their motel doors or the grassy areas in front.

But vacations weren't for everyone, or so he had heard. There were always some who felt safer, if not happier, at home.

He gazed down the beach to where it narrowed, eventually disappearing into a tumble of stone. There was the main part of Innsmouth, the old docks, the church towers and the sprawling meeting halls. Several buildings near the edge had actually tumbled into the sea, leaving a slope of woody debris soaking up the ocean salt and a splay of broken uprights. Surely he was mistaken, but he had a vague memory of the same ruins, the same collapse, present when he'd been here as a child.

A broken chorus of voices rose with a sudden flight of black birds as if riding their backs into the air. The voices dissipated with the scattering paths of wings. Whitcomb had no desire to venture into that part of town, thinking it a far more dangerous place than this poor strip of sand.

He caught sight of a familiar sign and, walking closer, caught himself in a tease of a smile. By the Sands: Miniature Golf. His family had discovered the place their second day there and even his mother had seemed to enjoy herself. It appeared to still be in business. He found himself passing through the gate without considering.

At first he thought the fellow taking money was the motel clerk from the night before. They might have been twins. Then he saw that this one was a little taller, not as fat, and he hid one arm inside a voluminous sleeve. He handed the fellow a dollar and was pointed to a rack of balls and clubs beside Hole #1.

It was the usual layout of obstacles, ramps, windmills, passages through miniature buildings, and wide metal curves the ball could cling to for a left- or right-hand turn. But there were local touches as well: a giant brass frog with a wide mouth—a ball entered the mouth and shot out the anus in some random direction. A water obstacle with leaping mechanical fish—periodically a fish would alter its trajectory by some mysterious means and snag the ball. An array of dilapidated buildings—he couldn't really tell if the destruction was cosmetic and faked, or actual damage incurred by the miniature buildings because of exposure and lack of care. He didn't remember many specifics about this miniature golf course from his previous visits decades ago, but it seemed that some of these features might be new to him—except for the frog. Now that he thought about it, the brass frog had been here before.

The last few holes had been invaded by sand. But that fit the golfing theme, did it not? Sand traps designed to defeat even the most professional of golfers. At hole fifteen the sand trap moved, and the ball dissolved amidst a swirl of greedy silvery grit, ending his game.

As he left the golf course he found himself staring at the ocean, the endless repeating waves, the long curving edges of foam, that meandering line where dark gray sea met an only slightly softer sky. As a boy, he'd thought that line dividing the air and water impossibly high, an instability that threatened everything he held dear. Now it seemed worse, and he thought he could detect structures inside it, only vaguely covered by the water—long reticulating lines, horizontal and vertical edges, the boxy shapes of some lost city drowned beneath the waves.

It made him feel empty, void of substance, and he realized he hadn't yet eaten and had gone to bed without dinner the night before. There had been a few small cafes, he remembered, accessible only from the beach, and he continued walking in the direction of that denser part of Innsmouth, hoping one might still be in business.

He closed his eyes at one point, having walked far longer than he had hoped, and near to exhaustion. He did not remember finding the restaurant, or sitting down, or ordering. But the next thing he knew he was blinking rapidly, and he was holding a large spoon, and warm and slippery things were washing down his throat. He almost choked when he realized it, and had to down a large glass of water which tasted a bit too salty and whose color was less than assuring. His teeth felt unstable, his tongue sore, the inside of his mouth scraped.

He only vaguely remembered the meals he'd had when his parents brought him here as a child. He remembered feeling ravenous the whole time, and devouring hotdogs and something else—some sort of pita-like concoction—from beach-side stands. His parents ate hardly anything at all. His father had been drinking, not as committedly as he would after that vacation, but enough that it made him quiet, grumpy, and without appetite. His mother—he was never sure if his mother ate anything during that trip. He vaguely remembered sitting with them in a small restaurant like this one, only cleaner, brighter, and watching her dab at her mouth with a cloth napkin, always dabbing, touching her lips with it, her teeth, and a redness coming away on the cloth.

He looked down into his soup, or stew. Very little was left, a small bit of tail sticking out of a thick, gray broth. He pushed the bowl away, looked around him. There were other patrons in the small cafe. This shouldn't have surprised him, except that he had seen no one except the motel clerk and his near-doppelganger the miniature golf attendant since his arrival the night before.

There were five, no, six others, huddled over their food. Thickly dressed in layers, high collars, some with weedy mats of hair slapped on top their heads. Some with stocking caps, despite the warm day. All looked vaguely ill or hung over, here to recover, perhaps, from the night before. The fellow closest to Whitcomb had a similar soup bowl in front of him, filled with gray. Periodically he jabbed his fork into the liquid as if attacking.

The walls looked greasy, with large spots by the tables along the perimeter, as if people had rested their heads there, soiling the dingy green paint. He saw a tall man in a muscle shirt asleep at one of those tables, perhaps a sailor given the theme of his tattoos—fish and whales and frogs and waves and some things tendrilled, perhaps vegetation, perhaps not. His torso leaned against the wall, one arm pressed beneath his chest, his head lolling, cheek smeared flat.

The sailor suddenly woke up, startled, glared at Whitcomb and pulled his head and arm away from the wall. Sticky pale threads ran from his flesh to where bits of him still clung to the wall, including part of a bluish anchor design.

Whitcomb stumbled out of his chair and went through the door. Had he paid? No one shouted, no one chased him. But he stopped himself out on the beach, thinking that if he hadn't paid, the proprietor would catch up to him and he could apologize, explain that it was a mistake, and pay what he owed, pay double what he owed. But no one came.

He looked back down the beach searching for his motel. He had no idea how far he had come. He also hadn't realized that he'd been walking up a slope, this part of the beach being noticeably higher than from where he'd come. From here he could see the entire stretch of it, hundreds of yards, and the way the waves came in, taking greedy nibbles. And all that had been ruined. And how the sand moved, minutely, but seeing it all together like this, multiplied, so that for the first time he could be sure, all that sand, everywhere, was moving.

He must have fallen quite hard, because he was suddenly on the ground, eyes and mouth gaping. The sand edged around him. He shut his eyes, trying to force it out.

He'd awakened that night, all those years ago, because of a noise or a dream of a noise. Someone crying, someone lost. Bits of his memory from that time had wandered off, but this memory, at least, he had found.

His father lay passed out on the bed. Whitcomb was on the rollaway, shivering—he'd always been so skinny as a boy, and easy to chill. As he sat up he'd realized it was because the motel room door was open, and the ocean breeze was coming in, and the sand. He'd looked around for his mother then, but she was nowhere to be seen.

He'd wandered out. His feet must have been damp, because he could remember the sand sticking to them. He remembered looking down, all that clinging sand making his feet look frosted, sparkling in the moonlight.

Out on the beach there was a tall, thin form. He'd recognized his mother's pale yellow gown. She was swaying, and the wind was lifting her gown, and he'd thought he should turn away because he shouldn't be seeing this.

She'd turned her head then, and her mouth was so red, and he'd thought she was looking at him, but it quickly became clear she was gazing at the ground behind her, the sandy beach, which was moving.

She'd tried to get away from it. She never would have left him if she could have helped it. She'd always been devoted to him, despite her flaws.

He didn't know where she was running. He'd only been eight,

but even then he'd understood that the ocean wouldn't have helped her.

The sand trailed up and her gown began to fall away. He was embarrassed and closed his eyes, but forced them open again as the hazy softness of her went dark. Later his father would hold the empty gown and ask him if he had seen anything. And he would say he had not, because he had not.

Whitcomb opened his eyes and saw the drift of tiny particles on the beach in front of him, felt them float in and out of his mouth, in and out of his ears. Red bits and soft bits, and an endless streaming of sand.

A lifetime later he sat out in front of his room, taking in the ocean, taking in all the sand. He was missing pieces. He could not remember why he had come here, just that it had been a compulsion, beyond important, but that memory was useless to him now. As were all other memories, scoured and taken and blown away by the wind. But it was almost a relief to see them go.

He gazed down at his sweatpants, which were almost empty now. He began to smile, but could feel that even bits of his smile were gone.

RED RABBIT

He found her on the back porch again, watching the yard through the sliding glass door. He didn't want to spook her, so he made some noise as he left the kitchen, bumped a chair, and made a light tap with one shoe on the metal threshold that separated the porch from the rest of the house. Then he stopped a few feet behind her and said, "What are you looking at, honey?"

"The rabbit. Matt, have you seen that rabbit?

"That was yesterday, Clara. Remember? I went down there, and I scooped it up with a shovel, and I dropped it into a trash bag. Some wild animal got to it. Rabbits can't protect themselves very well. That was yesterday."

"But it's back." Her voice shook. "Can't you see it?"

He followed her gaze to the lower part of the lawn, where it dipped downhill to the fence. Shadows tended to pool there, making the area look damp even though it hadn't rained in almost two months. Beyond were a field of weeds and wildflowers, and the line of trees bordering the old canal. Beyond that was the interstate. You couldn't see it, but you could certainly hear the traffic—a vacillating roar that you could pretend was a river if you really tried.

The skinned and bloody rabbit had appeared there yesterday at the bottom of the yard, eased out of the shadows as if from a pool. And here was another one, its front legs stretched out toward the house, its body gleaming with fresh blood. This must have just happened. They must have had some sort of predator in the yard.

"I see it," he said. "Something got another one."

"Something terrible is happening," she said. "I've been feeling it for weeks. And now this rabbit—I see it every day. Sometimes just after sunrise, sometimes just before sunrise. I thought I was going crazy, but now you see it too. What do you think it wants? Can you tell me what it wants?"

Matt looked at her: her eyes red and unfocused, lips trembling. She was somewhere else inside her head. She was wearing this old green tube-top thing. She'd never looked good in it. Her back was knotted, her shoulders pushed up, her arms waving around as she spoke. He figured she must be crazy tense if he noticed it—he never noticed things like that.

He felt sorry for her, but he also felt scared for himself. The woman he had loved had been gone for years, and now he was left with this. He wasn't a good enough person to handle something he hadn't signed up for.

"It's not the same rabbit, Clara. There must be a predator loose in the neighborhood. Probably just a big cat or maybe a dog. It's just a dead rabbit. I'll go get the shovel and take care of it. There's nothing to get upset about."

He didn't really understand how her mind worked anymore. But maybe his being logical helped her. No one could say he hadn't tried.

"There's blood all over him," she said. "He's all torn up. Can't you see that something terrible is going to happen, that something terrible is happening? Can't you see it?"

She continued to stare at the rabbit in the yard. She wouldn't turn around and look at him. It felt creepy, talking to her back all the time. He didn't dare touch her when she was like this, like a fistful of nerves. He didn't think she'd looked at him full in the face in days.

"It was a wild animal. It had a savage life. And something got to it. It's not like a cartoon, Clara. Rabbits can't protect themselves very well. Real rabbits in the wild, their lives are short and cruel."

They hadn't had sex in a long time. He'd been afraid to touch her. You can learn to live with crazy, but you can't touch it. He couldn't let her drive, and when he left her alone she called him at work every hour to complain about some new thing she'd suddenly realized was wrong. Their GP kept prescribing new pills for her, but he was just a kid, really. Matt was sure the fellow had no idea what was wrong with her.

"I haven't been feeling right, Matt. Not for a very long time. Something terrible is going to happen—can't you sense that?"

"I know that's what you feel, but just go lie down. Let me

take care of this, and then I'll come join you." But he knew she wasn't hearing, the way she stared, glassy-eyed and the edge of her upper teeth showing. He stood in front of her and whispered, "Go inside now. Please." When she didn't respond he stepped closer to block her view of the yard and put one arm around her, gave her a bit of squeeze.

"Honey, just go inside and lie down. I'll join you in a few minutes. Maybe I can even figure out what's killing these rabbits, and I'll deal with the thing. You just go inside." Hopefully she'd be asleep when he was done. When she was asleep he could grab a drink, watch some TV, relax and unwind for once.

He grabbed a shovel and a trash bag and some gloves and started down the slope of the lawn. He'd generally neglected that part of the back yard. The ground there had always been mushy, unstable. He didn't know much about ground water, septic systems, any of that stuff. But he figured it must be some sort of drainage issue, maybe because of the old canal, or maybe because of an old broken septic system, something like that. It didn't smell too bad, just a little stagnant most of the time, a little sour. Only sometimes it stank like rotting meat. But they couldn't afford to fix it whatever it was, so he'd just tried to ignore it.

The carcass wasn't where he had seen it. In fact he couldn't find the rabbit anywhere. He thought about that mysterious predator, and went back to the house and grabbed the rake that was leaning against the wall by the sliding glass doors.

He stood still, the rake held in both hands in front of him, raised like a club. He still didn't see the rabbit. He felt unsteady, and shortened his grip on the handle. He imagined that the predator, whatever it was, had dragged the body off somewhere. Some of the more dangerous animals in the region—coyotes, a wildcat or two, once even a small bear—had been known to wander out of the foothills and follow the canal into the more populous suburbs. He crept down the lawn toward the fence, afraid he might lose his footing. The grass looked shiny, slippery, as if the earth beneath were liquefying.

He detected a subtle reddish shadow as he got closer to the fence, and then saw that it was a spray of blood. The body had been pushed up against one of the fence posts, eviscerated, but still clearly some version of rabbit. He was glad Clara couldn't see this. It must have suffered terribly, ripped and skinned alive, all gleaming, bright-red muscle, damp white bone, strings of pale fat. But the muscle had no business being bright red like that, like some kind of rich dyed leather. He'd skinned squirrels with his dad—he knew what a dead, skinned animal looked like, so dark and bruised. But this? This looked unreal.

He bagged it and trashed it, then brought out the hose to wash away the blood and any loose pieces of meat. That's what you did with this sort of thing. That's how you handled it. You cleaned up the mess and then you went on with your life. Later he grabbed his binoculars and studied the field and the trees beyond, checking for any signs of movement. He saw nothing. If he had been ambitious he would have climbed over the fence and walked through the field to the row of trees that bordered the canal. He could have followed that canal into some other place. The water might not be running through the canal anymore, but it was still a passage to something, wasn't it? But he wasn't ambitious. And he didn't want to go there.

Matt drank and watched TV until about midnight. The house was a mess—Clara hadn't cleaned in weeks. He couldn't abide a messy house, but he worked all day—he didn't have the time. But if he had the time he knew he'd do a great job. It wasn't that hard keeping up a house—you just had to understand how to manage time and not let it get away from you. He hadn't signed up for this. He'd tried—and you owed your wife at least to try. But everybody had limits. You couldn't expect a man not to have his limits.

She didn't wake up when he crawled into bed with her. Good thing—she'd ask about the rabbit, and he didn't want to talk about that damn rabbit anymore.

He woke up once and saw her standing at the window, looking out onto the back yard. He started to say something, started to ask her what was wrong, but he stopped himself. He was tired, and he knew what was wrong.

He woke up alone. He didn't like waking up alone, but he didn't want to answer any of her questions. He fell back asleep, and when he woke up again the room was bright from the sun coming through the window. He'd overslept, but at least it was the weekend. Nothing important ever came up on the weekend. They'd stopped doing the important stuff a long time ago.

"Clara, you up here?" She didn't answer. "Clara!" Nothing. He got his pants and shoes on and went downstairs. He still couldn't find her. He felt a little panicky, and he was mad at himself for feeling a little panicky. He made himself be methodical. He went back upstairs and searched each bedroom as he went down the hall. He wasn't sure why they had all these bedrooms—they didn't have any kids. They had way too much house, but he'd gotten such a good deal on the place.

He felt a pressure building behind his eyes. He tried to shake it off. He went back into their bedroom and looked in the closet and in the master bathroom. He got down on his knees and looked under the bed. There were several socks, another larger, unidentifiable piece of clothing. He made a note to sweep under there later.

He called again from the top of the stairs. "Clara! Are you in the house?" Nothing. No steps, no rustle, just the soft hum of the refrigerator. He went downstairs and jerked open the front door, a little too hard. It banged against the rubber bumper mounted on the wall. He hadn't realized it before, but he was beginning to feel pretty angry. Maybe she couldn't help it, but this was ridiculous.

She wasn't lying on the front lawn again, thank God. And the Subaru was still there, which was a big relief. Matt thought about getting in his car and driving around looking for her. But she could be anywhere, and besides, he knew that once you started chasing after someone like that it never ended, not until you'd given yourself a heart attack. She was a grown woman—he shouldn't have to be searching for her.

He made himself stop. Most things got better that way: taking a break, waiting. People needed to be patient, not make such a big deal out of everything.

He went out to the porch and sat down. That's when he saw her kneeling down at the bottom of the yard, her back turned to him. Just like she always did. Her shoulders were heaving.

He slid open the door and stepped outside. "Clara?"

She didn't speak, but he could hear her crying. Then he saw

the blood streaks on her sleeves. He started running. "Clara!" Not again. Not again.

He came up behind her and grabbed her by the shoulders, twisting them to stop her from whatever she was doing. He grabbed both of her hands and raised them, trying to get a good look at her wrists. Her forearms, his hands, everything slick with blood. "Where's the knife, Clara!"

She looked up at him, wide-eyed and dull. "No knife. I didn't see a knife."

He couldn't find any cuts on her wrists, her arms, her hands. He looked down at her knees, and then the grass, and then the bloody bits he was standing on. He jumped back in alarm. It was another rabbit, skinned and gutted, its flesh weeping fresh blood.

"It's back!" she said, her voice rising. "It's back!"

"Dammit, Clara. It's not the same rabbit!"

She stared at him, her face tilted. "But how can you tell it's a different rabbit? How do you know for sure?"

He started to explain, but what was there to explain? "Because this is real life. We live in real life, Clara! Just stay right here. I'll get something to cover it with, and then we'll go wash you up, okay?"

He ran into the garage and grabbed a drop cloth, and on his way out he grabbed the rake, too, just in case of, just in case he needed it. But when he got back Clara was gone. The rabbit was still lying there, but there was no sign of Clara in the yard. How could she have moved so quickly? He stared down at the rabbit. It looked like all the others, as far as he could tell. One huge eye, pushed almost out of its socket, stared up at him.

He looked around the yard, the edge of the house, inside the house. He couldn't find her anywhere. He gave up. He imagined her walking around the neighborhood, her shirt bloody, her arms and hands bloody. Somebody would call the police. Well, the hell with it. He'd done everything he could.

Matt left the rabbit and went back inside. At least he could clean himself up. At least he could get that much done.

After his shower he grabbed a jar of peanut butter out of the fridge and stood at the kitchen window digging two fingers into the jar and eating the peanut butter right off them. Looking through the window into the porch and then through the sliding glass doors made the yard seem a pretty safe distance away. He could still see the fields and the line of trees beyond, and he was sure he'd be able to see any movement out there if there was any. But there wasn't any. After a while he collapsed into that old chair on the back porch and sat watching the yard for a couple of hours. It was midafternoon by then and he hadn't had any lunch. He supposed he could find something in the fridge to heat up, but then maybe Clara would come home. Fixing him something might occupy her, keep her mind off things.

He was actually pretty surprised she hadn't shown up yet. If the police had picked her up they would have come by now. He was used to her being anxious, but she usually snapped out of it after an hour or so and managed to get going on whatever needed to be done. He'd call some of her friends but that woman Ann had moved away six months ago and he didn't know any of the others, if there were any others. Clara never made friends easily, at least not since he'd known her.

He couldn't get over those damn rabbits. Whatever had gotten to them, it must have wiped out an entire den. Why had the thing left its kills in his yard anyway? Like a house cat dropping the mouse it slaughtered at your feet. But you had to trust your eyes —most of the time it was the one thing you could trust.

Clara needed to be back soon. She'd always been this timid thing, couldn't protect herself worth a damn. Terrible things happened to timid creatures like that. She knew. That's why she kept saying that. Well, terrible things do happen, Clara. It wasn't too hard predicting that.

He must have dozed, because the back yard suddenly looked dimmer. That shady bit down by the fence had grown, spread half-way up the yard toward the house. Lights were popping on over at the neighbors'.

He sat up suddenly as a chill grabbed his throat. "Clara!" he yelled as loud as he could to scare it away. Still no answer. He listened hard now. The refrigerator still hummed. It was like he was living by himself again.

He could check with all the neighbors, but the last thing he needed was for everybody to know his business. He could call the police, but would they even take a report? Maybe if he told them Clara was a danger to herself. She'd cut her wrists more than once, but she'd always botched the job. Timid people like that, he reckoned they intended to botch the job.

He thought about talking to some young policeman, trying to explain how Clara was, trying to explain about the skinned rabbits, how they must have a predator in the neighborhood, and how the cop would act deliberately patient, and condescending to this older guy who had just called in about his missing wife, who'd only been gone a few hours, probably on some impulsive shopping trip. Matt couldn't bear it.

She'd been a lovely girl when he'd met her—pretty, and shy. She'd made him feel like he was about the greatest man in the world. Then she got nervous, and then she got old, and surely she was crazy now. Maybe if he was truly a good man he could handle that—he'd stick with her and make the best out of a sad situation. But people had to be realistic. Good men were few and far between.

Flashing red lights broke through the trees on the other side of the field. They made it look as if parts of that line of trees bordering the old canal were on fire. But then the wind shifted the branches a bit and he could see that he was mistaken. There were scattered fires on the interstate beyond. And many more lights and faint, but explosive noises. People shouting maybe. Or cars being pried open like clamshells to get to the meat inside. The Jaws of Life, that's what they called them. But only if the people inside were still living. If not, then they were the Jaws of Death, weren't they?

The radio was right by the chair, so he could have turned it on. But he'd rather wait until Clara showed up and then they could learn together what terrible thing might have happened over on the highway. Matt supposed it was an unhealthy thing in people, how listening or watching together as the news told the details of some new disaster tended to bring couples and families together.

He sat and watched the red flashes and the burning and listened hard for the noises and the voices until it was dark enough for the automatic yard lights to come on. The gnawing in his belly was painful but he had no interest in eating, assuming eating was even the sort of remedy required.

He could see everything, except for that shadowy region down near the fence. He could see the rake where he'd left it, and the folded-up drop cloth. But there was no sign of that rabbit. Something had moved it, or maybe—and the idea made him queasy—it hadn't been completely dead. Skinned, but not dead. Crawling around suffering.

As Matt's eyes grew weary he found himself focusing on that area of shadow. It had always seemed odd that the longer you stared at a shadow the more likely you were to find other shadows swimming inside it. Something moved out of the edge. In the border between dark and light a skinned body lay in the slickened grass. Bleeding heavily, and this one much too large for a rabbit. Stripped to muscle and bone, it was an anatomical human figure made real. The skin over part of one breast remained. And when it reached its scarlet arms toward the house it called his name.

ACKNOWLEDGEMENTS

"City Fishing," "Angel Combs," "The Poor," "Preparations for the Game," "Little Cruelties," "The Men and Women of Rivendale," and "Hungry" appeared as part of the collection *City Fishing* by Steve Rasnic Tem, Silver Salamander Press, 2000.

"A House by the Ocean," "Wheatfield with Crows," and "The Cabinet Child" appeared as part of the collection *Here With the Shadows* by Steve Rasnic Tem, Swan River Press, 2014.

"Crutches," "Leaks," "Houses Creaking in the Wind," "Escape on a Train," "Among the Old," "In the Trees," and "Underground" appeared as part of the collection *The Far Side of the Lake* by Steve Rasnic Tem, Ash-Tree Press, 2001 (repackaged as *Absent Company*, a Crossroad Press / Macabre Ink ebook).

"Out Late in the Park," "The Figure in Motion," and "An Ending" appeared as part of the collection *Onion Songs* by Steve Rasnic Tem, Chomu Press, 2013.

"Twember" appeared as part of the collection *Twember: Science Fiction Stories*, *Imaginings* vol. 7 by Steve Rasnic Tem, NewCon Press, 2013.

"Origami Bird," "Firestorm," "When We Moved On," "The Company You Keep," "The Bereavement Photographer," and "Invisible" appeared as part of the collection *Celestial Inventories* by Steve Rasnic Tem, ChiZine Publications, 2013.

"2 PM: The Real Estate Agent Arrives," "The Carving," and "Jesse" appeared as part of the collection *Ugly Behavior* by Steve Rasnic Tem, New Pulp Press, 2012.

"Miri," "Vintage Domestic," and "Grandfather Wolf" appeared as part of the collection *Out of the Dark: A Storybook of Horrors* by Steve Rasnic Tem, Centipede Press, 2016.

"Between the Pilings" originally appeared in *Innsmouth Nightmares*, edited by Lois Gresh, 2015.

"Red Rabbit" originally appeared in *Borderlands 6*, edited by Olivia & Tom Monteleone, 2016.